LEECH

HIRON ENNES

TOR PUBLISHING GROUP

NEW YORK

This is a work of fiction. All of the characters, organizations,
and events portrayed in this novel are either products of the author's
imagination or are used fictitiously.

LEECH

Copyright © 2022 by Hiron Ennes

A Tordotcom Book
Published by Tom Doherty Associates / Tor Publishing Group
120 Broadway
New York, NY 10271

www.tor.com

Tor® is a registered trademark of Macmillan Publishing Group, LLC.

The Library of Congress has cataloged the hardcover edition as follows:

Names: Ennes, Hiron, author.
Title: Leech / Hiron Ennes.
Description: First edition. I New York : Tordotcom / Tom Doherty
    Associates, 2022.
Identifiers: LCCN 2022010454 (print) I LCCN 2022010455 (ebook) I
    ISBN 9781250811189 (hardcover) I ISBN 9781250811196 (ebook)
Subjects: LCGFT: Science fiction. I Gothic fiction. I Novels.
Classification: LCC PS3605.N556 L44 2022 (print) I LCC PS3605.N556
    (ebook) I DDC 813/.6—dc23/eng/20220304
LC record available at https://lccn.loc.gov/2022010454
LC ebook record available at https://lccn.loc.gov/2022010455

ISBN 978-1-250-81120-2 (trade paperback)

Our books may be purchased in bulk for promotional, educational,
or business use. Please contact the Macmillan Corporate and Premium
Sales Department at 1-800-221-7945, extension 5442, or by email at
MacmillanSpecialMarkets@macmillan.com.

First Tordotcom Paperback Edition: 2023

Printed in the United States of America

0 9 8 7 6 5 4 3 2

For Budna,

WHO HOWLED WITH ME

DURING THOSE SUNLESS WINTER DAYS

LEECH

I

THE SIGHT OF THIS old train car saddens me, though I cannot quite articulate why. There is something unnamable about the rattling of the empty wooden seats, so like the pews of a deserted church, that puts me in a lonely humor. It is an unusual feeling, since I have never in my life been alone.

Jagged mountains rise and fall outside the window, dotted with white trees and the occasional lodge long since abandoned to the wild. It has been one hour and forty-two minutes since the last snow-shrouded sign of civilization crawled across the landscape, and it will be fifty-four minutes before the next appears. This is not accounting for delays, accidents, breakdowns, avalanches, or seismically induced derailments.

The only other occupant of the car is a young boy, bundled so heavily he resembles a sphere more than a child. He sits alone because he failed to follow his mother off the train at the penultimate stop, but he does not appear distressed. The conductor had promised to deposit him at the correct station on the return south, and he shrugged in reply, biting shyly at the forefinger of a well-chewed glove.

The train stops twice so workers can clear snow from the tracks, adding, according to my timepiece, forty-one minutes to the journey. It is not so deep into winter that such a delay will prove fatal, but I will arrive on the dangerous side of dusk. Perhaps that is for the better. The man I plan to meet at the station is not likely to be punctual, especially since he does not expect me. He may not even yet know of the death that brings me north.

The snow-laden firs bow their heads and shed motes of light as the sun slips between two western peaks. The boy squints out the window, drawing intricate outlines of mountains in his condensed breath and wiping them away with equal enthusiasm. I study him at play, noting his movement and development, his flushed cheeks, the herpetic sores at the corner of his mouth. He is a charming creature.

He meets my gaze and reddens, balling his hand in the palm of his four-fingered right glove. I suspect come nighttime the ride will only get colder, so I remove my own gloves and offer him a trade. Wordlessly, he compares them to his current pair. He slips his hand inside and, finding them to be close enough to his own size, accepts. As the train once again bellows and lurches, his complacent smile reveals dark gaps of missing teeth. He spends the rest of the trip removing the gloves, twisting the fingers in knots, untwisting, reversing them, and wearing them again. By the time my destination comes into view, he is chewing away at one leather forefinger.

The train whines to a stop. As I bid farewell to the child, I suddenly long to trade places with him, as easily as we have traded gloves. I would like to ride back south in his place, to assume his unworried demeanor, to occupy the capricious brain developing in his skull. Perhaps, one day, I will.

But for now, I must address my own mind. I must follow the eddies of darkness where the flow of my thoughts has been interrupted, where a gap has opened and swallowed a portion of my memory. Only a corpse is left, a body I should have seen die, but whose agonal moments slipped past with nothing but a tense, vague unsettlement.

I collect my things and disembark. Workmen drag several dozen boxes of supplies through the snow, and I follow their tracks to the three-walled shack that passes for a railway station. The shelter offers little respite from the cold, and I shiver between crates and containers, massaging a numb forefinger and curling my frozen toes in their inadequate shoes. The train reverses course, black smoke billowing in its wake, and disappears back into the maze of mountains. Silence falls with the dusk, and the encroaching shadows color the snow an endless, featureless blue.

Baker arrives with predictable lateness, and in his usual manner: bathed in the exhaust of his snow-treading vehicle, balancing sidesaddle on a torn foam seat, with a small branch of pine—a poor substitute for the cigarilles he has vowed to eschew—poking aslant from his frosty beard. At his back creaks a sled of his own making, a rickety contraption of wood and metal on which he hauls supplies between the station and the town.

Suppressing an unexpected pinch of anxiety, I watch him rattle up to the shack, smoke wheezing from the machine's trembling tailpipe. I raise a hand in greeting.

Baker slides from the seat. He looks to his left, then his right, as if hoping to find someone who can explain my presence. He, of course, does not recognize me.

"You're of the Institute, I s'pose," he says.

I nod.

"Hell of a fast arrival. Been but two days back the château sent the letter." He speaks hard Franco, and though this young tongue of mine is unused to its phonemes, I am familiar with the language. "Just nay thought—lor, never mind. I'm Baker."

I pretend I do not already know. He extends his hand and I take it.

"You lost a finger there," he says. "Can 'quire summore gloves in town. Nay far. Any luggage?"

"No."

He raises a bushy eyebrow. "Supe, crawl in the back. I can come

tomorrow for these. Wild animals nay stealing the baron's new
porcelain while we're away." He pats a crate with a furred glove
and motions for me to climb into the dilapidated sled. When I am
safely inside, he blows two pillars of smoky, condensed breath
from his nostrils and starts the engine.

I squint at the rusted track of the machine as it flings oil-stained
snow, grooves glinting like knives, and I try not to imagine a body
crushed under it, tangled and torn beyond recognition. I know
better than to conjure such thoughts, but phobias, like immunities, are acquired early and are difficult to erase. Despite logical
input from a conscious mind, a body fears what it fears.

The ride is unpleasant, but it is not long. In a few minutes an
orchard of smokestacks appears beyond the treetops, ringed by
the slanted tin roofs of miners' homes. The pines part, ushering us
down a corridor of crooked stone buildings braced with ice. We
wind through the snowy streets, past half-buried warehouses, past
belching chimneys and pumping turbines that are denied sleep
even in the dead of winter, and up the slope of a looming hillside.
At its crest, we cough to a halt before a wrought-iron gate. Two
men emerge from a crumbling guards' hut, one wielding a shovel
and the other a rifle. They exchange a few words, glancing at me,
then force the gate open on hinges rigid with cold. The taller one
waves us in, gun dangling from his shoulder like a broken limb,
and we sputter onto the unkempt, frozen grounds of the Château
de Verdira.

Of a hundred windows, only a dozen are lit. The château, likely
a sister to the luxury hotels that once dotted these mountains, has
mostly crumbled into darkness, its outer wings abandoned to the
elements or repurposed to house animals in winter. Only the cen-
tral tower, a looming, crooked thing, is alive tonight. It arcs over
us, as if bending to allow the single eye of the highest window—
the baron's, of course—to scrutinize approaching visitors. Bathed
in the weak light of the manor, Baker leads me up the snowy steps
to the oak doors. He raps thrice, and in a blur of marmot-furred
coat, retreats to his vehicle. The engine roars, the gears scream,
and he disappears into the dusk.

I knock twice more before a maid answers. She narrows her

eyes at my inadequate topcoat and unfamiliar face, and wordlessly invites me out of the cold. Sylvie is her name, but she will introduce herself to me later, after I have proven trustworthy. For now, she saves the smiles and curtsies, and bids me wait under the jade dome of the foyer. I remove my hat and count the cracks running through the stone to pass the time, but only reach ninety-three before she returns to present me with the Baron de Verdira's only son, Didier.

He barely resembles himself. His handsome face seems to have withered in my short absence, and behind the cracked glass of his pince-nez, his eyes are colored with fatigue.

"You must be the replacement," he says. "I didn't think you'd come for another few days, at least. And at this time of evening—sweetest hell, I hope you didn't walk up from the station."

"Baker was kind enough to escort me," I say.

"Had I known you'd arrive so quickly I'd have sent someone to retrieve you. And certainly well before nightfall." He attempts, valiantly, to smile. "You must be exhausted. I'll have something hot made for you. Come rest in the salon and I'll pour you a drink."

I peel off my gloves and coat, dropping them into Sylvie's outstretched arms. "I would much prefer to see the body first."

"Surely that can wait."

"I am afraid not, sieur."

Didier's eyes glide over mine, probing for the reasoning behind my urgency, but I have nothing to offer him. Somehow, I know even less than he does.

"If that is what you wish," he says. "We've laid him out in the cold so—well, you're no doubt familiar with the . . . process of decay."

"I am."

Didier lifts an oil lamp from its sconce and bids me follow, unaware that I have traveled these halls for years. He guides me through the distal veins of the château, through darkness thickened with cobwebs and dust. We wind down creaking staircases, past rows of rooms that have not seen an occupant in centuries, to a tall, unadorned metal door.

"I'll get the houseboy to bring you his old tools, if you want to . . . open him up." Didier struggles with the lock for a moment. "But with his wound, it's not hard to guess how he died."

I do not remember a wound of any sort. "Regardless, I would very much appreciate the tools."

He nods and pushes the door open in a wave of freezing air. We step into what may have once been part of a kitchen, but now serves as meat storage. Legs, torsos, and strips and mounds of venison and pork hang from hooks in varying states of disassembly. Steel bars bend across crumbling sections of wall, keeping any wandering carnivores, including hungry townsfolk, from worming their way in. On an iron butcher's table, supine and blue with cold, lies a body familiar to me.

At the sight of its sunken face and the dark puncture wound on its neck, a multitude of voices echoes in my mind, some worried, others calm, all rational. A hundred mouths whisper twice as many questions, and for a moment—not the first in my life, though it is rare—I am at a complete loss.

"Who is responsible for this?" I ask.

"I have no idea," Didier replies. He lingers by the door, eyes averted. "Nobody had anything against him, except for my father, perhaps. But he has something against everyone, and he can barely get out of bed to eat, much less drive a scalpel into someone's throat. I can't help but suspect . . ." Didier pauses. "I suspect he did this to himself."

I say nothing. I cannot confirm nor controvert his theory, since I have no recollection of the event. I was not there, and that is what terrifies me.

"I'll be back in a moment," Didier says, and disappears.

I take a breath, quieting all my voices, and inspect the corpse's exterior, noting every detail to be stored in my hall of recorded deaths. I observe the blackish toes, the atrophic genitalia, the missing fingernails and molars—all expected signs of the unique condition the body carried in life. There are only two things out of the ordinary: a clean puncture on the anterolateral neck, and a series of thin black marks divaricating from both eyelids. The former is clearly the immediate cause of death, but the latter may be an underlying one.

I am mulling over the potential significance of the discolored vessels when Didier returns with the houseboy in tow. The silent young man hands me my bag, then watches intently as I don my gloves and mask. I would like to ask him a few questions, since in my experience servants often have a better grasp of the goings-on of their masters than the masters themselves, but I know he cannot answer me.

I address Didier instead. "Tell me what happened."

He fidgets as I peel back an eyelid to examine the blackened conjunctiva. "Well," he starts, "he fell ill about a week ago, maybe more—influenza or some such, perhaps. We didn't think much of it."

I did not, either. "Strange," I mutter.

The body's pupils shine with a disturbing color, but I do not know if it is a result of trauma or a chemical reaction. One voice suggests simple postmortem opacification of the cornea, while another suggests an infection. Images of my books, open to their relevant pages, appear before me, but I cannot focus on the words at the moment. These eyes are occupied.

"I found it strange as well," Didier continues. "He was the last person I'd expect to see so ill, but he was showing his age of late. He took to bed for a few days—"

"How many?"

"Hm . . . three, I believe. My father's fit lasted as long."

I reach for memories of the past week. They are filled with nights of blurred, confused malaise, consistent with a seasonal virus. The symptoms are familiar to me, and not particularly worrisome. I have been ill before. No human body is impervious to invasion.

"Time of death?" I ask.

"I'm . . . not sure. Émile—this fellow here—found him the morning before last, at about six. He was still warm."

I glance back at the servant. His dark eyes are fixed on the corpse, wide but dry. He crosses his arms, distress evinced only by one gray hand tightening to a fist.

"What do you know about these marks?" I ask.

Didier's gaze falls to the corpse's sunken cheeks and the color drains from his own. "I don't know anything. His eyes were darkened for . . . a fortnight, maybe. I didn't look closely at them. I presumed he was tired. Each time he came to my father's room, it looked a little worse."

With a sound that could turn the hardest of stomachs, I scoop out the body's left eye. It does not yield easily, and as I tug it away from the clinging extraocular muscles a few ropes of dark fluid drip from the discolored sclera. A black, hairlike substance that I cannot identify clings to the severed optic nerve. The socket is tangled with the stuff, and it holds fast when I apply my blunt forceps. My mind fills with theories and memories—of necrosis, gliomata, masses of hair I sometimes pull from children's stomachs—but each thought dissipates as readily as it appears.

Behind me, Didier squirms. I know he does not enjoy sights like these. Even when he ascends the tower to help clean his father's tubes and replace his filters, he cannot hide his aversion. But he lingers to answer my questions, shuddering with cold and discomfort.

"Did you notice any uncharacteristic behavior?" I ask, prodding the mysterious substance.

"He acted as if he had a headache, and he was shivering quite a bit. He was not entirely . . . present, at the end. He muttered to himself, but he often did that."

"That sounds correct," I say. Fatigue, myalgia, blurred vision, impaired cognition and communication are common symptoms of a thousand nonfatal pathogens. Foolishly, I did not consider the possibility of a more malicious infection.

After exploring the optic canal, I manage to grip the growth with the tips of my forceps. It resists me at first, but I twist, plucking tiny tendrils from walls of connective tissue. A substantial part of the thing pulls loose, and the hairs widen, meeting in black confluences toward what must be the body of some sort of organism. With a soft popping sound, I pull it from the bone, past the socket, and into the cold air.

A muffled gasp escapes Didier's throat—then another, quieter exhalation tumbles from Émile.

"A container, please," I say, as dangling black offshoots twitch at the end of my forceps.

The servant fishes a thin phial from my bag, angling it with mercifully steady hands as I place the creature inside. By the time I secure a lid over the glass and remove my gloves, it is already dead.

Voices spell out caution and curiosity in equal measure. Some propose the hairlike processes are fungal hyphae, others suggest tactile flagella, and still others are unsure, turning the pages of a thousand biological texts as they scour the breadth of my knowledge. All, however, spiral toward a similar, terrifying conclusion.

It appears I have a competitor.

II

THREE HUNDRED AND THIRTY miles south of Verdira—give or take a few due to the unpredictable and sometimes catastrophic tremors that wrinkle or stretch the landscape like a tablecloth—there is a snowless city where the reds and browns of the earth shine like rivers. It is a network of sunbaked brick and ruby cobblestones, alive with oil-scented wind and the constant hum of electricity. It is the vault which holds the surviving knowledge of the known world, a hub where the spokes of the railways meet, and an altar at which keening poets leave their hearts. I can easily mirror their sentiment. Inultus is where I have left my brain.

Encased in a domed skull of marble and jade, my library is a maze of time-eaten tomes, of ancient journals and accumulated specimens, a repository of every medical and biological fact left to humankind. If there exists a description of a black organism fond of nestling in the optic canal, if any long-dead expert once etched an illustration of a creature small as an infant's finger, dozens of limbs tapering to hair-thin filaments, it would surely be buried in those overstuffed shelves.

As I stand petrified in the iceroom of the Château de Verdira, staring at the motionless contents of the phial in the houseboy's hands, the library is alive with noise. Shoes click across the moon-lit marble; the spines of books unopened for centuries creak in pain as their pages are revealed once more; the timbres of a hundred worried voices billow out the windows into the warm air. The dry, electric pulse of the city carries a jolt of panic from the Interprovincial Medical Institute, conducts it over tiled rooftops, between tall bursts of reddish fronds, and across the rattling paths of trolleys that howl like tomcats in the night. Confusion diffuses across the city, sweeping into every physician in Inultus within a fraction of a second.

The silent shock propagates unseen by the majority of the city—at most, a patient might look on his doctor's face and mistake the frown for a poor prognosis, or a surgeon's hand might pause before resuming its impeccable cut. Though most of my hearts have risen to my throats in palpitating unison, my stethoscopes do not stray from rib cages, my eyes do not leave my books.

Only one body, exhausted from a day's work in the Inultan governor's aeronautic laboratory, gives way under the weight of my surprise. In the dusty red light of the dirigible bay, I stumble, the stretcher's handles slipping from my grasp. My patient cries out as he hits the floor, limbs splayed, jointed in places every textbook left on Earth says they should not be. He rolls over, groaning with such force he unsettles a hive of starlings nesting in the ventilation shafts.

"What is wrong with you?" The stretcher's other carrier, a hard-faced engineer, bends to help his fallen comrade. "Ten minutes past you lift half an engine off this man, and now you can't lift *him*?"

I look to the cloud of birds spilling out of the laboratory's walls, circling the gargantuan, half-assembled dome of the airship. I hesitate, considering an explanation, but nothing comes to me. I only push the injured technician back onto his stretcher and resume the burden of his weight. "Forgive me," I say.

"Forgive me." In the small, freezing room in the Château de

Verdira, my voice sounds flat, muffled. "Émile, I am going to ask you to keep hold of that phial for a moment."

The young man nods, pinching it in cautious hands, as if its contents might spring back to life at any moment. He affects calm expertly, as any servant of the château can, drawing his mouth into a thin, taut line.

I do not think he notices the way my forceps tremble as I lay them on the table. It is subtle, no more than a slight twitch in these steady fingers, but I am glad I have entrusted him with the delicate work of holding the phial. None of my hands have shaken like this in at least half a century.

A patient once told me that there are as many ways to die as there are drops in the acid sea. I disagree. Though the sea is vast, I am certain it is finite.

It is simple to attribute death to one ailment or another, to moon-ague or blackworm, to sepsis, ischemia, murder, suicide. In truth, each is an accumulation of proximate and ultimate causes, sudden and gradual, accidental and intentional. When one of my bodies expires, I can always trace the reasons why, often down to the cellular level. Occasionally I initiate the process, if a host is injured beyond repair or debilitated by age. But when I destroy a body, I do so from the inside, minimizing pain and spillage. I do it with the same reluctance as a person facing the inevitability of cutting off their own gangrenous toe. They do not take blades to their own parts without exhausting all other options, and neither do I.

This death was not of my conscious doing. It could have been an accident, an assault, or a damaged cerebral cortex desperate to escape the pain of infection. I know better than to direct all my suspicion to something as simple as a bloodstained scalpel. I have been in this business too long to mistake death's mechanism with its cause.

Of course, I keep the organism contained. The glass phial sits

securely in Émile's hands, reflecting the flickering lights of the château's sconces like a lantern. He does not look at the thing, but
keeps his eyes raised, as if he believes the old adage Sylvie repeats
to Didier's twin daughters at bedtime: so long as one never looks a
monster in the eye, one is safe from it. If I did not know him quite
well already, I would say he appears more resolute than fearful.
Before a new guest to the Château de Verdira, he is dedicated to
formality. He will soften to me in time, but I allow him his rigid
decorum. If there is one thing that defines a good servant, as the
baron says, it is his ability to suffer his offices nobly.

Émile leads me to my old rooms, situated at the heart of the
manor. It is a humble suite, but I do not demand much. One chamber for living and sleeping, one for bathing, and one for my books,
microscope, and other necessities. All three are connected to the
château's fickle electric wiring, and all three, I hope, have been
thoroughly scrubbed of bloodstains.

Émile ushers me into my firelit chambers and places the organism on my shelf, beside rows of familiar tools and medicines. He
retreats from the phial, not quite willing to turn his back to it until
he reaches the doorway. He stops to bow on the way out, and I
tell him not to bother bringing supper. Though this stomach can
rumble loud enough to shake loose the stones in the walls, it is
strangely still. Exhaustion and worry have silenced it.

In the moonlight of Inultus, a profusion of brains is at work.
Some of them urge me to dissect the organism immediately, begging for a sample to be sent to the city. Others insist a quarantine
is best. Still others send me flashes and snippets of words and diagrams, faded pages of ancient texts. My thoughts are disjointed,
blurred with the distance between my subject of study and my
books, but I do not panic.

The brain I have brought here is analytical and inquisitive. It
works well, and works elegantly. It retains useful information and
discards irrelevancies with consistency and precision. These hands
are steady, these eyes are sharp, this constitution is strong. This
host is one of my best.

But it is certainly tired. While I remain awake, poring over my
books, while I tend to the unfortunate technician I dropped in

the dirigible bay, I crawl into bed. Curled up under the covers, warm and limp like a sore muscle, I close these eyes and watch the moonlight pass over the stained-glass windows of my library. I count seventeen ticks of the grandfather clock in Verdira before the palm-scented air ushers this body into a deep rest.

III

"PEOPLE DIE," THE BARON says. "You're here to replace my doctor, not mourn him."

The old man wheezes and shifts on his pillows, bathed in soft exhaust. A chorus of machines hums and whirs around him, pumping fluid through the crude fabric of tubes weaving in and out of his skin. When he lowers a stained handkerchief from his bluish mouth to speak, a foul odor escapes. "Just throw him in the furnace and be done with it."

Didier has accompanied me to his father's bedside, perhaps because he thinks he can defend me against the old man's verbal attacks. He does not know I am already accustomed to the baron. This is the second time I have had the displeasure of introducing myself to him.

"Monsieur," I say, "with your permission, I would preserve the cadaver in the iceroom and conduct a thorough autopsy."

"What more is there to see? The bastard finally got tired of emptying bedpans and took the quick way out." The baron pauses to cough, or perhaps laugh, into his handkerchief. "He'd easily be able to poke himself in the—well, whatever vessel it is that goes to the brain."

The puncture had, in fact, not been as precise as I would expect from a deliberate act of self-annihilation, but a shaking hand can miss its mark.

Didier clears his throat. "It is still unclear if he . . . did this to himself."

"Who else could've done it? Émile? The twins? *Me?*"

"Of course not," I say. When it comes to ordering executions, the baron is as creative as he is prolific, but even he hesitates to cross the Institute. At the very least, he would secure a new physician before disposing of his old one.

"Surprised he didn't end himself sooner." The baron wipes a string of mucus from his nose. "Fifteen winters in, and he finally breaks."

"Pèren, *please,*" Didier hisses. "There is reason to investigate further. Evidently there was something—something growing inside . . ." He wavers at the conversational precipice, glancing to me for assistance.

"I discovered a retro-orbital mass," I say. "Perhaps some sort of neoplasm or parasitic growth." Even after a night of digging through my library, I am still unable to pinpoint the specifics. As we speak, a hundred fingers sweep along lines of texts, but none has been lucky enough to land on a satisfactory diagnosis. "It is a disease unknown to me, and there is some possibility it is contagious."

"Well, who's it spread to?" The baron hacks into his handkerchief and tosses it to the floor, where Émile, swift and silent as a passing thought, swoops in to dispose of it.

"No one, as far as I can detect," I say. "All who have come into contact with the corpse appear healthy. And since no one else in the household has reported symptoms, I suspect the infection was contracted somewhere outside the château. Perhaps outside Verdira proper—"

"Oh, *supe,*" the baron says. "Let the winter kill it. Only a dog-brained lunatic would wander outside town this time of year anyway."

"With all respect," I reply, "even the lunatics are under my care."

The baron does not seem to hear me. "We should've seen this coming. He never lived the most salubrious lifestyle, did he? Always wandering out too close to dark, always with his face uncovered. Not in fine fettle, not at all. Last time he was up here he left a fingernail in my kidney." He motions with a gnarled hand to a round, whirring machine. "Fucking incompetent."

Of course, I would never have been so careless, but I allow the baron his indulgences. Of all the riches he possesses, the right to complain is his most treasured. "If you are feeling ill, monsieur—"

"Right as rain. I'm in perfect health, no thanks to your predecessor." He takes a moment to pick me apart with his cloudy eyes, once a sharp blue but now faded to a chalky, yellowish gray. "And you seem about half as capable as he was. Heaven's shit, what was the Institute thinking, sending you here? You look like you spat out your maman's tit sometime last week."

"*Pèren*—" Didier starts.

"What sort of rocks does the Institute pull you out from under nowadays?"

"I must insist—"

"Shut up, Didier. I'm asking a question. What sort of rocks?"

I have heard this query before. A thousand elderly patriarchs have hurled similar questions at me, attempting to gain a foothold over me, to crack me open and account for the invincible queerness of the Interprovincial Medical Institute's physicians. The interrogations often hinge on aspects of my outward appearance, the darkness of my skins, the perception of my sexes, the wrinkles on my faces, or my invariably small size. I do not know if any of these factors particularly matter to the baron. He has asked me this question before, in identical words. It is, apparently, at the forefront of his arsenal of interrogative half insults.

Just to see his eyebrows rise and the needle gauges on his machines twitch, I supply the same answer I did the first time I met him. "Whichever rocks are easiest to turn over."

The baron shakes with something that resembles laughter.

"Just as insufferable as the last one, aren't you?" He pauses to catch his breath, lips curled back over gray teeth. "Can't imagine it'll be long before you end up like him."

I can almost hear Didier's overtaxed joints pop as he tenses every muscle between neck and ankle. "Pèren, that is no way to speak to your physician—"

"I'll give you half a day to cut the corpse apart," the baron says. "Then dispose of it. There are already too many useless bodies in this house."

"Monsieur," I begin, "half a day is hardly adequate. I must first—"

"Spare me your disquisition, doctor. Just take care of this little disaster and don't bring it up in my presence again. I've already got enough to worry about, running this shit show." He throws out a bluish hand and shakes it until Émile deposits a clean handkerchief into his palm. "Now, if you please, remove yourselves. Houseboy, you too. You reek of dog."

We all bow to the baron and retreat, sidestepping clusters of tubing and vibrating machinery. We emerge onto the tower's spiral staircase, and when we descend far enough to evade the baron's still-sharp hearing, Didier releases a sigh.

"Please forgive him," he says. "He's only so surly because he's in great pain. He's . . . well, I hate to think of it, but I believe he's very near the end."

Didier, like the rest of the household, certainly does not hate to think of it, though the baron's death is nothing more than a distant possibility. Conservatively, I give him another forty years before he expires. It would not surprise me if he lasted well into Didier's final days, surviving on nothing but unyielding spite. I have seen it happen before, with sicker men than the baron.

I have a sizable collection of patients like him, whirring and wheezing across the habitable land, from Misulah to the coast, knee-deep in their own graves but unwilling to sink further. They pay generously for the opportunity to prolong their suffering, and I do not challenge them. I have dozens of clinics to upkeep and hundreds of mouths to feed.

"Everyone dies differently," I say. "Some more gracefully than others."

"And this week has done no favors for his mood." Didier shakes his head. "Doctor, I would like to move quickly past this . . . incident. I want a swift and painless transition, as I'm sure you do. So if you need anything from me, anything at all, do not hesitate to ask Émile."

"I will. Maeci, sieur."

"He always knows where to find me. He's well-mannered, and quite competent. Though I hope you do not mind a bit of fur. Here—" The houseboy grimaces a little as Didier rakes a gray tuft from his sleeve. "He helps tend the kennels, you see."

"I see."

"Send him out for anything you need from town. You needn't leave the château. In fact, it's best if you don't. With winter rolling in, you don't want to find yourself caught outside our walls. It would be a great shame if we were to lose two physicians in the span of a week."

In a small clinic on the prairies, a brain with a paranoid predisposition tries to decipher that as a threat, while another laughs at the suggestion. Didier does not threaten—at least not nearly as adeptly as his father.

"You will not lose me," I say, with all sincerity. This particular host might succumb to the freezing storms and debilitating illnesses the winter brings, but I will not.

Émile does not, or perhaps cannot, speak. This in no way precludes him from being an excellent conversationalist. He spells his thoughts clearly through his frowns and nods, the forthcoming twitches of his eyebrows, the bending of his elbows and wrists. He is a master quip-smith, a clever composer of difficult questions, and, though rarely expressed, a smiler of considerable skill.

He slides back into the role of doctor's assistant with ease. He has helped me many times before, holding down the twins for their vaccinations, adjusting the baron's levers and dials, clutching the trembling hand of Didier's wife during her ill-fated parturitions. Émile himself may not recognize the familiarity of his situation, but his hands do.

While I take apart my body, he hovers at my side. His gloved fingers tap against cartilage, measure the lengths of cross sections, tilt the bistoury to ask in bluish glints where and when to cut. He hides his revulsion well, but I have known him long enough to recognize the subtle furrows in his brow, to catch the uneasy way he purses his mouth to nibble at the inside of his lip. His dark eyes keep wandering to the corpse's sunken face, to the parasite's thin, severed limbs clinging to its enucleated orbit. He is accustomed to seeing that face animated, seeing its mouth smile and its wrinkles move thoughtfully along its forehead.

It saddens me too, to deconstruct an old host, to reduce its complex machinery to parts, to erase its singularities. Like every body, this one has sustained its fair share of injuries, unique as the whorls on its fingers. Every scar is known to me, every fracture, burn, and laceration, every sign of decay that my occupancy has inflicted. I have used this one well, but it would have enjoyed many days ahead, had it not been for a wayward lancet.

There are no signs of a struggle, and the angle at which the blade entered is consistent with self-infliction. Human anatomy is woven into my brains as deeply as instinct, so it would be difficult to miss the common carotid with any hand of mine. It is entirely out of my character to stoop to such methods of eliminating a body, but I cannot deny the evidence laid before me. At this moment, without an inkling as to who would kill me or why, I must surmise that I did this to myself, without my own knowledge.

When I am finished taking samples, when I have examined myself thoroughly, I throw a thin sheet over my disassembled corpse. I nod to Émile, and we remove our coats and masks. All that cannot be sterilized is left to burn with my body.

The houseboy helps me carry the specimens back to my chambers. We stain and plate the tissue in apprehensive silence, arranging oil lanterns around the small shrine dedicated to my brass microscope. It is an ancient, maladjusted piece of machinery, a plaything compared to those back home, but I try to have one at hand wherever I am. It is always practical to have a window into oneself.

If you cut a host of mine and smear my blood, or if you magnify a thin sample of tissue under decent light, you will see, briefly, before decay takes hold, a spatter of perfectly spherical white flecks. Should you tell those tiny motes to smile, you will see their host's lips upturn in obedience. That is because, at the innumerable little cores of my being, I am something of a pleaser.

When I lower my gaze to the microscope's single eyepiece, I spy the shriveled fragments of my own cells, as expected. I can see no traces of any other invader, no black hyphae or curled flagella. Dermal, mucous, pulmonary, gastrointestinal—I place sample after sample under the scrutinizing lens but I can make out no certain pathology. My new competitor apparently knows how to cover its tracks.

In my library, two long-fingered hands dance along a typewriter, spelling out the words my mouth forms as I linger over my microscope. There is not much I can commit to paper, since I am limited by my equipment and what chemicals are available for staining, dissolving, and preserving. *Mass is 2.5 cems long, 17 grs*, I type. *Microscopically, at first glance resembles septate hyphae, though higher magnification reveals a more complex striated structure. I cannot immediately assign it to any taxonomical category. Some characteristics suggest fungal tissue, others animal. No available information on its reproductive habits or method of transmission. For now* . . . Here, my fingers pause as I mull over the possibilities. *I will conclude only that it appears to borrow attributes from several different kingdoms. Perhaps even my own.*

"Whichever that is," I mutter. The remnants of the world's once-vast knowledge have so far failed to produce an answer to that question, despite my unabating search. "I suppose I could send a sample of this creature back to Inultus. Baker can weld a secure box for it."

A few mouths back home shout an adamant yes, but more warn me of the foolishness of sending a possibly contagious pathogen back to the city before I know a thing about it. I must concede I have a fair point.

Smearing a cluster of tissue from a distal appendage reveals fragments of a filamentous structure. Resembles muscular fiber. Possibly necessary for motility, possibly as a mechanism for invading a host body. Flagellates, spores, larvae, or other recognizable infectious cells are notably absent in the collected human tissue. The only pathological abnormality is the macroscopic organism itself.

One hundred and seventy-two miles southwest of Verdira, I am pulling a whiteworm the length of my arm from the throat of a caravanner's son. "Perhaps what I see now is all there is to see," I tell myself from across the barren prairies. My patient, the poor child, unclenches his fists and tries to force a smile around the body of the worm. He does not know I am not speaking of his parasite, which I anticipate is still coiling much of its length inside him. "A whiteworm even of this size begins as a single infective cell, floating upon the surface of still water. But many of its cousins do not undergo such radical transformations."

"An whay es y'tell em that?" the patient's mother asks, leather-armored hands squeezing his shoulders. "Just *pull*."

I can see my reasoning. Perhaps this tangle of tiny black limbs has always been exactly that. Perhaps when I first encountered it, I thought it was nothing more than a hairball spat up by one of the château's perpetually gagging cats.

"But I would *remember* such a thing," my mouth in Verdira blurts, drawing a curious glance from Émile. A writhing tangle entering one of my hosts by any orifice would be a notable occurrence. I would recall seeing it, ingesting it, feeling it burrow under my skin—were it not for the gaps in my memory. Somehow, that tiny creature has carved holes into my brain, both literally and figuratively.

It is absurd to think this thing lived in me for days—perhaps even weeks—severing my carefully crafted neural circuits, and I did not notice. I had spent fifty years dancing along those veins, seeing through those eyes, riding the tides of emotion and logic contained in those wonderful networks of axons. I had inhabited that body as thoroughly and faithfully as any tenant, sharing it with billions of other occupants, with kingdoms and communes

of delicate flagellates and sturdy rods, outposts of mites and pro-
tists, trading, talking, battling. But now I feel as if I am walking
through a house I once knew well, only to discover the halls and
staircases have rearranged themselves in my absence.

My sigh, heavy enough to echo from Verdira all the way to the
southern floodlands, seems to startle the houseboy. He jumps to
attention, tweezers in one gloved hand, basin of disinfectant in
the other.

"Émile," I say, "I take it this is the first time you have encountered a creature like this?" I do not need to gesture to the phial.

He nods.

"It is . . . novel." Most of my other mouths pipe in with more
descriptors, some reasonable, some not, and I realize I ought to give
the specimen a name. A hundred voices leap forward with suggestions: *Macrosporidia, Pseudomycota,* Discovery 814-Verd, To-Be-
Determined #290—no, #289, brine lamprey was classified last week.
"Whatever it is," I say, half to myself, half to the servant lingering
beside my host in Verdira, "it is certainly clever, if it can move
through a body without leaving evidence."

"There may be evidence I cannot yet see," I assure myself from
a clinic on the oily coast.

"You will inform me," I turn back to Émile, "if you encounter
anything unusual around the house." He raises an eyebrow. "Anything more unusual than . . . usual."

This elicits an amused frown from him. He nods.

"I suppose I should dismiss you." I glance at my timepiece, and
then again, as if its restless face can tell me where five hours and
twelve minutes have fled. "It has been a long afternoon. Go and take
some time for yourself."

He turns to the exit, no doubt heading for the kennels, where
he will commiserate wordlessly with his wordless friends. But he
pauses in the doorway, fingers bending shyly, as if they want to
spell something for me but do not quite know how.

"Do you have a question?" I ask.

His lips disappear into his mouth.

"What is it?"

He looks to his feet, then the wall, and his fingers fall still.

"Is it about how my predecessor died?"

He brings his hand to his own neck.

"That is my conclusion as well. But if you know something else, I implore you to come out with it."

He shakes his head.

"Well, then. I appreciate your assistance, Émile. Please inform me if you discover anything of interest. Or if you fall ill."

He gives me a solid blink of acquiescence, but neither of us anticipates him coming to me in a state resembling that of my old body, with sunken, blackish eyelids and a dizzied expression. I have never seen the boy take sick in his life.

His perpetual health is one reason among many that I had once thought to take him back to the city with me. But Didier staunchly refused, despite my offers of generous compensation. He had cited only one reason, one that still makes little sense to me. He had frowned, wiped his spectacles on his shirttails, and said, "Those who are born here die here, doctor. It's just the way it is."

As Émile disappears into the darkness of the hallway, I cannot help but wonder if I have missed a valuable opportunity. His eyes are sharp, his mind sharper, and if the origin of his muteness is neural or psychogenic rather than physiological, it is likely I could repair it. But he is too old now, and there is no shortage of bright, talented human beings available to me. I do not need Émile, and I like him enough that I would rather not obliterate him.

IV

SUPPER—PROPER SUPPER—is a once-weekly affair in the Château de Verdira. Six days out of seven, the large oak dining table stands perfectly set but perfectly empty. From early evening to midnight, bells are rung from all habitable corners of the mansion, servants scurry from kitchens to bedrooms with covered plates, and I sup in the merciful quiet of my own chambers. But on the final day of each week, the baron is scrubbed clean of crust and fluid, adorned in his finest blankets, hauled into his wheeled recliner, and carried down from the tower on the backs of sweating servants. Bags of urine and serum swinging like pendulums from his armrests, he is pushed through the château's winding halls and deposited at the head of the table. In preparation the twins help one another into their velvet dresses and attempt to separate the tangles in their dark curls, their mother douses herself in perfume I can smell from here to Inultus, and Didier consumes at least three-quarters of a bottle of gin.

Tonight, he has asked me to join him for apéritifs in the salon. The invitation, arriving an hour before suppertime in Sylvie's outstretched hand, contains an apology for the infelicitous nature of my first days in the château, and a promise that a taste of the salon's fine spirits will acclimate me to the house and the family that occupies it. What I have surmised from nearly fifteen years of living here, however, and what Didier in forty has failed to, is that no amount of alcohol can make his family agreeable.

As I button my waistcoat and tie my cravat, I glance at the small phial glinting beside my microscope. The organism inside looks much the same as when I first pulled it from my decaying tissue. Motionless and confined to its airtight prison, it seems perfectly harmless, but I do not relish the thought of it sitting here unguarded and unobserved. Because I cannot convince myself not to, I reach out for the container and turn it in the candlelight, examining it thoroughly for cracks before slipping it into my pocket.

At the same moment, in the Inultan aerostat laboratory, a pipe of toxic exhaust swells and bursts. A man screams, another rushes for help, and a cloud of yellowish fumes churns with such ferocity nearly all my skins can feel it. By the time I reach the salon, the acrid billow has burned through three machinists, the governor has been summoned, and my body in Verdira has broken into a mild sweat.

Didier, sunk into a seat so plush it seems to have halfway swallowed him, attempts to welcome me. Already several drinks deep and trapped a fair bit deeper in the cushions, he struggles to scoot forward, hand outstretched. I take it, unsure if he is honoring me with his touch or asking for help to stand up.

"What would you like?" he asks. "Pastis, gin, sherry?"

"Water," I answer.

"Just like your predecessor, then." He smiles. "Is temperance enforced by the Institute?"

"I suppose it is." I am not fond of intoxication, especially when it begins to spread between brains.

"What the *fuck* just happened?" the foreman shouts. I am on my knees, wrapping a mechanic's scorched shoulder, ears ringing.

Didier reaches for a brass bellpull. "Let me call someone to get you a glass."

"That is quite all right." I pretend to explore the salon, shuffling across the cracked marble to an ancient bookcase that has not, I suspect, seen a book in several centuries. Verdira is not a place of written words. Oral tradition ruled here, at least until the last Montish storytellers were slaughtered in the château's garden.

"Yes, the crystalware is just to your left," Didier says. "Right there. And the bottles are—well, you seem to know where you're going."

"I have been in many salons like this one," I say.

"I suppose you have." His face falls. "I must apologize on behalf of our humble château, doctor. It is much improved from when my family first discovered it, but I'm afraid it's still in quite a state of disrepair."

"Yet it has its luxuries." I drink, soothing cold spreading from this mouth to my fume-burned throat in Inultus. "The water is fresher here than anywhere else."

"Oh, certainly it is. And soon we will have it running through the pipes. Our mechanist is expanding the circuitry, too—you'll see, doctor. If the wheatrock treats us well, in five or so years the château will be as it once was. Fit for the world's greatest men to walk her halls."

I give him a supportive smile. Didier has dreamed for decades of a château half a decade distant, filled with noble guests, artists and politicians and magnates. Rebuilt, bright-lit, washed clean of its massacres and ghosts. Even with a few hundred brains at my disposal, I cannot envision it.

"We have just raised the new chandelier in the dining hall," Didier smiles. "And at the moment I am having some cave-grass tapestries restored. I don't suppose you have ever been introduced to old Montish art?"

"Do not let that man take me on another tour of his collection," I warn myself from a roaring trolley.

"Here and there," I say.

"They're in quite a sorry condition, but once cleaned they will look absolutely magnificent. They truly are masterpieces, doctor. Quite dissimilar from the ceramics or sculptures in Inultus— weaving is such an underappreciated art in the south, I've found. They do not much understand the beauty of utility, or vice versa."

A crack runs along the glass face of a pressure gauge. Hot air screams through a pipe opposite me.

"I see I am boring you," Didier laughs.

"Not at all, sieur." I seat myself opposite him.

"And how fares your investigation, doctor? Sylvie tells me you've been spending time in the iceroom. Examining . . ." He pauses, perhaps unwilling to guess aloud exactly what I have been doing to my corpse.

"I had a thorough look at it, yes. Unfortunately I have not discovered anything of value."

"With regards to his wound?"

"Or the infection. I cannot pinpoint its source."

Didier's thumb taps against his stubbled chin. "Perhaps he brought it from Inultus, when he first came up."

"If so, it must have an incubation period of fifteen years," I say. More than enough time for me to locate and expel any parasite, no matter the size. I am a magnanimous sharer, but there are some offenses I do not tolerate. "Not impossible, but unlikely."

"Odd that he was the only one with symptoms," Didier says. "Perhaps he acquired his illness doing something the rest of us didn't. Or going somewhere we haven't."

I swallow a mouthful of water and my thoughts slip into a dark cavern. My vision narrows to a tunnel, ringed by ridges of stone like the rib cage of some colossal, petrified animal. It is a place only I have been, and I do not want to go there again. "I intended to ask around the château to discover if anyone has seen a similar organism before."

"Good dead gods, I'd *hope* not. I certainly haven't."

Two jolting smells meet my nostrils, first a plume of chemical smoke from the aerostat lab, then a cloud of perfume wafting in from the salon's doorway. One is followed by a call for evacuation, the other is followed by Didier's wife, hair piled high, dark silk shining over the globe of her stomach.

"Tippling again without me, damour?" she asks.

"Hélène." Didier's smile is joyless, fragile. "Can you not see the good doctor and I are having a chat?"

"Of course not," she answers, gliding to the shelf of bottles and looking it over with narrowed brown eyes. "I see two people sitting across from each other, and the thought that they might be conversing did not, in fact, cross my mind."

"Yes, well, we were about to discuss the ghastly intricacies of medical autopsy, were we not?" He looks to me for help. "Surely a topic that holds little interest for you."

"As it does for *you*?" Hélène laughs. "You'd faint three words into a conversation about the 'ghastly intricacies' of anything." She reaches for a decanter of liqueur and pours a generous volume into a faceted glass.

"Must you *really*—"

"I was looking for you, doctor," she continues, slipping onto the chesterfield and raising the glass to her lips. "But I couldn't find you amid this chaos over our dear dead physician. You'd think his was the first corpse found in this miserable old house, the way the servants are acting out."

"Hélène, you should not be drinking," Didier says.

"There's a development on my skin that might interest you, doctor," she continues. "A boil, right here." She lifts her arm and wrestles with her loose sleeve, rolling it up to her shoulder. "Touch it. I swear it's started leaking."

"*Hélène!*" Didier hisses. "I beg you, chérin, for the sake of propriety—"

"Go on, it's right there—oh, look at those smooth hands of yours, fresh from the cradle. And with all your fingers! So nice to see a fetching sapling among all these frostbitten trees."

"Are you already drunk?" Didier clutches his forehead. "You shouldn't . . . especially not as you are."

"Oh, *please*. You know well enough that when I was heavy with the twins I was much heavier with beer."

"Don't speak of such things, not in front of—"

"Our physician?" She laughs. "The only person who has any business prying into my maternal health? Dead gods, mayrin. A nip here and there helps me get through it."

A mild breeze wafts through the windows of my library, fluttering the pages of a thousand ancient journals, and despite them all, I cannot argue with her. Hélène's attempts at producing a sibling for the twins have failed far more spectacularly than anything described in the old texts. Her stillbirths are complex and fascinating, uniquely disastrous on a cellular level. I have preserved several of the unfortunate creatures in my collection of specimens, and they are often at the forefront of at least one of my brains. It is difficult to pass by them without pausing to marvel.

"Touch it," Hélène continues, gesturing to the alleged boil. "It's right here."

"Stop that," her husband says.

I lean in to examine her smooth, flushed skin. "I do not see anything."

"Did I ask if you *saw* anything? I told you to touch it."

I palpate her axilla and ribs, and find nothing appreciable, much less anything that could express any sort of fluid.

"I cannot *believe* you," Didier moans. "Leave, now. I command you to leave."

She smiles. "Damour, can you not see I am engaged at the moment?"

"I am afraid your skin appears perfectly healthy," I tell her.

"It's those damn *dogs,* doctor," she says. "I can't be in the same house as those things, they ruin my complexion. They're not natural. They're not natural and neither is this cold. I keep telling Didier it's not good for my health, you know, none of this is good for my health, but he just won't listen—push harder, it's in there."

"I apologize," I reply. "I cannot feel anything."

"Then you're as useless as the last one." She lowers her arm, unrolls her sleeve, and reclaims her drink. "May his poor soul warm itself in hell. Did you find out who killed him?"

"No, madame—"

"Not much of a mystery, I'd say—but you should keep your eye on that servant."

"Which, madame?"

"You know. That Montish one."

The thought of Émile driving a scalpel through my throat is horrifying only in its absurdity. "I am sure he has nothing to do with it," I say.

"He was always so quiet," a patient in the Whesler Isles groans as I sew up the knife wound her sweet, shy nephew has carved into her. In Inultus, an engineer explains to the governor the mechanics of pressure buildup over prolonged periods of time.

"Of course it wasn't him," Didier says. "He would never. He doesn't have it in him."

"He's a *thief,* mayrin," Hélène snaps. "Slinking around like a dog—it wouldn't surprise me in the least to learn he bites like one, too." She pauses to sip her drink, smile fragmented behind the crystal facets. "Now that I think on it, Émile and our dear physician spent quite some time together before his death, didn't they? Too much time. Perhaps it was a lover's spat—it wouldn't be the first in this household to end in blood, would it?"

Her husband turns a mortified shade of red. "How *dare*—"

"There was no such quarrel," I put in, if only to quell the rising hostilities. I like Émile as I have liked many others, but I would not engage in such acts with him, even if I were capable. "I suspect it was suicide."

"Was it?" Hélène's meticulously plucked eyebrows rise almost in pleasure. "Well, I suppose no one can blame him. Just burn his body and forget about him. Your replacement will do the same to you when this place drives you to kill yourself."

"For hell's sake, fayme," Didier mutters, slumped in defeat.

"Madame, I was hoping . . ." I pause, finger brushing the container in my pocket. "I wanted to inquire if you recognized . . ."

Unprompted and untouched, a liquor bottle flies from the shelf and dashes itself to pieces on the floor. My question dies on my tongue.

"Oh dear." A lump travels down Didier's throat as he watches the glass spin across the chipped marble. "How do you suppose they managed that?"

"Wretched girls," Hélène sighs. "They know they're not permitted in the salon."

The electric lamps stutter, the candles flicker in a sourceless breeze, and for a moment the room is engulfed in darkness. Slowly, the door creaks open. A tangle of dark hair floats in, two small bodies sprouting like stems from its middle.

The twins are not physically attached at the scalp, but they might as well be. From the moment they slid from their mother, one breech and the other vertex, each boasting a full head of thick hair, the girls' skulls have found myriad ways of trying to adhere. I can spend hours separating them, extricating their curly heads from one another when my services are not needed elsewhere. I find the process time-consuming but amusing. I have separated many twins in my life, but I have nowhere else witnessed the spectacle of their convergence.

"Girls," Didier says, attempting to wriggle out of the soft gums of his armchair, "how many times have I told you to stop with your pranks?"

"You know how they make your papa nervous," Hélène says. "And—hell's sake, how did you get tangled again?"

"We were beset by ghosts," one twin says.

"They chased us down the stairwell," says the other. Their tones are identically earnest, but their faces share the same impish grin. It reminds me of myself when more than one mouth smiles at once.

"We're hurt." The first lifts her arms and proudly shows us a collection of tiny red marks, stark against her ivory skin.

"I have the same pattern but backward."

"Gods' corpses, it's obvious you pricked these yourselves," Hélène sighs. "Go clean up before your grandfather gets here. At least roll down your sleeves. Here, let me—I swear you'd be dead without me." She ushers the twins out of the salon and down the hall. Candles and lamps writhe at their passing, but when they are gone, the flames burn steadily once more.

"Those girls have such wonderful imaginations," Didier tells me, gulping the remaining quarter of his glass and reaching for the one his wife left behind. "Though I sometimes worry about them. They are always running amok, chasing ghouls and wraiths and what have you."

"It is not uncommon for children to believe in such things," I assure him. "Ghosts, monsters, or unseen friends." I do not add that the twins are well beyond the age at which those imaginings should disappear. Their poltergeists are substantial enough to send them to my chambers with the oddest complaints. If it is not sudden, transient blindness, it is memory loss; if it is not an intense bout of cacosmia, it is an inexplicable bite mark. Their ghosts are almost corporeal, prowling the halls for passersby on which to lay decidedly physical hands.

"Yes, well, we have tried to train it out of them," Didier says. "Burning through so many governesses has cost the household a fortune. It took the girls eight weeks to break the last one—by the time she fled back to the train, she swore she could see specters, too." He laughs bitterly, peeling himself from his chair, one limb at a time. "Their antics are a touch macabre, but perfectly harmless, I assure you. As a disciple of science, I imagine you will be immune to them."

He is only half right. The girls have posed a delightful challenge as long as I have known them. For years I have attempted to pick apart their minds in every sense but the literal, and they have evaded explanation or diagnosis. "In truth I find your daughters rather charming."

"Do you?" His face softens. "They really are quite clever, and have an uncanny knack for legerdemain. Unfortunately they are just bored enough to use it. It will be good for them to have the company of another child. I am hoping for a boy this time around."

He gives me a warm smile as he shows me to the door. If I did not know him so well, I might have mistaken his hope for anything but false.

By the time we make our way from the salon to the dining room, the twins are already seated at the table, hands folded in their laps. Safely disentangled, they exchange excited whispers, heads slowly gravitating back together. Hélène watches them, occasionally batting the tips of their curls away from one another.

The squeak of rusted wheels marks the baron's arrival. His shining girth, more rubber tubing than flesh, spills over his armrests as a servant delivers him to the head of the table. A few armed guards, the constable at their head, stir in the shadows around him. They circle the dining hall in silence, weaving between oak pillars and disturbing the tapestries. When they flush out no threats, they disappear again into the corridor. It is a straightforward but meaningless ritual. No one has made an attempt on the baron's life for years now.

When the guards are gone, the old man's eyes fall on me, occupying the foot of the table, too small for my throne-like chair. "Didier," he starts. "Are we going to make this a habit?"

"Our physician is a professional, not a servant," Didier replies. "A professional deserves a place at the table."

"Yes, well, far be it from me to decide who gets a seat at my own table." He lifts his serviette and coughs into it. "Let's hope you're better company than the last one. He proved to be something of a bore. Always sitting there staring into space like there was something fascinating about the ceiling."

"It is rather a nice ceiling," I offer. "The beams are carved so skillfully. A wonderful—"

The baron snorts. "If you compliment the chandelier, I'll have you hanged in its place."

"*Pèren!*" Didier hisses. "Doctor, you must forgive him. He likes to jest."

"I never jest," the baron says, lifting his bony hands so a server can massage them with a steaming cloth. As each of us are handed our own towels, Hélène leans toward me and nudges my arm.

"What was it you wanted to ask me?" she whispers. She looks me over, taking in the wrinkles in my waistcoat and the unnatural bump in my pocket. "In the salon, before the children interrupted."

I shift, suddenly very aware of the little container pressing against me. "It can wait until after supper."

"Of course it can't wait! It'll eat away at me until dessert if you don't tell me."

Hélène will not last until dessert, but I shake my head. "It is best we do not discuss it here," I whisper. "For the baron's sake."

"For the *baron's* sake!" she hisses gleefully. "What a topic it must be if we can't speak of it in front of him."

I shift as her hand drapes over the arm of my chair and brushes my trousers. A spike of anxiety twitches the hair on several of my necks, and I drop my embroidered serviette over my lap. Hélène's smile widens, but she withdraws her hand, directing it toward a large spoon as the first course arrives.

"So." Didier turns to me. "I take it you're settled in? Are the accommodations to your liking?"

"Quite satisfactory," I answer.

The baron scoops a heap of stew into his mouth. "Even if they weren't," he begins, "no one is about to haul all your dreck to a new room. Bastard servants are too lazy. Can't even carry me to the dining hall without dropping an organ of mine."

"For the love of hell," Didier mutters.

"And that's without all my parts. Stuck-up fucks refuse to bring my colon—now, how's a man to eat without his colon? I'm no scholar, but I happen to know it's an integral part of the human digestive apparatus."

"Dearest pèren." Hélène smiles mirthlessly. "Forgive us if we don't find the stench particularly appetizing. It's only fair to the rest of us."

"*Fair?* You get to bring your colon wherever you go." The baron releases a pungent cloud of derisive laughter. "I suppose I shouldn't expect you to condescend to muster up a little sympathy. Not an ounce of feminine tenderness for an old man—"

"Pèren, how do you like the new porcelain?" Didier asks. "It arrived on the last train. Salvaged from a liner off the Whesler Isles."

"This shit?" The baron does not pause to examine the porcelain before developing a distaste for it. "You'd think our forefathers would've had the self-respect to eat off plates of higher caliber. Why, those hacks in the city could've made something better—"

I recognize the advent of a lengthy monologue, so I lean back in my chair and lift my attention to the crystalline reflections of the chandelier. The smell of supper fades into the smoky air, the baron's speech blurs to a deep drone, and I return to Inultus, bathed in the glimmering red light of evening.

Before me lies a gargantuan textbook, faded pages illustrating the shapes and habits of a thousand of the world's parasites—bloodsucking, egg-laying, skin-devouring, ranging from harmless amoebae to fist-sized ticks. There is no sign of my newest discovery, nor anything I can guess is even a distant relative.

I close the book with a soft sigh, lifting a hand to stroke my lon-gest and most significant beard. "No signs of infection anywhere but my optic tissue," I say to myself. "So the eye is the likeliest portal of entry."

"Yet surely it would have left some sign of trauma," I reply from a caravan on the dusty plains. "Punctures in the sclera, abra-sions, lens displacement."

"Hm. I was overeager to remove the eye during autopsy. Any damage can be blamed on my own tools."

"And should it have burrowed through the orbit, or the sur-rounding tissue, it would have triggered a marked cascade of in-flammation."

"Transient or permanent blindness."

"A considerable amount of pain."

"A memorable event." I look deeply at myself, into myself, into eyes of brown and yellow and blue. "So why do I not remember it? Why do I remember nothing of that body's death?"

"Perhaps I did not want to remember it," I reply quietly. "Per-haps I was only thinking to hasten it."

I frown at myself, hands rising to my respective throats. Even in Verdira I must pause, laying my spoon at the edge of my bowl. I have lost eyes before, lost limbs, lost entire bodies, but the aches of old injuries do not seem to lessen the sting of new ones.

"You're staring."

The sharp whisper jolts me from my personal discourse. I lower my gaze and see Hélène, focusing on me as her father-in-law bel-lows in the background. In my negligence, I have let the serviette fall to the floor, and her hand again crawls toward my leg. Perhaps she has spied a glint of the phial's lid, and she thinks I am with-holding something interesting—at least more interesting than the baron's rambling. Or, worse, she has mistaken the elongated bulge for arousal. In my profession I have certainly seen stranger-looking erections than the thin, cylindrical protuberance in my pocket.

"What is that?" Hélène asks.

I am beginning to regret my decision to bring the organism with me. "Madame, not now. I will speak with you later."

She smiles, drawing her painted lips back from her teeth, and her hand darts forward, closing over my pant leg. I attempt to twist from her reach, but she holds fast, thumb tucked into my pocket. I do not know if it is surprise or desperation that tightens her grip, but as I tumble from my chair, I hear the sound of stitches ripping. Time protracts as the little container slips out of my pocket and flies through the air, rounded glass arcing along a shallow parabola.

All of my hands are fast, but these ones are not fast enough—they grasp empty space as the tube spirals downward, twirling past Hélène's recoiling fingers. I grit at least a dozen sets of teeth as a high-pitched crack resounds through the dining hall. A fissure crawls up the side of the glass, and as it spins to a stop, tapping musically against the uneven stone, I see the lid is the only force that holds the two halves of the phial together.

A heavy quiet descends on the table. The only sounds are the wet smack of Hélène's mouth falling open, the trickling of cold blood draining from Didier's face, and the soft, distant scream of a woman—a patient in Misulah entering the second stage of labor.

"You . . ." Didier starts. "You should not have brought that to the table." He rises, pale to the point of bluishness. He grasps for a serviette as if intending to fan himself with it.

"Brought what?" Hélène asks. Her gaze is fixed on the small tangle of black inside the container, but she seems more intrigued than horrified. "What *is* it?"

I cloak my hand in my serviette and kneel to scoop up the phial. It does not seem as if the creature has slipped through the cracked glass, but I wrap it as tightly as I can. I feel the baron's poisonous gaze bore into my back, and I know I have no choice but to answer. "I am not sure," I say. "An ocular parasite of some sort. I have never seen anything quite like it."

"Doctor, this is not the place," Didier nearly growls.

"I did not intend to . . ." I take a deep breath, knowing an explanation is not worth the effort. "Madame, I had intended to ask if you have seen anything like this before."

"Of *course* not!" Hélène half laughs. "Sweetest hell, where did you *get* that? You didn't . . . good dead gods, you didn't pull that out of Old Doc, did you?"

"I did."

The twins slide from their chairs and float toward me. "We want to look."

Their mother catches one of their four shoulders, arresting them. "Don't," she says. "You have such dreadful images in your heads as it is."

The baron holds in his words a moment longer. His bony fingers are folded under his second chin, jowls spilling over his knuckles. His eyes are unusually clear, and that does not bode well for me.

"I do hope you were not planning to introduce this to our food, doctor," he says, finally.

In the hallway, the riflemen shift. I can almost hear the constable's husky voice, the tapping of impatient boots. "Of course not," I say. "I simply . . . I did not want to leave it unattended, monsieur baron. Forgive me."

"Are you that frightened of a little bug?" he hisses. "You should be more afraid I'd call the constable in here and have your feet shot out."

"Not in the dining hall," Didier says. "And you know our doctor would never—"

"Shut up, Didier. You, bring me that stupid thing."

I obey. I open my hand to him and he snatches the phial from my grip, unfolding the serviette and holding the glass up to the chandelier's light. "This is it, then? This is what has you scared so shitless you can't let it out of your sight?"

For a moment I am afraid he will toss the phial and let gravity finish its work, or he will snap his bony fingers, summoning his men to blast both me and the organism to ribbons. He only hands it back to me with an amused grimace. "I know you've only just arrived, so I will do you the courtesy of warning you," he says. "If you so much as mention this thing in my presence again, I'll have you thrown out into the night."

"Pèren . . ." Didier starts, but does not have the heart to finish.

I nod. It does not take much to elicit a threat from the baron, but on principle he tends to make good on them. He will have me dragged back inside well before the cold does its work—this body is less expendable to the baron than it is to me—but I do not look forward to treating my bleeding pores and thawing the ice that will stiffen my joints for days afterward.

With permission, I take my leave, carefully cradling the phial in my serviette. I pass the curious guards and retreat into the safety of the corridors, only half relieved. This stomach is still roaring inside me, but I have suffered far worse suppers at the baron's table. I have seen tears, screams, unretractable vilifications, and, in one memorable case, several piles of colorful vomit. Something, some insult, accusation, or accident, will inevitably drive the baron's guests, one by one, from the table. It is exactly how he prefers it.

Nobody can reasonably expect to survive until dessert, but still, I am disappointed in myself. I have never before failed to make it past the first course.

V

WINTER, LIKE EVERY OTHER season, is not kind. With each few turns of the broken moon, another hazard avalanches from the mountains, past the foothills, and along the miles of weaving railroad. Vernal storms bring in jittering throngs of patients with lightning-marked burns starting from erect hairlines and ending at short-circuited mechanical limbs. Summer brings heatstroke, suffocating throats choked with spores and pollen, insect bites the size and color of apples. Meteor season brings the harvest, and plagues of blight that drift down from the clouds to colonize the crops. But winter is the cruelest, especially in Verdira—it brings viruses, frostbite, starvation, and the kinds of darkened thoughts that drive scalpels through carotid arteries. The cold does the ill no favors, nor does the brief and sickly sunlight that, in the deepest weeks of the season, only graces the whitened peaks for a few minutes of the day.

Winter is taking its first deep breath—I can feel it from here to the southern floodlands and back—and soon will come the great exhale. The heaviest snows will blow with it, always sooner than expected, always deeper than expected, and I will be confined to the Château de Verdira until they pass. The days will shorten to slivers of sunlight; even now, the sun sets early. If I hope to venture out and return safely in the fraction of light left to me, I must be quick. Wherever I find myself at sunset, I will have to stay, unless I want to risk night winds so sharp they have been known to tear travelers to bloodied shreds.

Even with the baron nettled at my misbehavior, he will have to call upon me sooner or later. If I am absent, if this body is blinded or killed by the winter night, it may be a week or more before another arrives. In the meantime I will have no substitutes, no equals. There will be no one to properly care for Verdira, no one to soothe the baron's irascible pain, no one to stem the havoc that little black parasite might wreak in my absence. Of course, I only have myself to blame for that. I have carefully engineered it that way.

Whenever I set foot on new ground, whenever a village grows large enough to warrant a clinic or a ruling family commissions my services, my first task is to remove any and all local pretenders to my profession. Salesmen and charlatans disappear upon my arrival, fleeing the shame of exposure, succumbing to mysterious sicknesses, meeting with accidents, or promptly retiring. I then assume their roles and honor their work, misguided though it may be, by absorbing their cleverest methods and discoveries into my own practice. I preserve any useful books or tools, I adopt their patients, and I carve myself a new, healthful niche.

Verdira is no exception, though I arrived unusually late to the settlement. I was not present when the protean mountains split open to reveal a path to the north, nor was I there fifty years later, when the mines were restored and the railroad snaked into the foothills, nor even fifty years after that, when a remarkable green pebble destroyed the Inultus I knew and rebuilt it a hundredfold grander. By the time I stepped off the train, most practitioners of local medicine had been conveniently massacred. There were no more apothecaries, no more Montish midwives that sang old hymns at the mouths of the mountain caves. The only one left who dared call himself any sort of physician was an amateur herbalist who, exhausted after decades of bearing the town's medical burdens, eagerly stepped aside for me.

They call him Priest, but only because he has taken up residence in the old church at the end of Verdira's longest cobblestone lane. As far as I know he harbors no belief in a deity, but he is full to the brim with parables. He is the closest thing to an old Montish raconteur this place has left, and he may remember a tale or two about an indigenous retro-orbital parasite.

The organism, upgraded from a fragile phial to a sturdy, thick-glassed jar, rattles in my bag as I approach the crumbling church. The steeple, angled and warped by the vagaries of time, sputters smoke through broken windows. The carvers must be at work. Most of them are old miners, too frail to descend into the earth for wheatrock, too spry to refuse to be of use. So they sit and fashion ornaments of jade and rhodonite, churning out rumors as quickly as hairpieces and spectacle rims and teaspoons. They etch silhouettes of ghosts that haunt the château and beasts that prowl the winter night; they manipulate and embellish ancient Montish legends as dexterously as their trinkets. I am always charmed by their creativity.

When I enter the church, the carvers' hands fall still, their voices fade into cautious silence. Wrinkled, opaque eyes follow me across the nave, and a few heads nod in recognition. Almost everyone can tell a body of the Institute when they see one.

Backlit by the flames in the altar, surrounded by tools and uncut stones, lounges the head of this congregation. He turns as I approach, neck creaking like pines in the wind.

"Ay vulà, the replacement," he rasps. He does not greet me with touch, as Didier and many other descendants of Inultus do, but instead brushes a finger between his tufted eyebrows in an old Montish salute. "I'd bid welcome to Verdira, though nay make the night any warmer."

"Perhaps not," I reply, mirroring his motion. "Quite the time of year to arrive."

Priest's knar-like nose bobs above his nearly toothless smile. His Franco is even deeper than Baker's, full of the mountain's gravel. "Dreadful temps. Soon'll be too much snow to escape. Might flee south while you can."

"I have considered it," I answer. I wonder for a moment if the sickness that took my old body might have originated from behind Priest's rheumy eyes, but nothing about his face strikes me as un-ordinary.

"Lor, what brings the Institute t'our petit chapel?" Priest asks. "Abandoning the poor baron in his malaise?"

"I have come to ask about something," I say.

"Odd thing, a disciple a science here to query the dead gods."

"I am here to speak to you, not them."

"Oh?"

"About the château's previous physician. My predecessor."

"Wae," Priest sighs, frowning. "Nay much to say. Nay seen him since winter began. Bizarre he got sick, much less dead."

"Yes, quite," I say. "Especially considering what I found inside the skull." When I reach into my bag and reveal the jar, Priest leans in, cloudy eyes narrowing. I keep a tight grip on it, hoping not to reenact the events of the previous night.

"Hell's that thing?" he asks. "Resembles cave grass."

"It is not cave grass."

Priest glances at me. "Nay s'it *were* cave grass, just s'it *looked* like."

A strange sort of dread bubbles inside me, and I can feel several of my stomachs threaten to turn. I banish the images that suddenly emerge in my memory—the mouth of an adit, a blade sawing through flesh.

"*Just go there,*" a body snaps all the way from Misulah, currently occupied with stitching a diver's eel-bitten toe back together. "I already know the worst that can happen."

Priest's eyes follow the jar as I place it back in my bag. "Honest, nay seen a thing like it before. Presume it killed Old Doc?"

After some hesitation, I nod. "I have been told you are very knowledgeable about Verdira and its history. I wanted to know if you have heard any stories about an organism like this."

"Hm. A few warning-tales in my time. Countless 'bout the

dangers en grotte, but nay so small as that thing. This's ventigeau country. Tall monsters roam here."

A carver, close enough to overhear, clicks his tongue. "That's what took my nephew last winter. Tore right through him. Nay found the pieces, they were too small."

"There's a château servant who's got the mountain in him," Priest tells me. "Dark eyes, a pet small. He mighta heard a tale or two from his maman when he's in her belly. Trouble is—"

"He does not speak," I finish. "Yes, I have asked Émile."

"Nay even write an answer?"

"He was less than forthcoming."

"Wae, figures. Boy's got a good hand, but uses it seldom. Saves his words for gods, mostly. Whichever ones habited here. Thinks I can deliver his notes upward."

"I do believe that was the historical function of a priest," I say.

"Nay tell the poor child, but I just burn 'em. Would read 'em, were't any business a mine. Or if I could read." He coughs into his gnarled hand. "Gods nay could help that boy if they were still breathing. Watch him, médsaine. See he's all right."

"He is the healthiest of all of us," I answer. "It is the rest of the town I worry about. If you will indulge me, I would like to examine you and your carvers."

"Wae, bensûr."

As Priest and his workers prepare themselves for my probing hands and cold stethoscope, the hum of chatter escalates once more. Tongues flap even as I depress them, throats chirp out the latest gossip under my palpating fingers.

"Now what'd the baron pay for a prim thing like you?" an old lapidary asks as I pry open her eyelids, searching for slivers of black tissue. "A caboose fulla jade?"

"Gold," suggests another.

"Nay seen a soul come outta the château since the flu rolled in. Médsaine, how many're dead from it?"

"Nay matter. Even dead they'd still rule us."

"It were wheatrock, weren't it? City's always after the ugly little gem."

From the corner of an eye, I see the farmlands swaying in the dry Inultan breeze. Orchards and cornfields, windswept barley bleeding into the sun-petrified ruby hills, roots replete with re-fined wheatrock. Clearer but still blurred by distance, the pock-marked slope of the governor's back comes into view, blocking the fields. Half naked, with his recurring cysts opening under my lancet, his groans of pain ease seamlessly into his monologue: ". . . the third accident in a month, doctor. It's those fucking saboteurs from the naturalist collective. I swear to the cursed fucking moon they've infiltrated the aerostat bay. Someone in our lab works for them, they *must*. You'd think a group like them'd know enough to move past their superstitions—"

"Inultus needs wheatrock to survive, just as you do," I tell the jade carver. "More so than you."

"They survived before it," the man answers. "And I got a hard time believing a place rich 'nough to buy all these trinkets is des-perate to use wheatrock to grow anything."

"Nay even seen the place," another says. "May be just a blague."

Priest shakes his head. "Never believe anything you nay can see."

"Never."

"What do they expect us to do, build a *boat*?" the governor hisses. "Can't row any farther than the Wheslers without your hull disintegrating. And they're the ones killing their own scientists in the fume wastes—*shit*, have mercy, doc." He flinches as I force out the last clump of lipid debris from under his skin. "East is fucked, west is fucked, south is fucked. North is especially fucked. Only way left to go is up."

A Verdiran ciseleur coughs, launching sputum into the roaring fire. "Tell us, médsaine, does Inultus even exist?"

"If we want to take flight we've got to cut all our tethers," the governor growls. "We'll have to smoke out every last one of the bastards. Clear the lab—hell, the whole city. Round up that surly lot and have them killed."

"Surely that is not necessary," I reply. In truth, I am somewhat fond of the loose assemblage of historians, mechanics, and scien-tists that calls itself the naturalist collective. They are outspoken, but delightfully inquisitive. I am partial to any mind as curious as my own, so long as it does not overstep its bounds. "They cannot pose so great a threat, governor."

"Ha! You're still young, doctor. You don't truly understand necessity."

"You right, médsaine?" Priest recalls my attention to the church. "Look a pet distrait."

I finish my last examination and return my tools to my bag. I am starting to accept that no one in this town, besides my old body, has ever encountered this damnable little infection. "I am feeling overworked," I say.

"Already?" Priest shakes his head. "Ay winter nay proper here yet." The fissures of his wrinkles deepen in the somber firelight. "Nay let the peaks get you down, médsaine. Just keep your eye low, keep sighta the ground."

"Nothing worthwhile aboveground anyway," says a carver. The others click their tongues in agreement.

My fingers in Inultus tap away, marking the occupants of the church as asymptomatic—just as I have for the baron, his family, the miners, the refiners, the barmen and servants and cooks and mushers and tailors. Didier's words in the salon echo through a few of my skulls, veering me toward an unpleasant conclusion: I must have contracted this disease in a place where no one else in Verdira has been—at least no one still alive.

I stand.

"Parting?" Priest asks.

"There is only so much daylight left," I reply. "I would like to see Baker before dusk."

"Wae, s'pose he'll need his heart tuned. Saw him spitting such smoke yesterday, thought he'd taken up cigarilles again." Priest returns his gaze to his meticulous carving. "'Dieu, doc."

"Adieu, Priest."

I am halfway to the door before he says, "Pleasure to see you again."

My step falters. I almost turn to address him, but I hold my silence and retreat into the winter air. It is likely a mistake, a slip of his tongue, or an automatic, meaningless nicety. Perhaps it is his

nature to be cryptic, or perhaps he really does recognize a fundamental similarity between my hosts. Even if he has unraveled one
mystery of my private life, he is no danger to me. Otherwise he
would not be alive today.

I am lucky—no, I have had the foresight—to be indispensable
to people like Priest. The systematic collection and isolation of all
medical necessities has guaranteed my survival, so that even those
who dislike or distrust me must call on me in their hours of need.
After all, what use would I be if everyone knew how to dress a
wound or remove a growth, if everyone had a steady hand and
an intimate knowledge of the body? Just as I need others, I am
needed. To be needed, I suspect, is fundamental to being human.

Baker says something I do not process.

The sun creeps across the western peaks, and the chimneys of
the château spill smoke into the clouds. At the base of one of those
stacks, in a powerful furnace, the diced remains of my corpse
burn. I tell myself that I cannot possibly smell whatever bodily
particulates float in that low, gray sky, but that does not quell the
bubbling rancidity at the back of my throat. In a sunny examining room on the western coast, a host that once had the habit of
chewing and swallowing its fingernails says aloud, two knuckles
deep in a man's rectum, that to absentmindedly ingest one's own
dead flesh is not terribly abnormal. Not without some amusement,
I feel the patient's sphincter tighten at the words.

"Excuse me?" I ask, realizing that in the stretched, looming
shadow of the Château de Verdira, Baker is ushering me into his
cabin.

"I asked if you're cold."

It should be easy for him to guess, glancing at my thin overcoat
and snow-wet leather shoes. "Yes," I say. "Maeci."

He pulls me out of the snow and into his den of smoke and
steam. He closes the door behind me, retreating to his collection
of jittering kettles. "Lor," he starts, "how is the . . . uh . . . how're
things going?"

"Middling," I answer.

"Ah. Find out who stabbed Old Doc?"

"Signs indicate Old Doc."

"Wae, looked like he was having a hard time. Verdira does that to southerners after a while."

In my largest surgical theater, four of my hands saw through a man's femur. I find the sound grating, for some reason. "I am here to examine your heart, Baker. And to ask if you had an electric lamp you could lend me."

He raises an eyebrow. "Going somewhere dark?"

"I have heard they work well in many environments," I answer.

He retreats to a corner to dig through a giant bird's nest of scrap metal. "Wae. In the wind and underground 'specially. Old Montish called it bad luck to bring fire into the caves, though that didn't stop us. You're nay gonna ask for a ride somewhere too, are you?"

"I was going to, yes."

"Well, can't. Barely got 'er working to haul supplies from the station. Nearly died coming back here. The machine, nay me. Well, maybe me." He raises a rusted electric lamp and sets it on his workbench, coughing up a puff of blackish smoke. "You're uh . . . familiar with my condition?"

"Yes."

A kettle moans in agony, oozing a dark, viscous fluid from its spout. Baker stumbles to the stove and adjusts the knobs, waving away the vile smell. Between the fumes and the rusted mounds of metal piled in every corner, his house is not the most sanitary of operating rooms.

"You bring any extra tubes from the city?" he asks.

"None to be found. The plastiophages were bad this year."

He sighs. Since he is inevitably the one called when the baron's support systems malfunction, he is intimately acquainted with the machines that demand all the spare wiring and plastic around. "Eating everything up, aren't they?" he mutters despondently.

"I brought you a tube that will last six months at maximum. It is unfortunate, but after that you are going to have to scavenge."

"Damn. We emptied out the last nearby ruin more'n a month

ago. And I'm nay going any farther than the old nuke plant this winter. It's gonna be bad. Already cold enough to kill half my motors, nay gonna let it kill me too."

"We will find some plastic by mid-spring," I assure him. "For now, please remove your shirt and seat yourself."

"Always cutting to the chase, just like Old Doc." He grins. "Your Franco's parf, too. Where're you from?"

"Inultus."

"No, I mean, where are *you* from?"

I glance down at my hands, and then they are long and pale, flipping through pages in my records hall. There is always one host or another down there. I take a moment to reach for the relevant tome. I pause, but not so long that Baker loses the thread of the conversation. He has dealt with me before. He is familiar with my occasional lapses and nonsensical mutterings, as if I am speaking with someone who is not there.

"Just south of the city," I conclude. "Satgarden." I snap open my bag and retrieve my gloves.

"Oh? Always wanted to visit the place."

"That would be ill-advised." Though this body cannot go back—all hosts are barred from returning to their familial origins—I can make out the sloping tin roof of the Satgarden clinic. A few patients shuffle in from the factories and satellite gardens with severed arms, blackened lips and lungs, skin torn off by excitable machinery. A patient losing an appendage is a daily occurrence in Satgarden. Some even manage to lose the same one twice. "It can be dangerous."

"Wae," Baker sighs, lowering himself to his tattered rug. He slides as easily into our old routines as Émile. "Still, I'd like to see it. To count how many ships and machines come down."

"Most of them sink into the mud-river." I pause to take his pulse. Four hundred revolutions per minute, as normal as could be. "It is far more likely to see a machine resurface after a few centuries than to see one fall for the first time. And once one does, you have no idea what it is planning."

He wears a cautious frown. "Don't trust machines, doc?"

Not even the governor's most skilled engineers truly trust machines. They have swallowed too much of the world's knowledge, poisoned too much of its life. "I trust yours," I answer. "It has served you well."

"Wae, it has. Four years now."

"Longer than any other of its kind. How has it been lately?"

"Middling," he smiles.

I examine his chest, his perpetually wind-bitten cheeks, and his eyes, bright gold and free from any signs of infection. "Fever, nausea, dizziness, headache, fatigue?" He shakes his head. "Any discomfort around or behind your eyes?"

"Nay."

"Very well then." I remove the relevant tools from my bag—a thin tube of rare, bendable plastic, a small syringe, a portable electrometer with sterilized probes. "Are you prepared?"

"Much as I can be." He stretches himself on the floor and puffs out his chest like a mating bird. Slightly to the left of his sternum, awkward as a third nipple, sits a nub of rounded silver. I twist it between gloved fingers, cracking the dried discharge and flaked skin, and with a short hiss, the head comes loose. I give Baker a warning nod, adjust my grip, and pull.

The tube slips out, covered in fresh and clotted blood. Baker's neck twitches, his head slumps back, and his heart ceases to function.

Did I die this time? he always asks when I am done. I would like to answer him honestly, but I am never sure on what side of his brainlessness and pulselessness I should draw the line of death. That is one function I have never experienced. I have passed away many times, but I have never died.

Somewhere behind me, the kettle screams. I take a breath, my heartbeat thumping in my ears as I slip the sterile tubing from its case. I lean over Baker, pushing its end into the cavity. When it clicks into place in his heart, I fill my syringe with blackish oil. My timepiece ticks away, but I manage to refill and lubricate his machinery well before he is in any danger of hypoxia. I remove the syringe, twist the silver mammilla back into his chest, and restart his heart.

Every muscle in Baker's body rigidifies, and his eyes roll

back—in the whites I can see branching vessels, but no black marks, no sign of disease. Almost immediately, his convulsions relent, and he groans back into consciousness.

He raises his head and smiles at me. "Lor . . ." I prepare for the usual question, but he just lifts his eyes to the ceiling and releases a sigh. "How 'bout some tea, then?"

Evidently Baker is not curious about life or death today. "You would like something to ease the pain as well," I say.

"Wae." He sits up, wiping a drop of blood from his chest.

I pretend not to know where Baker keeps his tea leaves, and he points them out with a shaking finger. I remove the kettle from the stove, and it is something of a relief to see clear water pour from its spout.

"How did it look, doc?" he asks.

"Fine." *As always*, I do not add. "That tube will last you half a year. Less if you exert yourself, and much less if you resume smoking."

"I'm done with that," he assures me.

I dissolve a few mils of dark liquid into his drink, and drop in a clump of sugar to reward his sportsmanship. He has always been one of my more tolerant patients.

"A little sweetness almost masks the taste," he says, raising the mug to his lips. "Do all your kind carry sugar in your bags?"

"Mostly for adults," I say. "The children handle their medicine quite well."

"That's 'cause they're easier to hold down." Baker chuckles, raising a hand to massage his chest. "Nay can throw a punch worth shit. 'Cept Didier's kids. The last time I saw Old Doc I'm pretty sure the girls gave him two black eyes. Precious doves, them."

"Hm." I wrap Baker's tube for disposal. "Did you notice anything else unusual about his appearance or behavior before he died?"

"Nay, but he was pretty sick. Pained-looking, jittery, normal for a bad flu."

"Did he say anything to you?"

"He mentioned something 'bout boarding the train back south, but we all fantasize 'bout that, 'specially when the snows start."

Baker looks into the ripples of his tea as if searching for something. "Did you know him well?"

I pause. "I did."

"Can't really say the same. Barely saw him for most of the time he was here. I half believed his real name was Doc, or Sawbones, or Leech—"

"An unkind term."

"Wae, he certain didn't like it much. Nothing but polite 'bout it, though. He was a good man."

This gives me pause. "Good?"

"Well, good as he could be, for his station." He runs his fingers through his beard. "Fast to show up in the face of every disaster. When the . . . when the north mine collapsed in autumn, he insisted we drive through a storm to get there. My heart still hurts from it." Baker takes a sip. "When I had to stop and wait it out, he kept going on foot. Got struck twice, didn't slow him."

I recall the event with marginal clarity. The dry storms that roll through the hills never fail to blur events in my mind—on the worst days, I can feel the warping of the grid on which my thoughts travel, like tracks melting under the searing wheels of a train. I do not recall much, but I distinctly remember that I was not, in fact, struck.

"I heard of the incident," I say. "It was unfortunate so many did not make it."

"Wae . . ." Baker's eyes glaze a little. "With poor Cass, and the boys . . . nay the first time something like that has happened 'round here, with '97 and all. But it was the first time for him. I wonder if that was how he got in such bad shape. I don't know if he's had so many people die on him like that before."

I think of the bodies lost in the darkness, and I can only count myself lucky that my own had not been among them. "It is a common human tendency for a great number of people to die all at once, and of the same cause," I say. "It is hardly surprising. We have all seen it happen."

"I'm sure *you* have, being from Satgarden. But he told me he was from Misulah. So much nicer there, 'cept for the moon-ague."

"Misulah?" I murmur. I cannot recall ever disclosing that information to Baker, but he does have a habit of fabricating details.

"Poor man," Baker sighs. "Never thought he'd die so soon. But with him looking so sick . . ." He scratches the metal plug on his chest. "Tell me it's nay contagious. Whatever it was old Stanislas had."

I am quite adept at regulating my autonomic systems, but I cannot stop a hundred hearts from skipping a beat at once. In a panicked shuffling of papers, I leaf through memories in my records hall. "An interesting name," I say, carefully.

"Wae. He told me just before his sickness got real bad." Baker shrugs. "Figured he might've known what was coming. He was always keen on the Institute's service-before-self thing, but no one wants to die nameless."

My hands hover over my bag for a second before I snap it shut. "I have no reason to believe this disease is contagious, and I have no reason to believe it is not." I open the door in a flurry of freezing air. "But it is best to be wary. Report anything unusual to me."

"Will do."

"And maeci for the lantern."

Back in the snow, I clench one hand around my bag and the other around the electric lamp, furiously commanding them to stop shivering. Perhaps it is only the bad weather rolling in, obscuring the air between my faraway selves, but a lonely ache begins to pulsate in this forehead.

As far back as I can possibly remember, in any place, in any host, I have never had a name.

VI

THERE IS ONLY ONE season in Misulah. All through the year, the rains fall unrelenting, the air is choked with heat, and the winds burp listlessly along the water like the belches of some beast bloated with a rotten meal. The passage of time is marked only by the variable acidity of the water and the comings and goings of mosquite swarms so thick they blot out the sky. It is one of the pleasanter climes of the known world.

My clinic creaks above the water on viny wooden stilts, filled to the brim with half-drowned children, victims of moon-ague, and divers with aquatic predators still latched onto rubber-clad ankles. My patients in that sprawling town often pay for their treatments with treasures they find underwater: rusted electronics and plastics, sealed jars of ancient medicines, confiture, or other remarkable objects. Sometimes, they pay me with their children.

It is not uncommon in places like Misulah, where the infra-structure is unstable and the labor dangerous. In the floodlands a child can expect to grow into a boatman or diver, a harvester of stinging aquatic nettles, or a stilt-builder riddled with splinters. I offer security, mobility, opportunity. My clinic there is large, my bodies well fed and healthy. I reside in the households of powerful families, and I can be spied on the decks of watercraft adorned with gold as often as on the swampy commoners' boardwalks. Though the parents who leave their children at my doors know they will never meet again, they are reassured the young bodies they brought to life will thrive in my care.

In the orange morning light of my library, a few of my persons sift through my records. My recently severed host was indeed from Misulah, acquired as payment for a successful amputation. The child had been around twelve, with an ideal degree of neuroplasticity, and clearly healthy enough to survive integration. It was relatively uninteresting, with uniquenesses and irregularities like any other. When it came into my possession, it had ten fingers, eight webbed toes, a deep-rooted fear of fire, and a mild case of mange. It had been partially blind in its left eye, but after a year of diligent neural pruning, I had fixed the problem in its entirety.

The only thing remarkable about that body, besides its death, was its name. Though the patients I serve may find it useful to address a host by some moniker or another, I do not. I keep meticulous records on the size, shape, and health of all of my hosts, of course, but titles are of no use to me. I am no child that must assign pet names to its own parts. I am perfect in severing any neural connection that may weave a sense of individual identity. At most, in the throes of sickness or fear, my bodies may revert to old instincts like nail-biting or stuttering.

There is only one thing I can blame, one variable that has appeared in that host and no others. And I can only think of one place that might have produced such a variable.

In the silence of the candlelit château, I trace paths on a map. My finger winds past abandoned chalets and work sites, looping from a sickness to a surgery to a grove of wild anti-inflammatory herbs. North, west, then north again, along a route that has not seen direct sunlight for weeks now. It is a dangerous wilderness, and without Baker's vehicles to help me traverse it, I have to resort to the last feasible method.

I am not fond of the dogs, and they are not fond of me. They can smell something odd about me, some quality that sends their ears twitching and their hackles rising down their white backs. It is as if they cannot quite fathom me, as if they do not comprehend how my bodies differ from others'. Of course, they are as alien to me as I am to them. They are nothing like the dogs illustrated in the ancient texts: squat or hairless, long-faced or wrinkled, with flopping ears or bulging eyes, as diverse in their imperfections as the people that bred them. They are large, wolflike things, sharing their grayish hair and dark eyes with the people that weathered the world's storms alongside them deep in the mountains. They have flourished in Verdira, undiscovered for centuries, untouched by the genetic manipulation that haunted their past. They are reliable brutes—fast, strong, and certainly preferable to skiing. I can only hope they do not provoke this body's innate anxieties like the shining treads of Baker's machines do.

I wriggle into a too-large parka and grab my lamp. After squinting at a relevant text from my library, I fill a bag with empty jars, collection phials, forceps, masks, and gloves. I glance at my sample of the black organism—no changes—and when I convince myself it will be safe without my constant observation, I lock it away in my cupboard.

By the time I slip from the château, the clouds reveal patches of icy, predawn blue. My timepiece suggests five minutes before ten. I pull my hood over freezing ears and follow the sounds of eager barks to the sled. Émile lingers in the shadows of a crumbling wall, looking a bit like a dog himself, dark eyes shining from the halo of his furred parka. A bone whistle, capable of piercing the sharpest wails of Verdiran snowstorms, hangs on his chest by a sturdy strap of leather. As he readies the sled, he raises his fingers to touch it every few seconds, as if to make sure it is still there. It is the only voice he has.

"Has anyone seen you come out?" I ask him. He shakes his head. "Good. Sylvie will assume your duties for the day."

Émile rests a hand on a nearby dog and nods, though I do not know if it is to me or the animal. Those creatures often seem to anticipate his requests, adjusting their course before he whistles for them to turn, sitting for him well before he commands. He is, I am sure, the best person to accompany me on my journey north. I only hope that we return before Didier notices he's missing.

"He *did* encourage me to ask Émile if I required assistance," I holler to myself from a clinic on the acid coast. My patient flinches, and I remind myself, futilely and for the nth time this century, to stop talking to myself aloud.

Émile helps me onto the sled, and the lead dog rolls her head to give me a black-eyed stare. A deep growl stirs in her throat, her torn ear twitches, and for a fraction of a second I believe she recognizes me. The hackles of her companions fan out in suspicion, but drop when Émile's whistle sends them pulling at the gangline.

It is only about a half hour by sled to the north mine, which gives me little more than three hours to investigate, pack up, and sled back to town before night falls. It may prove risky, but the dogs are fast, and though they do not trust me, I trust them.

We run under the arcing shadows of mountains, between silent copses of trees aching with snow. The wind stings my face, and the earthen pants of a dozen dogs puff into the air, lit by the rising sun's feeble glow. A confluence of clouds rolls over the hilltops, and I begin to feel unsettlingly localized. The farther northward I stretch, reaching this isolated body toward the mountains and the mines beneath them, the more the voices in my head dim to whispers, the more the visions behind my sight blur into nothing but snow. I grit my teeth and close one eye, holding tight to the barest outline of a familiar window, concentrating on a passage I'm reading in the distant foothills. But the images and sounds come and go, and I know it will only get worse.

The ruins of lodges, shacks, and metal towers pass us by. We traverse the scattered clusters of abandoned settlements and châteaux, poking their highest spires from the permanent crust of ice. Some of the more isolated buildings, untouched by time, likely house centuries of treasure. In summer, braver Verdirans will venture to the empty north, to camp and hunt, to explore the ruins and return with books, plastics, photographs, alcohol. But in winter, we all know better than to tarry too long in one place. No one wants to meet what lives in the night out here.

During the warmest, stormiest week of the previous autumn, when the last snows of spring began to melt and the first snows of winter began to fall, Baker tumbled through the front door of the Château de Verdira. He swept through the halls uninvited, knocking servants from their feet, and though I cannot recall exactly what I had been doing when he burst into my chamber, I remember the look on his face. His nostrils spat columns of panicked smoke, and his heart whirred so loudly I could almost hear it from Inultus. The sight of his yellow eyes, wide with worry, is one of the last images I can recall clearly.

We scrambled onto his automated sled and rumbled north, too hurried to bother with any supplies other than our professional bags—his full of wrenches and radiation-detecting equipment, mine full of blades and bandages. He rode to see the machines, whose limbs and pneumatic columns lay crushed under collapsed rock, and I rode to see the miners, who were in much the same condition. Didier, mopping sweat from his collarbones, stayed at the château, laboriously jotting down every expense, every loss, every ounce of wheatrock, jade, steel, and human flesh lost in the accident. I can only assume the sums were tragic, since after a full night spent tallying in the office with Didier, even stolid Émile had emerged shaking with emotion.

I barely remember clinging to Baker on the back of his sputtering engine, bouncing over the soft, grayish snow in an attempt to outdrive an oncoming electrical storm. "What a time," he had muttered, clawing at his chest. "What a damn time for the sky to fall."

A few miles from the mine, both man and sled wheezed in pain, creaking to a stop and succumbing under the weight of the squall. Several attempts to revive the engine failed. As the clouds descended and darkened, striated with silent lightning, Baker began to tremble, clutching at his heart as if it were trying to escape his rib cage. I helped him retreat to the safety of an abandoned lift terminal, gathered my things, and continued on foot.

It was not the first accident at this particular mine, and it was not the first without a known cause. It may have been the grumbling of an angry earth, agitated by centuries of small apocalypses. It may have been the electrical stirrings of the storm, which are sometimes known to rattle veins of metal and water beneath the ground. At the time, I could expend no effort identifying the source of the disaster. I had to occupy myself with bone-setting, stitching, comforting, and in one case, sawing the remaining three-quarters of a miner out from under the debris.

Crawling with my serrated blade before me, I followed the workers' instructions. Some of the survivors braved the dusty adit with me, voices trembling through their masks as they guided me downward. I know the last thing they wanted was to reenter the dark, but the echoing cries of the lone survivor urged us onward. They gave me everything I needed—a sturdy carbide lamp, ropes, a helmet, a pair of too-large boots—and waited at the mouth of the collapse as I slid my small frame through the cracks. The others cleared away rocks behind me, using what broken machinery they could, and I navigated the thin passage where the throat of the mine had constricted. I cannot recall most of my journey, though there are still flashes of nonsequential scenes in my mind. Hundreds of miles from the rest of me and muffled under a thick slab of mountain, my thoughts were vague and tangled, confined to an isolated body. For long, terrifying minutes, I had only one life, one pair of eyes and one pair of ears, filled with the hollow, agonized cries of a familiar voice.

Many patients, in times of stress, will recount dreams haunted by images of their bodies falling apart. Sometimes they tell me stories of paralysis, or rotten extremities dangling by thin skeins of flesh. Most commonly, they talk about their teeth painlessly and inexplicably falling from their gums. These dreams never fail to horrify their dreamers, and I can understand the discomfort in watching one's parts detach. But never do these dreamers experience what it's like to be the limb that rots away, to be the tooth that falls from the mouth.

The few memories that remain from my descent into the dark are unclear, blurred with streaks of blood, the flickering of a lamp, the strike of a match. I remember clearing a path for myself in the rubble, slipping through the cracks others could not, following the crescendo of desperate hollers and the sharp, deep smell of a dying fire. I remember reaching her, seeing Cass's face, the dirt-streaked, crooked-toothed smile that could not conceal her pain. I remember the insurmountable weight of the dislodged boulder that pinned her, and the sound of a saw shearing muscle and bone. It was a poor decision, but the only one that could have been made.

"If I live," she kept muttering, wearing that uneven smile, "I'll owe the Institute my firstborn."

I do not know how long she had been down there before I arrived, nor what panicked mélange of neurotransmitters made her chatter so vehemently as I extricated her from the wall of rock. She inundated me with nonsensical questions, perhaps her way of clinging to a shred of hope, of the possibility of a future—"How's everything back home?" "How's the wheatrock doing?" "How long until we get sunside?" Even after the others had cleared a wide enough route for her to be passed back through, even with all the binding and disinfecting, even with a clean cut, she was in a poor state. We all were. Nothing more could've been expected.

That night, after we had dissolved her corpse safely in a vat of drainage and returned to Verdira with the survivors, Didier wasted no time dispensing vague and unprovable accusations of sabotage.

"Didier can suck my metal nipple," Baker had responded belatedly, halfway through his sixth pint. "Fuck him, blaming the miners, blaming Cass. Knows absolute shit 'bout her. Knows shit 'bout how hard she worked." His hand trembled as he called for another drink. "She was wicked strong, doc. *Wicked* strong. She could lift me over her head like it was nothing. Once rescued me out from under my own set of treads. Musta been a ton, at least, lifted it up with one arm. Why couldn't she—why in hell's name couldn't she—" He had begun to weep, tears foaming and off-color like his ale, smelling pungently of motor oil. "Fuck, I was gonna marry that woman. I coulda built her a leg. Coulda built her a leg and she coulda been fine."

I could not help imagining the possibilities if she had not bled to death in the throat of that cavern. I would've been quite glad to take Cass's firstborn. No doubt it would've been a hardy specimen. And even if it failed to survive integration, I would still appreciate the gesture. A corpse, especially a fresh one, is a fine gift for my laboratories.

It is almost universally accepted that the safest place to be is underground. When death comes, it comes from the heavens, as electric storms, falling satellites, mosquites, plagues, and blights. It descends from the luminous eyes of ventigeaux, tall as trees, it rolls down the mountains as avalanches, it torches in burning arcs from the stars. Even the moon has not survived that heinous sky.

The Verdiran caverns have offered protection for centuries, growing and changing under the force of human hands and the mountains' shifting pressures. The Montish weathered the world's end in the safety of these dark halls. For every blast that leaves a miner dead, a thousand come and go unharmed. I should not be afraid, but I am.

I do not know what has changed since my last visit to the mine. Storms and the rumbling earth are known to rearrange entire sections of the mountainside within the span of a season. It is what makes these tunnels so abundant in new discoveries, so rich with freshly turned and untouched deposits, but it is also what makes them dangerous. There is little that cannot be mined in Verdira, but there is nothing that can be mined easily.

This particular adit leads to the only deposit of wheatrock in the known world. This unremarkable half-moon of darkness is where the cave grass grows in abundance, undulating in the subterranean drafts like kelp in the acid oceans. The soft green stone that nourishes this unique flora also yields unprecedented growth in other life—wheat, potatoes, barley, soil microbes, harvest pox, and, if my hypothesis is correct, one unnamed organism I pulled from my own eye socket.

I slide out of the sled and sink up to my knees in the snow. Electric lamp in one hand, medical bag in the other, I shuffle toward the black mouth of the mine.

Émile lingers by the dogs, arms folded across his chest. I wade a few more steps and turn, motioning for him to follow me. "We are only going to have a brief look inside," I say. "We will be back out in half an hour at most."

The confidence in my tone astounds even me. Normally I am able to tread strange or dangerous ground because I have a few hundred brains to aid me. But now, I can only hear the faintest whispers of my other hosts' voices. This body is no longer expendable, and I am suddenly quite sure that I will not be able to enter the mine without Émile.

"We'll be fine," I assure him. "And Sylvie will send help if we fail to return." I cannot imagine how distasteful her master will find my misappropriation of the château's dogs, sled, and houseboy, but I suppose suffering Didier's disapproval is better than death.

Émile does not react, so I raise the lamp, showing off its electric bulb. "We are not going to start any grassfires, either. We are as safe as can be."

He raises an incredulous eyebrow—he still thinks I do not know what I am doing, that I do not know how little time we have. I see he is not going to move, so I decide to invoke my strongest argument. "Fine. I shall go alone. But I am sure the baron will have plenty to say if you return to the château without his physician."

Émile's eyes widen, his arms fall to his sides, and something like conviction crosses his features. He glances back at the dogs, at the layer of snowflakes dotting their raised hackles, and follows me.

As darkness arcs over us, gaping like the open mouth of some massive animal, my thoughts seem to shrink. With each step into the adit, they contract in my head, arriving half-formed and disconnected, devoid of feedback or moderation. They are nothing but glimpses of cavern walls and imprecise memories of a familiar path. Any knowledge I forget here will be lost forever, and I will have to rely only on what thoughts are formed in this single brain with its many talents and flaws.

I do not know how people like Émile can bear it, being alone every hour of every day. They cannot make decisions based on logical consensus. When they talk to themselves, the ears that listen invariably belong to the mouth that speaks. They will never know the true sounds of their own voices, nor will they smile at a passing scene or pleasant thought drifting in from miles away. But somehow, they survive.

And so will I. At the very least, I have Émile beside me, and I can count on his company when I cannot count on my own. Every few steps I glance back to make sure he follows, pushing through the darkness with an equal measure of surety and reluctance.

"The place has changed a bit," I mutter, perhaps too loudly. By spring it will change a bit more. New veins of ore will open, new wealth will be excavated and deposited at the baron's feet. Fortunately, the drift I am looking for has not moved since autumn. A few stones have shaken loose, dunes of dust have accumulated on the uneven ground, but familiar humps of equipment rust in cavernous offshoots, each a mark on my vague mental map.

Damp stone and mineral wheatrock smother my only sense of smell, and a chill wholly separate from the cold trembles down this lonely spine. I push forward in spite of it, guided by the feeble light of the buzzing bulb. The ceiling dips, and I crouch, squeezing myself along the narrowing gullet of the warped drift. By the time the tunnel opens and I reach the vat in which we dissolved Cass's body, my pulse is thumping in my ears. I do not dare shine my light at anything but the main passage, and I force my attention forward, deeper into the cavern. Lamp first, I crawl through jagged tunnels, numerous and labyrinthine like the foramina of some great rocky skull, until I squeeze through the final, narrow crack into the chamber where I found her.

I am certain Cass and I were the only living things to occupy this newly turned pocket of earth. Yet when the dim lamplight illuminates the drastic changes that have overtaken this place, a condensed puff of breath forces itself from my lungs. Émile starts at the sound, and cautiously accompanies me forward, examining the wall of rock before us.

"Careful." My voice emerges hoarsely from my single, constricted throat. "This is certainly not cave grass."

It is thick, black, and it crawls from every pockmark in the stone, limbs sprouting from fissures and radiating across boulders like the vessels of a sickly retina. The light reflects a greenish sheen of moisture on its surface, and as I move my gaze along its fractal pattern, a bubble of bile rises in me. I cannot tell if the vile odor originates from the raw deposits of wheatrock around me, the strange substance on the impassable collapse, or the abandoned corpses I know lie just beyond it.

I set down the lamp and dig through my bag. "We'd best wear our masks," I mutter. "Unfortunately they won't protect us from the smell." I don my gloves and retrieve my forceps, stepping toward what I can now see is a thick colony of interconnected organisms.

Instinct tells me to flee, to scramble to the safety of the sunlight, but I bury the thought. This is why I came. This thing, this elongate, slimy collection of soft branches, is the entire reason I have subjected this body to solitude and risked its life. I will not let myself be frightened off before I can collect a sample.

I suppress a gag and ready my trembling forceps. Émile's equally unsteady hands struggle to open a jar while I map out the growth, determining a good place to cut, grip, pierce, or pull. My instrument glows in the lamplight as it follows the tangled, trembling limbs, converging and diverging like nodes in an elaborate network.

The organisms shudder slightly in the windless air. Thin appendages seem to beckon me forward, and I pause, contemplating a cluster of tissue somewhat isolated from the rest—a fist-sized knot, latched to the others by thin, stretched tendrils. A part of me, eager and scientific, tells me to prod it, to ascertain whether this mass is one of many individuals or merely one component of a larger whole. But the more present me, the me whose only heart flutters mercilessly, knows I do not have the neural resources to analyze this thing right now. I cannot hold more than a few thoughts at once in this single head.

I reach out, slowly, breath held, and clamp my forceps around the creature. I adjust my grip, hoping that some voice will flare in the back of my mind, to offer me words of advice or encouragement. I hear nothing but Émile's breathing. Cautiously, I begin to tug.

It resists. The strings of strange flesh are malleable but tough, and it is only after several attempts that I manage to twist a lump of tissue from the stone. My captured sample twitches as I pull it from its substrate, leaving a green-black spiderweb of moisture behind. It looks like a larger variant of the thing I pulled from my own eye days before: dark, cold, limp like a softened sea urchin. My sole heart pounds desperately in my throat as I carry the specimen toward the open jar in Émile's hands.

I am halfway to him when a tiny shudder ripples down the appendages in my grip. I blink it away, dismissing it as a trick of the lamp, but when I open my eyes once more, I see movement, as immediate and irrevocable as a crack shooting through glass. I do not have time to cry out as a dozen black arms suddenly bristle, curling outward like thick, angry whiskers. Before I can react, a pair of tendrils whips toward me, past the metal of my pincers, and latches onto my hand.

A freezing sting shoots across my skin. My only fingers drop the forceps, my only heart jumps into my throat, and I stumble backward, knocking the lamp onto its side. A curt snap rends the air as the bulb shatters, plunging the drift into darkness.

VII

SOMETHING IS UNDER MY glove. Crawling, slithering in freezing filaments across my skin. A sting of pain or panic, cold as ice, jolts up to my elbow. I gasp, staggering through the darkness. Single mind reeling, completely blind, I fling myself toward what I think is the passage back to the adit. I try for the narrow crack, miss, and try again, plunging my wriggling body through the bumpy slit of stone.

I rake my glove against the rough surface of the rocks until it curls loose, wet with either my blood or the organism's. I can see nothing, but I can feel blades of air whip against my face as the creature flails its many limbs, I can feel it cling to my skin in icy pinpricks, I can feel it pull against my nails as if it is trying to uproot them. I smash my hand into the wall once more, and the freezing sting lessens for a moment. Without quite knowing what I am doing, I clamp my shaking fist around the organism, squeezing until something gives way. There is no pop of bursting skin, no crack of bone, but when the flesh softens, I give in fully to this body's instinct. I release a cry that is not mine, that is too savage to have come from any of my throats, and I hurl the thing into the darkness.

I hear it hit the wall only a few paces from me, and I stand motionless, itching to run, hand still stinging from its touch. Somehow, over the deafening pounding of my heart, I can hear the creature move. I can hear its long, thin limbs patter against the rocks around it, shifting the dirt where it landed.

For the first time in as long as I can remember, I am afraid I will die. A single, horrified voice—this body's and this body's alone—screams in my head to run. I stagger through the darkness, ears ringing with panic, looking for light, for one speck of promising light that might lead me back to the entrance. I stumble blindly, scraping elbows and knees on rocks and machines, abandoning the lamp, abandoning Émile. My feet spring forward of their own accord, my hands grope for purchase, my throat spits wordless gasps. This body is beyond my control.

Its raw instinct alone propels me through the darkness. I know each step it takes may only lead me deeper into the earth, or deposit me into the open air of an empty shaft, but I cannot stop. If this brain is snuffed out here, I will not remember what happened, and I may make the same mistake again, sending bodies and bodies and bodies down the throat of this cavern, into the greedy villi of the creatures that lie in wait. I cannot die, I must keep going, I must reach the mouth of this cave, no matter what mangles me along the way—

Something latches onto my arm. A harsh cry jumps up this trachea as the painful pinch tightens, yanking me with surprising strength. I flail, stumbling back into something soft, something warm. A hiss of voiceless breath assures me that my captor is Émile.

I want to tell him to let me go, to separate himself from me, that I have been contaminated, but before I can manage anything other than a pained gasp, he reluctantly grips my sleeve—the clean, unaffected one—and tugs at me. I am too exhausted to resist him and too desperate to distrust him, so with one last useless glance over my shoulder, I let him guide me. I stumble in his wake as he marches, steadily and with uncharacteristic confidence, through the tapering corridors of the subterranean maze.

Lampless, propelled by something more profound than my primitive fear, Émile leads me onward. I do not know how he finds his way. It could be old Montish instinct, a boon of his sensitive black eyes, it could be a doglike sense of smell, it could be luck. Whatever guides us, physiological or metaphysical, it does not lead us into the rusted jaws of old machines, nor into the pitfalls of shafts. Each step we survive is one more than I expect.

After what must be minutes but what seems like hours, I spy the distant glow of snow-light. It is blurry, a grayish suggestion against the dark walls of the mine, but it flashes like a beacon. The half-moon of the entrance enlarges, and as its light reveals a path forward, this throat spills a cry of relief. I close my lips and muffle the sound, however, when I catch a glimpse of my swinging right arm.

I detach from Émile and throw myself through the threshold of the adit, into bright, sunlit white. Just as blind as I had been in the dark, I fall to my knees, plunging my hand into the snow. As I wrench my arm back and forth, a stain of dark blood spreads from my sleeve—not red, not mine. It is blackish, thick, splattered from the tips of my fingers up to the elbow of my coat.

Clenching my teeth against the cold, hands shaking, I rip off my parka and toss it away. Curious eyes of sled dogs follow my movements as I gather handfuls of snow, trying to wipe the stains from my palm and wrist until the skin is raw, until I cannot feel anything other than the painful, purifying cold. Right when I am sure I have washed every drop of that protoplasm from me, I notice a few spots on the thigh of my trousers. Seeing no other option, I unwind my belt and begin to remove those as well.

A hesitant hand touches my shoulder. Deerskin pants curled down almost to my knees, furred boots nearly kicked off, I struggle to stand, struggle to regain my composure. Émile stares at me for a moment, dark gaze wandering from my shivering arms to my discarded clothes, then to the stains in the snow.

"I . . . forgive me," I pant. "Keep your distance . . ." My words freeze on my tongue, the wind stings my back, and I realize there is no point in saying anything more. Émile retreats to the sled and dives into our supplies, emerging with a deerskin blanket.

He wades back through the snow and throws it over me, leading me in a wide circle around the contaminated parka. As my hands fumble again with my belt, he lowers his eyes to it, lips flattening into a thin, nervous line.

"Don't worry," I tell him. "I will keep these on. I was merely . . . I panicked. That is very much unlike me, I assure you."

He nods. I suspect he already considers my behavior uncharacteristic of a physician of the Institute, though he surely thinks he's known me only a few days.

"I simply have not . . . I simply have never encountered such a thing." I wrap the blanket tighter around me, glancing back at the bloodstained snow and my coat half-buried in it. "You would think my profession would prepare me for the unexpected." In spite of the fear and the cold, a bitter chuckle forces its way up my throat. The sheets of snow muffle the sound, and even when I strain these ears, it is the only voice of mine I can hear. "Did you see it?" I ask Émile. "Did you see it . . . move like that?"

He shakes his head. A bubble of doubt boils in my gut, and I wonder if my panic had only conjured an illusion of the creature latching onto me. I had no other brains or eyes to ascertain the situation. Were it not for the blood, I would happily dismiss the event as a fabrication of a lonesome, frightened brain. But as it is, I must contend with the reality that I am isolated, far from safety, shivering knee-deep in snow, and stained with the internal fluids of a creature that may have killed me once already.

I turn my eyes to my hand. The skin is unbroken, and wiped clean, but it stings with cold. I carefully move each finger, just to ensure they still function, and clench them under the blanket. Then, when I am certain I am unharmed, I return my gaze to the adit. I dare not go back inside, but I cannot leave without doing so. If I had come merely to discover this infective organism and flee from it, I would not have brought my specimen jars.

Something stops me from stepping back toward the mine. It is not Émile's worried look, it is not the sudden fanning of the dogs' white hackles, but a small puff of snow near the mouth of the hollow, moving toward me like a trick of the eye. Émile does not seem to notice it. He only climbs onto the sled and whistles for me to do the same.

But I am paralyzed. Not with cold, nor even with horror—it is with dismayed fascination that I watch the sliver of black break the surface of the snow. The creature's dozen limbs drag the remainder of its body from the adit, mangled and torn, a steaming trail of black blood in its wake. I cannot take my eyes off the thing as it heaves toward me in halfhearted leaps, alarmingly quickly, sputtering liquefied tissue as an engine might sputter exhaust.

The dogs begin to wail. They snarl and pull on the gangline, not toward south or safety, but toward the approaching organism. Paws dig at snow, growls rumble through the valley, and I hear Émile's desperate whistles, mouthed and blown through his bone carving, calling for obedience. They struggle and howl more violently with every gliding movement of the creature.

A single, desperate voice in this skull tells me to retreat, to crawl onto the sled with Émile and flee, but I stand my ground. Here in the clarity of day, where I can feel the traces of my other persons behind me, where I can view the strange, injured organism in vibrant white light, I find my courage returning. I throw off my blanket, freeing my arms, and holler at Émile to fetch a jar. I do not take my eyes from the thing as it slithers my way, I only extend a hand behind me, hoping the houseboy will place what I need into it.

When a flash of pale hair reenters my vision, it is not Émile's. It is a line of bristling hackles, a pair of ears laid flat against a furred head. Black shapes dance against the snow—two dark eyes, a nose wrinkled over exposed teeth, spindly tentacles flailing as they rise to meet the dog.

I cry out, reaching for the blurred chaos of black and white, unsure which opponent I plan to protect. But the fight is over in an instant. With a jolt of muscle and a flash of sharp teeth, the lead dog clamps her jaws around the creature. Dark slivers tremble from the canine's slavering mouth, and I can only watch in bewilderment as she bites down, vigorously, decisively—then again, teeth meeting teeth in a clear snap. Then she lifts her head, black blood running from her serrated lips, and with one eager gulp, swallows the organism.

By the time I regain enough control of this body to step forward, the only remnant of the creature is one lonely appendage, twisting mechanically on the ground like a despondent tail detached from a Satgarden itch-lizard. I stare, paralyzed, as the limb turns in slow spasms, dark fluid staining the snow around it. The lead dog saunters back to her damaged harness while I, arm still outstretched, whisper, "Émile."

He appears beside me, jar in one quivering glove, a pair of tweezers in the other. Before I can direct him, he leans down, pinching the tissue into the container and twisting the lid. He raises it to the light, and we both watch the thing writhe for a minute, thrashing, probing the glass as if searching for the rest of its body. When it finds only its inadequate self to cling to, it curls into a ball and stills, undulating only enough to assure me it is not dead.

I can breathe again. These shoulders drop, these shivering hands reach for the blanket as knives of cold wind cut at my back. I rewrap myself in the deerskin, rubbing some warmth back into these palms, and turn to Émile.

"I thought you had control over your dogs," I growl. "What happened?"

He always seems to understand the thoughts and intentions of the pack, but this time, he shakes his head.

"That did . . . that did not go as planned," I mutter, eyeing the lead dog. The poor, stupid beast pants eagerly, wearing the smile of a well-fed predator. Distantly, I hear laughter—likely my own. Perhaps a part of me finds amusement in the absurdity of the situation. This far north, I cannot be sure. "We have to do something about her, Émile."

His stare is intense, horrified. He is asking me exactly what I have in mind, and I don't know how to answer him. We can't leave her in the wilderness, contaminated as she is. And we can't take her back to Verdira for the same reason.

"We shouldn't cut her open now," I mutter. "If she survives the run back to town, I might be able to induce vomiting. Or . . . we could allow her to incubate it." I lift my eyes to the sky. The low

clouds billow a shy shade of pink, a reminder of our limited sunlight. "For now we'd best get back to the château. I will examine
her then."

Émile moves his gaze from the bloodstained snow to the lead
dog, wagging at the front of the line. He scratches behind her
torn ear and kneels to reattach her to the gangline, examining her
for injuries. When he is satisfied with her condition, he glances
back up to me. Myriad expressions cross his features, but the most
prominent by far is exhaustion.

"Agreed," I sigh, pulling myself into the sled.

The animals, hackles lowered and tongues lolling, are eager
once again to run. Even the lead, not in the least discomfited by
her ordeal, paces and howls with the rest of them. Émile's attention lingers on her for a second before his bone whistle sends her
off.

As we wind down toward Verdira proper, Émile keeps a watch-
ful gaze on the dogs. I try to keep my own vigil, narrowing my
eyes against the sharp wind and cradling the jar in the crook of my
elbow. The thing inside, I realize, remains shamefully unnamed. In
Inultus, it is considered improper not to know an acquaintance's
name and title upon the second meeting, so I decide to rectify the
situation when I am again within thinking distance of the city.

The black appendage lies curled and still, image warped by
glass. I reprimand myself for daring to think that it might resem-
ble an earthworm, blind and small and harmless. Though the
poorly lit image is already hazy in my single-brained recollection,
I know I will not forget the size of the colony I saw in the mines,
the nodes and crawling limbs intersecting to form a whole, like
boughs to a tree, or cells to a body like mine. With the corpses of
a dozen miners and a rich wheatrock deposit to nourish it, it's no
surprise it's grown much larger than the dry, pathetic specimen I
pulled from my expired host. I am afraid that the samples I have
now may prove to be only hairs plucked from a giant's head.

I remind myself not to indulge in panic. Humankind has lived
for millennia in close company with giants. It once sailed the open
seas, over the heads of the titans in the depths. It pierced the sky and
fell back down, bringing with it all its monstrosities of machinery.

And it will meet more, when I help it take to the air again, when we reclaim the world that was lost to us.

Many of the giants I have seen with my own eyes I have also safely quarantined in myth, and this one will be no different. I will rebury this monster. I will consign it to a footnote in my texts. I must, because I have made thoroughly sure no one else can.

VIII

THE SUCCESS OF ANY parasite is proportional to its harmlessness. Some are intelligent; they avoid detection, allowing their carriers to lead healthy lives until obsolescence. Fewer, in brilliant acts of symbiosis, foster dependence in the host. But too many are loud-mouths and fools, instigating aches, diarrhea, fatigue, bleeding, or other braggadocious symptoms. Most parasites cannot think far enough ahead to maintain the well-being of their host, much less their host's entire species. Usually, such foresight is not necessary, unless humans are involved. They tend to hold grudges.

To infect too many at once or to infect violently invites eradication, though in many cases it cannot be helped. Host bodies have a slew of defenses against invaders, and sometimes the war can only be won by cruel means. It is this cruelty that has, in the past, made it easy for me to identify and eliminate my competitors. The body's many battlefields are always marked with scars.

This one is no exception. After nearly a decade, it still bears the stigmata of my presence—a dark pockmark on its abdomen, a scar on its lower lip, slightly loosened teeth and brittle nails, a slowly growing stain on its pituitary gland. I am good at what I do, but even I am detectable.

Strangely, *Pseudomycota emilia* is not. Our encounter in the mine has left no infective marks on me. There is a blackish spot on the fleshy base of my right thumb, which at first I fear may be a persistent stain from its blood, but turns out to be nothing but a shallow bruise. The skin is unbroken, there is no swelling, no erythema, no pain. Only the reassuring sting all healthy hands feel when reintroduced to warmth after exposure to winter air.

The organism appears to have left even fewer signs on the lead dog than it did on me. Upon returning to the château, after we had resettled the others into their kennels, Émile held her face and stroked her ears, breathing reassurance into her neck as I examined her. With clear eyes and a pink-tongued smile, the dog appeared perfectly healthy. She did not vomit, nor did she show signs of indigestion or irritation. Even the samples of saliva I have under my microscope now, scraped from her teeth and tongue, bear no traces of her strange meal.

With each symptom I cannot see, with each of *P. emilia*'s clever evasions, I must contend with the possibility that this creature, this pretender to the throne of my taxonomic kingdom, has managed to do what I never could.

This body is again in range of my larger thoughts, and most of them are occupied with self-chastisement. I should have spent more time underground, I should have collected more specimens, I should have investigated how and why the thing sprang from the mines. But part of myself—primarily the part in Verdira, still stinging from the cold—understands the strain of that moment. This brain tries its best to make the others comprehend, but it is like trying to teach a left hand to do what a right does naturally, and from three hundred miles away.

Just audible over the clouds rolling through the prairies, my muffled voices encourage me to remove the appendage from its jar, to vivisect it, to ingest it, or otherwise allow it to crawl into this body so I can meticulously note all of the effects. But these suggestions are only passing impulses, thoughts that arrive skewed and distorted, as if seen backward through a spyglass. I remind myself that if I want the advantage of an expendable body, a larger fraction of me will have to ride the train north.

A timetable lies at the edge of my vision, open across a desk in Inultus. The pages are barely legible, full of movement, falling apart and reassembling with each breath, but I can see clearly enough that it will take several days to get more bodies here. Until then, I must busy myself with containing and observing *P. emilia*—"An awful name," crackles a voice of mine, fragmented by the miles stretching between Verdira and the Whesler Isles. ". . . I can think . . . ter one."

"After whom should I name it, then?" I mutter. "Myself?"

I do not reply. I close the timetable, contemplating how best to reposition myself. Seven bodies can be spared from Inultus, two from Misulah, four from the townships and settlements on the grasslands, and one from an outpost near the eastern fume wastes, whose patients had left on an expedition the previous week and failed to return. "I can collect myself here," I think aloud in the buzzing hive of the Inultan station. "The ride to Inultus should take less than two days, but to gather an adequate number . . . may take more time . . . not ideal . . . snow . . ."

I strain my ears, but my voice dissipates under another's.

"What did you do?"

A familiar outline appears in my doorway, tall, broad-shouldered.

"Émile is quite distressed," Didier continues. "So much so he's rendered himself useless. He ran into the kennels and he's not coming out."

"Oh," I say. "Good."

"*Good?* I need his assistance upstairs, and he's hiding under a pile of animals like an old Montish caveman." He raises a hand to his forehead. "Sylvie tells me you're responsible."

"I am."

"What did you do to him?"

His suspicion surprises me. He has always held me in high regard, but there may be some quality about this body he implicitly mistrusts. "I have done nothing," I say. "Émile is quite all right. It is a dog that worries him."

"What did you do to the dog, then?"

"You wish to lay the blame somewhere. I understand." I nod in the direction of the two jars on my shelf. One specimen lies motionless, kinked appendages frozen in a cringe like the legs of a dead spider. The other clouds the glass with moisture, wriggling in a pool of melted snow. "There are your culprits."

"What . . . is that the thing you found inside . . ." His face whitens as he approaches the shelf. "And this one is *alive*? Sweetest hell, you didn't pull this from anyone else's brain, did you?"

"No."

"Then how many of these things are just . . . crawling around out there?"

"None, I believe." I hope. "These are the only known specimens in Verdira at the moment. Well, these, and the one in the dog."

"*In* the dog?" The muscles tense in his angular jaw. "Doctor, you haven't been . . . conducting experiments on them, have you?"

"No," I answer, though a few distant brains are mulling over the idea. "The dog and the pathogen came into contact accidentally, and recently. I would like to document the animal's condition, at least until prodromes appear. That is why I asked Émile to keep an eye on it while I'm working elsewhere."

"No," Didier says. "No, absolutely not. I don't want him sitting in there breathing in that . . . illness." A shudder runs visibly from his head to his ankles. "I want that thing out of my house. Which dog is infected? I'll have it shot and disposed of properly."

"Please do so," I say. "But wait until I'm done with it. At least until the symptoms manifest and the vivisection is complete."

"When will that be?"

"It's difficult to know." If I am to assume I had contracted the parasite while failing to rescue Cass, it took at least four weeks to incubate, though that particular host was blessed with genetic resilience common to the infection-hardened people of Misulah. I cannot say if a dog will last as long. "Until that time, Émile will keep it safely contained. I have left him with all the supplies he needs, and he knows how to use them. I assure you, we have done all we can to isolate any infective material. You are likely in no danger."

"*Likely*." Didier shakes his head. "Winter's already bad enough.

With the collapse, and Hélène as she is, and now this thing . . .
how on Earth . . . where did you find it?"

I hesitate. "Outside."

"Outside the château?"

"Outside Verdira."

"Where?"

"It is best," I think I hear myself say from my clinic in the floodlands, "to pull a tooth quickly."

I look Didier in the eye. "In the north mine."

He stares at me. When he realizes this is not some gauche jest,
he begins to turn a frightening shade of red. Fortunately he is
not the kind of man who explodes. He only simmers and melts.
"*How?*" is all he rasps.

I don't know if he's asking me to justify myself or asking how
I made it to the mine and back in such a short day. "I'm afraid I
don't understand your question."

He does not seem to hear me. He deflates, sinking against the wall
and picking at his cravat. "That's not possible. That's not even *possible.* We've been pulling wheatrock from there for decades now—
the Montish have for centuries. We've never seen anything like that.
How can it be there now? Hell, it wasn't even there last autumn."

"I suspect it's been underground for some time," I say. "It may
have been inaccessible until the collapse dislodged a portion—"

Didier has already moved on, pacing, firelight glinting orange
along the rims of his spectacles. "No one got sick before. Not with
this thing. No miners, no machinists, no carvers. *Shit,* of course
it's the wheatrock mine. Of all the earth's goddamn holes, it had
to be that one. Not the first problem to crawl from that evil pit."

"Sieur . . ."

"This was deliberate. It has to be. Someone must've planted it
there, it must've been—" He pauses abruptly. He closes his eyes
and takes a deep breath. "It'll move again. The mine will move
again, and all will go back to the way it was. An aberration, that's
all." He removes his pince-nez and wipes them with a loose shirt-
tail. "It seems every other year we have an incident in that cursed
place. And every time we've recovered. We've gotten back on our
feet, haven't we? Yes, every time. We just need some sort of plan."

"Institute persons will arrive on the next train," I say. "The mine will be quarantined until spring, and operations suspended until the Institute deems it safe to recommence."

"Oh, dear hell, I meant a *sensible* plan." Didier tugs at his collar once more. "You can't just shut everything down. No, that's a terrible idea. It's the only source of wheatrock we have."

"The health of Verdira is at stake," I say.

"The health of Verdira is *forfeit* if we cut off our livelihood. And the city's, too."

"Inultus has lived without wheatrock before," I say. I fail to mention how much of that life was lived in the shadows of cyclical famine, or how much the population has expanded since then. "It can do so again, at least for a time."

"How long a 'time' will you subject us to, doctor?"

Between isolation, excavation, disinfection, and in the worst case, partial or total destruction of the mine, the numbers multiply in my heads, clumsily, muddled by what I am now sure must be an electrical storm passing between the mountains and the city. "Anywhere from weeks to years."

"*Years!*"

"Surely there must be other deposits. There is reportedly a vast network of—"

"You don't have to explain my own business to me, doctor." Didier's smile is defensive. There is a little of the baron in it. "We can't just close the mine down and look for another. Perhaps you have not heard the tale of the last people who suggested my father halt his operations, but if you like you can find their bones in the château gardens."

I nod. Priest is proof the baron's personal physician is not immune to his violence, but even he would think twice before opposing the Institute. The baron needs me far more than I need him.

"You're used to living under the open sky," Didier continues. "You don't know the earth. It's good to us. It's temperamental, of course, but reliable. Everything will move back into place by spring. Everything will be as it was. It'll go back to the way it used to be."

I bite my tongue. I will have far more bargaining power with a few dozen bodies beside me. For now, I will have to go behind his back.

"Besides," Didier continues, "the mine is as good as quarantined already. No one would dare go there this time of year—at least no one in their right mind. So long as you keep those creatures contained, there's no way for this illness to spread." He pauses. "Is there?"

I blink, and see the dark canopy of hairlike tentacles, tangled over a crumbling wall of rock. I imagine them peeling apart and dropping thin-legged nodes into the darkness, a thousand invaders woken from dormancy by my incautious hand. I try to recall how many paces it is between the site of the collapse and the mouth of the adit, and then how many paces it is between the adit and the town of Verdira.

"Perhaps you are right," I mutter. "With this weather it is easy to keep anyone from going up to the mine." Keeping anything from coming out, however, may prove to be an entirely different matter. Even with more than one body, I will need help.

"If I may ask bluntly," Didier starts, "what in all earthly hells compelled you to go into the wilderness? Even with the dogs, even in the day, you could have gotten lost. You could've killed yourself—killed Émile. Do you know what lives out there? Have you ever seen a ventigeau?"

I have, once, from the baron's tower, impossibly tall, white as a ghost. "No," I answer.

"No, you couldn't have," he sighs. "With you experimenting on the dogs and endangering our houseboy, I don't know if my father will kill you before the winter does."

"Both are possible," I admit. An odd twinge of fear stirs in my gut.

"I must apologize, doctor." Didier's voice softens. "I don't mean to alarm you. I simply have not been clear enough with you. If you're planning to conduct any more . . . ambitious research, please inform me first. I am not my father, I will not punish you for asking. I meant it when I said the château was happy to provide you with what you need." He gives me a weak smile. "And it looks like you may need some rest."

I glance at my microscope, then through the arced doorway into my bedchamber. "I suppose I am rather fatigued. I feel a headache coming on."

"With this winter, who can blame you?" Didier says. "I can open a nice thick wine for you."

"No, maeci. I must . . ."

The thought hovers at the tip of my brain as a word hovers at the tip of a tongue. It may be the distance from here to Inultus, or the muffling effect of the clouds down south, but for a moment I feel separated from myself, as if I am still enclosed in the darkness of the wheatrock mine. I close these eyes, concentrating every cell of this body on home, but even when my own voices fade again into hearing, the thought I am looking for has already passed.

IX

WHEN THE RATTLING TRAIN first carried me north to Verdira, the town was barely smaller than it is now: a few hundred workers, and a few dozen more to keep them in line. The patient burden was not particularly heavy, but Priest was more than ready to pass it on to my shoulders.

Though he was bereft of an education, Priest's experience as a midwife and wet nurse had afforded him some knowledge of obstetrics, and he was eager to share tales of difficult births and the merits of old Montish herbalism. My first summer in Verdira, he guided me through the stone streets under the midnight sun, pointing out wheatrock refineries and furriers' workshops, instructing me in the region's unique patois. He introduced me to my new patients, told me he'd assist in whatever way he could, and dispensed advice I have never forgotten.

"S'a pet a knowledge I'd offer you, médsaine. Help you survive here. Primary—never disobey the baron. Secondir—never leave shelter on a winter night. Tret—if you think it's dawn, s'nay dawn yet. Ay, last but important: remember the château nay meant to be lived in."

Since Franco had been new to my ears, I thought I had misheard. "Pardon?"

"Wae, médsaine, thousands a years château were solely for sledchennies ay their whelps. S'posed to be for them alone, so they can dig ay run in the gardens, protect the clans habiting 'round the ville. Wae, a pack's howl-song's the only thing keeps the ventigeaux at bay. We forget that."

"I have not heard anything of the sort."

"Bensûr you nay have," he'd replied. "I learned from a Montish. Ay she knew more'n she ever shoulda known."

As far as I could tell through his thick speech, his informant had been trustworthy, knowledgeable, and, by merit of being dead, an excellent keeper of secrets. Priest had delivered and nursed her, and watched her grow into a healthy girl of remarkably boyish mien, at least to non-Montish eyes—the people of the caves, Priest informed me, made little distinction between sexes. She'd been an easy birth, and like her mother, had retained her fetal tail. An odd trait, but plenty of my patients, and some of my own bodies, possess such harmless malformations.

Hair cropped short, long-limbed, and gray as a stone, the little girl would slip onto the château's grounds, up its walls and through its windows, past the dozens of guards hired to prevent precisely that kind of intrusion. Priest would often find her sneaking cheeses from the manor's pantry, or in the playroom of the young master, hands stained green with wheatrock as if she had burrowed in straight from the mines.

"Nearly scared my tits off't first," Priest had laughed, before introducing me to the relevant Franco slang. "Find her in Did's room one day, ay find him gone the next. They'd disappear for hours on end. Loved each other like hell."

Priest never alerted the guards to her presence. When the baron came roaring down the halls, demanding his son for some pressing reason or another, he would lie on their behalf, offering reassurances that Didier was safe and disciplined, practicing his shot with the gendarmes or studying mathematics under a governess the baron forgot he had already expelled from service. For years, Didier and his friend would play, unimpeded by the complexities of caste and dialect, unrestrained by propriety.

She seemed to know more about the château than even its inhabitants. She knew the curses buried in its frozen flower gardens, she knew that muffling a dog's howl would bring a terrible storm to its towers. She had an explanation for the ripples of cold air that would paralyze the maids and butlers, she had seen the ghosts of the people who built those halls, and she knew never to look in a mirror in that place, lest her reflection move without her.

"Ah, petite Útolie were a raconteur like no other," Priest said. "Halfa what she said were mad, but the other half'd save your life. Every old history I know 'bout these hills come from her. Ask me to tell 'em to you sometime."

"I would be delighted."

"Collected plenty. 'Til the baron found out I'd let his son play with a cave rat." He laughed. "He had my knees shot out ay banished me from the château. Stories ended there."

I would learn later that there was quite a bit more to that narrative, but Priest was not about to tell a stranger the rest.

"Ah, hard habiting en château. You'll see things you nay wanna see. You might spy a ghost a someone you love in a corridor. Ay in a winter night you may hear a cry that sounds human. S'only a ventigeau outside. Nay follow it. Nay follow anything that tries to lead you."

I had nodded earnestly, just to satisfy him. Though later I would learn that some of his warnings were indeed true, many struck me merely as a familiar iteration of a universal folklore. I have lived many places, and I have heard of creatures worse than ventigeaux, beguiling monsters that still sometimes make the hairs on one or two of my necks stand on end.

In Misulah there are tales of mermaids, similar to humans in every way except for their evil eyes, blue and bewitching, devoid of pupils. In Satgarden they speak of automatons that crawl from the mud-river and copy the first person they find, adopting their looks and habits until entire households are replaced by soulless contraptions. In the naturalist collective's eastern outposts, on the precipice where our knowledge ends and the poisoned world begins, there are multiple reports of long-armed shadows, hunched and beckoning, that lead inquisitive explorers to fume-choked deaths.

There is one element to these tales I find particularly disturbing. It both dismays and fascinates me that, no matter where I travel in the habitable world, I find accusations of human mimicry and infiltration. Conjurations of familiar specters, doppelgängers, androids, beautiful succubi who drink their victims dry in the night—though the latter, after some investigation, turned out to be nothing more than a mobile colony of bloodsucking ants.

I cannot quite understand these fables, nor can I discern their use. I suspect they are born from the peculiar, specific anxiety that there is something fundamentally fragile about humanness. The dread that perhaps, if one takes time to peel back the skin of another, they will find an imposter, a machine, or stranger still, something like me.

A terrifying thing happens in my sleep.

My mind is drowned in images. Hundreds of them come in quick succession, but they are not the kaleidoscopic overlays that characterize my sight, they are not logical, parallel inputs from a thousand retinas. They are isolated, fleeting, nonsensical, and utterly beyond my control. I can only approximate the unorganized march of warped thoughts as dreaming.

I roll from sheets dampened with sweat, and for a sinister moment the darkness of my room threatens to throw me back into the northern mine. I scramble to the lamp, eager to turn the rocky ribs of the cavern back into cobwebby walls, and turn the writhing organisms back into the hands of a harmless clock.

When the light coaxes my traitorous chambers into view, I allow myself to take a deep breath. The jars of *Pseudomycota* shine on my shelf, undisturbed, unchanged, unbroken. I am safe, for the moment.

My heart slows a little, but with each beat a dull agony pounds through my head. This brain feels like a misused muscle, struggling to juggle unwieldy thoughts between its hemispheres. It longs for relief, for other brains to divide and carry the weight of its sudden visions, but as it reaches toward Inultus, it can only touch my most peripheral thoughts. A misplaced scalpel, a time-eaten map of the world as it once was, green and blue and open, a chilly wind rattling the wagons of a caravan.

Just as a distal nerve may propagate a jolt of agony, I fling distress toward the city. My thoughts are in disarray, but I can feel my swell of worry in Inultus, I can see my feet carry me across the mosaics of the train station, I can sense my larger self stretching northward as this body stretches south, like two edges of a wound trying to reconnect.

An image persists in this brain: a fading echo of a ghostlike dog, strings of black blood dripping from her mouth. I long to understand that vision, to interpret it in its entirety, but to try now would be like having a body perform surgery on itself. I must wait until my mind is whole.

For now, I focus on what a single body can do. First, it can steady its breathing. It can slow its heart. It can forget about home for the moment and concentrate on tying its shoes. It can open its bag, insert saws and lancets of all sizes, forceps and specimen phials. It can stalk the sleeping halls of the manor all the way to the kennels and return within the hour. Then it can crawl back into bed for the remaining six hours and forty-four minutes until dawn, and hope that nothing horrifying happens again in its sleep.

Émile will not be pleased with me. He might, if he is feeling particularly defiant, even try to stop me. He will not dare touch me, he will not dare use force, but he will certainly attempt to dissuade me in his compelling, voiceless way. When he is adamant, he is difficult to ignore.

The halls are silent, abandoned to a nightly chill even the thick walls cannot keep out. I hurry through the dark, but no matter how quickly I fly down twisting corridors, I fail to escape my dream of the lead dog, eyes bright and clear, just as I last saw her. Her echo stumbles after me, whining and coughing in that curious, muted way dogs do. As I reach the stairs descending to the kennels she lowers her head and retches, depositing a half-digested meal onto the floor. I refuse to contemplate the image. I do not want to see that organism, maimed and soaked in gastric acid but tireless as ever. I do not want to think about it crawling out of the bowels of the animal and into the bowels of the château.

I can only curse myself for not having thought of it sooner. I had dislodged the creature from its substrate, smashed it against a rock wall, and thrown it across a tunnel, and it still managed to follow me from the wheatrock lode to the adit. There is no reason to believe that a few bites of a dog's teeth could destroy it. Had I the proper breadth of neural tissue at my disposal, I would have warned myself of the possibility—no, not a possibility, but an encroaching certainty—that the body of the vile thing is still motile, wriggling somewhere in or around the lead dog.

I suppose the best place to start my search is in the gastrointestinal tract. I do not know nearly as much about canine anatomy as I do human, but I know where a meal begins and ends. If I find nothing, I will move to the eyes, and then the brain. The death will be swift, the procedure thorough, the cremation immediate.

The kennels occupy the distant tip of the château's east wing, a collection of guest rooms that must have once bordered on luxurious. Now, as I push open the steel door, the place is darkened, dusty, its carpets and upholstery soaked for years in the scents of dander, urine, and feces. Tufts of fur float like snowflakes in the air, and a chorus of whines blows through the hall as loudly as any wind.

I make my way through the crumbling corridor. In the rooms on either side of me, behind splintered oak and chicken wire and rebar, dozens of tails rise in suspicion. Black eyes stare through metal mesh, ears perk forward, teeth cease chewing at baseboards, ripped carpets, and end tables. One animal slides halfway off its bed, back legs stretched out over the ancient mattress, and releases a deep growl.

A dozen paces from where I stand, I hear a response. The sound of shuffling draws my eyes to the door at the end of the hall, scratched and chewed and swinging in the frozen air. Cursing any servant who would carelessly leave an occupied kennel open, I place my bag on the floor. A painful lump travels down my throat as I kneel, reaching for a lancet, a saw, anything that might defend me from the dog I know will leap into sight as soon as it smells me.

A voice, sharp and agitated but decidedly human, emerges from beyond the doorway.

"This is not the time. With this illness—oh, don't start. Someone needs to break your bad habits."

I pull my hand from my bag and rise, tilting my ear toward the hovering words.

"They're *diseased*. They'll spread it to you. To all of us—do you not care?"

I see Didier well before he sees me. He slides through the doorway, gaze locked on something behind him. His cravat is pulled over his face like a protective mask, and one gloved hand is wrapped around the houseboy's bare wrist, tugging urgently. Émile, not so cautiously dressed, only digs his heels into the carpet.

"What is *wrong* with you?" Didier demands. There is something odd coloring his voice, something angrier than fear. "Now *come,* or I'll have the constable—"

When Didier spies me, he freezes in place, dropping Émile's wrist. The houseboy appears no less startled to see me here, in the middle of a winter night, dangerously close to the outside world. His eyes fall on my medical bag, and a grim frown tightens his lips.

"Good evening," I begin, cautiously.

Didier blinks the surprise from his face, but he cannot quite rid his voice of it. "Doctor, what are you doing out here?"

Pretending to have lost one's way is a tactic that rarely works in the best of circumstances. "Émile," I say, instead. "I need—"

"What could you possibly need at this hour?" Didier asks. His tone is dark with suspicion. "You shouldn't be wandering at night, doctor. Not in the older halls, where the wind can still get through."

"Émile," I repeat. "I need to see the lead dog. Where is she?"

The wrinkles in Didier's forehead deepen. "You came here for the dog?"

I nod.

After a protracted second, he releases a humorless laugh. "You just couldn't wait to cut it open, could you? All the better. I want that thing out of my kennels. Who knows—*Émile!*" The house-boy stops in his tracks, abandoning his conspicuous attempt at escape. "Don't you dare. Show the good doctor to the animal, then clean yourself up and get back inside."

Émile hesitates, lower lip disappearing into his mouth. The house-boy knows me too well. He knows why I have brought my bag.

"Go on," Didier continues. "Get the dog." When the young man does not respond, he loses his tenuous smile. "Go. Willful-ness does not suit you."

"It is quite all right." I brush past them, slowing to make sure Émile gets a good view of my stern frown. "I can find her myself. She is the one with the torn right ear."

I pace the length of the hall, glancing through lattices of wood and metal. My first pass yields nothing. All the animals' ears are intact, they are either too small or too fat, their coats are blem-ished with grayish specks or scars, their tails are crooked or their stances submissive. Dread swells in my gut. I retrace my steps, then do so again. Slowly, with the heavy sluggishness of an over-taxed mind, I come to realize what Émile has done.

I sweep toward him, gritting my teeth. It is bad enough to be outwitted by *Pseudomycota emilia.* I will not stand to be outwit-ted by its eponym as well.

"She's not here," I say.

"What?" Didier's hiss is barely muffled by the cloth over his mouth.

We both turn to Émile, but the servant's expression is as plain and unreadable as snow.

"I know you are worried about her," I say. "But you should be more worried about the rest of us. I need to see her."

He does not respond. He betrays no regret, no fear, no triumph.

I must give him credit. He did have the foresight to know I would return, well before symptoms manifested, to vivisect or otherwise hurt the animal. He may even have considered the possibility that *Pseudomycota* would pass unharmed through the dog's digestive tract, and anticipated I would arrive at the same conclusion. But the fact he beat me to it flushes my only face with anger.

Fortunately, this particular skin is dark enough to hide it. "You are a kind young man," I say. "You care for the dogs, I know. You do not want to see any of them harmed. But she is a danger to all of us, including the other animals. So show me where you hid her."

"You heard the doctor," Didier nearly whispers.

"I only want to examine her," I say, though the deceit in my words is painfully apparent. "I have only come for a few samples. Take me to her."

The servant stands in impervious silence.

"That dog is diseased, Émile," Didier says. "You know that. And you don't want to be responsible for spreading it."

Finally, something of a pained look crosses his face.

"Where is she?" I ask.

The black pools of his eyes flick toward the end of the hall.

"I have searched that room already," I tell him. "I know she's not in there."

His eyebrows arch in a plea. I sigh and acquiesce, trudging once more to the doorway and glancing through. I see no dog, just an old, hard mattress, deformed under the weight of generations of sleeping canines, a worn carpet, and the frame of a dresser so chewed and scratched it resembles kindling more than furniture. "She's not here—" I start, but the glint of the window catches my eye. The glass reflects fragments of torchlight in its warped frame, wooden sashes dappled with toothmarks. The frost on its panes is jagged, recently disturbed.

Slowly, I turn back to Émile.

"You released her." Even I am surprised at the surety in my voice.

"You *what*?" Didier squeaks. He grips the houseboy by the shoulders and wheels him around. "You let that animal get infected with that thing, and then you *let it go*?"

A lump travels down the young man's throat.

It is all I can do to contain my frustration. "Was she acting ill?" I ask.

He shakes his head.

"When did you do it?"

His fingers spell four hours ago.

"*Shit*," Didier hisses. "Shit, I can't *believe* you."

"Maybe . . ." I cannot be sure if I am relieved that *Pseudomycota* is out of the château, or horrified that it's now free in Verdira, traveling far and fast on four canine legs. "Émile . . . perhaps you wish to explain yourself."

I try to mask the anger in my voice, but Didier makes no such attempt. He steps forward, baring his teeth. "You reckless little— are you—do you have any idea what you've *done*?" His cravat, dislodged by the pressure of his breath, dangles from his face as he lowers it to Émile's. "What will you do if she bites someone? You saw that thing in the iceroom. You *saw* it! How would you like to have that creature inside you?" His voice escalates, in volume and pitch, frozen breath blowing like steam. "You saw what it did to the old doctor! And it'll do the same to you—and the rest of us, do you not understand?"

"Didier, wait—" I start.

"She's going to *spread* that thing! You could've killed us—"

Didier raises his arm. Émile doesn't flinch. He just stares in quiet resignation as the back of Didier's hand meets his face. A sharp smack resounds through the kennels, followed by a silence even the dogs do not dare to break. Émile stands firm, eyes closed, turned cheek reddening as Didier strikes him again.

"Stop, sieur—"

My voice barely glances off him. Another curt blow to the face and Émile staggers, releasing a short gasp. One of my meager two hands twitches, nails digging into my palm as I stop myself from reaching out for Didier's wrist. I struggle for only a fraction of a second before I realize I do not have to compromise my own safety by laying a finger on the heir to Verdira.

He is already stumbling back, eyes wide, as if he has been struck himself. His hand falls to his side, shaking, and he lifts his eyes from Émile to me. He is wordless, mouth agape in terrified bewilderment. I have not seen Didier with such an intense look since the birth of his children. At least, his surviving children.

"I . . . I am so sorry," he murmurs, eventually, to no one in particular. "Something came over me, something made me . . . it's not me. I'm terribly sorry."

I do not know how to respond. I have never witnessed such behavior from him, nor had I even imagined it. He is right, this certainly isn't him.

"It's all this . . . what's been happening," he says. "It was under control. I had it under control until a moment ago."

Neither the blows nor the explanation seem to move Émile. He stares at the ground, knuckle-shaped blushes on his cheek glowing an indignant shade of pink.

"I recommend you get some sleep," I tell Didier. It is all I can say.

"Yes . . . yes, that is what I need," he replies, running a hand through his hair. "I'll get my father's men to start the search at daybreak."

The incessant winds whistle along the hall like cold breath through a flute. "Perhaps," I venture, too hopefully, "the night will take care of it for us."

"One of these dogs? Not likely. They've survived generations of Verdiran winter. We'll have to shoot it. And burn it. Burn everything it's touched."

"If it comes to that," I say. I suppose the useless, charred corpse of a dog is better than a surge in zoonotic cases of *Pseudomycota emilia*. "And if . . . and should the parasite somehow exit the host—"

"I will inform the town," Didier says. "I'll put a gun in every hand that can hold one and give orders to shoot at anything not human. That dog and whatever's in it will be dead by tomorrow." He nudges the small of Émile's back, shoving him toward the door. "And you're going to help. Come along. You've a hundred notices to write before dawn."

Émile does not resist, but slows to glance over his shoulder at me. As I attempt, and fail, to read the meaning of his dark stare, my anger shrinks from a flame to an ember. A cacophony of whines emerges from the kennels, but even they cannot drown out the sharp clap of skin striking skin that lingers in the air.

X

THE OLDEST OF ALL Priest's ancient tales is that of a nameless Montish boy. He lived back when the ashes of the world's great catastrophes were fresh and warm, when life was easy. Those were the days before people needed to stuff their blankets and clothes with dog fur, when one could walk alone on a winter night, and the ventigeaux were nothing more than tall, clement elk.

Only such a time of plenty could've produced a boy with such unwarranted happiness. His heart was so bright with hope and love that it could not be contained within him, so instead it manifested as a torch, which he carried with him wherever he went. At night he left it in a sconce on the wall. In the day he held it in one hand, always nurturing its flame, never allowing it to flicker out.

Every morning he would descend into the caves to search for precious stones, since those were also the days when the mines were abundant and obedient. But the sleeping mountains were waking up again, and through the widening cracks came the quakes and gaseous leaks, the poison cave grasses and the living shadows who gorged themselves on jade and wheatrock. When these beings laid eyes on the boy and his torch, they were both disgusted and intrigued. They hated his warmth, yet they envied it; they were afraid of his light, yet they followed it wherever he went. Jealous of his goodness, the shadows stalked him through the caverns, conspiring to swallow his heart, to snuff out its flame, to separate his soul from his body and devour him entirely.

"Ay so they did," Priest always finishes.

The first time I heard the story, I had expected a more cohesive narrative. I had expected a confrontation of some sort, a game of wits, a battle between the boy and the devils that lived in the darkness under the mountain. I was taken aback by the abruptness of our hero's end, name lost to the ages but ignoble death preserved in memory. That was before I learned all Montish stories ended that way.

"Have I missed the empratesse?" I had asked Priest. He had taught me the term earlier that week, a curious word, which translates roughly as usefulness, but is only applied to fictions and non-existent objects.

"Nay sure't has one, médsaine. Maybe's to warn against being too bright when others want brightness. Maybe's to keep kids from bringing torches into caves ay starting grassfires. Important lesson to learn, that. Start one, you can wake even the sleepiest mountain. Nothing worse underground'n a grassfire. Worse'n a blast. Least a blast is over'n a second. Grassfires'll last for generations if you let 'em."

At the time I was unsure if I had merely misheard his Franco. "Generations?"

"Well, you'd know something of it, as a physician. Some disasters go on for decades. Some is just passed down in the bloodline."

A gunshot rips across the clouds, rumbling through my aching head. The billowing snow has softened the noise so I cannot tell from where it has come, but I imagine somewhere beyond the château, where the woods are slowly but surely swallowing the gardens.

I choose to interpret it as a good sign. So long as the shot was not fired by the constable, who fires with unfailing precision at exactly what he does not aim for, there is a good chance the bullet has met its mark. If I am fortunate, I will have a dog's cadaver safe and sound under my scalpel come nightfall.

Nearly all of the baron's gendarmes are prowling the streets today. Verdira's supply of firearms has dwindled somewhat since the last massacre of its workforce, but somehow Didier has scrounged enough to send every man out bristling with weaponry. I can spy dozens of them at the perimeter of town, investigating every leafless copse and flurried mound of snow. They march in the long shadows of warehouses and peer from their perches on rooftops, escorting denizens as they scramble to make their final preparations for the deep winter hibernation.

A gust of wind ruffles my overcoat, and I catch an echo of Inultus: the turning of a page, an exchange between two soft voices, as automatic and rhythmic as a heartbeat. I strain my ears, concentrating, grasping onto the feeling of home, but the sounds flee as quickly as they came. A cold ache pounds in my head, and I long to touch one of my own persons, to rest a hand at the nape of a neck and know it belongs to me, to lay my bodies across one another as comfortably as one crosses their arms.

I do not know what is untethering my thoughts from each other, and I do not know what I will say to myself once I reconnect. No doubt I will be appalled at my irresponsibility, disappointed that this brain could not contain a single pathogen. If my sharpest intellects and implements are currently boarding the train at the Inultan station, there is a distinct possibility I will soon be cut with both.

The thought turns my stomach, though it shouldn't. To the best of my ability, I am kind to my bodies. It makes little sense that I should feel protective over this one in particular. Still, I find myself wringing my hands on its behalf.

I sidestep a pair of chatting gendarmes, and my mind returns to the icy street. At the end of the lane, sinking brick by brick into the snow, is Verdira's best and only pub. It is Domenche, the day of the blasted sun, when Priest celebrates the week's end by abandoning his congregation in favor of libations of wheatrock ale. Baker, that creature of habit, will be with him, cards and gambling chips in hand.

A gust of heated air welcomes me into the building. A recklessly large fire blazes in the old stone hearth, and miners gather around it, voices crackling as loudly as the burning wood. The barkeep is on his knees, stoking the flames, and does not greet me as I slip by. I wade through the stony shadows to a little enclave of petrified oak beams, choked with a pungent gray haze.

For half a moment I cannot believe my only nose. "You are not supposed to be smoking," I say.

My voice tears Baker's attention from the cards on the table. He looks over his shoulder, one bushy eyebrow raised, and his cigarille nearly drops from his mouth. "Oh shit, doc. What're you— how'd you know where to find me?"

"Baker, tell me you've not picked up the habit again. We've— you've spent years trying to wean off those things."

"Ay what would *you* know 'bout those years?" We lock eyes, and for a moment I fear he will spark and ignite, but he only sighs, a billow of black smoke pouring from between his teeth. "Wae, I know. Sorry, doc. S'just . . . heat's so nice, and the season's so damn cold already . . . just doing it this once. Promise."

"Wae," Priest says. "Day's cold 'nough to freeze a ventigeau."

"Why you even down here, doc?" Baker asks. "Baron's organs break again?"

"No, but yours will if you keep smoking. It is damaging to your vasculature."

"*Vasculature*," he laughs, half-guiltily raising the cigarille to his mouth. I can tell by the rubicund bulges of his cheeks that he has already had quite a bit to drink. "It'll only last me half a year anyway."

"Let a man warm hisself, médsaine," Priest says, motioning for me to take a seat. "Either he smoke'n here or march snowside for that rabid chennie."

"Ay I'm nay gonna march," Baker growls. "Nay with the constable. Bastard dragged the château's houseboy by a while ago, made him hand out the orders to shoot." He waves a little paper decree, written in Émile's immaculate hand. "I ordered him to go fuck himself, torturing a kid like that."

"Who'd the poor wretch bite?" Priest asks me.

"Nay matter," Baker replies, before I can. "Constable'd look for any excuse for a hunt like this. Lives for the drama. If I could stand to look at the ugly fuck's face I'd wager he had a grin on it."

"Does love to shoot," Priest admits, drawing a card.

"Even so, man could aim at the ground and miss."

"You nay reckon't were he that gave Émile a sore face?"

"Maybe. Could be the baron."

I slip into a chair and fold my hands under my chin. "It wasn't the baron."

"Wouldn't be," Priest agrees. "Nay gotten off his ass to beat anyone since he lost his legs."

"So it was Hélène," Baker concludes. "Makes sense. She's had it out for Émile since she caught him stealing from her."

"Not her, either," I say.

"Shit, nay the *twins*, was it?"

"No. Didier."

Baker's grin is incredulous. "You blagging? He'd sooner break his own hand than bruise someone with it. He'd never. Believe me, I've been the château's machinist for years. Did's been driven halfway up the walls by all the shit that goes on in that madhouse, and he nay take it out on no one. 'Specially Émile."

Priest's wrinkled lips downturn in a cautious frown. "I seen Didier get violent. Once. 'Round '97."

"You didn't," Baker replies. "Nobody has. Nay even then. Hell, far as I heard he refused to point his pistol at the door as they were breaking it down. They woulda killed him and he woulda just stood there, waiting for it."

"Nay what I'm on 'bout," Priest mutters.

"Can't blame him, how his girl out there threw the first rock through the château window. Were I him I'd've never got over it, either." Priest tries to interrupt, but Baker has already gathered momentum, dealing out words as sloppily as the next hand. "You heard 'bout the blast of '97, doc? Nay from *them*, you'd never hear it up on the baron's hill, but from down here."

"I have," I answer, if only to spare myself a graphic retelling.

"The barber or the butcher's version?" Baker asks.

Both, repeatedly. "I can't recall."

"All lies, either way. Those bastards weren't there. Nay know shit 'bout the blast, or the skirmishes, or the mines. Chock fulla wheatrock but cursed as the broken moon." He gathers his cards. "But there you go, doc. That mine is keeping us alive, ay it wants to kill us all. What do you do 'bout it? Just the state of living in Verdira, maman used to say. Your play, Priest."

The old man leans over and lays a card faceup, eliciting a string of obscenities from his opponent. "Lor, médsaine, I know you didn't come just to scold our poor mechanic."

"No," I answer. I blink, hoping I will catch a glimpse of Inultus, but all I can see are whorls of smoke. "Baker, I have come to request your assistance."

"Supe, so long as it's nay the baron's organs. What do you need?"

I am thinking of a massive door, several doors, steel tunnels and walls, domes for equipment and laboratories, drills and bombs powerful enough to reshape the core of the wheatrock mine. But those plans are not feasible, at least not until the snow melts. I need something quicker, something fit for winter. Something with enough firepower to melt that damnable tunnel to smooth, impassible glass. "Baker, you know more about explosives than most of the governor's engineers," I say. "And the Institute would like to make use of your expertise."

"Oh?"

"I need you to seal off the wheatrock mine."

Baker stares at me a moment, tipping slightly on his chair, before he breaks out into a wide grin. "You want me dead!" he laughs. "Seal off the wheatrock—where the fuck did that idea come from?"

"Caution." In my mind, the little limbs of *Pseudomycota* writhe through knee-deep snow as easily as water. "No, necessity."

"I got less love for that place'n anyone," he says. "But it's only a curse, doc. Don't lose your head. Wait till spring ay then you can suggest closing it off to the baron."

"Springtime is a good season for a funeral," Priest says. His sardonic smile forces my fist to clench under the table.

"Lemme guess," Baker continues, "you heard some sorta story 'bout the miners' corpses walking ay now you're do-gooding 'bout it."

"No," I answer.

"Someone started a grassfire ay you're worried it'll spread?"

"*No.*" Anger stings my eyes, my voice quavers. Though I reach out to myself, desperately, there are no other brains to relieve the pressure, no other jaws to clench or teeth to grind. Every feeling is here, concentrated in one head. No wonder it feels as if it might burst. "I'm worried about a pathogen. The very same that killed my predecessor."

Baker's eyebrows rise. "You said he offed himself."

"No death has a single cause." A cold bead of sweat gathers on my forehead as Baker and Priest exchange glances. "You must listen to me. I am a scientist and a physician, your *only* physician. I am the voice of the Institute in this colony, and if you refuse my request, they will certainly have something to say about it when they get here."

The red whiskey-glow of Baker's face fades as blood drains from it. "You're serious?"

"There is something in that mine, Baker," I say.

"Always is," Priest mutters.

Baker quiets him with a look. "So . . . the baron knows 'bout this thing? He's gonna let you close it?"

"You know him better than that."

"So you're asking me to start a fight between him ay the Institute." He shakes his head. "He'll hang me ay use my pieces in his machinery. I don't mind the hanging, but the thought of my own poor heart keeping the bastard alive brings the taste of oil to my mouth."

"More Institute persons will arrive on the train in a few days." I fold my hands, hoping they will stop trembling. "And more bodies means more protection, from both the baron and this disease."

"A pet late in the year for the train—"

"As soon as it arrives, you are going to help me isolate and

destroy that pathogen. The Institute will compensate you for anything you need to quarantine the mine. But you'd best start now if
you want to have something ready by the time the train comes."

"Oh dead gods. You really *are* serious. Look, doc—we can't. If
we dam the flow of wheatrock we all starve. Ay that's if the baron
nay murder us outright."

I know I should not redirect my ache of frustration onto Baker,
but I do not know what else to do. I am small, I am alone, and
I cannot stop myself. There is only one card I can play that will
ensure his cooperation. I have to lie to him.

"Baker, do you know what really killed Cass?"

The baron's tubing is clogged again.

I kneel by his bedside, twisting caps from his external lym-
phatics, enveloping myself in clouds of foul-smelling air. It is a
ritual I must perform every week or so, and I cannot escape it. I
cannot even excuse myself for something as urgent as dissecting
the corpse of an infected dog, since the baron's gendarmes had
returned at sunset with nothing but a sighting of a wandering ventigeau and a few mild cases of frostbite.

I know there is not much left for me to do but wait. Wait for
Baker, wait for the train, wait for the dog. I can study *Pseudomycota* as best I can and keep the household healthy in the meantime, but I am having trouble doing even that. The clouds over the
mountains have only thickened, and my every sense is muffled,
heavy. I cannot hear myself think, and even with something as
simple as scraping the baron's tubes, it is somehow more difficult
to direct two hands than a thousand.

"Hurry up down there," the baron says. "Dinner is no doubt
being served this very minute. If I don't get some food in me soon,
I'll shrivel up and die."

The world would be far better off if he did.

The thought, abrupt and unforgivable, takes me by surprise. I
pause, wondering if it's my headache or my isolation that is invit-
ing such bitterness. Perhaps it is guilt over my earlier cruelty, when

I reduced Baker to tears with the name of a dead woman I was not supposed to know.

"You can wait, pèren," Didier says. He is currently occupied with his preprandial drink, a bottle of thousand-year-old red with an unnerving congealment of opaque wax on its surface. "Here, have something to fill your stomach."

"What the hell dreck is this?"

Didier lifts the bottle and attempts to read the antiquated script on what remains of its label. "Sauvig," he says, too confidently. "Cashade Hees Venery."

I can't be bothered to correct his misreading. Usually only historians can parse through the nuances of dead Angalis.

"It'll do," the baron says. "Make me some."

Didier is not as skilled as the house's sommelier, but he dutifully pours the ancient wine, agitating the glass to disperse the crystalline film on its surface. His hands move swiftly in the firelight, the tips of his knuckles slightly swollen, ringed with subdued red. From this angle I cannot tell if they are burned, or marked from their encounter with Émile's cheekbone, but they do not seem to bother him.

"Ah, it's a thick one, isn't it?" the baron sighs.

I return my attention to an encrusted lymph capsule. The state of Didier's hands is a question this brain should ponder when it can share the cognitive effort. When Baker and I have isolated the mine, when the lead dog has been retrieved and vivisected, and when I can think clearly again. *P. emilia* is not a problem one human brain should tackle alone.

"Maybe you'd like some, doctor," the baron says. "It'll steady your shaking little fingers."

I cannot wait to be surrounded by my own bodies, to be myself again. Things will stop unraveling when I am myself again.

"Are you listening?"

The dog, the mine, Didier's hands—all these disparate symptoms will coalesce into a single condition, easily diagnosed when viewed from many angles at once.

"Doctor!"

I lift my head, mind catching up with my ears. "Monsieur?"

"I heard a little something about you today." He shifts, loosening my hold on the congested metallic sponge that passes for his spleen. "The constable tells me you've been exchanging a few 'jours and 'dieus with that old priest of ours."

"Really?" Didier wears an almost disappointed frown. "You'd best stay away from him. The man is dangerous. He's a manipulator."

"He's my patient, like you or any other," I reply.

"It'd be better to let him die," the baron says. "A pair of blasted knees wasn't good enough for him. Should've beheaded the poisonous little liar decades ago."

"He does not seem so bad to me," I can't help but mutter.

Didier takes a gulp of wine and chews on it for a second. "He doesn't. That's his poison."

"Indeed—" The baron pauses to heave a series of violent coughs. His filters buzz for a moment, his dials tremble, and he spits something into his handkerchief before tossing it to the floor. It falls with a commanding wet thud, but no servant appears to pick it up.

"Don't you dare reach for that, Didier," the baron barks. "Don't debase yourself. Émile! Where's Émile? Where's *anyone*?"

Didier's eyes snap to me. We both know he's not going to tell his father about the château's unfound canine. "Everyone we can spare is at the windows, watching the night," he says. "A ventigeau has been spotted in the garden."

"In the garden?" the baron snorts. "The *garden*! This time of year. Hah." He swallows the last of his glass in one gulp. "Thought I heard gunshots, but the sun is much too high for that. Much too high."

"It was small," Didier says. "Just an early one."

"What the hell is wrong with this winter?" The old man shakes his head. "It's too fucking cold already. Too cold. Someone put more logs on the fire."

Didier sets down his glass. He makes his way to the hearth and kneels before it, rattling the ornate screen.

"I didn't mean *you*," the baron says, but his son does not appear to listen. "Hell, you should be out there with the others. Especially if there's a ventigeau about. You're a better shot than any of those bastards." When Didier does not reply, the baron turns back to me. "Well, he used to be. Now I reckon the maids have probably surpassed him. Such a shame."

I do not answer. It seems pleasanter to direct my attention toward his crusted tubing.

"Used to take him back in the hills with the rifle in summer," the baron continues, undeterred by my silence. "Have him try at cans and bottles. He was better than me at that age. First hunt of the season and he takes down a buck, but when—" Here, he releases a phlegmy cackle. "—when we get to the carcass and he sees what he's done, he turns downright green. I think he's going to faint. I tell him that it's only blood, to pull himself together. I try to smack some sense into him, but he just falls to his knees and vomits—all over the buck." The baron's laugh devolves into a wet cough. "Took it home and cleaned it off, but he refused to eat it. I told him to have some pride, that if he didn't eat his own kill he'd never eat again. The boy starved himself for three days, but eventually his hunger overtook his misgivings. It always does."

Didier only stares into the fire, transfixed.

"That's what's wrong with him, doctor. He's always hungry but refuses to eat what's given to him." The baron leans over the bed, rapping his knuckles against my already pounding head. "You done down there yet?"

I pull myself to my knees, cradling three phials of blood and a beaker full of dried fluid. My samples look as expected: clouded, coagulated, and chronically mistreated. "I am."

"And?"

"You must stop drinking the way you do. In addition—"

"Stop drinking." The fattier parts of the baron tremble as he laughs. He is one of the rare men I've known to at once boast several chins and skeletal cheeks, to maintain a ladder of protruding ribs and a rounded paunch. "What shit advice. Stop drinking. A man needs his fluids—I thought you were a doctor."

I place my tools back into my bag, releasing a heavy sigh. "This is what you hired me for."

"I hired you to take care of me, not command me, you precious twit. Now, help me out of this bed. Didier. *Didier!*"

The man squats by the fire for a few moments longer, eyes locked on the flames. Another bark from his father and he slowly unfurls. "I'll . . . fetch someone to carry you down to the table," he says, and floats out the door.

"Feckless bastard," his father spits after him. "Used to be so full of vigor, doctor. Energy, passion. You know, that kind of shit. Now he never lasts three courses at dinner. Always gets spooked by the time the meat comes."

I say nothing. I happen to know that the last of Didier's passion blew away on a summer hillside nearly two decades ago. Or at least that's how Priest tells it, but he is, allegedly, a poisonous little liar.

I want to sleep.

I lie supine in the quiet of my chambers. After checking and checking again, I've assured myself that *Pseudomycota* is safely contained in its jar. The infected dog is far from the château, and the northern mine even farther. There is no reason why I should not take this opportunity to rest.

The blankets are bunched up under my chin, and one bare foot hangs off the side of the bed, as this body prefers to sleep. The body is as comfortable as it can possibly be, but an incessant, violent anxiety twists in its gut, jolting me awake as soon as I drift off. Every few minutes, my eyes snap open, looking for any sign of Inultus beyond the cobwebby ceiling. My vocal folds chirp and moan, trying to send a message to my ears back home, and I am enveloped in painful tingling, like a paresthetic limb. I can see nothing and hear less. I can only break the deafening silence in my mind with a solitary, quiet whisper.

"Please do not let it happen again," I say, though I am not sure to whom I am speaking. "Leave me be. Do not let it happen again."

But it happens again.

I see a quivering dark body, alone. It is still in the sexless state of prepubescence, and when it opens its mouth to cry, I spy a dark gap between its front teeth. I reach out several hands to comfort it, and assure it that although there might be some pain, it will not last long. The intensity varies from person to person, I explain, and there is a chance there will be no pain at all.

This body is healthy, and when I lay it down on the examination table, smooth and naked, I cannot be more pleased. Ten toes, ten fingers, sight in both eyes, no major impairments, a quick, adaptive brain, and as far as I can perceive, only a few reversible neurological defects. It is truly a wonderful thing.

It attempts to speak when it sees the size of the needle, but it is paralyzed now, numbed with a potent concoction. I grip a bit of skin on its stomach, the only fat it has—adipose tissue, I explain, as if it will not know soon enough, is a prime medium for me. Soft, welcoming, high in energy, it provides the ideal starting point for my journey to the brain. As I slide the needle in, the body releases a soft sob. It bites its lip, a sphere of blood welling where tooth meets skin. I allow it to express its discomfort, though I know I will be feeling the bite tomorrow.

It begins to cry, so loudly even my ears on the outskirts of Satgarden can hear it. I cannot predict if this child will take or not. I have seen bad nights end with a new pair of pristine eyes, and good nights end in cremation. I have seen survivals writhe well into late morning, and I have seen deaths so swift and painless that when I open them up in my laboratory, it is as if they died of nothing at all.

I watch the body from several angles, watch the thrashing of its brown limbs, the wails of its bobbing throat. It cries out for its mother, which is common. It cries out for its aunt, which is far less common. After a minute, or a week, the body quiets down, dark fingers twitching into stillness. An intense sigh of disappointment heaves through several of my lungs. I note the time of death, though I cannot read the clock on the wall, and order the corpse down the chute.

I glance away, and when I look back it is a different body on the table. This time a gray-skinned child with a growth on its lower spine, long and flexible like a degenerate limb. As the operating table is tilted toward the furnace shaft, the body lifts its dark eyes to mine. Suddenly, I know I have made a mistake. This one is still alive, but I cannot reach it in time, I cannot stop its fall. I try to close my ears to the sounds of it tumbling down the flaming chute, but I have too many ears to close.

Something shifts again, and I see the bioluminescent sails of a Misulah schooner, I see a white dog, I see a dozen illustrations of *P. emilia,* deformed, horrible sketches from my least talented hands. Then, the many angles of my sight narrow and coalesce into a clear picture of a badly bitten lip.

When this body wakes, it is standing. Heart frantic in my ears, bare feet freezing, I am leaning against the south wall, one hand on the stone as if I have been reaching out for myself while I slept. When I regain control, I push my fingertips against the mortar, stretching cell by cell toward Inultus. For a moment, far beyond the ceiling of my small chamber, I can make out a dozen of my own faces, I can smell the musty pages of ancient monographs and journals, hear the ring of a wrench as an engineer smashes an old motor back into rumbling functionality.

I hug myself, pretending these arms are another body's, and close my eyes. Down south the winter is passing pleasantly over-head, and I can make out the barest outlines of a building, ringed in pillars and bloodred ferns swaying in the night breeze—my heart, my marble heart, the Institute. From this angle, from this distance, I do not know if the Inultus I construct is a mirage, or if I can really see the streetcars and palaces, the ruby cobblestones and steaming bathhouses.

Blurry pictures whip through my head, of bubbling mud-rivers, of children jumping among the half-sunken wrecks, squeezing into passages and crevices larger treasure-hunters cannot, extending their hands to receive compensation for their discoveries, or in some cases, extending bloodied limbs so I can cauterize or reat-tach them. A flood of emotion stills me, and I realize that I miss Satgarden, even the dismemberments, even the misfired shots of defensive machinery, even the ancient infections that leap from the tips of rusted metal into the broken skin of salvagers. I miss everything.

A violent shiver dislodges me from my memories. The hearth has burned to ashes, and my toes have begun to pale. I crawl back to my bed and wrap myself in my deerskin and wool blankets, and though I can feel my warmth returning, the act seems futile, like bandaging a frostbitten finger already on the verge of detachment.

XI

As far as I have learned from the scraps of history left to us, no human being has ever been able to kill a ventigeau. Hundreds of Verdiran hunters have gone into the roaring storms with rifles and noble aspirations, but they have never brought back even a fraction of one, dead or alive—no hooves or teeth, no hides or chips of antlers. Instead they leave their segmented corpses strewn across hillsides, sometimes arranged in a half-intelligent pattern and perfectly preserved as if to serve as a warning.

"See, médsaine," Priest had told me, shortly before my first winter in the château, "ventigeaux nay eat people, only *hunt* people."

With antlers sharp as knives and breath as terrible as the iciest storms, the creatures can slice through flesh as easily as air. Those unlucky enough to have witnessed such a spectacle claim that the ventigeaux, after dismembering their prey, will dig through the remnants of the corpse. With thin hooves and long white muzzles, they scatter and rearrange the bloodstained smears of viscera, then do so again, and again, as if searching for something. Whatever it is, they do not find it. No one has ever seen a ventigeau devour a human, but as soon as they are finished with one, they are more than keen to move on to the next.

Little Útolie knew everything there was to know about the creatures, which was, regrettably, not much. She would often take Didier to the château's abandoned periphery to watch them scream their storms, and though Priest could not approve, there was little he could do to stop them. By adolescence they were swifter and craftier than the old man had ever been, and easily fled to wherever their private fancies took them.

The ventigeau, according to her, was a spirit of longing. It had to be—it was the only explanation for its deathlessness, its aversion to eating its prey, its perpetual dissatisfaction.

The first ventigeau had been a man, once. He had been a romantic, an ancient Montish astronomer of the first generation to slip from the caves and look once again upon a sky that had tried to destroy his people. While his siblings observed the stars with due suspicion, he opened his mind to their beauty, to their vastness, and was captured in their thrall. Like many fools, he fell in love.

One night, in his endless pursuit of the stars, he climbed Verdira's highest and most hostile mountain. He had hoped to touch them, to find a winding route into the sky, to step from the broken earth and into the vacuum. But he found only the mountain's crest, and the sole path forward led back down. He could not accept this, so he stood atop the peak for days, stretching toward the stars in desperation. He reached so violently his joints cracked and dislocated, his muscles broke and repaired and broke again, elongating to absurd lengths. His face grew thin and terrifying; great long bones sprouted from his head, extending skyward. By the time he realized he had deformed beyond repair, he had already frozen to death.

That was why, the young raconteur would say, it was safe to watch the ventigeaux so long as one was under a roof. Walls could not stop the creatures, but they would go nowhere they could not see the cursed sky, where they could not stretch their antlers toward the starlight.

"Sole story a hers I nay concore," Priest admitted. He maintains the ventigeau is an embodiment of a curse placed on a dead man, damned to seek his own body forever, never finding it among the living.

I have developed my own theory, though I have no more proof of it than others have for their dead men and curses. I have only caught glimpses of the creature. I have never studied its reproduction or feeding, I have never collected a sample of its flesh or bone. But my brains are only human, and they often find falsehoods and uncertainties as useful as facts.

It would not surprise me to learn that the ventigeaux are like the starlings of Inultus: biological mistakes birthed by millennia of reckless experimentation, human or otherwise. It is impossible to settle the ventigeau safely into any taxonomic niche, even among ungulates. It is an orphan, like the Inultan starlings, like androids of myth, like *Pseudomycota,* like me. Perhaps that is why it devours as it does, endlessly searching for itself, abandoned by the hand that created it. I do think longing is the right word for it. Longing, perhaps, or emptiness.

"Activity is continuous. Severed sections retain motility. It appears undirected. No indication of phototaxis." I turn in my chair, and the squeaks of its claw feet send a jolt of pain from one ear to the other. "Have you taken note of all I've said?"

Émile nods, eyes locked on the gilded book as his hand rapidly copies my words. He's parted his hair today, curled bangs combed down over the discolored side of his face. His contusions are not severe, and most are localized to the inferior rim of his left eye. Didier's aim might be true, but he does not hit hard.

I return to my specimen of *Pseudomycota* and the twitching slivers of tissue I have shaved from it. Mutilated, stained, pinned between glass plates and illuminated with a buzzing lamp—I almost feel a pinch of sympathy for the creature. My own cells are familiar with these particular tortures.

"Immersion in half a mil of Institute-issued disinfectant appears to damage tissue, but movement is conserved."

I pause, listening for the distant click of a typewriter. There is only Émile's pen, scratching away at the paper he's pilfered from Didier's study.

"I have yet to observe any regenerative or reproductive capacity, though considering the possibility of a definitive animal host . . ."

Far away, I catch an indistinct memory of a helpful passage. I close my eyes, trying to produce a clear image of my library. I know where the relevant book lies. I know the floor, the section, the shelf. All I must do is tread up the curving marble stairs, through a corridor of mist-lit glass, past a collection of ancient journals . . . when I find the tome tucked safely on its shelf, I open it, urging the pages to appear. For a second I dare to hope that I am actually seeing through my own eyes, actually standing in the safety of my own halls.

But I am not. The only picture I can conjure is torn and faded with age. A terrible coldness stirs in my gut, but I read on, pressing this body to remember words its eyes have never seen.

I know there are five illustrations on the page, each an exaggerated diagram of the Misulah moon-ague at a particular stage of its life, shapes so disparate that at first it is difficult to believe they belong to the same organism. It is a process that takes place in the safety of a mosquite vector, under favorable conditions. When the cell receives the signal, it will elongate, its nuclei will migrate to its extremities, and it will grow a dozen or so thin legs. Then it will pull itself apart, limbs carried along currents of blood like the seeds of a dandelion, ready to begin the cycle again.

I sigh. "Well, I can't know anything about what *Pseudomycota* does inside a canine host until the constable and his men return. And only if they don't come back empty-handed again."

I can't help but think that if those soldiers' bodies were mine, a synchronous organism of eyes and ears and rifles, they would've already recovered the dog and quarantined every straggling cell of *Pseudomycota*. But as they are now, they're scattered, isolated beings, driven mostly by fear of losing their only biological vessels. "That is the problem with autonomous bodies," I mutter. "They all think they're the only one."

A sharp, accusatory exhalation from Émile snaps my thoughts

back to my chambers. I have a retort for him on my tongue, but when my eyes meet his, I find he is only asking me a question.

"What? No, don't write that down." I push away from my desk. "I don't care for trite commentary. Only write what is necessary." I remove my gloves and massage my forehead, leaning over Émile's shoulder to ensure he has composed everything to the Institute's satisfaction.

Notation of the Observable Characteristics of Isolated Specimen of Pseudomycota.

Émile's flourished handwriting is quick, confident—save for the loops in *Pseudomycota,* which I slowed to spell out for him. I omitted its second name, of course. He does not need to learn I have rewarded him for saving this body by attaching his name to a parasite.

Reacts favorably to a nutrient bath of wheatrock, though no notici *noticeable growth to date. Specimen is 5 cems, 4 mims long. Survives at subfreezing temps equally well as at Institute standard.*

"Strike that through," I tell him. "Ambient temperature is much lower than standard, isn't it? It's freezing in here."

He flicks the pen. He does not seem particularly cold, but I've heard the Montish never do.

Exposure to animal tissue elicits no response. Porcine and ovine tissue: no response. Canine oral tissue: no response *mild aversion, otherwise no response. Exposure to 0.5 mil of unseparated human blood, courtesy of the baron: no response. Intensified light: no response.*

"There's no motivating this creature," I mutter. "It favors wheatrock, perhaps, but we knew that already, considering where we found it. There's no explanation for why it would pursue me in the mine." I bite my lip, frowning at the unforthcoming little monster. "Émile, when the train comes . . ."

He raises a bruised eye to me. There is something odd in his stare, but I don't have the mental acuity to interpret it. Not while my single brain is thumping against my skull with every heartbeat.

"Are you sure you don't want a liniment?" I ask him. "I really should inspect your eye properly."

He shakes his head. He has never been fond of being palpated or smeared with salve. For years he has made a habit of disappearing at the mere mention of an examination.

"Very well. If that is what you prefer." I slip toward my shelf of painkillers, reaching for an opaque bottle. "I take it you've been to the kennels today."

He nods.

"And are the other dogs behaving normally?"

Another nod.

"Of course," I mutter, before I can stop myself. "I suppose I shall know if they're sick when they mysteriously escape the château."

He releases a quiet sigh, startlingly close to a sound of defiance.

"No, Émile. I won't stand cheek from you. Not when that animal could be halfway to the next town south, biting everyone she meets."

He raises his free hand, but I stop him before he can fabricate some excuse.

"Spare me. I know you better than you'd think." I agitate a tube of viscous analgesic and squeeze a dollop into my mouth. "You should thank me. There are far worse punishments than taking notes on my behalf. You're fortunate I need four hands down here, or you'd still be out in the cold with the rest of the baron's men, chasing that damn dog."

Utility is your only shield against the world, mackinita, offers a voice inside my head. It is not mine, but I do not know from where else it could've come. Perhaps an echo of a talkative patient, eager to dispense advice.

The houseboy shifts, ready for more unkind words I may hurl his way, but I think I have exhausted my supply. Suddenly, I am too tired to take my frustration out on him.

"I apologize," I sigh. "I did not mean to be short with you. You did such a foolish thing, but you thought it right at the time." The bitter warmth of the painkiller has started moving from my tongue to the tight hinge of my jaw. "I've just been so fatigued lately. I've come down with a queer insomnia, and that does my memory no favors. Believe me, I wish I did not need you to record my observations for me."

He asserts he is quite willing to help. He has told me before, in no words, that assisting me is not the worst of his household chores. That honor is saved for tallying the château's ledgers, when he is locked in Didier's office for days at a time, checking and rechecking the sums and purchases and losses of the entire mining season.

"Émile . . ." I hesitate, looking him over, studying his solemn frown, his discolored cheek. I try to remember the last time I examined him thoroughly, and realize it had been years ago, when he had come to me to request a dangerous and unnecessary procedure. "Has Didier struck you before?"

He lowers his eyes, hugging his arms to him. The shake of his head is slow, but deliberate.

I believe him. I have never observed any such behavior before, nor any marks on Hélène or the twins. "Let's hope it is an aberrance. Perhaps this winter is breaking him. It's almost broken me already."

I clench and unclench my teeth, shivering with sudden cold. Though my headache is gradually subsiding, it feels as if my brain is being stretched, hyperextended, pulled in two directions. I struggle to my feet. A draft descends, without a source and without mercy.

"I'm going to prepare a bath," I say. "I want you to stay here. Keep an eye on *Pseudomycota*. Submerge the severed pieces in caustic solution and then store them with the living specimen. Write down anything you see, even if you don't think it's noteworthy. When you're done with that, I want you to clean everything in this room. Every instrument must be disinfected, all surfaces wiped, and everything with upholstery washed thoroughly."

The way he tilts his head reminds me of the dogs.

"Yes, it will take a while. If you get tired or bored, you may sleep, or find a book on my shelf that interests you. If Didier comes around looking for you, I'll tell him you're occupied. He wouldn't want to interrupt the work that is keeping his household alive."

Émile nods.

I linger at the door, all shivers and gooseflesh. "You are welcome to come down here, if ever you feel the need to escape the
ledgers. The other physicians should arrive in a few days, if the
train is swift. Before then there will be plenty of work for you
to do."

His frown relents, and he gives me a purposeful, grateful blink.

"It's not for you," I reply. "I'm merely keeping you away from
Didier's fists until the train comes." I give him a smile, though I
do not mean a cem of it. "If you're going to be my second pair of
eyes, I'd rather not have them swollen shut."

"See, doctor? It's moved. It's gone from here, to here." Hélène
points out the path of her ostensible boil, tugging open her silk
robe. "It's just beside my breast, right here."

We sit in what used to be the west tower of the château.
Though many of its floors have been shaved off by some disaster
or another, the suites are tall and spacious, with marble hearths
stretching to the ceilings and spiral staircases twisting between
mezzanines. Hélène has claimed it as her chambers, a comfortable, private place for her to force me to massage every cem of her
perfectly healthy skin.

"I don't see it," I say.

"Here, look, the heat brings it to the surface." Robe bunched at
her waist, she angles her bare skin toward the hearth. A fire as tall
as any of my bodies dances violently behind an intricate grating,
decorated with the metal leaves of an extinct vine.

"Please be mindful not to burn yourself," I say. In truth, the
winter's chill has seeped so thoroughly into me, a burn or two
sounds almost pleasant.

Her shoulder nearly touches the hot iron, but she does not seem
to notice. "Can you feel it now?"

The only protrusions on her torso are the bumps of normal
collarbones, two swollen breasts, and one surprisingly large bulge
where a fetus, well past Hélène's usual due date, still grows. Soon

enough, a human organism quite short of completion will pass from her as painfully and emotionlessly as a kidney stone. It will then go to the furnace, a mess of external organs and half-formed skull. There will be no ceremony, and no delay before Hélène sets herself to trying once again.

"Forgive me, madame. I can feel nothing."

"Then your fingers don't work, clearly!" she says, closing her silk robe. "I had *thought* you were worried about some sickness spreading through the house, but evidently my health is not a concern. I'm sorry for wasting your time."

If she was so sorry, she might try to grow a real boil for once.

The thought emerges unbidden, unfamiliar, but startlingly clear. I blink, trying to assess which of my tongues might've made the quip, but for the moment, I have only one.

"You are not wasting my time," I say weakly. "I only . . . I would venture that your pregnancy is your most significant condition."

"Oh, no." She nearly laughs. "Really, it's fine, doctor. You haven't had the displeasure of seeing the process, but they all come out quite quickly. Maybe this one will be interesting enough for you to bottle up and send to your friends in Inultus."

"Please don't speak like that, madame—"

Suddenly, unprovoked, the fire dies. It swells briefly, casting the room in a sickly orange glow, then shrinks to a pale ember. A freezing draft curls down from the flue, the candles flicker, and we are engulfed in darkness. Only a weak beam of torchlight trickles in from the hall, widening as the door to Hélène's chambers creaks open.

My heart drops into my stomach. Jerking unsteadily into the room, filaments frayed in the dim light, is a monstrous tangle of *Pseudomycota*. It is not my specimen, not the severed, pathetic thing I have tucked away on my shelf—it is far too large for that. I clench my teeth, legs tensing. I don't know if I should run, hurl myself at the creature, or accept that I have been defeated, that the dog has already spread the disease, that Baker's hurried efforts were for naught, that the entire colony has already detached from the cavern wall and followed me south.

"Oh, it's you two," Hélène sighs. "I should've known you'd figure out a way to sabotage my fire."

The torchlight shifts to reveal two pale faces, and the colony of *Pseudomycota* contorts into the twins, attached, as usual, by the head. They linger in the doorway for a moment, and I fall back into my chair, unclenching every muscle from my neck down.

"Sylvie!" Hélène shouts toward the adjacent suite. "Get in here! We need more light! And you, girls, come here and let me untangle you."

The maid appears and restokes the fire while the twins seat themselves in front of their mother. "You can call us by our names, you know," one says.

"We *do* have them."

"What's the point," Hélène mutters. She grabs a tortoiseshell comb and rakes through fistfuls of her daughters' hair. "Now, what foul mischief led to this?"

"We weren't doing anything bad." They flinch. "Honest. We were just running down the hall—"

"Looking for places to put our talismans."

"Talis*men*."

"And we crashed into Émile and got tangled."

"He knocked us over."

"Accidentally."

"Of course it was Émile." Hélène clicks her tongue. "That little wretch has always been impertinent with you. We should've shipped him off to the city ages ago, when we had the chance."

"We like him," the twins say. "He's nice to us."

"He's *nice* because he has to be," their mother replies. "Leave that boy to his own devices and he'd slit all our throats in our sleep."

I slouch on my stool. My heart is only now slowing, and my forehead is damp with cold sweat. As I watch the girls fidget in the growing firelight, I can't help but reprimand myself for allowing my fear to mislead me. It is not like me, not at all.

"There, that should do it," Hélène says. "Now, girls, I expect you not to get tangled again."

It's this brain. It's competent, that's true, but it is too used to operating in parallel with hundreds of others. Alone, it can be easily deceived. It can believe that a mobile colony of parasitic organisms could waltz through the château's halls unnoticed.

I take a deep breath, calming myself. A part of me knows that no matter what befalls this body, I will survive. Another part insists this is not true. My headache flares, my sight blurs briefly, and my mind struggles with itself, unsure which part of me it belongs to.

"And no more of these deathly pranks." Hélène's voice brings my attention back to the room. "No more wailing down corridors, and absolutely no more pigs' blood on the walls, do you understand?"

"They're not *deathly*," one girl says.

"And they're not pranks," says the other.

"They are, and everyone finds them ever so distasteful. Frightening, even."

"The doctor doesn't." They turn to me, a single, knowing smile spreading between them. "You're not afraid of anything."

"You've never been."

I blink. "Pardon?"

They grin at me, eager, earnest. "Maybe it's because you're dead already."

"Or not human."

"*Girls!*" their mother hisses, swiping at them with her comb.

A nervous chuckle rises in my throat. I tap my own hand, reassuring them, and myself, of my solidity. "See? Still living. And as human as the cells that comprise me. Just like you."

"Forgive them, doctor," Hélène says. "They're rude little things, but it's only because they haven't been socialized properly. They're lonely, locked up in this old manor with no other children."

"We're not lonely," the twins say.

"Of course you are," Hélène replies. "No playmates, no governess. Only servants and gunmen for company. It's no environment for a growing child. They're so dreadfully cold all the time, and they barely see the sun. They have no friends—"

"We have friends."

"Spiders and imaginary specters and two-headed mice do not

count as friends. Doctor, would it not be healthier for them to live somewhere warm? To leave Verdira?"

"I suppose so," I sigh. "Where did you have in mind, madame?"

"Must I have a place in mind? Inultus, the plains, the floodlands—send us out to sea or into the fume wastes, I don't care. As long as we're not here."

"We can't leave," the girls say, clawing at their mother. "Papa would be so alone."

"Your papa will get along fine without us. We'll leave him some props and stuff our dresses with straw, and he won't even know we're gone."

"Surely he deserves more credit," I say, massaging my temples. "He would miss all of you terribly."

"Oh, he may," Hélène laughs. "But he'll find another wife, he'll find more children. Everyone's expendable, doctor. When miners die, the château just ships in more from the plains. When our physician kills himself, we simply buy another one." There is no warmth in her smile. "That is one skill in which my husband excels. No matter what he loses, he'll always secure a replacement."

XII

THE SKY IS CLEAR, except for a few trailing clouds in the south, striated the grays and yellows of a cadaver. A halo of stars winks around the narrow, gravelly collection of the moon's extant pieces, and the sun passes between steeples of white mountains, painting the range with the pale glow of Verdiran dawn-dusk. Shadows of peaks move with it, pivoting across the snowfield like swollen hands on an unmarked clock. It is a rare, clement day, and I have utterly wasted all three hours of it.

It was a malformed idea to drag myself to the empty train station. I have shivered here with a small pistol at my side, a bag of tools and specimen phials, and a good viewpoint, but there is no sign of *Pseudomycota* or its canine host. Worse yet, there is no sign of myself.

Even in this clear weather, I cannot see anything beyond the hunched mountains. My only ears strain to conjure the distant scream of an engine's whistle, and my only heart is sore from the effort of leaping and falling as the flurries in the south mimic the clouds of a smokestack. Every time I close my eyes, hoping to see from a different pair, I open them again in disappointment.

It's all I deserve for having the audacity to expect the train to Verdira to arrive on time. Perhaps, like the old legends, I have stretched for a star I could not reach, I have carried the torch of unwarranted optimism too openly. Instead of tempting the shadows of the caverns, I tempt evening to fall, fast and hard and in bursts of icy wind.

If I stay out here much longer, I run the risk of becoming a cautionary tale myself. There is no Montish fable from which the hero emerges unscathed, untouched by humiliation, rape, mutilation, or death. Those Verdirans who are old enough to remember the times before the miners' revolt recall stories as unnavigable as the caves in which they were first told. Here and there some sort of *empratesse* can still be excavated from them, but most ancient narratives seemed to tunnel right under southerners' feet, obscured and uncatchable. The jokes burrowed even deeper.

"Ay the hymns're worst of all," Priest used to say. "Absolute piss. Nay spirit left on earth who can chant one correct. Didier 'bout could, when he were petit, though he nay comprehend what it all meant. Nay knew the right emotion. Nay do I, verily." Here, Priest would always sigh, breath tinged with regret. "Always been said Montish nay cry, médsaine. Even as babes—when I were a young wet nurse I fed dozens, ay all were silent as little graves, even when they come out. But you hear a chorus a midwives chant out a birth you nearly die from the feeling. *Strong.* Strongest heartshaking I ever felt. Could never deliver like the old wives could. S'a song I nay learned to sing true, even if my ear's trained."

I wish I could've witnessed such a birth, or listened to the slow hymns echoing through the caverns in deep, unblemished Franco. I would've liked to study Montish physiology, to inhabit one of their bodies and explore the changes their sunless subsistence on wheatrock and cave grass had left on their cells. I would've liked to unravel the miracles of their survival, to marvel, for the thousandth time this century, at the biological resilience of the human species. But I came too late. Thousands of years of subterranean adaptations and mutations could not save the Montish from an enfilade of gunfire.

"'Ey!"

The call pulls my eyes away from the vast snowfield. Beyond the ruins of the station, a collection of human shapes gathers against the pink sky. As they march toward me, I recognize the man at their head. His face nearly hurts to look at, even under a mask and goggles.

"Constable," I say, resting my gaze at his shoulders.

"'Jour, doc. What're you doing out here?"

When he speaks, it is through one mouth and half a nose, the other half of which had been lost a few years ago in a particularly brutal snowstorm. What remains of it only remains because he had stumbled to me in time for a partial surgical reattachment.

I can't help but think he'd be much prettier without the god-awful thing.

"You're not trying to leave, are you?"

I can feel his gaze on me, crawling like probing, painful fingers. The man may have the world's shakiest aim, but he doesn't need to resort to bullets when his eyes can do the job nearly as well. "No."

"Well, damn." His stare cools a little. "I almost shot you, what with your fur coat there. Thought you might've been the rabid beast that little dogfucker let outta the kennels."

I look at my feet. The snow is suddenly blinding, and a high ring oscillates at the threshold of my hearing. It is not the whistle of an oncoming train. "I do not think Émile fucks the dogs," I hear my mouth say.

The constable laughs. "Charming, aren't you? That makes two of us. What was your name again?"

"Service before self," I reply instinctively.

"Well, Service, it'd be a shame if you got snatched by a ventigeau out here, waiting for a train that's not coming."

"The train is coming. Perhaps not today. It's likely been delayed. Tomorrow, surely."

"It's not coming. Snow's too deep and it's only getting deeper. If it even left the city, it'd've been buried fifty miles south of here." He steps toward me, rifle slipping from his shoulder and into his hands. He gently nudges me away from the station with the end of its barrel. "You're not from here. You don't know the winter like we do. 'Bout this time of year stuck passengers have only just begun to eat each other. It'll be months before they start up the engines again, and then *we'll* be the ones who have to count the survivors."

"I hate that," grumbles one of the men behind him.

"It'll come tomorrow," I say. "And I have to be here to meet it."

"No, you don't," the constable says. "Won't come until spring. And baron'd kill me if I let anything happen to his devoted sitter in the meantime. Now, back to town you go."

Despite my high likelihood of dodging the constable's bullet, it will do no good to disobey him. My bodies are small, this one especially, and it will easily succumb to the force of stronger ones. I prefer to be led back to the château rather than dragged.

"It's coming tomorrow," I mutter. "It has to."

"Don't fret, doc," the constable says. "Spring'll be here before you know it. Hell, it'll be here well before we catch that fucking dog." A few gendarmes shake their heads. "You haven't seen it, have you?"

"No." My boots crunch through the dusk-pink snow, and the pain in my head intensifies.

"Hopeful winter's killed it already." He sighs. "Swear to the dead gods, if the baron'd let me train those chennies, they'd have brought back their traitor by now. Dogs should be hunters and guarders. They've got the teeth, don't see why they can't use them."

"They weren't bred for it," I mutter.

This elicits an ugly laugh. "Bensûr," he agrees. "It'll be a long road to get them good and tough, like chennies used to be. But they're animals. You prod any animal long enough, eventually it'll bite."

I am wrapped in every blanket in my chambers, shivering and exhausted. But I don't go to bed, I don't dare lie down. This body will only take it as an excuse to sleep. And I do not want to dream again.

Pseudomycota is my only company. The dead specimen lies untroubled, and the living squirms lazily in its bath of wheatrock nutriment, like a château mouser stretching and contracting in a rare patch of sun. It doesn't seem to care that it has been captured and scraped and plated and prodded. It has developed no fear of me or my glinting tools.

Something about it irks me. There's a secret to its invincibility, a reason why it is so calm, so unforthcoming, so content without a host.

"You're not a natural animal, are you?" I ask it. It has no answers for me, of course, so I pick up my notebook.

Easy to grip with Inultan brass design forceps model 884 084, Émile's curled handwriting reminds me. *Standard lancet produces a clean cut. No aversive response. No observable reaction to fungicidal tinctures or oils.*

"Nothing seems to move you," I mutter, turning the page. "So why would you . . ."

Intermediate and/or definitive animal host: unobserved.

"And that dog is long gone by now. The little fool let her go." I lift my eyes to *Pseudomycota.* "If I didn't know him so well, I'd suspect you made him do it."

It wriggles against the glass.

"The mechanisms of self-preservation and propagation can be remarkably complex," I tell it. "Do you know why they call it the moon-ague in Misulah?"

I take its silence for a no.

"When a mosquite bites, it deposits a colony of parasitic sporozoites. The skin swells, and the host begins to itch and burn. Water does not relieve the rash, nor does salve. The only thing that does is the night air. So the host will sit outside for hours at a time, moon-bathing, skin exposed, attracting swarms of insectile vectors. That gives mosquites the opportunity to bite again, and gives the parasite the greatest chance to return to its vector, where it restarts its life cycle."

The organism stills for a moment.

"So, then, what strange things do you command a host to do?"

Careful. A peal of laughter echoes in the back of my head. It's not my own. *You might find out that it tells its hosts to dream.*

Pseudomycota begins to writhe again, and I cannot stop watching the rhythmic slithering of a lone limb grasping for its body, its multitude of bodies. A bead of sweat makes its way down my cheek. For every thought I have directed south, for every shout and urgent summons, *Pseudomycota* may have sent a signal I cannot read, coaxing itself from the wall of the mine. Every mile of track I have traversed northward may be a mile traversed southward by my competitor.

Method of communication is not established, my notebook reassures me. *There are no telling chemical signals isolated from nutrient broths or plates.*

"Not that I would know with what little tests I can do now."

It does not necessarily communicate at all. Don't see yourself in it.

"Don't what?" I hiss. My sight is blurred, and I cannot tell if the words before me are in Émile's handwriting or mine.

It's nothing like you.

I turn the page too quickly. A sharp pain stings my forefinger, and I see a small drop of blood glowing at its end, red against brown. The thick, almost metallic smell of my own cells meets my nose, mixed with the earthy scent of paper. I stare at my finger, considering sucking away the blood, but soon my eyes are elsewhere, moving from the paper to the parasite.

Nothing like me, my mind posits. Much more accomplished.

Without quite knowing what I am doing, I lift my finger to the edge of the paper. The corner soaks up my blood, and I watch the stain spread elegantly through thousands of miniscule pores. It is a mockery of a proper laboratory technique, a mere imitation of what I could—what I *should*—be performing with my equipment from Inultus, but a single, suspicious gut drives me now, not a unified consensus of rational brains.

Shakily, barely awake, I retrieve my brass tweezers. I rip the bloodied scrap from the notebook, carry it to the jar of *Pseudomycota,* lift the lid, and drop it inside. Saturated and heavy, it falls to the bottom of the container in a tiny splash of red. I wait for several seconds, but *P. emilia* does not react. The disembodied arm simply twists and turns, making its slow, random way around the jar.

"You are marching as if you have somewhere to go," I say. "But you do not know where, do you? You're nothing but a mindless little leech."

I know that my own cells, perhaps still surviving in that bloody paper, are readying to defend themselves. I can already feel the hair standing on the back of my neck as my smallest components raise their chemical shields and attempt to warn the nearest host of the approaching danger.

Perhaps only by chance, *Pseudomycota*'s wriggling tip comes into contact with the paper. It stiffens, and in a series of sudden jerks, it ceases its march. It stills for a moment, then rhythmically, deliberately, it begins to turn.

I know I should scramble to write down what I see, but my gaze is glued to the creature, curling, writhing, twitching. I don't know how long I stare at the jar—perhaps a minute, perhaps less, but my eyes don't dare stray from the spectacle until *P. emilia* fully unfurls. When the thin arm of the organism stretches open once more, I see that it has destroyed the paper, and the blood on it, completely.

XIII

As soon as it is safe, I flee the château. The gray morning light is nothing more than a suggestion behind the haze of fog and frost, but it still pierces my skull like a trepan. Under my chewed gloves my fingers are striped with lacerations, and between my ears crackles an unceasing electric arc of anxiety.

Of course, I repeated the experiment. I dangled an abundance of temptations before *Pseudomycota*: clean paper, saturated paper, a few drops of blood from my stinging finger. The bloodless paper elicited no response from the organism. The paperless blood did.

I spent hours hunched over my desk as night wore into morning. Tides of pain rose and fell in my head as I exhausted my phials of biological samples, transferring *Pseudomycota* from jar to jar, tempting it with every sort of material from every source I had. The results did not change. No response to animal tissue. No response to my fingernails, my hair, my eyelashes, nor to scrapings from my skin. Nothing about the exterior cells of this body induces that unprecedented, violent reaction in *P. emilia*. It is only interested in the deeper tissues, only in the places where I live.

Either there is something about me that triggers a reaction in *Pseudomycota,* or the damn thing knows how to hold a grudge.

Gunshots pop in the distance. The silhouettes of riflemen follow me as I trek across the château grounds, climb over the half-buried iron gates, and wade down the hill toward the stout chimneys of Baker's hut. Even before I raise a glove to rap at his door, he appears from the darkness, smoky air churning at his feet.

"You shouldn't be out here," he says. "Dangerous, this late in the year. Ay what with that chennie loose—"

"The train didn't come," I say, desperately.

"Bensûr it nay did." His breathing is labored, and though there are plenty of worse scents drifting off him, I can make out a distinct undercurrent of tobacco. "Why'd you think it would?"

Because a dead, exfoliated cell is longing for its body. "Baker, we need to get to the mine."

It's too late now, mackinita. Nothing's going to fix you. I shake my head, blinking the voice away. I know they are the words of someone I have tried to forget.

"Told you, doc," he says, "I'm working on it. I got a dangerous amount a fire boiling in my kitchen right now."

"I need to go to the mine. Now. I need to bury that fucking parasite."

Baker's frown is suspicious. He leans past me, looking to his left, then right, as if expecting something to crest over the knolls of snow encircling his cabin. "I told you I'd help you. I thought that'd be enough."

"I don't . . ."

"Come in," he growls, ushering me into the dark. "Sit on that bench there."

I obey, trying my best to acclimate to the fumes of tar, woodsmoke, and volatile compounds.

"Hands to yourself'n nay touch nothing making noise. Anything louder'n a whisper'll blow you to bits, as a general rule." He slides over to a rattling kettle, fist clenched at his heart. "Though, you'd know that already."

"Why would I know that?" From excavations to avalanches, I have more than once witnessed the wondrous spectacle of Baker's explosives at work. But as far as he is concerned, that was a different doctor entirely.

"Been pilfering all the right things," he tells me. "Nay the stuff that could bring down the mountain, but a bit of all the right components're gone. Nay much volume, though. Wouldn't a noticed if I wasn't down digging in the stores already. Nay happen to know anything 'bout that, do you?"

"I have no idea what you're talking about," I say.

"Oh?" he snorts, eyes narrowed. "Look, you were convincing, doc. You made me think it'd be better to starve without wheatrock than die like Cass did, crawled all through with that evil cave grass. I told you I would do it. I was making everything ready. But I can't help you if you're helping yourself already."

I freeze, biting my lip. "I don't know what you mean."

He must sense the earnestness in my voice. He pulls the kettle off the stove and looks at me, beard bristling in confusion. "Nay? You're the only one 'round who knows what we're onto. You're the only one interested in sealing off the mine."

"Yes," I say. "But I swear to you, I've been nowhere near your stores."

He raises a hand from his heart to his mouth, and releases a black, foul cough. "Then who was?"

A chill crawls up my neck, despite the steam and smoke. There is an odd feeling inside me, deep in the inaccessible gaps and folds of my brain. It is familiar, and entirely new. Like waking up somewhere I didn't fall asleep.

"I have no idea," I say, honestly. I cannot even be sure I am not the culprit. I try to remember when I last slept, and cannot—each night is a protracted, half-conscious blur. And I have certainly seen stranger acts committed under the influence of somnambulism. "But it wasn't me. There's a reason I came to you for help in the first place. I don't know enough about your trade to do it myself. I'm only a physician."

He frowns, hand hovering over his heart again. "Then who . . . no one sneaking 'round at night, certain. Musta been in the day sometime. Or . . ." He collapses onto a bench across from me and absentmindedly scratches his silver nipple through his shirt.

"Dunno, doc. It's been . . . coulda been taken weeks ago. Coulda nay been taken at all. Could just be me forgetting. Winter's coming strong this year."

"It is."

"I nay've been so good lately. Last few days, all this thinking 'bout Cass is making my heart hurt bad. Nay can think with this heart."

My hands move toward my bag, and find only air. My stomach drops, and I feel as if I have somehow misplaced an arm.

"I keep thinking 'bout her, now my heart . . . Old Doc told me she bled out. I always thought she just bled out. Nay can believe he'd lie to me. He'd never lie."

Something inside me wants to tell him I do, I lie like a fucking snake, I just do it politely. I hold myself back. "Baker, your heart is hurting because you're puffing on those damn cigarilles again."

"I'm in here all day breathing in all sortsa fumes, ay you're worried 'bout a few cigarilles?"

"There are texts, and studies, and monographs—"

"Ah, those ancient things. Any younger'n a thousand?" He rubs the back of his head and sighs a billow of black smoke. "Just gimme something for the pain, doc. That's all I need."

"I can help you, I have only to retrieve my bag," I say. "I apologize. I have forgotten my most important tools. There is so much to do already, with that dog, and the mine . . ." A wave of freezing pain floods my legs, and I nearly collapse against his table. "Shit."

"Whoa, doc," he grunts, righting me. "Nay bump that—shake what's in that pot too much ay it'll heat. Heat ay it'll blow off your upper half. Here, just sit, nay move."

"Baker . . ." I groan, as the dizzying ache passes.

"Wae, doc." He kneels beside me. "You all right?"

"I am." I manage to sit upright again. "Forgive me. I am just . . . unused to this. I have . . ."

He sits expectantly, but I'm not sure what to tell him. I cannot explain this discomfort, and I am no stranger to discomfort. I have been hurt before. I have endangered my hosts before. I have sent the wrong colors, the wrong sexes, to the wrong places, and

I have failed to read the ill intentions of others. I have had bodies ripped from me and destroyed, as painful as twisting off a finger or plucking out an eye, and I have recovered. I have learned to reabsorb the afflicted persons back into the whole when I can, and eliminate them when I cannot. At my lowest I have been several dozen, at my highest I have burgeoned to several thousand. But never have I been whittled down to one.

"I will . . ." I take a breath, recovering myself—or what small fraction of myself is left. "The Institute isn't coming."

"I know," Baker answers.

"We can't wait for them."

"I know."

"Baker . . . finish preparing as quickly as you can. I just want to . . . I want to get it done. I can't have any more of that thing crawling after me."

His brow furrows. "Gimme two days, doc. Third dawn, be at my shed, early as it's safe. I'll have a batch compact 'nough for just us two to handle."

"Good." I stand, again intuitively reaching for a bag that is not there. *Nothing's going to fix you.* "I'll be back shortly with something for your heart. And my head."

He ushers me to the door. "I know it's hard, doc. Winter is always hard, the first 'specially so. Just focus on taking care of us, ay we'll take care of you too." His beard parts in a sweet smile.

"Yes . . . maeci."

"I'll borrow some chennies. Friends of mine have ones that can rival the château's. We'll make it there ay back. Ay after that, you're the one dealing with the baron should he find out."

"Understood." I linger at his door, single mind still occupied with the image of *Pseudomycota,* twisting its body through blood and torn shreds of paper, through my skin, my eye. I'd much rather be killed by the baron. "Keep safe, Baker. Don't go outside unless absolutely necessary."

"Nay worry, doc. Nay gonna, with that chennie 'round. Way it's throwing shit to chaos it may be a lycanthrope." He shrugs off my exasperated look. "Swear some turn into humans every twist of the moon. Montish blokes, completely naked, running on all fours through the snow. Seen it myself. Thought I was nuts till the twins said they'd seen them, too."

"The twins say many things," I tell him. "Most of which are decidedly insane."

"Contrary," he replies, nearly shouting over the gusts as I open his door. "Those girls're the only sane ones in that whole god-damn house."

There is something about the heavy stench of burned flesh that reminds me of home. If I breathe in the scent, deeply and thoroughly, it is almost as if I am back in the aerostat laboratory.

"It's bad, but not as bad as it could be," I tell the weeping jade carver. She sits in the shadowy corner of the nave, water basin at her feet, surrounded by the hunched and blanketed forms of the other workers. "I've seen worse. Six months ago I watched a man fall into a vat of exhaust and come out without his skin." The anecdote fails to comfort her. "Do not fear, he grew it back. Granted, he also grew a few extra nails in unexpected places, but his new skin has served him well."

"Nay many have talent like that," Priest puts in, gripping the unharmed hand of his carver as I peel away the last shreds of her burned robe. Blisters have begun to form, globular and pink and weeping.

"What happened?" I ask, soaking a cloth in cool water. It stings like ice against my skin.

"She were working like every day," Priest says. "Flame musta licked her robe hem."

"I was sitting too close," she says. "I just wanted to get a little warmer, is all."

"Well, you'll be feeling quite warm for the next while," I say. "From your ankle to your rib cage, at least." She cries out as I pour another dipper of water over her burns. "You were lucky this happened during the day. Had it been dark, I wouldn't have been able to come."

"I coulda done a pet," Priest says. "Bind it'n animal fat, the way s'always been done. Nay the Montish got burned too often. Much better treating frostbite ay such."

"I need more water," I say.

"Wae." Priest waves an arm at the small crowd gathered around us. "All, quit staring like perverts. Use yourselves ay get what the médsaine needs." The gnarled carvers back off, skittering along the aisles with the strange, bouncing limp unique to hurried geriatrics. "I hope this nay too much. I know you've only got two hands ay the town ay château are each pulling at one."

We can't put you back together, mackinita, says that doleful voice in my head.

"It's quite all right," I sigh.

"It's so cold," the carver hisses as I dab at her side. "Water's freezing."

"I know. I'm sorry." There are still a few rogue threads of half-burned cloth to be pulled from her blisters, but she will clean up nicely. For once, I consider it fortunate we are in such a cold, desolate place. Had she been somewhere like Misulah or Satgarden her wound would already be teeming with insects.

Someone pours a pitcher of water back into the basin at our feet, and I douse her with a few more cupfuls. She lifts her head and releases a tortured whine.

Priest kneels before her. "Keep eyes on me," he says. "S'all right. Médsaine here'll heal you correct. I'll give a hymn—look back at me, supe." Having cared for so many for so long before my arrival, Priest knows how best to distract a patient from her own body. It's a skill that I haven't mastered, even with centuries of practice. Perhaps I'm not truly cut out for this kind of work.

"Keep talking, Priest," I mutter as I lay a strip of gauze across a burned leg. "Distract us with a tale. Helps the pain, or so Medrah used to tell me."

I start, not quite sure what I've just said. Priest glances in my direction, and suddenly I'm sweating like my clothes had been the ones to catch fire.

"Just . . . a patient," I tell him, though I'm not completely sure. "A mother who liked to tell stories."

"Bensûr." He nods. "Mothers're always telling. It were some-one's maman who told all 'em here, but nay mine. You like the old northern tales, médsaine?"

"Can't say I've heard them." I have heard each of Priest's stories a dozen times. Except for his most intriguing one, which I have only heard once, and only on the condition I would never repeat it.

"Course nay," he says. "You nay been here long to hear them. Here's an old one, 'bout the times the sky were white ay the stars were black. For when the children were small ay needed to learn where the world came from—back when there were Montish chil-dren."

I nod, wrapping a length of the carver's leg. The woman stares at Priest expectantly, and doesn't seem to notice the tightening bandages.

"Kids'd ask why the world is what it is," he starts. "Ay the par-ents'd always point to the sky. Say that long ago, before the ven-tigeaux cut through the snow ay the wind tore trees outta the ground, the sky were white, ay the world were mostly on fire. The sky were so bright it were hard to look at. There nay were a cloud in sight, just shining white with a yellow sun. Only way you'd tell it were night were the moon'd come out, smooth ay round like a marble, nay a crack in it. Ay the stars were black—well, they nay were stars, were they? They were the thousand black eyes a dogs. Ay their noses. Eyes to watch, noses to sniff out trouble, a few black claws to put the trouble down. The sky watched the world's fires burn, its white fur kept in all the heat so the animals'd stay warm. But after a few hundred years, when all the trees were dead ay the world was too damn hot, too choked up with smoke for its own good, the eyes began to fall. They hit the ground in great blasts—huge, round black eyes blew holes right through the mountains, giant claws ripped through slopes ay carved out the couloirs. Great noses smashed into peaks so hard the impacts turned them inside out. For a couple hundred years no one could go nowhere without getting squashed by some giant piece a dog. So while the sky were falling ay chennie noses were shattering across the land ay leaving black bits a themselves everywhere you could look, the people went into the caves. Well, the fires only got worse when the sky-dogs fell, ay the smoke ay dust nay settled for decades—nay ask how many, I can't even count that high. But when the ash finally cleared ay it were safe to go outside again, the world'd changed. The ground were freezing, covered in the dogs' downy white fur, ay the sky, shit, the sky were a mess. It'd shed all itself except for a few tufts a hair, twinkling way too far up to be any use. The round, winking eye a the moon'd shattered, ay the sun were nowhere to be found. They didn't find it for months, the poor bastards. Ay vulà, the first winter."

By the time he finishes, I have wrapped the poor jade carver as well as I can. She glances down at herself and a pained look crosses her face, but Priest seems to have helped her through the worst of it. He's helped me, too, filling my head with dogs' noses instead of the wriggling tentacles of a subterranean parasite.

"What an absurd tale," I can't help muttering. My hands still shake with the freezing sting of water, so I blow into them. "Dog gods in the sky."

"It mighta made sense a thousand years past," Priest says, moving aside as a few carvers step up to take their injured compatriot to bed.

"Sense couldn't have changed that much," I say. I fold what remains of my gauze and tuck it into my bag, but not before retrieving a dropper and dousing my gums.

"You right, médsaine?" Priest asks.

"Just a headache. Analgesic was wearing off." I decide to squeeze a few more drops under my tongue before returning it. "Priest, keep a good eye on that carver."

"Wae."

"Keep her robes loose and her skin clean. Change the bandages often. Make her drink plenty of water. I'll leave some laudanum. But if anything goes wrong—in the day—send for me." I stand, cracking my spine into working order again. This body is far too young for such soreness. "And don't tell the baron I was here."

"Nay. Figure he's already cross with you for planning to wreck his mine." Priest's smile reminds me of the rogues in Inultus, sitting

on rooftops and playing their lyres, singing hateful things at passersby below. "Nay look so frighted, médsaine. I said naught to
him. Baron'd have me shot if I go a hundred feet a the château.".

"Perhaps that is for the best," I mumble.

"He'd nay believe a word I say, anyway." He brushes off his
robe and bends to help me remove the water basin. "How's Émile?
Poor boy's been in here tangling my day with a whole slew a
prayers I nay can answer."

"Has he?" I snap my bag shut. "Reckless. He shouldn't leave
the château if he can help it. Not this late in the season."

"Oh, he nay mind the cold so much as we, médsaine. But he
looks roughed, a pet."

"The past few days have been hard for him. For all of us." I
sigh. "But I believe he will be all right."

Priest seats himself on a pew and stretches his legs until each
knee cracks as loud as a handclap. "Ay the rest a the house?"

"Hélène and the girls are managing. The baron is indestruc-
tible, as always. Didier's been . . ." I hesitate. "Well, I'm not so
concerned for his constitution. He's robust as ever. He's the only
one in the house without an invisible boil or an extra limb or some
such thing. Though—"

I shut my disobedient mouth, but there's no missing the orac-
ular glint in Priest's eye. "Wae, he seems fitter'n the rest. Saner,
too, mostly. But you should know there's a wound in him, médsaine. Nay has it opened up since '97, but I'm worried it may be
again."

I perk my ears, despite their incessant ringing. "What do you
mean?"

He stretches his scarred knees again, massaging the spots where
the bullets had torn across them. "Best sit. Here's a story n'even
your predecessor knew, ay it's far less pleasant'n the last one."

I stare at the mirror, prodding the dark rings around my eyes.
They are swollen, unnerving things, accumulated over too many
sleepless nights. They should not bother me. It is better I endure

exhaustion than find myself trapped in a nightmare, or waking someplace I'd rather not be.

It's like closing your eyes and opening them somewhere else, I had told Medrah, years ago. I don't remember what I'd been referring to, then.

Nose nearly touching the glass, I stare out at me and into me, past rings of freckled brown irises and into the darkness of my pupils, where my traitorous imagination projects a hair-thin appendage wriggling across my retina. When I blink, I can almost feel something tickle my optic nerve.

"Restrain your wandering brain," I say to my reflection. "The last thing either of us needs is to fantasize our way into a panic."

My image bites its lip. The pain feels natural, almost comforting. "Wait for Baker. That's all we need to do. We'll be fine. We'll be safe." I look to my desk, where my specimen stirs. Trapped in its sturdy jar, there is no way it can get to me.

Unless it's already crawled from the mine. Unless the dog has spread it.

"Please," I tell myself. "She's gone. The constable has been shooting at nothing but flurries for days now. That dog is far into the wilderness. And we don't know if the parasite survived inside her. Right now we should worry about the town. The mine. We should try to get warm. We should rest. Close these eyes for just a moment."

Reluctantly, I look to my bed, but the thought of lying down sickens me. If I am lucky, I will sleep for a few seconds, and my brain will only subject me to a nonsensical vision or two: a dream whose greatest horror is its illogic, whose monsters are only objects in a void—a rifle, a surgical prong, a torn wine label with *Cascade Hills Winery* printed in curving gray letters. Benign, but not worth risking. I do not need such meaningless things cluttering my mind. My skull is already throbbing with pressure, like an abscess in need of drainage.

"Two days," I tell myself, shivering. "All I need to do is survive for two more days."

And then the rest of winter. The train isn't coming. I have only one body left to me, and it's exhausted, it's broken, it can't stop shivering.

There is only one way to enhance my chances of survival, one way to end this lonely pain building between my ears, but acquiring a new body is a delicate, painful process. I am not *Pseudomycota*. I cannot simply gorge myself on whatever is lying around. I cannot survive alone, without an intelligent mind—I am social, ethical, dependent and depended on, a symbiote. I am something that brutish little parasite cannot understand.

Deep in my gut, a knot of déjà vu begins to form. I know there is a memory struggling to resurface, but I can't remember it—I can't remember it because it's not mine. I cup my chin, racking this brain, but all I seem to unearth is the faint, stomach-churning smell of raw wheatrock, and the image of a dog's nose falling from the sky.

A quiet knock draws my attention to the door. I know it is Émile before the knob even turns.

"Avoiding work?" I mutter.

He doesn't answer. He closes the door behind him and leans against it, flustered but otherwise unharmed. He asks if he can stay here for a while.

Shit, look at those big dark eyes, emerges a voice from the tiny maze of my cochlea. Medrah's, talking about me. "Did something happen?"

He shakes his head. I cannot see any new marks on him, but he seems diminished, almost shrunken, as if he has lost some unshaped part of his body. I can understand that feeling.

"Make yourself comfortable, then. You can share the burden of staring at *Pseudomycota* all night."

He sinks into the chair at my desk. He looks over at the parasite, then back at me.

"Not smart to let it out of my sight," I tell him. "That thing has been active lately. It's after a warm body. Can't blame it, with this chill."

The way Émile glances aside makes me wonder if I have said something wrong. His brow is shadowed, and a bead of sweat drips down his cheekbone.

"Here, take some of this," I tell him, reaching over to grab a dropper from my shelf.

His eyes rest on my scabbed hands, still healing from my experimental feedings of *Pseudomycota,* but he knows better than to ask anything. He accepts my offer, leans back, and places a single drop on his tongue.

"You'll want more," I say. "It doesn't start working until the fourth, at least."

He shakes his head and swallows. The sound irritates me, for no reason I can fathom.

"Suit yourself." I squirt a few mils into my mouth and collapse before the roaring fire. Its heat seems paltry, halfhearted, utterly incapable of warming me. We sit in silence for a few minutes, and my lonely mouth cannot keep itself from speaking. "That thing just isn't natural."

Émile agrees.

"Can't help but think I've encountered it before. Maybe a long time ago. But I can't remember where."

He frowns. Before I can stop him, he reaches over and tears a page from my notebook. He scrawls in his flourished script: *An old patient?*

"Definitely not."

A book/drawing?

"No. This is . . . when I try to remember it, it's almost as if . . . I'm looking from a different pair of eyes. It's distorted, like glass."

From a dream, then?

I sigh. "Perhaps. I wish I didn't dream at all."

He raises the pencil to his mouth, mulling it over. Kind hell, he looks so warm.

From your childhood?

Despite myself, I laugh. Did I even have a childhood? I must've— no, of course I didn't. "You've got an interesting mind. Searching unexpected places for answers. I like that sort of inquisitiveness." Even through my narcotic haze, I can see the hints of a smile play at his mouth. "We may be able to make a doctor of you yet."

It feels as if my brain is being slowly, brutally pulled in half, each hemisphere stretching in opposite but aimless directions.

The baron is speaking of airships tonight, and I cannot remove myself from the table. There is nothing to see beyond the ornate roof beams and glittering crystal chandelier, even though the potent analgesic I swallowed before dinner is known to induce visual hallucinations.

"We should know by now not to look to the sky," the baron says. "It's the whole reason the world fell apart in the first place. And the second, probably. Hell, maybe even the third."

"Do you really think so?" Didier mutters dutifully.

I stare at my untouched plate. It is some sort of grayish pâté, stinking of wheatrock salt. It is a rich, fattening winter food that my previous tongue had enjoyed immensely, but whose smell my current nose cannot stand.

"That governor of yours probably thinks he's re-creating the glorious world of his ancestors," the baron continues. "Where does he think he's going to fly that stupid ship of his? Into space?"

"Of course not," Didier sighs. "Perhaps over the sea, or the fume wastes. It's only natural to want to see what's become of the lands around us. Isn't it, doctor?"

"Wherever we are, we want to be somewhere else," I mumble, staring at the centerpiece, which with every passing minute I am surer is only a pig's skull with dried flowers placed in the empty orbits. "We wish to be everywhere at once."

"Of course *you'd* say something like that," the baron laughs. "Every new province some wigged sod plants a flag in means a whole new province full of diseases you get paid to fix. Even better if they spread back to Inultus. You can't have people be too well. If no one needs bleeding, no one needs a leech."

"Perhaps you are right." I am too tired to find offense in his words.

"Well, there won't be any new provinces for a while yet," the baron says. "That ship won't get off the ground. The outcry in the city is so loud I can hear it all the way up here."

I squint beyond the chandelier, looking for Inultus. My imagination offers only the image of the naturalist collective lined up at the governor's door with their papers and artifacts and protests. *We're repeating a cycle that should be broken,* says a particularly prominent voice from a pair of dark lips, a voice that I cannot drown out in my head. *We've only ever used flight to kill, and I have the historical accounts to prove it—*

"It's been done before," I mutter. "It can be done again."

"And what makes you think we should?" the baron laughs. "Repeat the past, repeat past mistakes. Make note of that, Didier." His son only grunts, fork absently maiming his meal. "Me, I'm old enough to know not to chase old ghosts. I know the château'll never be what it once was, and there's no point in wasting our time setting up the wiring and the piping and the porcelain and all that dreck. It'll all get blown back down in the next big storm. Maybe next generation, maybe the one after that."

He sends a glance toward the twins, but their collective attention is locked on the glinting chandelier. They look like they've been getting as much sleep as I have.

A pang of guilt kneads my gut. At their age, they would be ideal. With their paired smiles and constant entanglement, I wonder if I manage to assimilate one, whether the other will simply follow.

"Only thing worth keeping alive is yourself," the baron says. "And your progeny, of course. Everything else falls apart. You girls can't tell now, but if you saw the trash heap this place was after '97—girls. *Girls!*" All four of their eyes return to him. "What is wrong with you?"

"A ghost tried to steal our eyebrows last night," one says slowly.

"It got half of mine," says the other, lifting her fringe to display the damage.

"Children," Hélène warns.

Their grandfather only laughs. "Well, shit, now you're going to have to paint yours on, just like your mother. And she sure as hell can't get them right. Pity *we're* the ones who have to look at them—"

"Didier." I lean forward, words concealed under the baron's loudening monologue.

"What is it?" he asks, fashioning a bib from his serviette as the second course arrives.

"Are you all right?"

"Am I all right? As much as I can be, considering."

"Your hands—may I?" He tenses as I reach for his sleeves, but he allows me to fold back the fabric to reveal splotches of inflamed tissue, white ringed with red. Some of the drier spots have already begun to crack and peel. "What happened? These burns look quite painful."

"It's nothing. I was only fixing the fire in my office and got a little overeager." His smile is hesitant on his mouth and absent from his eyes.

I take a deep breath, and my addled brain begins to hum. He doesn't smell anything like Baker's stores, but it must be easy for a man who lives in a château filled with soaps and perfumes to mask the scents of incendiary chemicals. Then again, I cannot fathom why Didier would need Baker's explosives, and why he wouldn't simply demand them if he did. "Should I get you some ointment?" I ask.

"You need not. I'm perfectly fine. In fact, with this winter my hand is the only part of me that feels warm." He laughs bitterly. "I was thinking perhaps I should throw the rest of myself in the fire, too."

"It is uncommonly cold," I admit.

"Quite. And all the hearths are lit. I've been wondering if fire itself has gotten cooler since last winter. It wouldn't be the strangest thing to happen around here."

"And you girls should've seen your mother on her wedding day," the baron laughs. "Plump and pink as a hog."

"I don't have to sit here and listen to this," Hélène barks, as she always does. She stands and throws herself toward the door, bunching her gown in her fists, but she is not halfway across the hall before the twins interrupt her. Wordlessly, they lift their noses, each fidgeting and gripping the arms of her chair. Both heads jerk forward simultaneously, and the twins release a violent, four-nostrilled sneeze.

The chandelier rattles, the candle flames wink, every crystal catches and releases a thousand fragments of light. I can't move my arms to push away from the table, I can't shout a warning—my mind is lead, my limbs numb. I can only release a gasp as the chandelier detaches from the ceiling, sails downward in a constellation of glittering glass, and shatters on the table.

In a deafening clatter, the metal base hits the centerpiece, launching bone fragments and flower petals in every direction.

Carrot soup and wheatrock pâté spill across the tablecloth. Goblets and plates and candelabra smash in a spray of crystal facets and hot wax. Half a bread loaf rolls to a stop at the end of the table, pierced with glass.

The silence that follows is cautious. We turn to the twins, and they turn to one another, as if to figure out which of their noses was responsible for ruining dinner before their grandfather had the pleasure.

"What the hell was that?" the baron asks. There is a shard of crystalware lodged in his jowls, but he does not seem to notice.

"*Girls!*" Didier stands. "How many times must I tell you? How many goddamn times?"

They turn their darkened eyes to their father, sniffling. "It wasn't us."

"This is beyond the pale, children," he growls, rounding the table toward them. "Someone could've been hurt."

"We didn't—"

"How did you do it? Crawl up the beams and loosen the chain while no one was around?"

Hélène spins on her heels and hurries back toward her daughters. "Didier, stop!"

"Do you know how much that damnable thing *cost*?"

"It wasn't us," the twins insist. One blows her nose on her serviette, and a string of dark mucus flies from the other's.

"Of *course* it was you!"

"Leave them alone, mayrin!" Hélène leans over them, checking them for injuries, caressing their cheeks. "Girls, you're not cut, are you? Look at me, let me see you. You're far too pale, little fleas. Doctor, look at them."

I do, analgesic haze shattered with the chandelier. A stream of black liquid runs from one girl's nostril and onto her bluish lips. The other leans in to wipe it away with the serviette, pallid fingers trembling.

"Doctor, help me put them to bed," Hélène says. "They're sick. They look so very sick, don't they?"

When I stand, my stomach stays seated. "Yes, they do."

XIV

THE TWINS WERE NOT Hélène's first attempt at children, but they were the first survivors.

An impromptu incubator, comprised of an old tub and kerosene lamps, was partially responsible for that. Baker, then a young, beardless novice, had juggled arcs of carbon while I copied my careful designs, one hand turning pages in Inultus, one scrawling measurements in Verdira. Baker had praised me for my impeccable diagrams, and I praised him for his impeccable handiwork.

He was as new to the château as I, a recent hire after word of his mechanical exploits escaped the mines. No one ever puzzled out how he could start an engine with no fuel or make a radio chitter without a signal, but the château was in need of a machinist, so they dragged him from the miners' dorms and repositioned him in the crumbling hut just outside the grounds.

"It's always give or take with twins," he had said, as I lowered the girls into their bed of blankets and warm air, already more hair than child. "Cass, you've met her? I used to dig with her."

"I have."

"She says the reason she was born so big was because she ate her twin in the womb. Shoulda shared the space, but she nay wanna. So she up and gobbled him." He had laughed, I had tried. "These girls're gonna be sweet as cherries, I can tell. Won't be able to lift a drill like Cass, but nay everyone should."

The children lay still as tiny corpses for days on end, soundless. Each doughy chest rose exactly when the other fell, as if they shared one breath between them. They did not squirm or fuss when I opened my bag of swabs and phials and extracted cells to be sent to my microscopes in the city—diploid, identical, perfectly paired.

Hélène was ecstatic. Even the baron, after three bottles of wine and some interrogation, admitted such a pair of tiny, weak creatures would have to do. Didier was the only one who did not seem to celebrate each pound the girls gained, or every rigid, enthusiastic movement that increasingly entangled their little heads.

"Only remind him of what he nay have," Baker explained to me, the day he came to dismantle the incubator and reclaim the bathtub. "Coulda married someone else. Shoulda. Shoulda been a pair of Montish kids in there." He wiped his mouth, leaving a smear of brownish grease on his lips. "Though they'd nay need the extra heat. Seem to like the cold better, even as kids. But you nay worry 'bout taking care of them at this point. All dead'n gone."

"I seem to remember seeing one with the butler."

"Oh, yeah, him. Keep an eye on him, doc. If he turns out anything like his parents he'll be trouble."

"It's just a sneeze, madame." Sylvie hovers over Hélène, trying to detach her from the twins so I can muscle my way in. "Mistress, only a sneeze. Let the good doctor look at them."

"You haven't gone outside, have you?" Hélène says, hands crawling across her daughters' foreheads. "You've kept to the château? What if it's that . . . thing? That black thing the doctor found—"

"We never went outside, honest," the twins reply. Plugs of cloth are stuffed into each of their nostrils. "And we haven't touched the dogs. We're only cold. We've just got a little ache, and we're cold." With a bed warmer at their feet, a fire in their hearth, and their mother at their side, they should have all the heat they need. But they still shiver uncontrollably, shaking from their toes to the ends of their untamed curls.

"What do they have, doctor?" Hélène asks, finally moving aside for me. She raises a pale hand to her throat to play with a gaudy jade bijou. "It's not serious, is it?"

I am quite sure the twins have not come into direct contact with *P. emilia*. The only specimen in the château is locked away in an oak cupboard in my chambers, and only I have the key. I have sanitized myself and everything around me each time I have handled it. I will not consider that possibility.

I listen to the girls' synchronized heartbeats and read their identical temperatures—both normal, despite their shivers and complaints. "Only a winter flu," I posit, too hopefully. "To be expected this time of year. You girls have not been getting enough sleep, and it is an unusually cold season. All you need to do is keep warm and get some rest."

"We *can't*," they start. "We don't have time—"

"Drink this," I say, retrieving a bottle from my bag and uncorking it under their noses.

"That's disgusting," one says, scrunching her face.

"We're not taking that."

"A few drops with honey and hot water and you won't taste a thing," I assure them.

"Sylvie," Hélène says, "go get what the doctor needs." The maid bows and sidesteps the twins' clutter of discarded clothes and books, slipping into the torchlit hall. "And girls, don't sit like that—look, your hair is already beginning to get knotty. Just lie down and stay still."

"Don't make us sleep in here," one twin says. "We'll be trapped. They'll trap us, the ghosts—"

"Oh, for fuck's sake!" Hélène snaps. "There are no goddamn *ghosts*. I swear to every dead god I will paddle you two into a coma if you mention them again."

The girls' lips pucker. "We were going to get rid of them."

"The only way to get rid of a ghost is to take it back to the place where it died and burn it," one says. "It's an old Montish trick."

"As soon as it sees where it died, lit up brightly like that, then it remembers it's dead, and moves on," agrees the other.

"Who told you that nonsense?" Hélène growls.

"Émile."

"He said this to you?" I ask warily.

"He didn't *say* anything."

"He just told us."

Their mother shakes her head. "Sweetest hell, if you think you can understand that boy, you're very sick indeed."

"When did he tell you this?" I ask them. I cannot banish the image of his hands, stained with traces of *Pseudomycota,* waving stories at the girls' faces.

"A while ago."

"Before winter."

"When he helped us hide fetishes to ward the spirits away."

"But they're not working."

"They haven't burned up any ghosts at all."

"They haven't even sparked."

"You stay away from him," their mother says. "He's probably the one who got you sick."

Sylvie reenters and sets a steaming tray on the pedestal table. I remove myself from the twins' bed, drawing her aside and slipping their medicine into her hand. The maid is nearly a full head taller than me, and she lowers an ear attentively. "Two drops of this," I tell her. "Both for one or one for both, it doesn't matter. Another dose a few hours before dawn. I will come by then to see to them."

She nods, and I return my tools to my bag. I know of a few dozen swabs, cultures, and tests which may rule in some common pathogens—but even with all of my equipment in the city, many of these techniques live only in journals, dependent on lost technology. It is infuriating, knowing exactly what to do, and exactly why I cannot do it.

My head throbs with indecision. I'm so used to being of many minds, and now I'm of two, wrestling violently in my skull. One wants nothing more than to rush to Baker's hut before the sun rises, to bury *Pseudomycota*'s mother colony under a mountain of debris. The other is driven to tell Baker to give up, to drop his explosives and hide away for winter, that the creature is already here, inside the town, inside the twins.

I rub my temples, my eyes, trying to wipe away thoughts that aren't mine. It can't be. There is no way they have been exposed. If this is not another one of their macabre pranks, it must be some other infection, a benign cold, an uncomplicated pneumonia. Or else *Pseudomycota* has figured out a way to slip out of its jar, to slither through the shadows and prowl the house unnoticed.

Dawn cannot come soon enough.

For a transient moment, I am home again. The smoke is thick, still hot from a recent disaster, but I can tell I'm somewhere near Satgarden. Nearby, the ruins of an old city jut from the dust and ash. The buildings are nothing but tall crosshatches of stone and rebar against a gray sky, and the ground is a sea of shattered glass. A few species of shrub struggle to grow in the wasteland, leaves as sharp as the soil. The mists are alive with the red lights and beeping voices of fallen machines, always dying but never dead.

I am in the fearful, fragile state of infancy, with no parent, no protector, no teacher. I have no control over the hosts in which I reside. For generations, stupid and helpless, I am passed from body to body with exchanges of blood or the desperate ingestion of human flesh. I am blind, powerless, insensate, as eager to destroy as to inhabit.

There is a kind of agony in witnessing the ugly, simplistic thing I used to be. It is as if suddenly, vividly remembering what it was like to have been a germ cell, jostling among inconsequential billions, a mindless, inhuman speck lost in the oppressive dark of a living body. Still, I cannot take my eyes away from the vile spectacle. Generations pass me by, travelers and settlers clothed in animal skin and carrying spears, swords, hoes, books, art, love letters. As they grow, so do I.

I see my own face across from me. Through four eyes, then eight, then a hundred, I see new buildings rise over the corpses of old ones. I see grasses shudder, roads crawl outward from this hub. Tribes and tribes of people make their way toward the glowing cluster of red stone dwellings that someone, whom I have long since forgotten, names Inultus. And there I am, books and needles in my hands, healing, cutting, culling, manipulating, and maintaining my homes as carefully as the rest of the people do theirs.

As I deepen my niche, so do the minds around me. Gathering halls and palaces spring up, decorated with mosaics of ruby cobblestones and glass, and I am introduced to the human instinct for aesthetics. The hills are cultivated, destroyed by blight, and replanted. The steam engine is reborn from the pages of an ancient text. Cycles of famine and prosperity wax and wane for hundreds of years, until a green pebble rolls down from the north and deposits itself in our fields. The city, like me, burgeons once more, its bodies nourished, its minds sharpened. It looks to the sky, to the impassable horizons of its ancestors. It reaches toward lost knowledge and endless discovery.

Or, at least, that is how the story should go. I know that is how it should go, but every time I push my mind toward that outcome, toward a history familiar to me, it pushes back. I know I am dreaming, but the dream knows it too.

It deposits me at the edge of a mud-river and turns my attention skyward, where a fleet of massive dog noses descend. As they crash into the earth, heaving waves of mud around curled nostrils, I duck and shield myself. I have only a single body now, one small, brownish vessel to carry every immeasurable detail of my genetics, my life. It should frighten me, but it doesn't.

It's only another job, only an order from whatever suit slithered down from the governor's palace today. *Atiey's mortal foes,* Medrah always called them, half joking.

In this new facet of my dream, I have one task. The governor's man told me to look for something. I don't know what it is, but I'm just little enough to fit into the kinds of places you might find it. So I crawl through Satgarden, above the roiling mud and broken metal. Warped propellers of half-dead machines spin aimlessly above me, as if they are groping to find the edge of an edgeless thing and push off into the sky. I slip under their circling shadows, along the rounded hump of a dog's nose, inching closer to the dark, spiral canal of the naris.

The world goes white, shooting knives of light through my head. The bright heat moves to my abdomen and twists inside me, pushing its way through my belly and leaving a bloated, wet feeling, like wheatrock soaked too long in a boiling pot. I try to run, but my legs are weak, numb, and I launch face-first into the gray smoke, wheeling and tumbling until I land on the floor of my silent, freezing room.

I wake with a jolt. I sit up on the deerskin rug, strangled by sweat-soaked sheets. As I move my legs, a different, uncomfortable dampness clings to them.

My hands shake as I scramble to light the lamp, and I can't help but curse this wretched body, this thing that's wriggled out of my control. I untangle myself from the sheets and throw them back onto the bed. I expect the sharp scent of urine, but what wrinkles my nose is earthier, almost pleasant—though just as unwelcome. My stomach turns when I reach down to investigate the subtle, undeveloped seam where my thighs meet. It's not urine, but something much more dismaying.

This body, like all my others, has been chemically desexed. For hundreds of years, and through thousands of pituitary glands, I've been free from the ailments that plague a reproductive animal. But when I peel my cotton nightclothes down to my knees, I find them clustered with dark red stains. At first they seem like some remnant of my dream, but the longer I stare at them, the more real they become.

I've spoken with countless adolescents, of every caste and sex, about this very matter. Some had been devastated, others elated, some confused, and others indifferent. No matter their reaction, I tell them there's no shame in it, no abnormality, that their anatomy will do what it will do with or without their approval. But now, with this cold sweat running down my forehead, I can't seem to take my own advice. Those children couldn't control their bodies. I can.

I strip my bed, pile the sheets in the corner, change my clothes, and stumble to my medical cabinet. By the time I manage to isolate two lumps of a congealed medication from a glass bottle and swallow them, my mind has gone numb trying to explain away what my uterus has done.

With cotton and gauze and tape, it's not hard to stem the flow. But this is a bleed I'll have to keep on dressing, one that will reopen in a few weeks' time no matter how perfectly I bind it now. I pace around my quarters, from my lab to my bedroom to my water closet and back, underclothes stuffed with slapdash dressage, trying to outwalk the twisting pain that wrings blood from me like moisture from a cloth.

I check on *P. emilia* and find it safe and unchanged. There is no way it could've escaped its jar, but I cannot shake the feeling that somehow that wriggling monster has managed to violate me in the night.

I have to leave. I can't think with all this nonsense in my skull. The smoke of early Inultus, the smoke from Baker's cigarille, the smoke of burned wheatrock—they're clouding my thoughts. A voice that isn't mine, meaningless and cruel, keeps echoing between my ears, like an insult yelled from a passing trolley. I am afraid it might be Medrah's.

The cold silence of the halls is almost peaceful. I trot through the château, trying to shake off the pain that clings to my head and abdomen, winding through the foyer, the dining hall, the salon, evading the shadows of the night watchmen on their looping route.

Somewhere near the grand hall on the second floor, I hear a hiss at the end of a corridor. I freeze for a moment, scanning the dark for the constable or any of his men. I see no one. I creep along the worn carpet and around a corner, drawn to the echo of labored breath. As an unearthly silver glow appears at the edge of my vision, I inwardly apologize to the twins for dismissing their ghosts.

I reach the grand hall and cannot move past the doorway. The windows of the château's façade are bright with starlight from floor to ceiling. Spiderwebbed cracks divide the glass into dozens of panes, each reflecting the expanse of untouched snow below, blue-lit by the pebbles of the broken moon. I have never seen such

a clear, lovely night, but it is not the strange beauty of the landscape that paralyzes me.

A figure lingers at the rightmost window, head lowered, eyes
closed, back pressed firmly against the freezing glass. My approach goes unnoticed; the figure only sighs and turns slightly,
angling his torso against the night. He rolls his arms, his neck, his
shoulders along the window. Even as I stand shivering in my wool
coat, he basks in the cold, glowing like a gray specter. It has never
ceased to amaze me how Émile seems to produce his own light.

When I speak his name, too loudly, he starts. He peels himself
from the glass, drawing his thin shirt tighter around him.

"You should be resting," I say, for lack of anything better.

His lower lip disappears into his mouth and he chews on it for
a moment, black eyes locked on mine. Then something seems to
give way inside him, and he blinks. It is dismissive, as forceful a
command as he can deliver.

"No," I say. "I'm not going to leave you alone."

His jaw clenches, and I can make out a thin stream of sweat
crawling down his cheekbone. The way he moves is stiff and unnatural, as if the fabric of his shirt stings him.

"You're in pain," I tell him, uselessly. "Show me, and I can help
you."

He shakes his head, and for a moment I'm sure that he's sick,
that he has infected himself and the twins with his own namesake.
But his eyes are clear, urging as insistently as ever for me to leave
him be. He is not ill, but he is not well.

When I reach out to him, he only pulls away. "I can help you,"
I repeat. "Just let me look at you."

Evidently this is the wrong thing to say. Quicker than a frightened animal, he turns tail and flees into the darkness. I am again
alone, frozen under the bright fragments of starlight, hand still
extended to the empty air where he had been.

The twins are inextricable.

Their heads have fused in their sleep, and they are fused still, despite Hélène's violent efforts to untangle them. Sylvie paces the room behind us, and Didier leans against the velvet stripes of the wallpaper, arms crossed, fists buried in the crooks of his elbows. Even Émile is here, disheveled, jacket unbuttoned and askew, toiling away at the fire. Despite his efforts, the room is bitingly cold.

"I don't know what happened," Sylvie says. "I tried to feed them their morning dose, like you said, doctor. But they can't sit up. They're so stuck they can't even lift their heads without hurting."

"Every time they sneeze it gets worse," Hélène says. "I've been with them all night. Look. *Look*."

A knot of fear rolls in my gut as she thrusts her hands into the black tendrils, long and thin like *Pseudomycota*'s, and pulls. The girls hiss in pain, and the hair seems to tug back at Hélène's hand as she struggles to extricate herself.

"Feel it, doctor," she demands. She grips my wrist, and I wince—it's just hair, it's only hair, you coward—jerking my arm away.

"Don't be so forceful, Hélène," Didier says, voice sharpened to a nervous edge. "Let the doctor work."

"We need to cut it off," Hélène continues. "Sylvie, get the scissors."

The girls each open an eye. "Don't cut it," they say. "Please, don't. It's not our fault."

"Stop," Didier says. "They don't need it."

"Sylvie, do as I tell you," Hélène growls.

"No, Sylvie, don't. They don't need it. Don't you move."

"Get me those goddamn scissors or I'll have you thrown outside."

The maid trembles, stuck in place for a moment, before choosing Hélène over Didier. She rushes out the door, avoiding his glare, as I grab the nearest stool and push it to the twins' bedside. I cross and uncross my legs, shifting, trying to escape the feeling of my own discharge. My hand shakes as I open my bag. My vision blurs.

"The ghosts are rattling the towers now," one twin says, opening her mouth for my dropper.

"They're trying to knock down the walls and move all the staircases around so we can't run," says the other. As if to illustrate her point, a soft shudder vibrates through the room.

Hélène does not seem to notice it. "Will you shut up about the fucking ghosts?" she snaps. "There aren't any goddamn ghosts, and there never were. They didn't get you sick. I'll tell you what did." She thrusts her chin toward Émile. "That thing over there."

The houseboy closes the metal screen and lifts his head. He is flushed, eyes ringed in purple, hair plastered to his forehead. He seems worse now than he did last night.

"Look at him, doctor, sweating like he is in this cold," Hélène continues. "He's sick, far sicker than my girls."

"Fayme, stop," Didier says.

"He looks terrible. Like he's about to collapse. And with him slinking around my daughters, telling them all those terrible stories about ghosts—look at him! Clearly he's not well. Get him out."

"Hélène," Didier starts once more, but his wife is not deterred.

She stands, tea gown bunched in her fists, and strides purposefully toward the servant. "He's got some filthy cave disease," she says. "I want him out of the house—"

"That's enough!" Didier steps between them, grasping her arms and holding her in place. The red and white tinges of his burns flex as he squeezes her elbows, wringing a cry from her. "He's done nothing wrong."

"Don't touch me," she snaps, struggling to escape his grasp. "I've seen him. I've seen him around here, always taking things, stealing from me. Bijoux, brandy. He stole my *brandy*. And now he's going to take my girls—"

"For fuck's sake, leave him be!" With an effortful grunt, Didier shoves her back toward the bed.

She shrieks, stumbling over her gown, throwing out a hand to clutch the twins' bedpost. She manages only to pull loose a handful of sheets, and she hits the floor with a pained gasp. She stills, mouth agape, face flushed, one arm crossed protectively over her rounded abdomen. For once, she has no words.

"M . . . mistress . . ." The small voice from the doorway breaks the silence. All eyes turn to Sylvie, one hand clinging to the knob, scissors dangling from the other. "There's something going on outside."

"What?" Didier growls, stepping over his wife and making for the door. "This early? There can't be."

Sylvie just bows her head as he trots past. I hurry behind him, fear unfurling in my gut, until we skid to a halt at the nearest window. Beyond the glass stretches the expanse of the town, or at least what the snow has not yet buried. I see the church spire and chimneys spitting smoke into the early-morning starlight; I see the unkempt castle grounds, the highest spearheads of the wrought-iron gates poking from the blanket of ice. Just beyond that, I can see Baker's hut, or what is left of it.

A column of dark fumes billows from the splintered wood. Its walls and roof beams are split, jutting into the winter air like a burst rib cage. The nearby snow is blackened with ash and debris, and even from this distance I see small fires still burning, eating away at the corpse of the little cabin.

My breath leaves me, and my sense with it. Shivers traveling through every cell, I turn from the window, clench my fists, and scramble for a way out.

XV

A FEW YEARS BEFORE I came to Verdira, an explosion shook the ground all the way from the wheatrock mine to the train station.

There has always been a saying among the Montish, *th'montegn indoremt say révilray*. The phrase attests that every cycle of calm is preceded and followed by a storm, that even mountains in deepest sleep will wake eventually. This time, the mountain woke in spring, when some unlucky flame met a snaking trail of volatile gas. The incident is only a footnote in this planet's history of disasters, but there is no one in Verdira who cannot tell you about the blast of '97. It was not so much the blast itself that made the year memorable—explosions tear through the mines every six months or so—but the ensuing revolt, which left the colony and its ruling family in panicked disarray for years after.

When a consumptive Priest told me the tale, dizzy with opium and lying on what he believed at the time to be his deathbed, he did not cast himself as the hero. Nor did he cast Didier, who was, if not at the center of it all, at least center-adjacent. Instead, he coughed out his story from the perspective of a tailed woman whose parents had died in the explosion and whose husband—or the man who might've been her husband had the Montish officialized their monogamy—would shortly have his brains spattered across an oak tree in the château garden.

She had not been underground the day of the blast. She had not been there to see the carnage, to smell the stench of smoldering flesh and wheatrock, but she played an integral part in the brief but violent uprising that followed. To this day, not even the folk historians of the Inultan naturalist collective can piece together why a hymnodist and raconteur, heavily pregnant with her first child, had placed herself at the head of the rebellion.

Regardless, Priest admitted, she was good at it. Her songs and stories defied the silent fatalism in which the miners had toiled for decades. Her tail, thin like a rat's and covered with fine, pale hair, directed the movements of the workers like a conductor's baton, crescendoing their mournful hymns into a furious shout. The curl of that strange appendage coaxed them into armories, into meeting halls, and into months of heated skirmishes that pushed Verdira to the edge of both destruction and liberation.

The summer was long and smelled of smoke. After months of gunfire and detonations, the woman led a parade of miners down the scorched streets to the château grounds. Torch in one hand, gun in the other, she had every intention of destroying that haunted place, of burning it down to its foundation.

The baron, with the cowardly shrewdness of any autocrat, had already fortified his tower in anticipation of this inevitable climax. He had his intractable progeny bound and locked away safely at its peak. He had food and weaponry stockpiled for weeks to come. He positioned himself at the apex of the booby-trapped stairs, flanked by lackeys and bristling with firearms. Behind the safety of the tower window he watched the miners trample through the grounds with torches and homemade grenades, and sent his men out to greet them.

As history would tell, the attack on the château was well planned, but not so much as its defense; the instigators were prepared, but not outfitted like the baron's gendarmes; the miners were numerous and resolute, but the mercenaries that arrived by the trainful were more so. Every explosive thrown at the building died against its stones, every flame set in its garden was doused, and the château remained standing, just as it had for thousands of brutal years.

It was no surprise that within the season the first whisper of retribution and deposition had wound down to a desperate, dying gasp. What was surprising was that the tailed woman, smelling of fire and clutching an empty rifle to her chest, was the only one to escape the massacre.

The man who had pulled her from the pile of unmoving miners had been the same aged medic who'd failed, during the explosion that spring, to save even one of his patients. He'd be damned, he told me years later through his bloodied cough, if he couldn't at least save her. So in the summer of '97, he betrayed the man who fed, clothed, and commanded him, and guided a half-conscious woman from the garden to the safe darkness of the church basement. Though her injuries were minor and she recovered quickly, Priest feared for her pregnancy. The Montish were hardy, known to walk the winter nights with relative ease, but everyone is fragile in the womb.

He sat in that basement for hours with her, arguing, listening to her contemplate aloud the fates of herself and her fatherless child, dry-eyed and intensely rational. She was unmoved by the thought of her own death, or even by the thought of her infant going with her, but to die now would prove nothing, it would solve nothing. It was, Priest hypothesized, the pointlessness of death more than the fear of it that convinced her to abandon retaliation and save herself. So she took Priest's hand and let him lead her down to the machinist's house, where a three-wheeled, large-tired engine waited for them.

The journey would be long, but it was safer than sneaking aboard a train overrun with soldiers. The late days of summer would offer plenty of light, and the snow was minimal, confined to the shade and easy to traverse. The storms of spring had long passed, and the ventigeaux hibernated in their freezing caverns, waiting for winter to arrive once more.

Their destination was a village in the rolling hills between the prairies and the mountains. Priest had a brother of a brother of a cousin raising pigs there, last he'd heard. It was a tiny settlement, far from the railroad, overlooked even by caravanners on their journeys to the coast. Though the woman's Montish coloration might draw attention to her, there weren't many ways for word of her to travel back north.

They made good progress. For the first few days in the wilderness, she sat behind him in grim silence, tail wrapped tightly around his waist. Despite her condition, she was unbothered by the bumping and swaying of the vehicle, and despite her situation, she was unwavering in her resolve. The deaths of her friends and family could not defeat her. In the end, it was something much more puzzling that did.

The third day after they had set out from town, a strange illness befell her. That morning, due to no ailment Priest could determine, she doubled over and began to weep. Her sobs were not like the dry cries of pain he'd heard from her before, nor the brief barks of sorrow or disappointment. They were silent, rhythmic things that wrung tears from her eyes so quickly and in such volume that within minutes she was kneeling in a puddle of mud.

Neither knew why she cried. It was her first pregnancy, so she could not know what this symptom signified. Between great cascades of tears, she told Priest that she was sure it was only an effect of the approaching birth. Strange things happen to pregnant people the world over, she assured him, as if he needed to be told. It was, she insisted, merely a consequence of sharing one's body with another.

Priest took it as a sign that parturition drew near. Weeping was an unexpected symptom, especially for this normally dry-eyed woman, so he watched her closely, let her rest when she needed to, and prepared himself to bring yet another babe into the world. But labor never arrived; the spasms that racked her were sobs, not contractions.

The farther south they ventured, the faster the tears came, and it wasn't long before she realized she no longer had the strength to give birth, even if it were her time. Every ounce of energy, every drop of moisture in her body had made its way to her eyes and down her cheeks. She drank the canteen dry. She stopped to shovel handfuls of snow into her open mouth. She reclaimed her tears with her tongue. It did no good.

In the span of a little more than a day, she withered like a leaf.

Her skin dried and cracked, her muscles wasted away, her eyes sank into her head, and she bent over like a crone, clutching the uncanny stretch of her swollen belly.

They had not even made it to the Verdiran foothills, and she could go no farther. She collapsed on a rocky moraine, and with her last breathy moan, demanded Priest to, as he would quote years later, "do your fucking job."

So he cut her open. It was not difficult, with her skin fragile as paper, to slide a blade across her abdomen, to peel back the withered muscles, and rupture the only part of her that retained any water. In a flood of amniotic fluid, a boy emerged, the last of his mother's water dripping from the tiny nub of his tail. By the time Priest stood, hands soaked, baby wriggling silently in his arms, the woman had desiccated completely. Even her shining wound was rapidly drying, and before Priest could even think about burying her, a strong mountain breeze descended the hillside and blew her into dust.

Priest realized he could not possibly continue. He could not feed the child properly, nor could he trust it to survive until he reached the next town. It had been years since his formerly abundant breasts had produced anything of nutritional value, but he tried his best. He attached the baby to his nipple and returned to the château a traitor. Of course, he received a traitor's welcome. The child was taken from him, his knees were shot out, and he was made to drag himself across the grounds bleeding, never to disgrace those halls again.

It is a classic Montish tale: tragic, directionless, with no clear moral. Priest offered no explanation, scientific or otherwise, for the content of the story. When I asked him why he thought the tailed woman had cried herself to death, he only shrugged, coughed into his gnarled hand, and answered, "Nay can know, médsaine. Just the way it goes. If you're born in Verdira, you die in Verdira."

When winter descends in earnest and the snow rises as inexorably as a tide, the second-story balcony of the château's façade serves as its front step. No one has bothered to cut away the balustrade or alter it for ease of passage. It has always been reasonably assumed that by the time the snows pile this high, no one in their right mind will leave the château at all.

So when I push open the heavy door and stumble out onto the balcony, underdressed and unprepared to take on the lingering night, my hips immediately meet a decorative bar of freezing metal. I double over, and a flurry of ice bites at my skin, worse than the stinging proboscises of floodland mosquite clouds. Didier stands in the doorway, shouting after me, but the howling gale carries away his words. I hear nothing but the wind and my own pained panting as I leap over the rusted balustrade, sink thigh-deep into the heavy snow, and begin to stumble in a crude approximation of running.

Every hair in my nose freezes to a painfully sharp point. The cold air rips down my throat and through my lungs, but I can't stop. I can't even pause to wonder what happened or why—my mind is surging ahead of me, toward the ruin of Baker's house, unwilling to wait for my body to catch up. My legs move too slowly, my eyes ache with frost, and I am thrust back into the helplessness of my dreams. I do not dare to hope this is only a nightmare, that this weak, desperate struggle through the deep snow is only a symptom of running in my sleep. It terrified me to know I was dreaming then, but it terrifies me far more to know I am awake now.

No one comes out to stop me. I can feel the gendarmes' eyes on me, gazing bewildered through the windows of the manor, and I know rifles are sliding from the slits in the guard towers, scopes trained on me. But there are no gunshots, no shouts, no threats. Unimpeded, I jump over the pointed tips of the wrought-iron gates and stumble down the hill.

My head is spinning, my mind reeling through the smoke. I can only hope the light and heat of the flaming debris will stave off the night, at least long enough for me to see dawn.

The skeleton of Baker's house smolders in a crater of snow. I reach the lip of the depression, glancing down to see that its sides have melted in the heat and refrozen into glistening ice. Fires and billows of silver smoke multiply in the conic reflections, and it is with a sickening vertigo that I slide down the glassy surface and into the splintered building.

I land on the warped corpse of a stove. Fire licks at my feet and gusts of heat tangle with the freezing wind, clearing the smoke, condensing it, and clearing it again. Waves of hot and cold crash over me as I stumble through the dizzying landscape of twisted metal and scorched wood. My eyes sting, my lungs struggle, but I still grope blindly through the maze of rubble, calling Baker's name.

When I come across the first sign of him, a gasp flees my throat. It takes a moment to realize what part of his body it had been—given the thickness of the muscular compartments, and the size of the bone protruding from the scorched meat, it is likely a part of his leg.

A few steps beyond that, I find the remains of a foot. Bloodied stumps of toes curl in the heat, singed threads of wool socks still clinging to blackened skin. That familiar smell of burning flesh meets my nose, and a maelstrom of panic seethes in my head.

Coughing and hacking, I follow the trail of the machinist's shredded body like bread crumbs. I stumble through the ash and debris to the north wall, now nothing more than a warped pile of splintered wood and melted teapots. When I blink away the tears, when the wind clears my sight, I fall to my knees.

Only half of the man remains. He lies against the back wall, under a smear of blood. His eyes and cheeks have burned away, revealing a row of crooked teeth in a fractured jaw. A few mangled scraps of his thighs are left, violently severed about the place where I had cut Cass so many months ago. The cage of his exposed ribs is splattered with motor oil, and between the glints of white bone I can spy his mutilated machinery shuddering. Even without its owner, even without any blood to pump, his stout heart still whirs away.

My own heart is drumming fast and loud in my ears as I crawl toward what is left of him. An absurd, prudent part of me tells me to salvage his parts, to rescue the plastic and metal before the heat destroys it forever. A better part of me tells me to run, to shut myself in the château and survive until spring, to forget about the wheatrock mine and the missing sled dog and *P. emilia*, to scramble out of this crater before any surviving explosives catch flame and disassemble my body as violently as they did Baker's.

But I can't move. The man's heart holds my gaze. Dozens of tiny gears whir and rattle, and the organ releases a high-pitched whine. Something darker than blood, thicker than oil, moves inside the warped plastic of a defunct pulmonary artery. Breath held, stinging eyes wide, I watch a long, whiplike appendage slither from the bubbling vessel. Blindly, it prods Baker's cracked ribs, probing, retreating, and probing again, before pulling the rest of its bulging mass through the tubing. As it wedges its fist-sized body between jagged ribs, I can't stop myself from muttering its name.

It is not its large size that stuns me, nor the question of how long it has occupied poor Baker's heart, but the way it moves, limbs twisting and contracting, rippling in the heat. Its arms glide with bewildering speed, expanding and retracting as it pulls itself from Baker and drops to the floor. It seems to be unfurling, elongating, growing and losing a hundred arms with every swift movement toward me.

Only when it is within a few cems of my feet does fear release me. I stumble backward, eyes locked on the creature, hands groping desperately for a weapon of any sort: a piece of debris, a plank of wood, or a bar of heated metal. My throat is seared silent, too choked to cry out, but that does not stop it from trying. A desperate breath cracks up my windpipe, but it can't decide whose name to call, who to fruitlessly beg for help—Baker, Atiey, Priest, the nameless dog gods of antiquity with their destructive celestial noses.

Before I can form a word, before my fingers can wrap around a bludgeon or sharp object, a boom shakes the smoldering remains of Baker's hut. A thousand layers of sound rattle the detritus and reverberate from the glassy walls of the crater, and I know, beyond a shadow of a doubt, that I am dead. The heat of the flames has touched Baker's surviving stockpiles of explosives, and the next series of sounds that tear through the house will be those of my spine shattering, of my jaw cracking open and my teeth flying from me like a broken string of lumpy Misulah pearls.

But as the next wall of sound rips through me, I remain intact. It is the writhing tangle of *P. emilia* that bursts, limbs flailing in a spray of black ribbons. The creature falters, flaccid body flattening against the floor as its disconnected parts twitch and struggle. I realize, with no small relief, that the sounds are not Baker's explosives detonating in uncontrolled bursts, but gunshots—one of which has slowed *Pseudomycota* enough for me to regain control of myself.

I don't linger to make sure the thing is dead. I turn and hurdle the debris, lifting my eyes to the edge of the icy crater. Two figures resolve in the haze above me, long shadows of rifle barrels jutting from each. Fingernails desperately clawing at the glowing ice, leather toes slipping and kicking, I scramble up the slope, back toward the night.

I am near the crater's lip, grasping for purchase, when a pair of rough hands grips my shoulders and drags me to safety. I raise my eyes and find that I cannot look into the face of my rescuer.

"On your feet," the constable pants, dragging me away from the smoldering hut.

As the heat of the disaster retreats, I am hit once more with the full force of winter. The wind tears at my skin, pricking needle-like at my narrowed eyelids. I take a breath to respond to the constable, but the icy pain immobilizes my throat and lungs. I can only release a puff of terrified air as he hauls me back toward the château.

The other man, rifle still smoking, face darkened with the deep shadows of starlight, is Didier. He says nothing, gloved hands clutching his gun, eyes locked on his home as if he's afraid it might disappear. I do not know if he or the constable fired the first shot at *Pseudomycota*, but I know Didier must've fired the second.

It's impossible to tell how long it takes us to reach safety. By the time we leap over the frozen balustrade I cannot feel any of my limbs. Streams of mucus have frozen to my upper lip, cracking and pulling at fine hairs as I gasp for air. The constable wrenches open the door and throws me inside. I roll across the carpet in a numb heap. I barely manage to cough out the last of the night air from my agonized lungs, and my bare hands are stinging and bloodied with cold. When the men squeeze through and slam the door behind them, I see they are not much better off. The three of us shiver violently for a moment, staring at one another.

The constable breaks the silence. "You stupid *fuck*," he growls. His hideous face is a blur of blood, his half-nose a deep, necrotic blue.

"Baker . . ." I breathe.

"What the fuck did you think you were doing?" His eyes burn against my cheek, and I have to turn away. "You stupid little shit—"

"Stop," Didier wheezes. He teeters near the door, face so wind-bitten it bleeds in places. "Doctor . . . are you all right?"

I make a small noise of affirmation.

"Good," he gasps, falling forward and collapsing onto all fours. He sways for a moment, fingers curling, rifle dangling, before he lowers his head and vomits onto the carpet.

XVI

THE SOUND OF THE château's panic does nothing to assuage my aches. Pain is split evenly between my brain, pounding to the rhythm of busy hammers, and my abdomen, where some invisible hand has grabbed hold of my uterus and is kneading it like dough. I stand in Didier's study, vainly trying to warm myself by his fire as he dispatches servants, ordering all doors to be locked, all keys delivered to the constable, all potential routes of escape boarded up. Holes in the walls will be filled, unused doors sealed and covered. Any cracks, crevices, or seams big enough for a mouse to slip through are big enough for *Pseudomycota,* I tell him, and he takes it to heart.

Hours pass, but the night seems eternal. As I stare at the wrought-iron leaves of the fire screen, my mind paints and repaints pictures of the tip of a cigarille, smoldering under Baker's nose, moving from one side of his mouth to the other as he grins. Had he dropped it from his teeth, had the lighting of a match gone awry, had he, in his absentminded way, ashed it into a cauldron of flammables—I don't know and I can't know. All I can do is curse between my teeth at his luckless, dead, stupid soul.

It is almost dawn, and the purple light of the sun is slipping shyly past the jagged peaks. The citizens of Verdira, I suspect, are just emerging to investigate the strange explosion, and I cannot predict what they will find. The animals of the mountains might've come to claim Baker as they did for the bodies of the Montish for centuries, or the heat of the disaster may have kept them at bay. Priest might be bending over the body right now, muttering something akin to a prayer, as Baker's friends gather his limbs and lash them together like a bouquet for burial. And *Pseudomycota* may be there, injured but alive, waiting for them.

A twist of guilt runs through me. I have no room to hope. I must consider every Verdiran outside the château infected. The whole village is dead until proven otherwise.

"What are we going to tell the baron?" I mutter, mostly to myself.

"As little as we can," Didier answers, scribbling a hasty protocol to be passed between the gendarmes. "An explosion is . . . not unexpected. You didn't know Baker long, but he's toyed with dangerous things all his life. He was an expert, but there's a reason he needed a second heart. He never treated himself with caution. Something like this was bound to happen." A defeated sigh rolls from him. "Pèren will not be surprised. Only angry, which isn't much better. A machinist like that isn't easy to replace."

I return my eyes to the flames. "The Institute can bring one up when the train comes in spring."

And what do you think that train'll find? asks a voice in my head. I have given up on deciding if it is mine or not.

"We'll have to stay safe until then," Didier says. He sighs, running a hand through his thick hair. His knuckles are red with new burns and flaking from old ones.

Suddenly, I wish he would burn my hands, too. They're still freezing, still tingling from the night winds. It would feel good to thrust them into the fire.

"Doctor," he starts, "did you know Baker had . . . that thing inside him?"

"No," I admit.

"Dead gods damn it. Clearly it was the dog. We were not fast enough to find her before she started spreading that disease. I would've hoped Baker trusted us enough to tell us if he'd been bitten, but apparently not."

"Any evidence of a bite would've burned away by now," I say.

"And hell knows who else he spread it to." Didier shudders. "Do you know if . . . if that disease had anything to do with how he died?"

I blink away the lingering images of his blasted form. The creature in his heart did not destroy his body, but it may have well been what killed him.

Shit. I should've guessed. I should've opened him up the moment he complained about his heart. I am as much at fault for his death as *Pseudomycota*. Maybe more so.

"It's . . . unlikely," I finally say. "Like you said, something like this was bound to happen."

Didier's face falls. "Such a terrible shame. He was a good man."

"He certainly seemed so."

"You must understand, though, that what you did was incredibly reckless. Did you really think you could make it there and back in that cold?"

I lower my head. I don't remember thinking at all.

"You're young, doctor. The young always think they're invincible. But I want you to know that if we hadn't come and found you, you would've died out there."

"I understand, and I thank you for the help." At another time, in another place, I would've at least argued that this body was dispensable. Now I only shudder to think that my consciousness could've been erased after half a millennium, snuffed out as easily and inconsequentially as a candle.

"In any case," Didier continues, "we're safe now. That thing isn't getting through these walls. By nightfall every door will be locked, every crack filled."

Doubtful. I stare at the fire screen for a moment, watching the metal leaves dance. In my mind, behind the shadows of Baker's corpse, I see Hélène falling, I see a bruised eye. "Didier . . . about your own health . . ."

A confused look passes over his face. "Is it about the vomit? It happens when I . . . with too much excitement. With guns, and violence and such. You should know. Pèren seems to enjoy telling you about all the embarrassing moments of my boyhood." He lays down his pen. "It's nothing to worry about. If I felt sick I would come to you."

"Regardless . . ."

He glares at me with sleepless eyes. "I assure you, I feel *fine,* I really do. I didn't touch that thing, I didn't get anywhere near it. There's no way that I wouldn't know that something . . . like that was . . ." He has to stop himself, turning his head and puckering his face like he has just caught a whiff of decay. "I simply cannot get sick. I am the only one holding this household together."

I know I can't argue with him, so I don't.

"I'll be fine. We'll all be fine," Didier says. "We'll be back in the mines come spring. And if not—well, it's not as if we haven't replaced our workers before." He turns to me. The surety in his expression gives way, and his face seems to fall limp, like a muscle after a strain. "It won't come to that. Your lot has put down many diseases like this. Pox and soot-mite and the like. The Institute will solve this problem."

"I will," I say weakly. "It will."

There is a horror in my gut, and a horrible sort of joy, when I think of the possibility that the Institute might step off the train to find *Pseudomycota* has colonized every body in Verdira. The first wave of physicians might not survive, but by the third or fourth the Institute will devise a way to protect itself. It will find this corpse, lying among a hundred others, eyes eaten through by long, thin appendages. It will cut me apart the same way I cut apart Stanislas, and I will be disposed of properly: just another used body tumbling down the shaft of the furnace, nameless and un-mourned.

"I haven't been crying," Hélène says. "It's just this boil. It's moved to my throat. It's blocking everything and choking me up."

The girls lie head-to-head, because they cannot be moved any other way. They are fast asleep, attached at the temples, four hands clutched tightly together. One breathes in while the other breathes out, sharing the air as they always have.

"Look, doctor," their mother continues. She has a drink in one hand, and the other is furiously wringing a clump of dark, curly hair. "It's falling out. I couldn't pull them apart, so I tried cutting it, but it fell out instead."

Small bald patches stipple her daughters' heads. The skin is red and raw, and when I lean in with my glass magnifier I can make out tiny spheres of dried blood dotting the follicles. I rub a globule of liniment between my fingers and apply it. The twins are too heavily sedated to notice.

"Is it bad? Will it spread?" Hélène asks. "Is it what Old Doc had?"

"He didn't lose his hair," I say. Stanislas had a healthy scalp, despite the damage I had done to the rest of his body. Consistently, irrevocably, I destroy everything I touch.

"Yes, but he told me different people present with different symptoms," Hélène continues. "Fucking heaven—Sylvie, it's too cold in here. Get us more logs." Hélène releases her daughters' hair to paw at the maid, clump of curled locks tumbling to the floor. "And bring us another drink while you're at it."

"Madame," I start, pointlessly. "As a physician I'm obligated to remind you that you shouldn't—"

"Oh, shut up, doctor. My daughters are dying. Sylvie, get her one too. She needs it. Look at the wretched thing." She stares at me a moment, dark, watery eyes wandering from my unpolished shoes to my overgrown hair.

"None for me," I say to the maid as she flees. As usual, she'll hear no words but those of her mistress.

"What, are you too *young*?" Hélène snickers joylessly. "How old are you, anyway? Surely too young to be a physician. And so *small*. Has the Institute been starving you?"

It has. For nearly ten years. "I am fed properly. Like all the others."

"They should've let you grow a bit more before they sent you out into the world. Especially here. You can't be skinny and shapeless like a boy and expect to survive winter. You'd think the world's body of medical knowledge would know that."

"You'd think so." I shift on my stool, returning the salve to my bag, but not before rubbing some on my own temples, across my eyelids, as if that could dampen the headache. Something is pounding against the inside of my skull, trying to escape.

Her eyes follow my movements, too carefully. "You're acting like this is your first, doctor."

"My first what?"

"Menses."

I think I can hear a cruel laugh, but it is not my own. "How would you—"

"Oh, please. You smell of it. You're hunched over ever so slightly, and every time you stand up you look where you sat just in case you've left behind evidence that you're human after all." Her smile is flat, accusatory. "You don't need to hide these things, you know."

I bite my lip. "I s'pose."

"I used to have the worst time with mine," she continues. "I—maeci, Sylvie. Here, doctor." I shake my head, but the maid closes my hand over a mug of heated liqueur. "Yes, the absolute worst. Every time I sneezed I thought one of my organs had slid out. Sometimes little organs *do* slide out now, but never any of mine."

"Madame, please don't—"

"I suppose it's proof that I'm *doing* something. Earning my keep, as my lawful father puts it. Seems like it's always up to him to define our keeps and how we should earn them." She takes a generous gulp and turns back toward her daughters. The steam of her mug seems to soften her, melting the smile from her face. "Still, breeding for the château is better than working in the mines, or carving, or refining. It's certainly better than being a machinist, like poor Baker, may he find the warmest hell there is."

"May he," Sylvie replies tonelessly.

"Well, drink. Go on. Sylvie, make her drink."

The maid tips the bottom of my glass toward my mouth, and I give in. The sweet, hot liqueur calms the twist in my abdomen, and for the first time in what seems like years, I feel warm.

"I was so happy, you know," Hélène says. "When I married

into this family. I was the prettiest bride in Verdira, wed to the handsomest man. I was so sure things would only get better."

A grave mistake, Medrah puts in.

"I thought that Didier would give me a villa by the sea. I could ride the train, I could go to the city and see the great palaces. All I had to do was produce a few kids for this cursed house and my work would be done. I could retire to a life of peace and pleasure." She pauses for a second, as if she is unsure what to say next, but her indecision vanishes when she lifts the mug again to her mouth. "Doctor, you might not know what it's like, being so young. Those in your profession never marry, do they?"

"No."

"I was told it would be sublime, you know. To be one with another person, body and soul. I tried at first, I really did. I tried to please Didier. I thought he was happy to be with me. He wept like a child on our wedding night, and I thought it was for joy. Stupid." She laughs. "Doctor, I believe I told you to drink."

I obey. The maid hovers over me, ready to top me off when I'm finished.

"This is his fault, you know," Hélène sighs. "He doesn't care about me. The man has only ever cared about one person his whole life, and it's not me. Even after I worked so hard to give him the twins. These two were miracles, and two miracles is two more than I can ever hope for. If I lose them . . ."

"You won't." *If you're gonna lie, mackinita, at least do it well,* Medrah says. I tell her to be quiet. "It's . . . only a winter flu. The alopecia is likely related to that."

"They can't die," she sighs. "The line will end. What are the chances I'll have any more, after a decade of producing nothing?" She finishes her glass, and her hand trembles as she raises it for Sylvie to refill. "No use digging in an empty mine, as my dear father says."

I hesitate, tipping my mug back, bathing my nostrils in steam. "Fuck him," I conclude, and for once, my unruly brain has nothing to add.

Hélène gives me a mirthless smile. "Would you look at that. Our kind doctor has a foul mouth. Sylvie, get us another."

"I'm fine, maeci," I mutter, but the cup fills in my hand, and I can't help but lift it to my mouth.

"Perhaps we should pour something sweet for my girls," Hélène mutters. "Try to wake them up. Sylvie—no, they're far too tired. This is the most peaceful I've ever seen them. Perhaps, if they recover . . ."

"They'll be all right, Hélène," I say. *Repetition makes truth.* That one was Atiey, not Medrah.

"If they are . . . I just want to get them out of Verdira. This place has driven them mad. It's the cold, or the vapors of wheatrock processing . . . I don't know, but it's given them such ghastly delusions. Before they fell asleep they told me they knew how to walk through walls, doctor. Through walls! Sweet hells, they can't stay here. I don't care if I see the little monsters ever again, I just want . . ." Her face falls, her voice falters. "They have to grow up somewhere else, while they still have the chance to grow. They have to escape this wretched place. I lost my chance a long time ago, and look what it's turned me into." She throws back her mug and flushes her throat with its contents. "I suppose Old Doc had it right. There really is only one way out of Verdira."

"Hélène . . ."

"He was a smart man, wasn't he? To work for the Institute you've got to have some brains in you." She sighs. "Rest in peace, poor sod. I'd make a toast in his name but I don't think he even had one."

"He had one." Somehow my drink has been miraculously refilled. "Stanislas. The Institute took it from him, but he got it back."

"To Stanislas, then." Hélène looks at me with something like pity. "To a man who took back his name, and fucking died anyway."

I don't know why I decide to ring the bell at this hour, whatever hour it is. I only know it's far too late to call him. Worse yet, I don't entirely know what I'm calling him for.

But he shows up at my door. It's a pleasant surprise, partly because I don't expect him to answer, and partly because in the few minutes between my summons and his arrival, I had forgotten I called him in the first place.

Émile hurries into my room with a worried look, hair disheveled, slick with sweat. When he sees me on the floor, halfway between the door and my bed, he heaves a sigh of relief.

"Sorry to disappoint," I tell him. "There's no emergency. No experiments, no accidents. I just . . . I need help with the fire, that's all." I congratulate myself on my improvisation and gesture toward the empty hearth, head swiveling on the end of my neck as if it might slide off and roll away.

Émile's lips pull into a tight frown, and he bends to help me rattle open the screen. Feet bare, thin coat clinging to him, he does not seem to notice the freezing draft as he lays down the kindling and begins to stack the logs.

"Are you not cold?" I ask him. He pauses to look at me, but the words in his stare are none that I know. I hug myself, shivering as he bends over the wood, lighting a small flame under the andiron. "Priest says Montish blood can keep anyone warm."

He doesn't answer. He only tends to the growing fire.

"I'm stuck in the body my maman gave me, unfortunately. Cold blood, thin skin, like an itch-lizard."

I spread myself along the deerskin rug, rolling toward the flames with the rest of the room. Émile stands, a blur at the edge of my vision. I reach out to him as he steps away from the fire, but I am so disoriented I can only brush the hem of his trousers. I want to tell him to stay, that I don't need him for the fire, I need him for his presence.

He makes for the open door, and suddenly I'm trembling like the last leaf at the end of a frosted branch. I can't tell him about the rest of the tree. I can't make him understand what it's like to be a stray hair from his head, sheared and left to blow away in the wind.

I nearly weep when he reaches the doorway. But instead of disappearing back into the hall, he closes the door and turns to me, fingers telling me that there is no point in starting a fire if all the heat will be lost into the corridor.

"Bensûr." I manage to smile. "'Course there's no point."

He steps again toward me, but doesn't seat himself. He only lingers near the bookcase, watching me with such intensity I cannot help but laugh. He thinks I'm keeping him here so he can clean up my vomit. He might have to.

"Fucking hell, Émile," I say, "there's no point at all. Baker's gone, your dog is gone, *Pseudomycota* is already here. Probably in the twins." Somehow, I manage to prop myself up on my elbows. "How, do you think? How did the little bastard do it? You didn't do anything that might've exposed them, did you?"

He looks hurt.

"I thought not, I just couldn't help but . . . you shouldn't keep playing with them, Émile. They're older now, and who knows what the baron will think. He wouldn't like it at all."

A solemn frown passes over his features.

"And what were you sneaking around for? Stealing Hélène's stuff. Brandy I can understand. But jewelry—were you hoping to sell it somewhere? In some other town?" I roll over and fold my hands under my head. "Well, no chance now, with that parasite crawling around. You'd never make it, no matter where you planned to go. Where *were* you planning to go?"

He doesn't react. He only spins, like the rest of the room.

"South, maybe. In that case, wait to come back with me. I'll take you to Inultus. We can go to Satgarden and see my pare— patients. We can make a physician of you. Have you ever considered practicing medicine?"

I don't bother to look at him for a reply.

"Don't. It's the kind of work that'll end up killing you. You'll lose yourself in it." Momentarily, I regain command of my own mouth. "Disregard that. Disregard everything I say. I'm not myself tonight. Don't trust me."

He stares at me, knots of concern deepening above his black eyes, and what little control I have is lost again.

"Trust me when I say don't trust me. Don't trust anyone as well dressed as I am, that's what Atiey used to tell me: Never trust anyone who's too well dressed. If they have good clothes they have good money, and there's no such thing as good money."

Émile folds his hands patiently behind his back.

"Just look at the Institute. Half its income comes from scrubbing the warty toes of tyrants like the baron. Can always find me standing behind them somewhere, ready to stitch them up, and everyone they hurt. Good business. So long as people are sick and injured, I've got a secure niche to live in. What more could I want?" I twist, trying to wriggle away from the ache that still pounds through me. "Of course there was more. So much I wanted to learn. About the world, about myself. But survival comes first." I lift my head and look him over, heart rising. He's not much bigger than I am. Perhaps, if I disable him, I could hold him down long enough to break his skin and slip inside. I could do it now, if I wished. I have everything I need.

Suddenly, I think I'm going to vomit.

"Shit." I fall back onto the rug, watching the ceiling turn slowly above me. If there is a creature living behind my retinas, I hope I'm making it feel as sick as I do. "What am I gonna do? How am I gonna find out if the girls are infected . . . I can't go around tearing people's eyes out. The Institute would be fine with it, maybe even the baron, but not if it's his family's eyes." I glance at Émile, and he averts his gaze. "You look just as bad as the rest of us. And you've gotta be running a fever."

He shakes his head, signing something I can't interpret.

I curl against the fire, and I'm positive I won't be able to move from this spot until springtime. I want to curse Hélène for putting me in this state, but I can't. This is my fault.

"You should stay here," I tell Émile. "Hide here, with me. I don't know what's making you run around the halls at night, but it can't find you here. The fireplace will keep lit. You can stay here."

Émile's face softens, and a sudden age seems to descend on him. I'm not sure how old he is, probably somewhere on the cusp of twenty, but in the shadows of my room he appears to me an old man.

"You can hide here as long as you want." I close my eyes, and cannot open them again. I can see nothing but the flickering rash of firelight seeping through my eyelids. As expected, there is no sign of Inultus. "Then at least you won't be alone."

He doesn't answer, though I don't expect him to. I have something I want to say to him, to warn him about, but my body outruns my mind, plunging toward sleep, and all I can do is spiral dizzily after it.

I wake up, and immediately regret the decision. I roll to my side, and the world rolls with me. A sharp pain jolts from my knees to my eyes, piercing my stomach along the way. I want to vomit, I want to outsleep this feeling, but my body does neither. Instead, resenting every muscle, I push from the deerskin rug and straighten my aching upper half.

My bedclothes are draped over me, and at my back the embers of the fire still glow. My brain, sore and throbbing like a wound, tries to remember why I am on the floor instead of in bed. The dim light illuminates the clock, pendulum curving as the walls around me slowly tilt, and I realize that it's far too early to be awake. But my dry throat and wooden mouth demand me to rise, groaning, and search for something to drink.

I discover a jug of water on the table, likely a gift from Émile. I gulp it down, not bothering with the crystal glass he set out next to it. As my throbbing head puts itself back together, I wonder if I should find him to apologize for my behavior, or thank him for enduring it. I can't remember what I'd been thinking, calling him to my room to take care of me, or if I'd been thinking at all. At the very least, whatever dark place had swallowed my drunken rationale has also swallowed any unpleasant dreams I had.

As I turn from the table, I see a few of my extra bedclothes piled on my chair. Beneath them, curled with his head to his knees, is Émile.

My sheets are bunched up under his chin, and one of his shoed feet pokes out from under the wrinkly heap, dangling over the cushioned arm. His hair falls over his face, and for a moment he resembles the subject of one of those old, rotting oil paintings that historians sometimes pull from buried wreckage, depicting long-limbed beauties draped over chairs like discarded clothes.

I blink. Such an absurd thought reminds me that, despite my sleep, I still might be drunk.

"Émile," I say. He does not stir at the sound. He's worrisomely still, but as I approach, a slight twitch of his exposed shoe assures me that he hasn't died in the night.

I say his name again. He only sleeps on, curled as tightly and comfortably as a sled dog basking in the summer light. I don't know what lifts my hand toward him. Maybe it's the same urge that impels the twins to disturb a cat when it has finally stretched out on the windowsill, poking at its paw pads and nose. Maybe it's the same impulse that comes over a parent when they suddenly tousle the hair of the child nearest them. Or maybe I reach for him because I know he won't squirm away from me, from my bright light or probing glove or the cold metal of my stethoscope.

The closer my trembling fingers get to him, the farther away the rest of my body feels. I gain distance from the ache in my head, the twist of my abdomen, the thoughts of Baker, the twins, of Hélène and Didier and missing dogs and stolen explosives and *Pseudomycota*. For half of a miraculous second, every cell of my being is solely devoted to the moment when my tingling hand will meet his shoulder, when I will gently shake him awake and again share this space with another consciousness.

But the moment does not arrive. Instead, my door flies open, and with a heavy, exhausted breath, Sylvie tumbles into my room. My hand falls to my side, Émile's eyes snap open, moving to the panicked maid panting in the doorway.

"Doctor," she gasps. "It's the mistress. She's doing it again."

"She's doing what?"

"She's having another one of those . . ." She pauses, hesitating to put a name to those baby-like things Hélène pushes out every half year or so.

"She's gone into labor?" I ask, reaching for my bag.

"I don't know. Whatever it is, it's worse than usual. She's calling for you."

I look to Émile, who only seems to shrink into my chair. "Well, don't just sit there," I tell him. "You know what to do. Fetch towels and hot water. And go get Didier. Maybe he'll condescend to hold her hand this time."

XVII

IN THE REFRESHING CHILL of the spring of '97, Didier realized he was madly in love with a Montish woman. The revelation only came to him, Priest assured me, because the baron had sat him down and informed him he was to marry someone else.

"Hélène were a calculate decision," Priest said to me. He spoke quietly, since the shadows of the jade carvers still circled us, gathering the towels and basins used to treat their burned workmate. They did not need to overhear a story that was not supposed to be told. "Verdira taught the baron his lesson 'bout how well kids a southern blood survive. Did were the only son to live past babehood, ay stole his maman on the way out. Baron knew, 'specially with the blast'n the trouble brewing, château needed a wife'd give it a whole gaggle of heirs."

Didier should've been ecstatic to receive the gift of a beautiful girl, hailing from a large family of large families, plump and healthy and ready to make her own. He had always been a complaisant young man, unfailingly polite and averse to confrontation—to the disappointment of his father and the relief of everyone else. But the news induced a fit of passion as unexpected and pathologic as an acute infection. He ran a fever. He wept so violently he doubled over and lost consciousness. He took to bed, barring the door to his chambers and refusing to emerge. When his father's men finally splintered his door to retrieve him, he was nowhere to be found.

He was, in fact, hurrying down the sooty streets, bathed in indigo midnight. The echo of the recent blast rattled under his feet, and the first hints of gunfire tittered like birds on the horizon, but he did not notice. His gaze, his entire being, was focused solely on a dilapidated stone building at the end of the boulevard, tall and crooked like the rest: the home of his first and only friend.

Later, when Priest was tending to her aches and pulling bits of cave grass out of her hair, she would tell him that she was not surprised to see Didier at her door. She invited him out of the street, sure that the tears that ran down his face were for the lives lost in the blast, for her, for the upheaval that was stirring in the distance. She had always told herself that Didier was not like his father, he was not like the constabulary, he could be reasoned with, he could be spared. But she was cautious. She knew that no matter where Didier went, whether he liked it or not, the gendarmes were not far behind.

When he collapsed in her arms, he said nothing about the mine, nothing about the smoldering violence waiting to erupt. He wept only for her, and for himself, for the snapping of a thread that he had not known was the last holding him together. Years of anguish writhed from him, finally broken loose from the château's relentless grip. He confessed. He prostrated. He poured the contents of his heart at her feet and pleaded for her not to grind them under her heel. He produced a ring of pressurized wheatrock pilfered from his mother's vanity, and tried to offer it to her in a southern ritual she did not understand.

She was a strong soul, strong enough to bear the burdens of others without breaking a frown, much less shedding a tear. But she could not stop her heart from sinking at his desperation. In a mo-

ment of weakness—that was the word she used with Priest—she
tried to console the baron's inconsolable son. She laid her hands
on his head and brought him into her lap, as she had done many
times before, when only the balm of her stories could soothe him.
She draped his shoulders in a tapestry of soft cave grass, stroking
back his curls and wiping away his tears. But it did not take her
long to realize what Didier wanted from her was not something
she was willing to give. Despite their lifelong companionship, despite all the kindnesses he'd shown her, the words and deeds and
gifts, his affections could not match those she had found in the
arms of a handsome carver's son. She firmly but kindly told him
as much.

Didier started to beg. He appealed to every ounce of her pity,
every confused ambiguity in her act of sympathy. He threatened to
hang himself from the orchard's oldest tree, to slit his throat with
a knife of obsidian, to incinerate himself in the château's furnace.
He was beyond reason, utterly helpless, and entirely at her mercy.
His heart was open, his hands empty. He didn't carry a gun, but
he didn't need to.

As she stared into his eyes, earnest and tear-filled, she recognized a glint of the inevitable. So she retracted her protests, drew
him close, and gave him a single word of assent.

He was nothing but gentle. When he laid her down on the tapestry, pushing her back into the woven strands of cave grass, it was
with an almost deferential tenderness. He entwined the end of her
tail in his fingers, just as she liked it, just as he had done when they
were teenagers, before she was sent to the refineries and he to the
top of his father's tower. He kissed her, slowly and earnestly, her
neck and collarbones and belly, filled out but not quite showing.
He did not know of the creature that grew there. He would never
find out that eight or so weeks ago she and the carver's son had
vowed to create something extraordinary.

He told her he loved her. He told her she was beautiful. He
showered her with heartfelt professions of devotion. He assured
her that he would never love another soul, aboveground or below, in this world or any of the warm hells that awaited them.

He promised he would never abandon her, he would never let the baron hurt her, he would die before he let anyone rip them apart again. He may have tried to make good on those promises, too, had he not been beaten into submission and locked away the moment the baron realized the miners' final march had begun.

She had felt no pain, or so she reassured Priest when her ordeal was over. She was in a strange, indistinct state, pulled in many directions by all the forces that occupied her. A new story sparked in her skull: a story of herself, her clan, her parents, her child, countless bodies enduring the thousand-year heat, the world's end, an era of sunless, howling winters—a million deaths dying inside her, all in service of the château.

She did not cry afterward, because she never cried. When Didier left in a flurry of nervous kisses, she brushed herself off, sang a healing hymn, and went to Priest for a salve. He offered her an abortifacient, but she assured him she did not need it. The life inside her, she said, the strange, beloved parasite that latched onto her and grew, would not cede its territory. Though it could not stop Didier from doing as he wished, it spurned any further claim to her biology. It would break whatever cycle he had attempted to continue within her.

She never told anyone but Priest of that day. But he saw the curse she cast with her eyes, unspoken but eruptive, a sleeping mountain waiting to wake. He knew she would reclaim the lives the château had stolen, the life it tried to steal from her. She would end the endlessly repeating seasons of toil and coercion. She would usher in the disaster that might, after thousands of years, finally crumble that cursed building.

"She never did," Priest sighed. "Revolt killed her with the rest. Ay the gash in Didier only festered worse'n ever."

When the story ended, my hands had gone numb from the balm I applied to the jade carver's burns. "And now it's dehisced," I said slowly. "Spilling into his conduct. Making him do things he wouldn't otherwise do."

"Wae'n nay, médsaine. Seems you missed the empratesse." Priest shook his head, wearing the same patient look he wore when

I first struggled through Franco. "Just said Didier had a wound in him. Never said he didn't put it there hisself."

Didier sits in the corner, pipe dangling from his mouth. He does not appear to be smoking, only crossing his eyes at the pinch of tobacco in the bowl, lighting matches above it and watching the flames flicker.

Hélène paces the length of her boudoir, drenched in sweat but still clutching a blanket around her shoulders. "It's this one," she says, not for the first time, bare toes curling in pain. "Oh, shit, here it is. It's this one."

"Take your time, madame," I tell her, bending to help Émile and Sylvie place the warm towels. "When you're ready, lie down on your mat." It is all I can do not to stretch across it myself and close my stinging eyes. I hope Hélène feels better this morning than I do. Considering how she waddles around the room, hands wringing, I can guess that even if she's escaped the hangover, she has plenty of other pains to replace it.

"Not this one." She turns and walks to the snowy window, shakes, and walks back. "It's this one, I swear," she tells me. "Now's the one."

"Chérin, just do it already," Didier says, match in hand. "You're usually a great deal more punctual than this."

"And where are *you* in a hurry to go?" Hélène barks, finally squatting over her mat.

"My study," he answers. "Autumn's shipments are still waiting to be tallied. And with what's going on outside . . ." He shakes his head, grimacing. "Let's say we'll owe the Institute something of a debt when they get here and rid us of that germ."

"It'll get them all, too," Hélène hisses. "And good riddance, I say. It'll just—" She rocks on her heels, pulling the blanket tighter over herself, even the parts of her I need to see. "I'm cold, doctor. Move me closer to the fire."

Didier does not take his eyes off his pipe as we help Hélène toward the flames. Sylvie gently wrestles the blanket back from her, despite her shivering and protesting, and I get a good view of her lower half, stretched belly striped with the leaf-shaped shadows of the intricate fire screen.

"Émile, support her shoulders." Reluctantly, the houseboy obeys, recoiling a little at the touch of her clammy skin. He has seen this process before, almost as many times as Didier or myself, but it never fails to affect him. Fortunately, he is not the type that lets the fearful parts of his brain command his hands.

"Don't let him touch me," she barks, even as she falls back onto him. "I don't want what he has." Another contraction flexes through her, and she curls her toes, gasping. "Oh, shit. I'm still cold, put me nearer to the hearth."

Half an arm's length is all we can manage. Émile is pouring sweat and panting with the effort, but Hélène does not seem to notice. "Closer," she groans. "Put me up against it. Put my back up against the screen, goddammit."

"You'll burn yourself," I tell her.

"I don't care. Just do it."

I look to Émile, then Didier. The latter has torn his eyes from his pipe and now watches us intently, match burning to a nub between his thumb and forefinger. "Just give her what she wants," he says. "Poor woman won't have anything but her way."

"Scoot back a bit," I tell Hélène. "I need that firelight to see. Émile, cover her shoulders and keep her warm."

"Get him away from me," Hélène begins, but reaches up to grab his hand anyway. "Oh shit, oh sweet hell. Why is it like this, doctor?"

"It's all right," I say. "You've done this before. Your body knows what to do."

"This one . . . this one is worse," she gasps. "Worse than the twins."

A violent shudder rolls through Hélène and into me. "Just keep breathing as you are," I say. I pull on my gloves and carefully push her knees apart. "Émile, support her while she lies back.

"Sylvie," I continue, "bring me those towels. Hélène, breathe. Yes, that's perfect."

"My dear, you shouldn't have done this at such a time," Didier says from the corner. I don't lift my eyes from his wife, but I can hear the strike of another match. "You should be with the twins. We already have so much to worry about, and now this—"

"Shut up." Hélène bares her teeth as fiercely as the dogs. "It's not like I planned for this. It's not like I planned for the girls to—oh dear dead *gods*—"

"Well, you could've held back a little longer," Didier says.

"Fuck you."

"Be quiet, Didier," I say. "This is the birth of your child."

He only shakes his head. "They're not children," he tells me. "I'm not sure what to call them, the poor things. You'll see soon enough."

Don't let that bastard patronize you. I look up at him, slumped in his chair, match burning cems away from his nose. "Are you drunk?" I hiss.

He raises an eyebrow. "Is my wife?"

Hélène contorts again, squeezing Émile's fingers. He tries to wrestle them away, but she only tightens her grip. She heaves something between a sigh and a shriek, and I bend between her legs. "Doctor, I'm dying," she pants. "I'm cold and I'm dying. This isn't like the others."

"I know," I tell her, though I don't.

"It *is* quite cold in here," Didier agrees.

I part Hélène's labia, probing the vaginal vestibule. Something dark—darker than blood—appears at my fingertips. I wipe it away, hand shaking, and tell myself the stain is nothing more than a part of her infant: a necrotized, external clump of tissue ejected before the skeleton and major organs. I know what this is, I reassure myself. I've seen it before.

Hélène cries out, and a small stream of dark liquid drips down her perineum. Her legs begin to shake, and my headache flares, icy pinpricks crawling from my temples to my eyes. Suddenly I am assailed by images—of Baker's heart, black fluid pouring from broken arterial tubing, of the lead dog crushing half-liquid arms of *Pseudomycota* in her teeth, of dark blood streaming from the twins' noses.

My sight blurs, my ears ring. When Hélène gasps, pushing herself back onto Émile, she's reduced to nothing but a dark spot between two long reddish legs. I push aside the stained labia once more and see something tucked within her tissue—it is obscured in the distended vaginal canal, but when I blink, I think I see a mass of hair-thin black filaments. Without taking my eyes from Hélène, my hand reaches behind me, groping for my bag. My breath sticks in my throat. My fingers brush something long and pointed, and I grip its handle. I am in a pained, dreamlike state, but I tell myself I am prepared for whatever Hélène pushes out of her. Whether it's a half-formed attempt at a child, or a writhing mass of *Pseudomycota,* or any other bizarre horror, I'm ready to meet it. But I'm not ready.

Hélène screams. My hair stands as she gasps, clenching every muscle in her abdomen. A minute passes, then another, then another, each as protracted as the last. And then, something crowns. A soaked tangle of black filaments, caked in vernix, bulging forward with every contraction. With a fierce groan, legs shaking, Hélène manages to expel the thing.

I am paralyzed. It's only hair, thick and curly as the twins' had been when they were born, attached to an unbroken scalp. The scalp, in turn, covers a fully formed, elongated head, free of growths, deformities, or blisters of exposed brain tissue. From there, an intact neck, wrinkling as I turn the head in my shaking hands, and from there, one shoulder—with an attached arm— then the other—another arm, or at least the upper half of one— then with a final, violent push, the rest of the baby arrives.

A round, red abdomen, from which an unkinked umbilical cord runs. Two eyes, a nose, a mouth, four limbs, five digits on each, a tiny penis. The sheer normality of the baby stuns me for a moment, and I scoot back on my heels, as breathless as the child before me.

Didier must see the look on my face, because he stands, giving me something of a pitying frown before he makes for the door. "You'll get used to them, doctor," he says.

The infant's cry stops him in his tracks. He turns slowly, and Sylvie rushes past him with a bundle of warm towels. She falls to her knees beside me and takes the infant, rubbing him down and draining his nostrils. As I clamp the umbilical cord, I cannot keep my eyes from the creature, kicking and crying vigorously as any normal child would. It is large, too large for its short gestation, red as its mother, fists clenched, toes curled.

"Is it alive?" Hélène gasps. Shaking, she lifts her head to look down the length of her sweating body at whatever horror I will present her. "What in hell's name is it?"

"A boy," I answer.

Didier's stubbled jaw falls open, his icy eyes are stuck wide. By the time he stomps back to us, his hands are trembling. "Hélène, did you really do it?"

She only closes her eyes, teeth flashing in the firelight. She does not seem to notice her husband, nor the squawking child I push at her breast. "I'm dying," she says. "Doctor, it hurts—everywhere, it hurts. I'm cold."

"You'll be all right," I say. I attempt to offer her the infant once more, and she only turns away. "You did it. Here is your child. Sylvie, will you take it—"

"Good dead gods, Hélène, you did it *now*?" Didier nearly shouts.

"We'll have to watch your bleeding," I say, and she nods, exhaling sharply. I palpate the skin below her navel, kneading the veiny, loose flesh as best I can. "You'll be all right. I'm here, you'll do fine."

"Let me see it," Didier demands. "I want to see it."

"Didier, *please*," I hiss.

To my surprise, Hélène breaks into a smile. She has her eyes shut tight, as if fighting against a strong wind. Her body heaves again, and as she delivers the placenta, she also pushes out a peal of wicked laughter. "*Now* you're interested in your children?"

"Of course I am," he says. "Damour, I was always—"

"Don't *damour* me, you piece of shit," she moans. "You don't care, you never did. You pushed me around, you did this to me! Fuck, doctor, it hurts."

"Hélène, I'm sorry, if I hurt you I didn't mean it, you know that—"

"Didier, will you *shut up*?" I bark. "Sylvie, take the man his goddamn son." She hesitates, eyes darting from Didier to his wife. Eventually she breaks, carrying the child toward her master in a grim ripple of towel and black dress.

"Somebody make it stop crying," Hélène says, rocking from side to side, eyes shut tight. "It'll drive me insane. Sylvie, make it stop crying. It's so *loud*."

The maid reaches Didier and offers the child to him. Slowly, he extends two shaking arms and takes it. "How . . ." he mutters. He looks it over. "It's ugly."

"All babies are ugly," I reply. "Now get out."

Reluctantly, he and Sylvie disappear into the hall. Émile stays, hands held captive by Hélène's.

"Doctor," she gasps. "I swear I'm dying."

"You're not bleeding much," I tell her. I begin kneading her uterus once more, rolling her flesh between my fingers. "Wait a while, we'll decide if you're dying in a few minutes."

"But I'm in so much pain—"

"I know, Hélène. It's a birth."

"I'm not worried about *that*, you goddamn fool!" she wails. "I'm not worried about a fucking birth. I'm worried about my fucking *boil*."

I glance to Émile. He offers nothing in return. "Where is it now?" I ask.

"It's behind my eyes, doctor," she says. "It's in my fucking head." She releases Émile's hands and raises her fingers to her temples, massaging firmly, smoothing and wrinkling the skin around her closed eyes.

"Lie back," I tell her. "Move your hands so I can feel it."

"You won't feel it!" she shrieks. "Fuck it, fuck Didier. Fuck you. None of you give a shit."

"Hélène . . ." As usual, I find no boil, but the pain in her voice is sharper than ever.

"Didier's never cared what I went through. All these years he's never cared." She is weeping now, through tightly closed eyes. "He and his goddamn ogre father just sit there and twiddle their thumbs as I destroy myself for them."

I wipe away the streams of her sweat with a spare towel.

"He never cared for any of us, only his little—*fuck!*" She digs the heels of her palms into her eyes, her temples, the hollows under her cheekbones. "My head, doctor, my *head*. It's right here, can't you see the damn thing?"

"I can see it," I lie. I glance over to my bag, to the many sharp tools inside, then back to Émile. He shakes his head.

"I had to be useful," she moans. "I had no choice."

"I know." Again, I stretch a hand toward my bag. "You did what you needed to."

"It hurts, the pressure is just—just get rid of it already."

"I'm going to."

"Where's Sylvie?" she demands. "Where's Sylvie? Where are my girls?"

"I can call for them," I say, gripping the bag's handle and pulling it toward me. Émile's eyes are wide, he is shaking his head forcefully now.

"Don't, oh, don't. I don't want them to see me like this—there's a horrible—"

Her face glows rubicund in the heat of the fire. She throws back her head, and a stream of blood paints a bright stripe from her nostril to her jawline. Eyes still shut, she thrashes.

"You should've taken it out," she cries, as my shaking hand descends into my bag. "Why didn't you take it out?"

With each word, blackish streaks of fluid appear along the curves of her lips. Her head rocks forward, her mouth falls open, and a half-solid globule of a bloody substance emerges, dangling on quivering strings of dark mucus.

I've seen this before.

"Émile," I whisper, though I don't know what I am supposed to ask him to do. He straightens behind Hélène, fingers tightening around her shoulders.

I grip something—forceps, a speculum, a bistoury—and pull it from my bag. I cannot take my eyes from Hélène to see what I have grabbed, and I wouldn't know what to do with it if I did. That insistent, demanding voice inside me tells me to move, to run, to cut her open, to do anything, but my limbs are not my own.

Hélène releases something between a cough and a scream, and hot droplets spatter against my cheek. Her jaw hangs open, and she howls, chokes, and howls again, tongue spasming behind bloodied teeth. In the inadequate light of the fire, I can see something move in the hollow of her pharynx, crawling across her tonsils and under her uvula. Long black appendages slither across the notches of her palate, digging into her flesh as they haul their body toward the outside world.

My mind is blank with panic, but my mouth moves without me. "Bite down!" I hear myself wheeze. "Bite down, Hélène!"

She releases a hideous moan, a low, animal thing. With a spasmodic choke she ejects the writhing, viscid mass from her throat. A dozen long appendages grasp her lips, small red beads bubbling where they pierce her skin.

"Bite down!" I shout at her, but she doesn't. Her eyes widen, glazed, staring at something beyond me, and the muscles in her face loosen. She releases a final, choked gasp, and her head falls forward, thin black appendages whipping from her slack-jawed mouth.

A fist-sized mass of *P. emilia* falls against her chest with a wet slap. It tumbles, limbs flailing, down the slope of her breast, leaving a haphazard trail of dark liquid in its wake. As Hélène collapses into Émile's arms, it squirms past her nipple and down her side, dropping from stretch-marked skin and landing with a spray of black blood onto the mat.

I do nothing. My tool slips from my fingers, and I don't bend to retrieve it. I don't call for a jar, I don't reach for the disinfectant. I don't obey the echoes of rational thought that still linger between my ears, disembodied from their hundreds of throats. Instead, there is only one voice, soaring loudly above the noise in my head: survive.

Time seems to slow as I stumble backward. My shadow, flickering like the fire behind me, falls across Hélène, across the creature that crawls beside her limp form. Black ooze drips from the mat and soaks into the threadbare carpet. For a moment, as I watch the creature's relentless march, the world blurs. The fire at my back disappears, the room disappears. Suddenly it is only the two of us. I'm thrown back into Baker's ruined home, into the mine, into the confines of a glass phial, positioned opposite *Pseudomycota* as if by some deliberate hand. We are pulled inexorably toward one another. I feel almost as if I should've known, somehow, that this would happen, that our recurrent meetings were immutable strokes of fate.

Then I see a woman, a backlit shadow, stomping her heel into the mud. I recognize the smell, the red light of the air, the familiar scrape of machines rolling in their shallow graves beneath the mud-rivers. I am back in Satgarden for a brief, blessed second. The smell of home, of trash and exhaust and soil, fills this little body of mine, and I almost fall to my knees before the silhouette in gratitude. But I can't move, I can only lock my eyes on what the woman has pinned under her heel, squirming and screaming like a tiny hinge tortured with rust.

See here, mackinita, you have to get it right in the middle, the big part of the body—Medrah twists her dark foot, boldly bare, and elicits another squeal from the creature. *Else its tail comes off and it's free to bite again.*

In the memory, I lift my foot to imitate her, and I lunge forward, heel poised. The sun throws my shadow over the itch-lizard, and though I lose sight of it, I do not lose the memory of where its body twists. With a muffled thump, I drive my heel into the Satgarden mud, into the venomous creature, into the stained carpet of Hélène's chambers.

At first *Pseudomycota* tenses, bulging out from under my foot so dramatically I half expect it to pop open like an overripe fruit. As I grind my heel into it, its little black arms wriggling and grasping at my shoe, the body gives way. My foot slams into the ground, and *Pseudomycota* bursts apart, dozen or so limbs twisting with the same aimless vehemence as a lizard's severed tail. I lift my foot and stomp again, catching the largest offshoot and smearing it across the rug in a line of thick black blood. As the creature twitches under me, I bend my leg once more, then again, then again, twisting, grinding, stomping, just like Medrah taught me, heel-first and relentless. I know she is watching me, head bobbing in approval as it always does, the smell of mud and oil and her pungent soap rolling off her olive skin.

Then she is gone. When she disappears, she takes a piece of my voice with her, wrenching a hoarse, half-coherent cry from my throat.

My foot continues to grind at the corkscrewing shreds of *Pseudomycota,* pulverizing it to a viscid smear. It isn't until I have reduced it to a slithering stain on the carpet that I allow myself to take a breath. I move my eyes from the splattered remnants of the parasite to Émile, who shudders with horror, and then to Hélène, who has ceased to move.

My heart drops. "Is she . . . she was . . ."

You didn't listen to her, I scream inwardly. You should've removed that boil.

"I couldn't find it," I whisper in my defense. My voice is raspy, tense, barely audible. "I had no reason to believe . . . I didn't . . . Oh shit. We have to tear up the carpet." I wipe the soles of my shoes against the floor, but then realize it will be easier to destroy them than try to wash away the still-living tissue of *Pseudomycota.* "Émile, douse the rug in disinfectant and throw it in the furnace. The goddamn thing is still alive."

He doesn't look at me. He leans over Hélène, carefully touching her forehead as if he has any hope of waking her. His trembling fingers leave crosshatched smudges of blood on her unmoving cheeks, over her half-open eyes, her parted lips, her jaw.

I know what we must do. I'm a heartless leech, but I know what needs to be done. "Don't touch her," I tell him.

He only clutches his mistress's face, dry-eyed and expressionless, pulling her hair away from her damp forehead. There is something almost reverent about the way he positions her corpse on the mat.

"Émile," I say. "We have to—"

My words catch in my throat when I read the question in his bottomless eyes. He is asking me what we are going to tell the twins.

"We're going to tell them the truth," I say, before I catch myself. "No, no we're not. You will say nothing. Don't let them read anything in you. They can't know, no one can know. This will only make everything worse." I swallow a lump and raise a hand to my face. When it comes away stained with Hélène's blood, a terrible shudder nearly turns my stomach. "I'll take care of Didier, I'll tell him—shit, *shit,* what about the baby? He could be . . . and I can't cut either of them apart, I can't do anything but—" I step out of my shoes and begin to pace, approaching Hélène, retreating and approaching again, nausea bubbling in my throat. The remains of *Pseudomycota* still squirm, desperate, seeking a body. It will not have mine.

"We have to get rid of her. Burn her, burn the mat, burn everything. Burn every object in this room, douse the walls in peroxide, lock the door, no, nail it shut. I want everything in here bleached or burned. Get rid of your clothes, get rid of mine, throw everything in the fucking furnace—"

Émile's stare silences me. His fingers form unintelligible words as his gaze darts from me to the fire, to the stain at my feet, then back to me. I watch a bead of sweat drip past his lips as they form a single, rounded syllable: *no.*

"What, you think we can *learn* something from this?" I growl, waving my hand at the twitching remains of *Pseudomycota.* "We can't. We can only protect ourselves from it. I don't know about you, but I intend on surviving until spring."

He shakes his head, motioning toward me, and I glance at my feet. Next to my abandoned shoes, *P. emilia* still moves, gradually shifting under the dancing shadows of the flames.

"What is it?" I whisper, but he has already covered his face with his hands. He digs his fingers into his skin, his eyes, clawing, rubbing, wiping sweat. He slumps back, hair damp, and releases a frustrated, wordless wheeze.

"Get up." I step toward him. "There's no point in sitting around here. She's dead. She's dead and the thing that killed her is already in the house. I don't know where, and I don't know in whom. All I know is that we need to hide that fact." I pull my coat tighter around me as a chill flows through the room. "So go stoke the furnace."

XVIII

"HOW DID YOU DO IT?"

Pseudomycota emilia does not answer. It only creeps up the curved glass of its container, probing. The way it curls and unfolds, undulating as boldly as an itch-lizard in mating season, makes me think that despite its mindlessness, it has somehow figured out how to gloat.

"How did you do it?" I ask again, tapping the glass. It doesn't respond to the noise, but traces the outlines of my fingerprints with its single, sightless limb. "How did you get into Hélène? Into the twins?" I pause, only half willing to whisper the final query. "Did you get into me?"

I push my palm against the jar, showing the creature my perfectly unbroken skin. "Did you slither into me at the north mine? Did you slip out of that jar and through my cervix while I slept?" I flick the glass, hoping the sound will unnerve it. It doesn't. "You're not so clever. You've made mistakes. Even you. You let your own hosts die, but you don't care. You don't even care. Disgusting."

It rolls over, ego untouched.

"How do you decide when to abandon them?" I growl. "When it gets too rough for you in there? Too dangerous, too painful? Have some fucking self-respect."

Like I do? The coward who can't live without a host body?

I turn from *Pseudomycota*, fold my hands behind my back, and begin to pace, stopping to glance at my reflection in my curved mirror. My eyes are dark, puffy, ringed in black. "Are you in there?" I ask the hair-thin limbs I can almost feel behind my retina. "Are you looking at yourself? Do you know you're looking at yourself?"

If it's there, it doesn't reply.

"Are you making me look at you? How would I know? How do I know you're not moving this body as much as I am?"

What absurd ideas you have in that head of yours, mackinita, Atiey had laughed at me, long ago.

I blink, and when I open my eyes again, I'm clutching a small lancet. It fits comfortably in my hands, but I find little comfort in it.

I grip it steadily, drawing it toward my face until the glinting blade hovers before my eye. I imagine how difficult it would be to perform this operation, and how easy. I could do it. I could cut out my eye and draw out *Pseudomycota* with a pair of sturdy forceps. I could dig around, half-blind but utterly determined to live, and tug out whatever strings of tissue I find. I could stand the pain for the sake of survival. Or I could go for my carotid artery, as Stanislas did.

The dark circles of my pupils shine in the mirror, but they reveal nothing. I watch for any sign of fear, any indication of *Pseudomycota* retreating as the scalpel approaches my cornea. The lancet is remarkably still, the grip is warm in my palm. Slowly, carefully, I rest the tip of the blade on the surface of my eye.

The sharp sting loosens my hand. I stumble from the mirror, scalpel clattering to the floor. Between the jolts of fear and pain that thunder through my mind, I can make out a cruel spark of amusement.

Did I truly think I could outwit it that way?

"No," I answer solemnly.

If I hurt myself it'll only crawl out of me, like Baker, like Hélène. It'll win.

"Or it'll die with me, like Stanislas."

Through the turbulent crash of blood in my head, I can hear myself ask why *Pseudomycota* died with him. Why it dried up with his corpse, instead of fleeing him like it did Hélène, like it did Baker. The answer is there, the obvious difference between him and the others. The difference between them and me.

I nearly laugh. I have always been a sore loser. If my cells inside my host had to die, they were sure as hell bringing *Pseudomycota* down with them.

"You deserve no better." I turn back to the parasite. "You're a low, evil little worm."

I cannot stop myself. I grab *Pseudomycota*'s airtight flask and sweep toward the fire. Barehanded, cut off completely from any other brain that can restrain me, I unlock the screen and hover over the flames. The repulsive monster squirms in its jar, springing to life as I move it toward the heat, twisting and writhing as if begging me to spare it.

Heartbeat in my ears, I kneel and painlessly place the jar into the fire.

At first nothing happens. Then, as I retreat from the hearth, the touch of flames tingling faintly on my knuckles, the creature begins to move. Its thin, almost gelatinous skin splits open in the heat, and bubbling lips of lacerations crawl along the grayish tissue. The membrane shines, dancing with light, and I cannot tell if *Pseudomycota* is dying or not.

It seems to boil, long, ugly arm curling up the side of the jar as if in desperation. As I lean in, I can see the hideous appendage split down the middle—a tiny, pinched fork runs through its length, peeling the membrane in half. The two flexible black needles of flesh paw at the heated glass, before they split in turn. The arms divide again and again, until each is so thin it is barely visible even in the brightness of the firelight.

The frenzy in my head dies down to a rhythmic, warm throb, and I reach into the fire. I know I must be burning, but as I wrap my fingers around the glass, the feeling is nothing but pleasant. I cannot take my eyes from the spectacle inside.

Pseudomycota's ends are comprised of near-transparent cilia, waving in the hot air like seaweed in the oils of the western bays. I tell my hand to stop shaking, to stop accelerating the process taking place before me, but it's far too late. The heat has been provided, the smoke has fed its instincts, and *Pseudomycota* has been agitated from its restive state.

The cilia detach. Tiny strands slither weightlessly through the air in the jar, imperceptible, ubiquitous, unstoppable.

I stand paralyzed for a second. Sudden, vivid images march through my head, tightening my hand around the glass. I see Hélène trembling on her mat, goose bumps raising every hair of her freezing skin. I see the spiral of smoke from a cigarille, a robe set aflame, a pair of burned hands. In the haze of smoke and fire in my brain, I understand. I should've seen it sooner.

I had been the first one to feed infected flesh to the fire. I can almost remember being inside the furnace, as if my cells in Stanislas's defunct brain had been alive enough to sense the smoke, the heat, the colonies of *Pseudomycota* still clinging to the perforations in his skull. I can almost feel the microscopic remnants of the parasite wriggling and splitting in the flames, borne upward by the currents of hot air, through the chimney stack and into the sky—a billion gametes, agile, small enough to creep through pores in stone and bricks, through the unsealed cracks in windows, the gossamer curtains of the château's bedrooms, the ducts and channels in the human eye.

I have infected myself, and everyone in this household.

I sink into my claw-footed chair, wondering how I could've missed it, how the huge flames in the château's hearths, the burns, the smoke, had gone unnoticed. If I had one other brain, just one, I would've known sooner, I would've seen things that had slipped me by.

Émile tried to tell me. He had insisted we not burn Hélène's body. He tried to convey what I thought I already knew, but I had been blind in my expertise. He managed to notice what I had not, guided by reason or luck or instinct. He knew the places where we should not bring fire, while I had marched ahead with the torch held high.

"Stupid," I mutter. "Unforgivably stupid. If only I had . . . if I had his . . ."

A cautious sort of hope pulls me from my chair, taking hold of me with the same grip despair had moments before. My gut twists in anxiety, or guilt, or shame, or something else entirely. I cannot name nor control the feelings that direct me now. Perhaps I've never truly understood human emotion.

I make my way to my bedroom, fall to my knees, and reach under my bed. As I pull out a wide metal box, thick with dust, the voice in my head repeats vehemently, insistently: don't.

He was the only one who didn't reach out for the fire. The only one of us who took off his jacket, who had his sweat-stained shirt buttoned only for propriety's sake, whose bare feet against the stone floors were not blue with cold, who leaned against the windows in the night for some relief from the heat. His must be the only body capable of resisting the inflammation that has taken hold of this house.

Didier will ask questions, warns that untethered part of my mind. He'll ask why his houseboy has suddenly changed. He'll make things difficult.

"The man is beside himself," I say. "He hasn't come out of his chambers, not even to see his son. He's crippled by his misery. He is no threat to me."

I lean over the box. I slide a small key into the lock, shivering with each click of metal against metal.

Don't.

"Montish bodies survive Montish diseases," I remind myself.

I can't do this. He won't take. He's too old. I'll kill him. It's evil, this is evil.

"We are beyond that now."

He'll die, and Didier will have me shot. He'll have me thrown into the night.

"He might. Better he kill me than *Pseudomycota*." I open the container and remove the smaller one inside. Another latch, another key, and I pull out the final box, lined with steel and rubber and cotton.

This is reckless. The Institute will not approve.

"I *am* the Institute!" I bark at my empty room. "I've lived five hundred years, and I'll live ten thousand more."

Slowly, carefully, I remove the tools I need. It is a set of instruments these hands have never touched, reserved only for the worst disasters, when every other weapon in my armamentarium has failed.

Everything is here, accounted for and stored meticulously by my persons in Inultus: sterile phials, a syringe, a set of curling glass pipes and absorbent beads, and a bottle of a powerful cleansing agent. At the bottom of the box, contained safely in a cylinder of soft plastic, is the last ingredient. It is a viscous, grayish sludge, trapped in layers of preservatives—even looking at myself in this state sends a pang of disgust through me. Helpless, ugly, inhuman, this cellular substance is all the things I am not.

"It will work," I assure myself.

I carry the items to my desk and begin to assemble the filtration system. I open the phial in which I sleep, slide the syringe through the layers of waxy, congealed preservatives, and extract the cells.

"I will live."

I will leave one body for another. I will escape this little thing crawling inside me, twisting around my eyes and constricting my thoughts. I will survive this winter. I will survive any way I can. *Pseudomycota* might be highly infective, but so am I.

XIX

THE DEATH OF HIS daughter-in-law does not put so much as a wrinkle in the baron's schedule. Preparations for the household's weekly supper proceed as planned. The kitchens are thick with trapped smoke, a pig is slaughtered in the southern drawing room, and I spy a servant throw a velvet mourning pall over the oak table as I pass by the dining room. The air is choked with the smells of burned meat and wheatrock, smells that disgust me but set the thing inside me to giddy activity. There is no room in the château free from smoke, free from the heat of the overstuffed hearths. Though I shudder with chills, I can see the corridors distend and contract in the waves of hot air. The house is inflamed, febrile with infection.

The halls resonate with the howls and pants of dogs and the wails of Didier's children. His son screams in the arms of a perpetually sobbing Sylvie, and his daughters are wrapped in down blankets in their room, terrified not because they have lost their mother but because they have gained her ghost. Hélène's body has since been fed to the furnace, but both the delirious, sickly twins and I can feel the invisible parts she left behind. They sense the billow of her dress and her jeweled coiffure, and I sense the long strings of infective protein and transparent membranes, borne by the currents of heat.

It is difficult for me to know what Verdira will look like come spring, but I can imagine. Several of me will descend from the train—but that's not me—and wait for Baker to arrive. Perhaps I'll wait for hours, perhaps less. I will likely spread out, sending a host to every nook and cranny of the place, clearing patches of ice and melting snow, where I'll find colonies of black tissue growing like cave grass in the open, crawling across stoves and chimneys and stores of wheatrock in the warehouses. I will find bodies preserved by the snow, mouths and eyes and ears and hearts burst open where *Pseudomycota* tore from them and into the fire. And I will find myself dead, my corpse in the same sorry state as the others. But then I will find myself alive, preserved in a resistant body, the only one who survived the onslaught.

Émile is more than eager to come to my chambers when I summon him. He steps through the doorway bearing a tray, coat unbuttoned, face flushed, eyes dry but ringed in sorrow. With snow and bodies piling up around him, with the dogs and Didier howling ceaselessly, he seems relieved to step into the relative calm of my room.

He follows me past my laboratory and into my living chambers. He sets his tray on my small table—cream, hot water, liqueur, and two mugs. As he looks around for the recipient of the second cup, I bid him sit.

"You need a break from all this," I tell him.

He bows his head.

"Just for a while," I say. "A hot drink is the least I owe you for all your work."

Reluctantly, he grasps a mug. He doesn't sit.

"Allow me." I gently pull the cup from him, and his face falls along with his arm, as if I have hurt him by depriving him of his duty. "I can just as easily pour for us. You *do* want some, don't you?"

He declines, but I pop open the liqueur anyway. "How are the girls?"

He motions that they have fallen back asleep.

"They're close to the end, then? It's such a shame. Though I suppose it's too late for regret. Far too late."

His lips tighten. His frown is troubled.

"I misread you, Émile," I say, stirring the steaming cup. "In Hélène's room. I misread what you were trying to tell me." I always do. "I was too caught up in my own assumptions. 'The idiocy of expertise,' my aunt used to call it. I apologize. I didn't understand you, at least not until recently."

He gives me a curious frown.

"Go take a look at *Pseudomycota*."

I know that vile organism is the last thing he wants to ponder right now, but he obeys. He slinks through the doorway and strides to my desk, hovering over the jar of transparent spores. I do not particularly care what he thinks about the changes *P. emilia* has undergone. I only need his eyes elsewhere for a moment.

It takes a fraction of a second. I hover over his mug, the thick alkaloid solution trembling and clinging to the end of my dropper before falling, invisible, into the fragrant liqueur. The cream hides it well, and it will only require a few sips, and a few minutes, to take effect.

When Émile returns, an unreadable expression on his face, I have his drink ready for him. He takes it in shaking hands, lifting his eyes to ask me what has happened to *Pseudomycota*.

"Airborne flagellates," I say. "I've never seen them before, but I have encountered similar methods of propagation. I suspect that is how it has spread." He covers his mouth. "You needn't worry. I do not think you are infected."

A shadow knots between his brows.

"You knew it was seeking the fire, didn't you? At the very least, you suspected. You suspected well before I did. And I was lucky enough to follow your line of thinking—hell, this is why I need more than one pair of eyes in this house." I seat myself and warm my hands against my mug. "Stay awhile, please."

He lowers himself into a chair. He glances down to the pale whorls in his drink, but he does not raise it to his lips.

"I appreciate you sitting with me," I say. "I don't want to be left alone with that thing, and you're much better company than Didier. I'd rather take my apéritifs here than watch him drink himself to death in the salon. It's the weeping that gets to me."

I raise my cup to my mouth, but Émile does not follow my example.

"Have a sip. It'll warm you." It hasn't warmed me.

A bead of sweat drips down his forehead, but finally, he drinks. The small bump of his throat rises and falls, and I release a short sigh. It should be an expression of relief, but it only tightens my chest and sends my heart racing.

I desperately want to tell him to stop, to throw the mug on the ground and run, but I can't.

"It's good, isn't it?" I say. "Almost enough to take your mind off . . . well, everything."

He folds his hands again and stares deeply at them, as if trying to read something written in the tiny creases of his knuckles.

"Do you not like it?" I ask, and to my relief, he takes another cautious sip. When he lowers the cup, his eyes meet mine, and he asks me a question I cannot answer. I hesitate, trying to parse out the meaning of his look.

"What?"

He stares at me, then past me, pushing away from the table. He circumambulates the room, returning to me when he has a pen and paper in hand. He sits, inserts the pen into his mouth, and chews thoughtfully. He lowers it to the paper, withdraws it, then lowers it once more. He composes his query, pen circling in neat little flourishes, and pushes the paper in my direction.

What is your name?

The question shouldn't torture me, it shouldn't tighten my throat with a muffled cry, but it does. I provide him with the only answer I have: "Service before self."

His face darkens, like I've disappointed him. Maybe he was expecting me to make an exception for him. Boys always think they're the one exception, Medrah had told me long ago.

He stares at his hands, then picks up the pen. *How did you know about Hélène and Didier?*

"Know what?"

You knew he never held her hand.

I smile as best I can. There is no escaping Émile's keen ears. At least I'll be able to use them soon. "The Institute is concerned with details like that. You know, the health of body and mind is dependent on every aspect of one's personal life. It's all there, catalogued in the library in Inultus."

It is not entirely a lie, and it is apparently convincing enough for him. He asks, with a few twitches of his nose, if we have a file on him as well.

"Of course we do. Yours is equally detailed. Every little thing we know about you is in there."

He seems unnerved by the information. He lifts his liqueur to his mouth and sips once more. That should do it.

Don't do this, I beg myself.

"Say, Émile," I start. "What would you think if I told you I wanted to invite you to the Institute? You're quite old for a matriculate, but we can make an exception for you."

Don't toy with him.

His eyebrows furrow, his lower lip disappears into his mouth, and I can tell his interest is not feigned. He knows as well as anyone how firm a hold the château has on its residents, how short the baron keeps his leashes. Like every other servant, he has fantasized about escape. There is no one in Verdira who hasn't.

Don't do this.

I don't want to. I'll be no better than that thing in the jar. But I have to.

"It's a wonderful thing, you know, being part of a larger whole. I think you might like it." Disgusting—"It's freeing, in a way. And you'll finally get to leave Verdira. We'll send you somewhere warm. Somewhere where you can go outside and not have to worry about getting chopped to pieces by ventigeaux."

He does not mirror my smile, but the edges of his mouth twitch. I would not expect an easy grin from him, though he is trying his best.

"I will warn you, it's a demanding profession. You'll never come back here, and you'll lose your name."

He reaches for his pen again. *This is just the one Priest gave me.*

"And isn't it important to you?" my mouth asks him, without me. Inside my head I can feel scratching and squirming, as if *Pseudomycota* has realized I am going to abandon it inside this doomed body and leap for another one.

He shrugs. *I was named after a rat that lived in the church basement.*

I laugh. "Then it's not much to lose, is it?" It is, by all the dead gods it is—I desperately want to tell him that. "Not much to lose at all, and much to gain for both of us."

Something of a bewildered frown crosses his face. His hand relaxes, slipping from the mug to the table.

"What I do is similar, I'd say, to your work here. Caring for people like the baron, people for whom you don't necessarily harbor much affection. You're used to it."

He looks confused. His hand flexes slightly at the table's edge, and his black eyes stare somewhere beyond me.

"And what a pair of eyes," I mutter. "A good, quick mind. There really was no other option. This is the only way either of us will live."

His head tilts back, and he stares at the ceiling, as if searching for something on which to focus, to use as an anchor to the solid, sensible world. They do this often, though usually at this point they're on their backs, secured, disrobed, and sanitized.

Émile loses his rigidity. His arms swing limp to his sides, and he slumps, head balanced on the crest rail of his chair. His eyes have stopped moving, glazed under half-closed lids, and his mouth hangs open, lips stained from his final sips of liqueur.

I spend a few moments watching the slow rises and falls of his chest, making sure his core has not succumbed to the same paralysis as his periphery. All appears normal, so I grab him about the wrists and drag him from the chair.

I know his eyes still function, I know his brain still whirs away inside his dangling head, but I do not have to worry about what he might see or recall. He will not remember the heels of his leather shoes dragging across the stone, and will certainly not remember the shaking, sweating effort of my small body as I throw him clumsily onto my bed. He will either remember nothing of this incident, nothing of his entire life, or he will take what he remembers into the furnace.

Stop. Don't do this.

It's too late. I am monstrous, I am repellant, but I will live.

I adjust his torso, grab his ankles, and lift his legs onto the mattress. I place his head gently on my pillow and pin his arms to his sides, arranging him as comfortably as possible. I wipe away the sweat that has congealed on his forehead and lift his lids to examine his eyes, the black pools of his pupils, the tiny red vessels, the ducts that are dark and hard where others' would be pink and wet. He has an unusual optic system—not the most significant of his bodily abnormalities—but I can detect no sign of *Pseudomycota*. It is my luck, and his loss, that he has always been so healthy.

When the paralytic wears off, he will struggle. They always struggle, though to different degrees. Sometimes the extent of their resistance is a small moan or a single kick, and sometimes bodies nearly break free of their restraints. I don't have leather straps at my disposal as I do in Inultus, so I will have to make do with belts, curtain ropes, and bedsheets. My slapdash restraints must be secure enough to ensure a flailing body will not harm itself or fall from the bed, but crude enough that the same body can easily free itself upon waking.

I've killed him. He'll die. He's gonna fucking die.

He won't die. He would not do something like that to me. He is sensible, and he knows me. He might, under duress, even confess to liking me. He would not resist me, at least not so much that the fury of his rejection would drive his body to shut down. He is too smart to make me complicit in his death, too kind to force me to explain to a horrified Didier why his corpse is tucked neatly in my bed. He knows better.

Slowly, I reach down and pull open his collar. A rope of muscle in his neck twitches—likely the strongest fight he can muster under these circumstances. It quickens my pulse to think how those will soon be my muscles moving, my breath churning in that voiceless throat. My fingers tremble, making the buttons difficult, but eventually I manage to loosen his shirt and pull it open.

I freeze when I see his twitching torso. As his physician, I know there are several unusual components to his anatomy, but this is an unexpected sight. He is perfectly ordinary in the curves of his muscles, the striped furrows of his ribs, his two grayish nipples, and, my ultimate goal, a small deposit of fat below his concave navel. But there is something terribly wrong with his skin.

His collarbones are bruised with ruptured capillaries. Rings of discoloration are scattered on his axillae and waist. A strange injury crawls across his shoulder, and as I wrestle him from his shirt, I see it is a curved pattern of raised, flushed skin. He draws in a pained breath as I push him to his side and run my finger across it, around his deltoid, down his scapulae to the knots of his spine. The burns are not severe, but they are complex and extensive, tapering in intricate loops and dotted with the distinct shapes of an extinct leaf: a facsimile of the household's ubiquitous fire screen. From neck to belt there is hardly a cem of skin untouched, and between long serpents of erythema lie the whitish echoes of older injuries, variations of the same pattern.

He has not been seeking the fire like the rest of us. If I am correct, and I must be, there is no reason he should be burned as we are. These marks are accidental, or not of his own doing. As I gently touch a raised scar, I realize I will never know. Émile will be gone by this evening, and he will take his knowledge of these injuries with him. The best I can do is make sure they do not happen again. I must take care of my bodies.

I leave him supine, push myself away from the bed, and return with the syringe. Carefully, with the gravity of any crucial procedure, I kneel at his side and disinfect his skin for insertion. When I am ready, I pause, taking in his face one last time, allowing him a few final moments to exist as himself. Then, after steadying my hands, I pinch a bit of his scarce abdominal fat between my fingers. I slide the needle under his skin, reaching a thumb to the top of my syringe and slowly depositing its contents into him. He does not move, he does not protest. His eyes are fixed on the ceiling.

I stand and gently rub the site of the injection, encouraging my cells to hurry. I can't wait to see myself again, to hear myself again, as only I can.

I belt the body's arms to its sides. I pull my sheet over the limp, pale torso, tucking its edges firmly beneath the mattress. For good measure, I tie a few of my blankets together and loop them about the body's waist, securing it tightly to the bed. When I am satisfied no amount of tossing and turning will dislodge it, I retreat, unwilling to watch the spectacle. I am lucky this one has no voice. Usually within the first few minutes they begin to cry out.

By the time the body starts to struggle, I am already fastening my waistcoat and securing my cravat. I stare at myself for a moment in the mirror, taking in my dark, tired eyes, my twitching lips and freckled cheekbones, my overgrown, unkempt hair. When I have everything buttoned and tied, I dust off my jacket and lock my room behind me. The bell for supper rings just as I enter the corridor, and I realize, with a small pang of guilt, that I have forgotten to bid Émile a proper farewell.

XX

ONLY DIDIER, THE BARON, and myself sit at the table tonight. The twins are tucked away with their metal bed warmers, and the newest addition to the family, thus far nameless, is firmly attached to a bottle of pig's milk somewhere in the maids' quarters.

The baron is content for once, his smile magnified by the shattered glass of the broken chandelier, which some enterprising servant has decided to repurpose into a centerpiece. Opposite him, disheveled and pale, sways his son. It appears half the gin in the salon has come with him to supper, and I wouldn't be surprised if it ends the night on the dining room floor.

The silence seems invincible, but the baron, in his decrepit strength, manages to break it. "Congratulations, Didier," he says. "I heard it was a boy."

Didier leans over the foul steam of his wheatrock soup, threatening to collapse into it. Somehow, he manages to lift his head and shoot his father a dark look.

"You should be happier," the baron says, shoving a gargantuan spoonful into his mouth. "You're a new father all over again. First son, that's a landmark."

"Don't start," Didier says tonelessly. "Not tonight."

The baron does not appear to hear him. "What do our darling twins think of him? Where *are* the twins? They should be here with us. I imagine they have all sorts of insane suggestions for a name."

"They're not coming." Didier is barely audible—though perhaps it's because I have begun to hear the heavy silence of my room, where my second pair of ears is rapidly falling under my control.

"Not *coming*? This is a time to celebrate, and you're letting them sulk in their room?"

"Pèren, stop."

"Go fetch them! They're your children—you can't just let them walk all over you like you let your wife."

"*Stop.*"

"Oh, are you *upset*?" The baron leans forward, lips pulled back over gray teeth, grin multiplied in the glass centerpiece. "You've got a new son. You've finally rid yourself of the wife you never wanted. Everything is going right for you—there's just no pleasing you."

Something dances before my eyes, a flicker of movement. It floats above the table, vague and diffuse, like the ectoplasmic orbs the twins see wandering the halls at night.

"Don't act like it's my fault," Didier says. "I was only ever good to her. Gentle with her—I was better to her than she ever was to me."

The light thickens. The candle flames pulsate with each of Didier's words, growing and shrinking and writhing. I can't take my eyes off them.

"And what good that did her!" the baron laughs. "It shouldn't be too hard to find you another woman. Hopefully the next will survive longer than your previous ones."

"Stop." Didier's voice is a distant echo. I twitch my ears—only two, so far.

"To be honest, we should've replaced Hélène long ago. Dead gods know *you* wanted to."

"Pèren—"

"But I had faith in her. I knew she would pull through for us and at least give us a boy."

"Will you *shut up*?"

The words arrive in my ears at several octaves, at several ages, angry and disappointed and soft and joyful. When I look at Didier's face, it changes—his spectacles shimmer in and out of existence, his beard disappears and regrows, falling from his angular jaw and corkscrewing back. I'm seeing a dozen pictures of him overlaid and blurred with a watery brush, like the ancient palimpsests Atiey used to study.

"She always said it was your fault," the baron says. "That all you gave her was disdain. And she struggled so hard to mold it into something living. Sad, really."

"Pèren, if you don't stop talking, I swear to all the good dead gods I'll—"

"You'll *what*?" the baron chuckles. His voice, too, is distorted.

When Didier stands, he leaves a trail of his own image behind. "I'll . . . I'll cut your tongue out."

The hoot of the baron's laughter shakes the air so violently even Didier trembles.

Look at that, Medrah breathes inside my head, *and tell me madness ain't a passed-down thing.*

It's environmental, Atiey replies.

Something is wrong, I interject, trying to wrestle my thoughts back into my possession. Something is going very wrong with Émile.

"I mean it." Didier lifts a hand to his forehead, and all I can see is its softness, the gentleness with which that hand had once stroked my hair, my cheeks, how it opened to offer me a stone, a congealment of wheatrock so old and pressurized it had cleared to a faultless emerald. It belonged to the baroness once.

"Sit back down, you little coward," the baron says, mouth blurring into a pink-gray smear.

I see dogs in the light. Dozens of them, mouths opening in heartwarming smiles, pink tongues licking at the burns on my shoulders as sincerely as they would clean the wounds of their pups. I see their eyes and noses, black as black can be, a tail wag-ging on a struggling white rump as I push the lead dog through the kennel's window, well before the doctor can arrive to kill her. I see Baker's cabin, his shed, his unguarded stores of volatile com-pounds, handfuls of which are easy to slip into my pocket. I see a large hand reaching to pull me close, to wrap around my elbow and hold me against the hot screen of the roaring hearth. Asking if it feels nice, if I am finally warm, if I like it. Of course I like it. I had to. If I didn't, I'd work up the guts to speak aloud.

"You enjoy this, don't you?" Didier growls. "You enjoy watch-ing everything fall apart. Everything I've held together for you, everything I've worked for."

His hand moves to the knife beside his plate. And suddenly it's not his hand but Old Doc's—no, he no longer called himself Old Doc or médsaine, but Stanislas. It is a spotted, swarthy hand, usu-ally strong and steady, but when it picks up the lancet, it shivers as violently as the mines in a magnetic storm.

"Everything you have, you have because I've given it to you," the baron says.

"Everything I have, I've *earned*. You stole my future, pèren, you stole everything from us. And now it's my money—my work— that keeps that repulsive cadaver of yours breathing."

"Watch yourself, Didier."

"I'm the only one stopping this cursed place from crumbling to ruin, despite your best efforts."

"For fuck's sake." The baron's eyes are locked on his son's fist. "Don't threaten me with that, you ingrate. You don't have the fucking backbone. Sit, or I'll have the constable come in here and shoot your knees out from under you."

Didier laughs. "Go ahead, if you want holes in your ceiling."

"Then I'll do it myself."

"You wouldn't."

I can't, Stanislas had told me, gnarled hands shaking over the black rings of his eyes. *It hurts too much. I'm so cold, I'm so goddamn cold and I can't get warm again. The fire frightens me.* The chill of a metal handle meets my palms. *If you're not going to*

*push me into the flames, then do this for me. You know what to
do. Right here, on the neck, here.*

I shake my head vigorously, raising my hands to my temples
and gritting my teeth.

"Oh, doctor?" All the versions of the baron blend into one gaping, monolithic mouth, gray-toothed and throwing strings of spit-
tle. "Do you have something to say? Do you have some vital input
to contribute to this conversation?"

Émile must be dying. I don't understand. I've had thousands of
potential hosts die at this pivotal moment, and none has suffered
like this. And they sure as hell haven't fucked with my head like
this. "No," I moan.

"Good," the baron replies. "Now sit down, Didier. Your meal
is getting cold."

His son remains standing, knife trembling in his hand. "You
killed Hélène," he says. "If you hadn't forced us to marry, she'd be
alive right now."

I'm sick. I'm guilty. I want to die.

"Well, I wasn't the one squirting all those monsters into her,
was I?" the baron barks. "If you want to blame anyone, blame
the doctor over there, rocking and groaning like an animal. If
you had any brains in you, you wouldn't have let a quack like that
anywhere near your wife."

I've let it control me for too long. Stanislas's wrinkled eyes are
red with tears. *I'm so cold, Émile. I can't get this ice out of my
head. I've tried everything, everything short of burning. Don't
make me do this to myself.*

"Sit, Didier," the baron growls. "Now. Or I'll make sure you
stay seated for the rest of your life."

I do. I regret it, but I make Stanislas do it to himself. As the
scalpel twists in his hand, I reach out to stop it, but the doctor
is quicker than an old man should be. The metal reflects a thousand images in the firelight, of myself, of the twins, of Hélène in
my lap, blood pooling under her, the sheen on her eyes reflecting
the creature that killed her, slithering toward the heat of the fireplace, before the trembling doctor lifts a foot and grinds it into the

carpet—and when the scalpel meets Stanislas's throat, as blood pours bright from the wound, I back up against the wall, voiceless gasps tearing at my throat.

Didier sits, finally.

I nearly fall from my chair in relief. I have never suffered such aggressive resistance, I have never been so overwhelmed by a new body. I have never had a mind burrow into me as ardently as I burrow into it.

I heave a sigh when my second pair of eyes scans my bedroom ceiling. I lift my head, a formless pain wriggling down my spine as I gain control of it. My shoulders rise, my toes twitch, and an intense warmth washes over me. I can't stand this sudden heat, these damp sheets, the suffocating air roaring from the fireplace. With sweaty, shaking hands, I begin to tug at the belts holding me.

Just as I manage to escape my bed, just as the last echoes of this body's memories leave me, just as Stanislas fades from view and his final words dissipate—*don't trust anyone without a name*—my body in the dining room and the one in my bedroom each gasp, and something breaks inside me.

My fists clench—all four of them—but as I stare down at my arms in my bedroom, the burned, bruised, trembling things, they move of their own accord. They grasp for a handhold, feeling their way along the stone walls of my chamber. The air turns sour in my new lungs, and my throat constricts. Voicelessly, painfully, my second body releases a breath so intense it might, in any other throat, have been a scream.

"Doctor, what the hell are you doing?"

The baron's voice tears me from my chambers and into the dining room. I shut my eyes again, trying to see from my other pair. I move my arms, groping for the bedroom around me, but all I can feel are these two hands here, clenched around the edge of the table.

"What is wrong with you?" the baron almost laughs, as I struggle to my feet.

"I have to . . ." I start. The world blurs and refocuses, and my stomach migrates to my throat. "I have to—"

"Do *what*?" the baron asks. "What sordid activity could you possibly need to do at the moment? The second course isn't even here yet."

I close my eyes again, wondering where my other body has gone. I try to see from its eyes, but my sight is mired in endless black. It's a miracle I remain standing.

Here come another one, Medrah says. *Get her ready.*

"Doctor, sit back down."

I see a streak of movement at the entrance to the dining hall. A figure appears under the curved arch, a blur of bare skin, of dangling clothes, of hurt and horror. Émile pauses at the doorway, mouth hanging open, wet hair plastered to his forehead above two black circles, wide and clear and certainly not mine. When our eyes meet, we paralyze one another.

Disembodied, we stare for an excruciating second, not quite ourselves and not quite each other. Then his eyes move, slightly, to my right. For a moment I can see what he sees: an archway of shadow on the other end of the dining room, an escape into the upper corridor, and from there, the freedom of the outside world. He steps forward, gleaming with sweat, and I can't bring myself to intercept him, to reach out a hand and call his name.

"What the hell are you doing?"

I don't know if it's Didier's voice or the baron's, but Émile doesn't seem to hear it. He sprints past the table, leaving a trail of light behind him.

Anger sweeps through me, sudden and unwelcome. It's my body that the little bastard has commandeered, my body that is sweating and suffering, my body that will die if it escapes into the winter night.

It's not my body. Neither of these are my bodies, I'm just a fucking leech—

"Stop him!" I wheeze, shaking against the table.

Breath heaving, cheeks rubicund with drink, Didier manages to do what I can't. He rushes from his chair and catches Émile, burned hands clutching burned skin. "Are you mad?" he barks. "Running about half-dressed—have you gone *mad*?"

Panicked and drenched in sweat, Émile gasps, and I squeeze my own lungs in effort. He struggles, pain shooting from his arms to mine, and he throws his weight forward, attempting, and failing, to escape Didier.

"What in hell's name do you think you're doing?" The baron's voice flies from a distant place: smoother, younger, without the incessant wheeze of his machines.

"Quickly!" Didier growls, wrestling with my rebellious second host. "He's gone insane. Doctor, help me!"

He falls onto Émile, onto me. One of my bodies collapses across the table while the other is thrown against the stone wall. Didier's fingers push into its shoulders, wrapping around its arms, squeezing its—my burns. When he touches me, while his hands tear at my raw skin, an agonizing dread rushes through me—both of me. A terrible guilt boils my gut, and I know that I have done this to myself; that I have given a look, given a nod, given acquiescence when I did not mean to; that I am at fault.

I think I see faces. Priest's face, hiding under the darkness of his robe, bringing his flock out of the light. I can see him burning the notes I have written, earnestly imploring whatever gods are left, in elegant letters, to *make Didier die*. I see the twins' grinning faces as I hand them the small explosives I have fashioned from pilfered materials, disguised as fetishes to be hidden in the cobwebby nooks of the manor. I see my own face, black-eyed, pulling my hair over the bruise Didier has given, mouth forming silent words in a Montish dialect I am not supposed to know: *th'montegn indoremt say révilray*.

Émile's lips move, but my voice emerges, spilling from the body hunched over the table, decisive and damning: "Don't touch me."

I raise two of my four hands and shove Didier from me, one fist striking his shoulder, the other his stomach. The burst of movement spends every ounce of strength I have left, and Émile escapes my hold as violently as he escapes Didier's. I collapse, thousands of bursts of light obstructing my vision, and my second body flees from me.

Émile tries again for the door. I can barely move, barely register the heat that flares through every cell as Didier springs forward, enraged.

"How *dare* you?" he shouts. His arm latches onto Émile again, squeezing the both of us. With each firm twist of his hands, the burning pain rises and falls, until it recedes into a sharp, phantom tingling.

"Stop!"

I am exhausted. I cannot fight any longer. When Didier wraps his arms around my shoulders, forcing me across the hall, I cannot feel them.

"What is *wrong* with you?" His blurred aura leaves a ghostly wake behind. "What has—did the doctor do this to you?"

The smell of mud, metallic Satgarden mud, permeates a part of me that is not my nose. *Out of all the smells in the world, your brain chooses mud,* Atiey chuckles. A feeling comes over me that I have not felt for the past ten or so years. I haven't kept count, since there hasn't been much space to keep count, not with every neuron firing and firing again and sending messages halfway across the habitable world—

"She's hurt you." Didier drags my second body toward the heat of the hallway, past the wary gendarmes, toward the fire. My heart falls, my breath comes ragged and tortured. I know where he's going, I know where he's dragging me, I know what he wants. "She's sick, you stay away from her. Come here—*come*!"

Both my bodies have gone blind. The smell of Satgarden mud is thick in my nostrils, the lights of a spinning propeller turn my vision to bright, painful pinpricks.

"They're sick. They're all fucking sick. We can't let them infect us." The genuine concern in Didier's voice infuriates me. He is fleeing down the corridor with my host, whispering in ears that should be mine. "Don't you dare—come here. Don't you ever run from me."

For a moment I'm in so much pain I realize why Stanislas killed himself.

"Do you hear me?"

I do. I want to tell Émile that I heard what he heard, that I saw what he saw. I want to tell him that I didn't mean to hurt him, I didn't mean for it to happen this way, what I did to him was for the good of both of us. But I can't open my mouth. I blink furiously, trying to banish the blurred sway of two glowing bodies, but they linger, each movement imprinted in my retinas, painfully bright like the afterglow of a pitiless sun. A tremor erupts in my head, familiar and terrifying. A sharp spasm crawls over me, spreading from my neck to my shoulders, forcing its rigid electricity into every part of me.

"I'll keep you safe. I'd die without you."

There is nothing that can halt the progress of this episode. I know, as a physician, and as a patient. I have been in this place before. I know what is happening, but I don't know why. I have fixed this. I *fixed* this—

Hold tight, mackinita, Medrah commands, and I do.

XXI

"Congratulations, doctor."

I can't tell if it's the baron's voice or the nauseating stench that brings me back. I lift my head, eyes throbbing with blurry light, waiting for the world to reassemble itself. Every muscle is sore, every synapse shudders with the tired confusion of overwork. My mind stretches itself awake, torturously puts all its parts back into place, tries to figure out how many minutes have passed and what my body might've done without me in the meantime. Twitching, talking, moving around, like I sometimes do. Or like I did before the Institute rearranged my brain.

Eventually, the pulsing lights clear, and the silhouette of the baron comes into view, haloed in tubes and wires. When he shifts I can make out two shining eyes, two rows of gray teeth spreading in a wide grin. No doubt this has been one of the more interesting dinners in his collection.

"You're the first one to make it to dessert."

He lifts his arms as a servant sets a small plate before him. A hideous green lump sits upon it, hard and smooth and oozing a sharp malodor.

As I rise from the black tablecloth, exhausted, my sight places all its lost components back into their proper order. The swirling colors begin to clear, and the object sitting before the baron fades into view.

"The thing about raw wheatrock is," he says, smile shining with saliva, "you have to heat up the knife before you can cut it." He beckons the servant, who produces a long utensil, blade glowing red. The touch of hot metal does not disturb either of them; the baron takes the knife and lowers it to the lump of wheatrock. "But once you do, it's exquisite."

The metal sinks into the soft stone, and a putrid smell forces a gag from my throat. The lingering haze from my syncope intensifies, and I feel as if I am falling in every direction at once. The world beats around me like a drum, and for a moment I fear descending into another fit. A swirl of brightness flits before me, transparent strands of *Pseudomycota*'s spores twisting in the air. I remember, suddenly, that I will not live through winter.

"I need to find Émile," I manage to groan. Wherever he is, he is not freezing like I am, he is not trapped in a haze of sickness. His body will survive this, and I need it. "I need . . ."

"You know," the baron says, "it surprises me the Institute would send an epileptic up here to care for me. The body of medicine must always be healthy, I thought. What happens when doctors get sick? I've heard they just disappear."

"I . . . don't . . ."

"Of course, I'll be telling the Institute about your ill health," he continues. "And I expect to exchange you for someone more competent." He lifts his fork, wheatrock deformed and slumped with heat. "But that is a problem for spring. Now, eat. The theater for tonight is over, so you might as well enjoy your dessert."

Though it turns my stomach, I can't keep my eyes from that lump of wheatrock. Strings of saliva dangle from the baron's thin lips, a bluish tongue curls behind gray teeth, but he doesn't bite down. The bubbling green blur droops over the sides of his fork, and something sharper than a shadow creeps from his mouth.

I sit petrified as a threesome of tendrils, thick as earthworms, emerge from between his lips. They probe the wheatrock with pointed, shining ends, curving, feeling, tasting. With the properest delicacy, they lift the stone from the fork and sweep it into the baron's mouth. His lips close around it, his jowls shudder in pleasure, and in one effortful spasm, he swallows.

My head swims, my throat itches to vomit. I have to escape this smell, escape the sight of the baron summoning another fresh-heated knife for his second bite.

"I need to go." It's all I can say. I push myself upright, grasping the wall for purchase, and make for the corridor. The baron doesn't stop me.

I stumble across the dining hall, aimless, enveloped in a dream-like fog. I can't stop my mouth from muttering Émile's name, trying to summon him to me, to bring a picture of him to my mind where there are only shadows, darknesses from a past that is not mine. Montish hymns vibrate through my head, stories jerk and sputter around my skull, echoing in Priest's voice. The sensation of burns crawls across my shoulders and back, and though I can't see through those black eyes, an echo of their sight still lingers in mine, showing me where to go.

The halls of the manor bend and curve like the vessels of a living thing, currents of air flowing from one fire-stoked room to the next, carrying the sounds of the baron's laughter, the baby's screams, the howls of caged dogs. The inhabitants of the mansion pass me by, the gendarmes, the maids, the ghosts, but I stumble onward, pushing through the thick haze. I follow the trail of memories Émile has left me, filled with scentless incendiaries etched with prayerful runes, tucked into the shadows of corridors and chambers and offices.

I cannot tell how long I swim through the arteries of the manor. There is no light from the windows to guide my way, no suggestion of dawn. It could just as easily be noon as midnight, it could just as easily be this year as the next. I could just as easily be dead as alive.

It's all I deserve, for what I've done. For succumbing to the Institute, for letting myself believe they could fix me when they couldn't, for letting myself believe I needed to be fixed at all. For giving myself over, for destroying thousands to keep myself alive, for wriggling through them like the little parasite I am, for trying to do the same to Émile.

No. I've done nothing wrong. I've only done what any other animal would do in my position.

But I'm not even an animal. I'm not even that. I'm lower than that, sucking one host dry and jumping to another when it suits me. Thankless, like a flea, less than a flea—a mindless disease, that's all I've ever been. I deserve to be devoured. I deserve to have *Pseudomycota*'s tendrils tear me apart, to fall to one of my own kind.

I will not. I will not waste five hundred years of adaptation, of sacrifice, of learning, of becoming human. I will not let these invasive thoughts turn to self-destruction. I will not let them cloud my resolve the same way my sight is shrouded in blinding, oppressive light.

Shit. I'm so tired. I'm so tired of fighting. Both of me, all of me.

"Where you going, doc?"

The smell of a cigarille and a face I can't stand to look at. Never liked looking eye to eye with authority, just like Atiey. "Upstairs. Study."

"Not allowed," the constable says. "Didier can't have you carrying your disease up there."

"I'm his doctor." My mouth moves like an atrophied limb. I barely know what I'm saying. "I'm his fucking doctor. If anyone can save him from infection, it's me."

"Compelling," the constable's mouth laughs. "But you need to go. Turn around."

I do. Numb, vertiginous, lost, I move away from the constable, smearing his hideous face back into the firelight.

A hundred emotions pull at me, memories and thoughts that shouldn't be mine—Didier's lips opening over mine, Priest's kind smile, the starlings back home, Satgarden, a gargantuan dog's nose tumbling from the sky. An old dumbwaiter that the twins showed me, long ago. It will be filled with fire soon, but for now it is big enough for this body, this weak, dying body, the last straggler of my teeming hosts. I pull myself through its hatch, ignoring the bags of flammable powder beneath my feet, and enter the walls of the château.

I reemerge into Didier's suites, pulling myself into an abandoned drawing room, powdered with decades of dust. I slip out into a murky hall, carefully following a memory that is not my own. One hand on my head, the other clutching the wall, I stumble down the narrow corridor.

I'm so cold, and I'm burning alive.

I turn again. I am at the bottom of a spiral stairwell, windows glowing with noonday darkness and midnight light, smoothed and dimmed by thick snow clouds. It is a staircase I have ascended many times before, but it is still strange, foreign to me. I don't know where this staircase will lead, and I know too well.

I climb it anyway. It is my body up there, and I will die without it.

The spiral stretches for miles. Outside the window, I can see the fire, the wind of a ventigeau, the teeth of Atiey's smile. *Pseudomycota* pounds against my skull, each limb a tiny fist sending a freezing ache from my eyes to my ears and back. By the time I reach the upper corridor and arrive at the door to Didier's study, I'm nearly blind with pain.

But I still see him. Through the haze, through my exhausted dizziness, I see his broad, bare back, the straining muscles that have held up what is left of this creaking château for years. I see the sweat rolling down his scapulae, the mounds of his spine, the crests of his undulating pelvis. He is hunched over the fireplace, breath heavy, and Émile is beneath him.

I cannot speak. I cannot move. I do not know if this image is a conjuration of a dying mind, a terrible memory, a nightmare, but every moment I stare, the figures become clearer, ringed in halos of firelight, pushing, withdrawing, and pushing again. Slowly, with an agonizing horror, I realize that I am seeing a wound, one I should've smelled festering for decades, opening once more, infecting Émile, infecting me.

Heat sears the shapes of a long-extinct leaf into my back—or what should be my back. One of my legs is lifted, one arm pinned to the fire screen, and I can almost feel his fingers cupping my coccyx, grasping at the base of a hairless tail. I can hear his breath in Émile's ear as clearly as if it were my own, echoing through the seasons, the years, reassuring me that I'm safe, I'm with him, I'm so warm, we'll finally be warm now. And through his words, I feel his desolation. I know he's trying to bury himself as desperately, as violently inside Émile as I had, with needle in hand, hours before. He thrusts us both against the fire, seeking the heat, seeking a body that does not belong to him; it is mine, it is my only chance of survival—

Then I see my own eyes, Émile's eyes, black as night. He does not seem surprised to find me here. Shoved against the screen of the hearth, hips tilted, he only stares at me from over Didier's shoulder. A sheen clouds his gaze, not with terror, not with agony, but debilitating, chronic resignation. He doesn't struggle, he doesn't cry out, because there is no point. He is limp, blank with acceptance of the inevitable. He is outside of his body, just like I've been for years and horrifying years.

I recognize his look. It is one I have seen on a thousand faces of a thousand unlucky children the moment the paralytic sets in, when they realize that their skins are no longer their own. It is the look I gave the Institute when they lifted me to the table, when they slid the needle into me. I can still feel the straps around my limbs, the pinch of metal, the last moment when my lungs, voice, eyes, hands, were my own. I can still feel the heated, pressurized lump where a foreign body invaded me, crawling up through my useless, helpless limbs. All I could do was cry for Medrah, for Atiey. All I could do was bite my lip until it bled and hope for it to end.

And now, finally, it will. As my sight narrows to a long, thin tunnel, beginning with me and ending at Émile, I know that we are mountains waking. I know I am not the Institute. I know that no matter what it tried to do to me, I am still, somehow, myself.

I shout. I can't control the words that are thrust from my mouth, or feel the shapes my lips are making. But Didier hears me. He tenses, a final shudder running through him, and he withdraws. He turns to me as Émile sinks onto the hearthstones.

"You," he croaks, horrified. "What are you doing here?"

I manage a painful step forward. My ears ring. Tears film over my eyes, blinded by the candles, the fireplace, Émile's radiating burns. I don't know if I'm more enraged at Didier or the Institute, but I cannot stop myself. I don't know why I would want to, after all these years of helplessness. So I let myself go.

I grope at the desk beside me, looking for a penknife, a bottle of ink, anything to cut or bludgeon him. My eyes do not leave him, swaying toward me, his mouth moving prolifically but silently, drowned by the panicked heartbeat in my ears. I do not need to hear him. I know that he's insisting that this is not him, this is not as it seems.

He shuffles toward me, skin glistening, chest heaving. His eyes are bright, furious, alive with movement. Serpentine bulges wriggle under the thin skin of his lids, curling and slithering as he blinks. Dark liquid pools at his ducts, then streams down his cheeks. His eyelids ripple, and shadows curl out from underneath them, long and thin and black like a second set of lashes. They sway in the billowing heat, unnoticed by their host, twisting along his cheeks, probing, dripping thin strings of dark mucus onto his bare collarbones, then retreating back into the safety of his orbit.

"Doctor, what the hell are you doing?"

One ice-blue eye is turned out, an orbital muscle pulled taut or snapped by the appendages of *Pseudomycota*. The other is on me, glinting, irate.

My hand finds its way to an object and grasps—some utensil or paperweight, hard, heavy. With every ounce of strength left, I throw the thing at him. It blurs through the hazy air, soaring over his shoulder and into the fire screen behind him, rattling the metal with such force it nearly shakes Émile back upright. I reach over the desk again, searching for something else to throw, but he gets to me before I can.

"What the *fuck* do you think you're doing?"

Right as I grasp the handle of a penknife, Didier lunges, raising a fist. I am on the ground. Blinding white pain pulsates from my cheekbone, radiating across my eye and into my ear. I am too aware of the mechanisms of damage—the pressure of vessels bursting, the chemicals that sear the webs of nerves across my face. I raise my arms, trying to deflect his hands, but he grabs my wrists and flings them aside.

He pins me, a knee on either side of my waist, and hits me again. Another flare of pain, then another, and I find myself slipping back into the early days, when Medrah first taught me to fight back. Blind, mad as an itch-lizard and twice as eager to bite, I drive my hand forward, penknife first—dead gods, what a fucking feeling to move my own limbs, after all these years—and Didier's arm meets mine. Through the narrow tunnels of my vision, I can see his face, speckled with the glistening arms of *Pseudomycota*. As his mouth falls open, dry lips cracking and splitting with black blood, a mass of whiplike appendages crawls from it, flinging toward me. I want to scream, I want to struggle and writhe and panic, but I know this is my only opportunity.

Dormant instinct rips through every muscle, a familiar growl rises in my throat. Pushing myself up to one elbow, I plant my feet and thrust him off-balance, as I've thrown many of my shrieking friends and snarling enemies into the Satgarden mud. Just as he flails outward, a hint of movement behind him catches my eye—a blur of hair, pinkish in the firelight, a streak of metal cutting through air. Before I can cry out, something small and dark collides with the side of Didier's head. His body stills, his face slackens, the thin black limbs still writhing inside his open mouth. A rivulet of blood drips from his ear and down his neck, rolling over the little hill of his clavicle. He stares at me for a moment, one eye rapidly dilating, then turns his head on his half-limp neck. Fragments of exposed skull shine white above his ear, ringed by a cavern of torn skin and curled hair. The bleeding is copious, and fast-flowing. It doesn't take hundreds of years of clinical practice to know the outcome of an injury like that.

Didier falls to the ground, and a pool of red expands swiftly under his temple. Long, thin tendrils wriggle from his eyes, his nose, his still-twitching lips. Behind him looms Émile, one shaking arm wrapped around his naked middle, the other clutching an iron fire poker. When he steps toward me, tail swaying, I know he's going to strike me next. The momentum of all the cold, passionless anger in his eyes will drive that poker into my skull, eliminating me at the source. Worse yet, I know I deserve it.

I lift my arms and cover my head, scooting backward, begging, wishing that I could give back all the bodies I have taken, all the lives I have stolen. Voices swirl inside my skull, some I know, some I don't, each from a different invisible mouth, trying to pull my only mind a hundred directions at once. But I can't move from this spot. I can't crawl to the door. I can't cry for help.

I don't know if Émile is going to kill me, if he's going to break my bones or poke out my eyes. Before he does, I want to tell him that I understand him, I know him, I was him. I know what he wrote on all those prayer slips he gave to the illiterate Priest. I know all the things he's done and all the things that have been done to him. I want to tell him I know what chemicals he's stolen from Baker and where he's hidden them. I want to tell him I'm sorry, that it wasn't me who slid that needle into him, it was something else, a festering wound inside me, in my bones, in my mind. But then I would sound no better than Didier.

"What the *fuck*!"

Blurred, oblique, rippling as if through a veil of water, a figure appears in the doorway. I can't see his face, but I know he's looking at Didier, crumpled and bleeding on the study floor. The snout of his rifle moves toward me, then Émile, then back to me.

"What did you do, you little cunts?" he growls.

The poker slips out of Émile's hand and clatters to the floor. He stills, tense, as I struggle to my knees.

"Don't move!" the constable shouts. "Stay down there!"

Somehow, my mouth escapes me. "No."

There is pain, there is horror, and there is joy, so much joy, at regaining my voice, at feeling every muscle in my face coordinate so subtly, so fully. At being myself again. At knowing my name again.

"I said *don't move*!"

I move. I lift myself, feeling every creak of my vertebrae, reveling in every stinging pain that crawls through my skin.

"Don't you dare! First shot is a warning. Next is in your head."

I raise my hands to touch my own body for the first time in many years, and the constable raises his gun.

"I'm telling you," he hisses.

Then, there is a whistle.

It is high-pitched, mechanical, shrieking louder than the wind. It's a sound that, weeks ago, I would've welcomed as a savior. Now, as it shakes through the study, it wrings my heart. It echoes louder and closer than any train could be, rippling the expanding pool of Didier's blood, rattling the windows, traveling up my spine and triggering a surge of terror. They're here, they've heard my calls for help. I have to run.

I pivot toward the door, and my shoulder erupts in pain. The echo of a gunshot rings through the room, and I stumble to one knee, a bright, thick stain spreading through my shirt. I raise a shaking hand to the injury, cupping the blood, feeling the warmth. As the world sways, it takes every ounce of my being to keep from laughing, from weeping, from falling to the ground and celebrating the sudden influx of pain, of terror, of feeling.

Truly, only the constable could fire a warning shot and miss.

XXII

I KNEW FOR A long time that Medrah and Atiey weren't sisters. That wasn't just because they were two different colors—siblings with the wild genes of Inultus sometimes come out as chromatically diverse as a litter of kittens. It was because they didn't act like sisters. They didn't fight like sisters are supposed to, and they sure as hell didn't kiss like sisters are supposed to.

The lie had come out half-formed, Medrah told me, one morning in the early days, when the governor's men had cornered them in a sweep for palace defectors. No, no, no, Medrah had attested, Atiey was homegrown Satgarden stock—a lifelong mud-rat, a cousin, a sister even. Born in that shack just behind the collection of tangled rotors, right over there. The gunmen did not seem to notice the way Atiey carried herself, the way she held her head high like she did not expect to lose it at any moment, the way her feet shifted on the unsteady mud. What began as a lie became a joke, and what became a joke sweetened to an endearing honorific.

I loved Atiey. She knew how to read and write, and her brain was filled with all sorts of facts and theories that would keep me up at night beneath the windowsill. She was part of my life since before I could remember. The story goes she'd come to Satgarden from the shiniest parts of Inultus to discover machinery, and instead discovered Medrah. So she moved her books and scrolls and tools and wires into our shack and continued her studies, mostly of flight, though I told her plenty of times the machines in Satgarden couldn't fly. She said she was interested in keeping it that way.

Atiey's thesis was going to change the world. She let me in on all the ways she was going to stop the governor's construction of that monstrous hot-air balloon, as she called it. Of course, all the while, I was collecting bits and pieces of old machinery to give to his polished henchman from the palace. Atiey hid whenever he came around, but in evening, when the metallic roars of Satgarden quieted to a low rumble, she'd come out with a little gun in her pocket, just in case, and show me the starlings.

We'd watch them for hours, swooping in murmurations, a thousand bodies churning in a unified cloud of night-lit feathers. Nobody knows how they act as one when they've got so many brains between them, she told me. But we found out, once.

She'd always end there, smirking, telling me to wait for her to publish. I'd always say I couldn't read anyway so there was no point.

"Let's just say that's where things went really bad for us," she'd continue. "Back when we could fly. When we thought what we built could save us from everything else we built. In the end, what we built won."

I never figured out what she meant. Half of what she said eluded my developing brain, and the other half, I'm pretty sure, were jokes. But she was always serious when she told me that ruin was ingrained in everything we made, waiting to get out. It was ingrained in the branches of our railroad, in the computers that devoured the world's knowledge and then rusted to death, and in the bones of the Satgarden machines, who, bereft of human commands for thousands of years, still discharged sprays of bullets and neurotoxins. Even asleep, even dead, they were set in their ways.

The day of the accident, I was exploring a hollow hunk of metal in the mud-river—a fallen ship, though of course at the time I couldn't know it was a ship. I also couldn't know how closely the dual curls of the craft's engines resembled a dog's nose, since I'd never seen a dog. All I knew was that the governor's shiny-shoed lackey had come down from his labs and offered a Satgarden fortune for whatever promising junk we brought him that day. Atiey told me never to take his offers, but great evil mackinae, I couldn't eat itch-lizard every day. I was a growing girl.

The ship rose from the mud-river at dawn. It was nestled under an arc of concrete halfway to the outskirts, hidden from other scavengers under a protective canopy of warped propellers and sheets of metal. The discovery was just one more in my long streak of good luck. I'd found some crystal panel the day before, and the day before that, a wide length of rubber I gave to the Interprovincial Medical Institute's clinic in exchange for a piece of crystalized licorice.

I remember spirals, two large spirals framing what must've been exhaust tunnels, like the ships in the illustrations Atiey showed me. It was there that I was sure I was going to find the best trinkets, the most valuable metals, so I crawled inside. When I reached the heart of the machine, I didn't have time to examine the bizarre collection of things around me. I grabbed a few tubes of plastic and a promising-looking disk, and got out of there before the mud-river swallowed it again.

It was, in fact, the rumbling of the ship descending that dislodged a piece of a rotor fossilized in the concrete arch above me—or that's what the foragers who found me told me afterward.

I don't remember much. Only a shriek of metal, a sudden, blinding pain in my skull above my ear, and the stomach-turning smell of wheatrock lingering thick in my nose.

It's mostly the pain that tells me I'm awake. It throbs from my shoulder outward, moving up my neck and culminating in a burning ache behind my eye. It blows through the clouds of Satgarden, drying the mud-rivers to dust and pushing me firmly back into my broken body. Slowly, the room comes into view.

I'm in my bed, supine. There's a familiar smell in the air, of aerosol disinfectant, of soap and plastic and fresh bandages. The fires are lit. The air is unbearably warm. Bodies shuffle around me, moving silently, coordinated like the ghostly legs of a giant spider. One of them pauses, a smear in the shadows, and floats to my bedside.

The blurred lines resolve into a gray-coated doctor, tall, pie-bald, probably once male. Behind the mask and glass goggles I can see a face I've recognized in the mirror many times—a face that my brain, at the command of the cells inhabiting my occipital lobe, had learned to think of as one of its own. I'm almost surprised I still recognize it. Somehow, the neural networks built by my disease, that pestilent Institute, have become my own.

"How . . ." I croak. Snippets of images return to me. The glint of a rifle, a thin tail swaying, a man motionless on the floor, black tendrils slithering from his mouth and eyes. I feel sick. "Where's . . . Émile?"

I shake—no—the Institute shakes its head, in that invincible, practiced way. "He survives, despite the baron's insistence that he should not."

"What's gonna . . ." When I try to turn my head, a dizzying pain foams in my skull. "What's gonna happen . . ."

"Please, not too fast," the doctor says. This one has always had a hoarse, soothing voice, easy to obey. "I must remember to rise slowly. Enough damage has been done to this body already."

I can see my image reflected in the greenish lenses of the doctor's goggles. I'm mostly bandages; the left half of my aching face is wrapped thoroughly, from my forehead down to my blood-stained shoulder. My one working eye is caked in mucus, and when I attempt a slow and painful blink, I can still make out an afterglow of my own shape, an echo of what the Institute sees. I shudder, thinking that maybe not every one of those little cells inside me is gone.

"The train . . ." I mutter. When I reach up to massage my head, the physician gently catches my wrist.

"The train will not arrive for another six weeks, at the earliest." The Institute pauses. I can sense a smile behind its mask. "So I took to the sky instead. Remember?"

My aching brain tries to parse the words, pierced with the echo of an otherworldly whistle. I recall the rattling of Didier's office, the lights blinking outside the window. "What . . . how? The airship?"

"We lost thirty-seven workers before it was airworthy, but urgency necessitated it." Its mask shifts, and I think it's frowning. "The aeronauts managed to dock on the eastern wing. Only a few rooms away from where I found this body."

I take a deep breath. I want to ask the Institute how it got that engine running. I want to ask how it managed to divert the governor's costliest resources just so it could fly to Verdira. I want to tell it I didn't mean it, that all the summoning and calls for help weren't me, only a desperate plea from a parasite on the verge of realizing its time in my body had ended.

"I was lucky to arrive when I did," the doctor continues. "Well before exsanguination. Still . . . I am not pleased with the state of this body. Worse, the constable tells me he is justified in harming it. He claims Émile and I tried to kill Didier." It pauses, no doubt searching for a reaction. "I am afraid I have no recollection of the incident."

I turn away. If the Institute expects me to fill it in, it'll be standing here till the next armageddon.

"I should remember, and I cannot . . ." The doctor closes its eyes for a moment, and I know it's trying to see through mine.

"Stop that," I say. I've endured enough of its invasions. Seeing through me, speaking through me, manipulating my limbs and organs to live, to satisfy its curiosities, to destroy its competitors and care for its allies.

"I can still feel it, slightly," the Institute murmurs. "But I cannot . . . I cannot see through . . ."

A body from the next room, hunched over the microscope, speaks up. "I cannot move those arms, either."

"Strange," the first physician says. "This one is no longer me."

"No," I say, voice shaking as badly as the rest of me. I push up on my elbow, pain shooting through my opposite shoulder. "No, it's not."

I can form the words of my own will, and that reassures me of their truth. Still, when I blink, the room disappears from my view only to reappear in another—blurry, colorless, weak. My body is too close to those with which I once shared that terrible disease. I can almost feel their cells reaching out for mine, eager to reinfect. I dread to think a part of me still belongs to the Institute.

"It was never you," I mutter, too softly for it to hear. "Not truly."

"It is worrying how little information I have been able to glean." The Institute's troubled, magnified eyes turn to itself, to introspect, to watch another body rifle through the mess I've made of its lab. "I have spoken with the baron, and the constable. I have read my notes, but still . . . I cannot truly say what has happened to me. It appears to me as if I had gone insane."

The doctor glances at me. When I don't give it what it wants, it leans back and strokes its chin, and another voice speaks up, this time from a body next to the bookshelf. "I recall an incident in the wheatrock mine. *Pseudomycota* had proliferated at the site of the autumn's collapse. It was likely something the earth overturned."

"Likely," I mutter. Every piece of land you see, Atiey told me a long time ago, is scar tissue. The world is diseased and inflamed, eternally breaking and healing.

"I know I returned safely to the château," the physician nearest me continues. "I do not remember much of the excursion to the north mine, though that is not unexpected, given its distance and depth."

"And the mountains' active geological and electrical activity," the other body puts in. "Upon my return my thoughts were quite troubling—or at least the thoughts I could make out. At the time I had surmised my communication difficulties were the result of a storm between the city and Verdira."

"But now you know better," I say.

"Now I know *Pseudomycota* is to blame." The piebald doctor pauses, looking me over. "The last thing I remember is an escaped sled dog. I lost coherence after that."

Maybe it's still not coherent enough to realize we're all swimming in a particulate mist of *Pseudomycota*. But given the sheer pungency of the room, I doubt the Institute left any surface unsprayed or any gust of air unfiltered. It's got a mask on every mouth and glass over every eye. It must've figured out something.

A knot of dread ties up my gut. "What do you know?" I ask.

"I know the wheatrock mine is the source of the pathogen. I know this body, possibly through my own neglect, managed to contract it."

The one at the microscope clears its throat. "As did much of Verdira, I suspect."

"And I know that I attempted and failed to propagate myself inside Émile," finishes the first. "Clearly I thought I would survive in him when I could not survive in this body."

My stomach turns so violently I can feel it in my throbbing shoulder. Almost worse than the memory of me lingering over Émile with a needle is the image of a dozen Institute bodies doing the same. They're going to pull him apart. They're going to pull him apart looking for the reason I targeted him. "Let me see him," I groan. "I need to see him."

"He is in a delicate state at the moment," the Institute replies. "And I cannot allow this body to leave my room. Surely I must— you must understand. The baron is quite adamant that you both be killed. As it is, this body and Émile's are the only ones I suspect are still uninfected. And this one, only because . . . well, let us say I—you were lucky to have me on your side, suppressing the organism before it spread from your eye. The others are not so lucky."

"Lucky?" I begin, but the physician reaches up to retrieve a small, sealed phial from one of its passing hands.

"You survived," it says, "though I am not sure I did." It closes its small fingers over the glass and leans forward. "You are no doubt surprised by the severity of your injuries."

"Should I be?" I ask. "Gunshot to the . . ." I try to turn my head, but I am too sore to discern the specifics of my wound. "Repeated . . . blunt trauma to the left eye . . . well . . . half my face."

"Ah, yes, you will have to forgive me," the Institute says.

Shit. I recognize that tone of apology. "For what?"

"I took the liberty of excising the infected tissue." It opens its hand and reveals a tangle of *Pseudomycota*, suspended in saline. Each twitching appendage branches over a strip of torn muscle, wrapping like a loose-fingered hand around a veiny, collapsed balloon of ocular tissue. The yellowish sclera fades into a ring of cloudy brown iris, freckled with dark spots.

It's my eye, all right.

I shudder. Not in disgust, not even in surprise—of course I knew that *Pseudomycota* was nestling there, and of course I knew the Institute would remove it, if it could. What shakes me is the physicality, the irreversibility of this moment. After nearly ten years, the full weight of my expropriated, mutilated body is finally pressing down on me. That's my eye, and I'll never see from it again. I had just gotten it back, too.

I reach out a hand and take the phial. The Institute seems charmed by the gesture, and lets me examine my eye and its parasitic attachment.

"A body needs only one to see, after all," the piebald man says. "And I am quite good at adjusting to such acquired defects." When it reaches for the phial, some odd instinct makes me pull it to my chest. The Institute does not seem to care. "Compared to the size of *Pseudomycota* specimens I have been collecting recently, it looks like I did a remarkable job of quelling the organism's growth. I suspect many infections disseminate, moving to the paranasal sinuses, the lungs, or the atria of the heart. I managed to keep mine—yours— localized, though I would guess it was not the pleasantest feeling to have that battle take place in your head."

"No," I mutter. "Felt like my brain was splitting apart."

"I am pleased this body is recovering. I have invested too much into it to hand it over to a hostile parasite."

I roll the glass in my hands, looking into the misshapen oval of my clouded iris. "You want it back."

"That is a conversation best saved for another time. Whether or not this host is best reintegrated or discarded is a debate that is taking place in the city."

I close my remaining eye. "It doesn't matter. *Pseudomycota*'s already killed you."

The physician touches my elbow. I can guess the look it's wearing: genuine, solicitous, irritating. "What makes you say that?"

"It's in the air," I mutter. "Spores, or gametes, or larvae. Probably slithered into your eyes the moment you stepped off the ship."

There is a pause from the Institute. I open my eye and glance at it, hoping to see any sign of surprise or defeat behind that impenetrable mask. Instead, it turns to glance at itself, and stands. "I know."

My heart sinks.

"It is likely that at least some parts of me have contracted *Pseudomycota* by now, but that is the advantage of having many bodies. There is not much that can be done for the rest of the household, or for the town, unfortunately . . ." The piebald doctor pauses to exchange some piece of information with a faraway host. "But I will lend aid if it is needed, until *Pseudomycota* is destroyed. Some patients are faring remarkably well. But others . . ." It pauses, listening to itself. "Yes. Perhaps."

"Perhaps what?" I ask, though I know the Institute is not speaking to me.

"Once mature, exposure to a sufficient heat source may impel the colony to abandon the host," it says. "Or extreme stress—" The piebald physician disappears through the doorway, chasing that particular brain's train of thought. Another takes its place, a mind unoccupied with thoughts of *Pseudomycota* and free to deal with me.

"Lie back," it tells me. It is a young body, perhaps younger than mine. Its eyes are round and beautiful, even behind glass. "Lie back and open this mouth, please."

I can tell the Institute is unused to talking to one of its own parts as it would a patient. "Please," I say. "Let me go."

"I apologize. I cannot." A gloved hand squeezes my cheeks, forcing my mouth open, and I know better than to protest. I only clutch my eye to my chest and grimace at the sour taste of a familiar medicine. "It is regrettable, but you know the steps I must take to ensure my survival."

I do. I know far too much about that.

"And so you should know I am planning to live for many centuries yet, even if I must dispense of some bodies in the meantime." The doctor closes my mouth for me, since it's already gone numb. "I only ask that you do not make it necessary for me to include this one among them."

All the fragments of my life are here in this bright dream. Bits and pieces of the Institute, of Satgarden, Atiey, Medrah, the other children. Even the governor's man with his polished shoes.

"It's too late, mackinita," Atiey tells me sadly. "Nothing's going to fix you. Except for them, maybe. They'll get rid of that lightning in your head and make you better." A staunch naturalist, she's always had faith in those scholarly types. "My cousin had a cousin once who could hardly walk. No balance and no strength, but sharp as a lizard's tooth. Institute took him in and fixed him up—he's been spotted working in Misulah."

"And he don't remember nothing of what they did to him," Medrah answers. "And nothing of his own family. Dunno, mimor, there's something odd about those medicos. Something very weird with 'em."

She's not wrong. We've all seen them from afar, seen the way they never need to look at each other, the way they move and speak, all the same, all with that insufferable pretense, the unplaceable accent.

I ask Medrah if they're going to open my head, if they're going to crack my skull and see what's short-circuited inside of me. If they'll keep me quarantined in a cell like the dogs in the château's kennels, sliding food under the door between experimental surgeries.

"Maybe," Atiey says, before Medrah can reply. "They're going to want to find out what happened to you, mackinita. Why you're the way you are now. You're a curious thing to them."

"And she act like she don't care!" Medrah half laughs. "Swear to goddamn mud, your atiey's got no moral compass. Or if she do, it sure as hell don't point north."

Atiey laughs with her, and they fall back together, clutching one another in the bubbling mud-river. I reach after them, lose my balance, and tumble into the tarry foam. Breath held, heavy, I sink through the black mud, until the river twists into a whirlpool. It condenses into a perfect circle, shining with stripes of oil and water, and retreats from my outstretched arm. At its edge twitches a length of skin, dappled with pores and wiry hairs. Something closes over the disk, a wrinkled lid, and I realize that I am staring into a gargantuan black eye, so dark I cannot tell where the iris ends and the pupil begins.

Hands that are both mine and not mine remove the magnifying lens and return with a collection of swabs. They dab at the filmy sclera, the hard tear duct, gently inverting the lids and scraping the conjunctiva. The eye twitches, paralyzed, pried open, as the sampled tissue is withdrawn. Two gloved hands plate the oil and skin and hair under the spotlight of a microscope, observing, prodding, discarding, and then returning to their captive eye for more. In the sharp, bright circle of the microscope's light I watch the transparent slivers of *Pseudomycota*'s progeny, squirming and wriggling, trying to escape some invisible force that shreds their membranes into ribbons.

I sit up in bed, gazing at the clock, but the dream goes on. In the glow of the lamp the long neck of a dropper shines, clutched in gloved hands. As it lowers to the eye a sphere of liquid grows on its tip, trembling, filled with the shadows of a slithering, swimming parasite. The black pupil twitches, and its owner tries to blink, tries to turn his face, but the Institute's hands hold him in place, lowering the diluted sample of *Pseudomycota*. When the sphere of liquid falls from the dropper and hits Émile's eye, I do not wake up. I realize I have been awake for hours now.

XXIII

THE INSTITUTE WON'T TELL me what medicines it's forcing into me. It's not hard to guess, given my near decade of practice and the memories of thousands of brains before mine, but I'm not gonna let the physicians in on that. I know what happens to non-Institute bodies who know a little too much about medicine.

The tincture is for the injuries in my head, they tell me. For the contusions and burst vessels in my cheek, for the complete enucleation of my eye, for any remnants of *Pseudomycota*, for the electrified lesion the Satgarden shrapnel left in my brain. Whatever it is, it helps with the pain. It doesn't help with the mild, vestigial delocalization.

When I close my eyes and make this drugged brain concentrate I see the hazy movements of what once were my other bodies. I feel light dancing along a dozen different retinas, vibrations running across hair cells, aromatics churning in nostrils. It is as if my neuroanatomy is still deformed in the shape of the Institute, imprinted with millions of microscopic dimples where its cells used to reside, each empty recess desperate to recapture the sensations of its nearby kindred. Maybe some fragment of the Institute survived the battle with *Pseudomycota* and still lives inside me, too weak to transmit signals but strong enough to receive them. Maybe the more potent medicines are spinning hallucinations in my mind. At this point I cannot afford to pinpoint the etiology of the images— only to hope that they will help me.

I see the twins, lying head-to-head, patches of blood-matted hair scattered on the pillow around them. They are ghostly pale, unmoving, faces framed in fine black tendrils, either their own or *Pseudomycota*'s. A pair of gloved hands pulls a dark sheet over them, and an itch in my nose tells me one of the Institute's bodies is allergic to a nearby cat.

In another room, the baby lies under a lamp, a cluster of hosts hunched over him. His little body is a blur, red like his mother's and completely motionless, drugged or sleeping or dead. There are a dozen voices talking at once, expressing thoughts I can't make out, proposing mechanisms and discussing the complications of a fetus gestating in the same body as *Pseudomycota*. Several debate the mechanisms of placental infection, several more juggle flasks and lancets and scissors. One can't stop humming to itself. I remember that one. There was always a song stuck in its head, though it was never able to identify it.

I lose the images when the shadow of a gray coat catches my eye. One of the Institute, my piebald acquaintance, has locked gazes with me through the doorway to the lab. For a moment I fear that it has caught me spying on it, that it can see hazily through my eyes like I can see through its, but it doesn't seem suspicious, it doesn't move to interrogate me. It only lingers at the doorway for a moment, examining me from afar. I recognize that look.

My fists clench under my sheets, sending a spark of pain all the way to my shoulder. Just seeing its pretentious face sends a fire through me. Or it could just be this unbearable heat.

In Didier's chambers, the Institute is reassuring the baron that once the investigation and containment of this outbreak is completed, he is quite free to execute Émile. "That *fucker*," the baron replies, unassuaged, shadows of thin appendages whipping behind his teeth. "That little dogshit. I should've had him slaughtered with the rest of the cave vermin. Should've slit his throat—and that bitch doctor of yours."

The piebald physician comes to sit beside me, attentive, curious. The Institute will always have time for a fascinating specimen like me.

"Are you sure you are well enough to speak?" it asks, kindly. "I will get you more—"

"What are you doing?" I demand. "Tell me what you're doing over there."

"Readying an assay." It pauses, contemplating some invisible thing floating above our heads. I can almost hear the voiceless chatter in the air. "Yes, it is rather crude. I will fly some samples back later."

"Samples of what?"

"Saliva, skin, blood, gastric acid. Some ocular tissue, yes." It cocks its head, listening for a voice I can't hear. "Isolating an antibody, enzyme—some defensive mechanism—something that must be particular to the Montish. And to a lesser degree, I suspect, their dogs."

"Shit." I pull my aching head from the pillow. "You're vivisecting him. You're gonna kill Émile."

"Of course not." The physician gives me a curious look. "At least not yet. I may not need to move further than his eyes. There is certainly something unique about them. His bulbar conjunctiva are a hostile environment for this particular pathogen. And since it is the portal of entry for *Pseudomycota*—"

"You tried to give it to him." The image of the slithering strands of *Pseudomycota*'s larvae rears in my mind. "You gave it to him, didn't you?"

"I suspect I did not succeed." The Institute turns its head again, caught up in its own thoughts. "Yes, perhaps the same qualities that make him resistant to *Pseudomycota* grant some resistance to me. And other pathogens, considering his overall health. I will need more—"

"Let me see him," I say. "I need to see him." Truthfully, I already can, at the edge of a doctor's vision. He is resting his tortured eyes, blood snaking through a plastic cannula. Like the twins and the baby, he's not moving, but I know him better than to think he's given up. He's probably planning his escape as much as I am. He's been planning his escape for many months now. "Let him go," I say. "He's been through enough."

The Institute seems puzzled. It must not know what truly happened in Didier's study. Or worse, it knows, and it knows better than to do anything about it. "You have a surprising amount of inquiries about him. Do you think you bear some responsibility for his well-being? Is it because this body was the one who attempted and failed to integrate him?"

My foggy mind clears for a moment. In a way, I suppose the Institute is onto something. I feel responsible for him because I know him better than anyone else, and I know him better than anyone else because the Institute had used my body to infect him. But the less the bastards know about that, the better. "He deserves to know what's happening to him," I say. "And why. You can't just march here and experiment on the household without telling them—"

"You called for me to do so," the physician reminds me.

"I didn't do anything!" I croak. "I *couldn't* do anything, not while you were in me, fucking everything up."

"Not while I was . . ." I can almost hear its fingers typing up a storm in the city, composing its first case study of this disconcerting new phenomenon. "Tell me, how long have you been lingering there, inside that brain?"

I almost laugh. "What do you mean? You think I was just sitting here, folded up and preserved and waiting to get unpacked? I don't live inside my brain. It's not some tool for me to use, like it is to you. I *am* my brain."

The Institute only dips its head, like I used to—like it used to do with my head, when it didn't quite understand. I sit for a moment, watching it think.

"D'you know why Stanislas killed himself?" I ask.

This seems to pique its interest. "I killed my body because it was in unbearable pain."

"That did help. But it wasn't why he did it. He did it because he knew what you did to him. He realized . . ."

I can't explain it. I can't explain how something in Stanislas's brain snapped back into place, how the revisitation of a single, potent pathway triggered a resurgence of memory, of habit, of figures of speech. I can't describe how it spread, how the same cells shifted into slightly different orientations, how hints and instincts and diverted conduits traced a picture of a brain remembering itself from the base of its oldest structures to the peaks of its intricate consciousness.

I settle for the short version. "He realized what you did to him. He realized every time he moved his arms, it wasn't really him. Every word he spoke, every thought that passed through his head, they weren't his. He remembered who he was, and he knew you'd taken his whole fucking life from him. He'd been helpless for decades and he couldn't stand the thought."

The Institute raises an eyebrow. "He had been colonized by plenty of other organisms before me. Many of which influence behavior and cognition."

"That's why you'll never understand. You know how to live in a body, but not how to *be* one. And you sure as hell don't know what it's like to have that body taken from you." My empty socket begins to ache, like my missing eye is attempting to tear up. "Ten years. For Stanislas, fifty. It's a kind of paralysis you'll never know. Watching yourself go through these motions, day after day, like a dream. Thinking thoughts you never wanted to, saying things you never thought you would."

"I . . ." It pauses for a moment. It raises a hand to its ear and pinches the lobe, probably a childhood habit it hasn't fully excised from its host. "I have . . . never encountered this phenomenon before. I am truly sorry for any unnecessary pain it has caused."

Unnecessary hits my ears like a mallet. I know too much about what the Institute considers needless and needful harm. I have seen its painful cures to worse ailments, its maggots and cauterization and culling.

"I assure you," it continues, "my habitation of human bodies is necessary. I am an intelligence, like you. I cannot exist without a mind to think. Who would I be? Where else would I go?"

"Extinct," I snap. "Just like you should be. Like every one of you should be. You and *Pseudomycota* and everything else that fell from the sky."

It looks at me like I'm mad. "I know you are in pain," it replies, "but your hostility is unwarranted. Clearly you are suffering. I will fetch something to calm your nerves." The doctor stands, since there are no nearby bodies to retrieve anything on its behalf.

"I don't need my nerves calmed," I say, but the host turns from me and retreats to the shelf where it keeps its bottles and syringes. "I need to go. I need to leave. I need to go home."

It returns to my bedside with a needle in hand and reaches for my elbow. "You will. When this is all over."

As the warm, heavy fluid fills my veins, the world slips from me. I want to struggle, but I know better. I know too much about medicine to think I'm ready to fight off this particular infection. As soon as I have time to rest, as soon as I can walk again, I will break free from these fucking parasites.

Suddenly, passionately, I want to hurt the Institute. "You're not much different from *Pseudomycota*, you know," my mouth croaks.

Don't, Atiey warns from a decade ago, after she had escaped the governor's palace for good, but before the naturalist collective took her in. *Don't let anyone in on how much you know. That upper hand will be the one that saves you.*

"I am afraid I do not understand what you mean," the doctor says gently. I can feel its other ears listening in.

"You read your notebooks, you know what you saw," I reply. My one functional eyelid droops. "*Pseudomycota* has it out for you. You saw what it did to your blood. You remember it coming for you in the mine."

"I read about it, yes," the Institute replies.

"You're two parts of the same thing." A cloud hovers over my head now, muffling my hearing. "Two mistakes of the same kind."

"It is nothing like me," the Institute says. "It behaves nothing like me, it looks nothing like me."

"As different as a bacterium and the phage that lyses it."

A long pause from the doctor. "Are you suggesting that *Pseudomycota* is my phage?"

"Yours, and probably others like you," I mutter. "Others who didn't make it this far. Who didn't survive the crash when they fell back down."

"What on Earth is putting such ideas into this head?" it grumbles. "I had thought it was somewhat of a sensible one."

"It does make sense, when you think about it," I grunt. The world has blurred to a darkened haze. "*Pseudomycota* got you out of my body. When nothing else could, it fought against you, and won. It cured me."

The last thing I see is a look of distress crossing the doctor's features. Horror, offense, disbelief. I smile. It's the kind of look that can make me rest easy.

I don't know if Émile can hear me, or if he ever will. I don't know if we'll ever share the same mind again, ever see from the same eyes. I reach out to him anyway.

Hold on for a little while longer, I tell him. Just until I heal a bit more. I'll come find you. I know the room you're kept in, I know the hallways, I know the locks. I'll get you out. Live through this. You've survived so much already, you'll survive whatever those leeches have in store for you.

It's too late to worry about the twins, or the baby. It's too late to save anyone but ourselves. Give up on Didier and the baron. Forget about what you think they deserve. I'm your only chance, and you're mine.

I'll come for you right before dawn. We'll go down to the kennels, where you've hidden your jackets and skis, your food and brandy, and prepare ourselves for winter. If we're quiet, and lucky, we might even have enough time to ready a dogsled. We'll be out by sunrise, and there will be no need for you to set your fires. We'll leave those incendiaries you've hidden in the walls, quiet and unlit. I'll get us past the eyes of the Institute. I'll use the scars they left inside me to blind them to our movements. We'll get out. We'll go south. We'll find my parents, we'll find help. We'll find a place for us, safe from the Institute.

I know you must hate me, hate the parasite that lived inside me, for what we tried to do to you. For the way we invaded and stole from you. I wish I could offer you repentance, retribution. I wish I could give the world back to the folk healers, the hymn-singers and midwives. I wish I could build a bonfire in the middle of the Institute's library, piling up all its books and journals, and throw *Pseudomycota* into the flames. I wish I could watch the transparent gametes slither into every one of its eyes and rip its bodies free the same way it did for me. But I can't.

All I can do is try to escape them. And I will try. I swear on my mother's true name, and my aunt's false one, on every evil fucking mackina in Satgarden, I will try my fucking best.

I can't save everyone, but I can save us. Maybe.

Didier lies on his bed, empty blue gaze locked on the ceiling. Tiny strands of *Pseudomycota*, half-dead, slither at the rims of his eyelids. His bandages are a blur of white and red, and his chest rises and falls with the breath of an external ventilator, likely one of his father's spares. The drone of machinery is only interrupted by the anguished voice of the baron.

"Fuck all of you, that's my *son*. He's the only one I've got. And with my grandchildren all—"

The Institute doesn't appear to be listening to him. Or, at least, nine out of the ten ears in Didier's room aren't listening. Instead, they're engaged with a soft-spoken engineer who has just informed them that several of the dirigible's main parts have frozen solid. Nobody's flying back to the city anytime soon, he insists. Especially not Didier, in his condition.

"We could repair them, or bring in replacements," the aeronaut says. "But only when things thaw."

The baron removes his handkerchief from his face and sprays the nearest physician with mucus. "What kind of wretched incompetents are you? It's your fault he's like this. You sent me a dud, a *butcher*. A broken fucking product. And you can't even clean up her messes, you can't even stitch a man's head back together!"

"It is a complex wound," the one nearest him answers. "It requires delicate surgical techniques and machinery we do not have here—"

"I'll not let this go unpunished," the baron snaps. "Your higher-ups will know about this. I'll have every one of you killed. Every one of you will pay for this."

"Daylight's barely bright enough to do maintenance work," the engineer continues. "Not long enough. We can chip away at things but they just freeze over again within a few hours."

There's a chatter of dispute going on between the Institute's heads, but I can't decipher any of it. I can't tell if it's thinking about wintering over, about leaving and letting Verdira rot, or if it'll incinerate an entire region to destroy a single pathogen. If Atiey is right, and she usually is, there must be some weaponry on that airship outside. Every machine that flies ultimately flies to kill, she always told me, whether its builders intended it to or not.

"You're the second host I've lost to *Pseudomycota*," a doctor says to me. It's the piebald male again—it has the sharpest eyes of the bunch. If it knew what was good for it, it'd keep them fixed on Émile, not me. "Though there is not much this one shares with the host from Misulah."

"Stanislas," I say.

It closes its eyes. Its fingers twitch, and I know somewhere back south it's sifting through its record hall, examining some scroll or another. "You are a body from Satgarden. You volunteered for integration because of an otherwise incurable head injury. You suffered from an uncommon form of epilepsy and auditory hallucinations."

I move my blanket and ease my legs over the side of the bed. The doctor grips my elbow, assisting me more out of curiosity than concern.

"I repaired them," it tells me. My bare toes grip the stone, and I dare to stand, leaning on the Institute's shoulder. "I repaired every damaged area I could. I kept everything under control. I healed you."

"Did you?" I growl. I take a shaky step—not too bad, so I take another one. "You fixed the wound but killed the patient."

"I would expect you to be more understanding," the Institute says. "You know firsthand the complexities of what I do. My work is replete with difficult compromises, none of which seem fair."

"I know." I can't help it. I'm smiling. The thoughts swimming in my brain may only be conjurations of narcotics. They may be the remnants of the Institute's presence, or the firings of a conglomerate of unorganized neural cells, each with their own needs and desires. "I remember being you. I remember being much more than you."

"I've got the future of this household to consider!" the baron hollers. "I have to look ahead, especially with everyone else looking behind. You fucks and your ancient machinery—"

Over the old man's bobbing head, in the blurred periphery of the Institute's vision, I can see the outline of a loosened stone. It's a stone Émile has removed and replaced many times, planning and measuring and carefully inserting a rounded metal egg, granular yolk ready for the spark of flame. Down the hall, in a dumbwaiter that hasn't functioned for centuries, the twins have placed a similar one, a fetish to ward off their ghosts.

"You can't control me in my own home," the baron growls. "You *need* me. You need my wheatrock or your whole fucking degenerate mess of a city will die."

I wonder, briefly, if the baron is speaking for himself, or if *Pseudomycota* is speaking through him, posturing for its competitor.

"I'm putting that animal down," he continues. "The constable will end him, quick and easy. Quicker than he deserves." The shadow of the man moves behind the baron's chair, nose nothing more than a pair of long slits. He's probably as eager to end Émile as he is to end me. "And then you perverted fucks can dig around inside him all you want."

"What do you remember?" the Institute asks me. "About me, about being more than me?"

"I remember discovering you," I say, easing myself across the room.

"When you came to my halls." It nods. "When you came to be cured."

"No. Before that." I take another step, shaky with pain. "I

discovered both you and *Pseudomycota*. I know where you came from."

This catches its interest. Several doctors in several rooms stop speaking, tilting their auditory cortices in our direction. "Where?"

I can feel its apprehension, I can feel its longing for a taxonomy as intensely as if it were my own. It was my own, once.

I smile. "From a dog's nose."

Sometimes, if the starlings were aggressive that season, Atiey and I would stay inside our little shack, and she would read me books about when the world was far too big. She hid them in the loose floorboards in case anyone from the palace came around to snoop, but at night she'd take out the whole stack. She'd stolen dozens and dozens of tomes when she fled from the collection of palace geeks that called itself Research and Development—it was called so, she told me, for the same reason Inultus's governor was called a governor and Verdira's baron was called a baron. Someone found the word in an old magazine, approximated its meaning, and decided to use it.

There were thousands of pictures in Atiey's books. She showed me model organisms: slime molds and ants and other creatures that appeared to make one mind out of many, or stranger still, no minds at all. She showed me pictures of what we built to emulate those things—swarms of metal bees spilling across the sky, vats of semiconscious liquids bubbling in agony, a township-sized, ultimately harmless mold that did nothing but wander from one end of the continent to the other, muttering to itself. She showed me the tools we built to send them into the sky. There were long ships and wide ships, dirigibles and rockets, and small, rounded floaters that were supposed to have eased through the stratosphere like pollen on the surface of water. Nobody knows what was inside them, Atiey told me.

But I found out, the day I lost my head. I wasn't inclined to parse through what I discovered inside that giant nose—after all, I had crawled into the ship only for the rubber tubing, frayed bouquets of wiring, and other small, profitable materials. I couldn't sell a well-preserved human corpse, so I skipped over it without a second thought. I couldn't sell what I couldn't carry, so I didn't pause to examine the screens that flickered in glowing halos above my head, rows of Franco and Angalis, words I couldn't read then and wouldn't understand now. I couldn't sell the strange smell, so I only pinched my nose.

Still, I remember them clearly. The neural pathways that stored these images have sat unused for nearly a decade, so they almost feel fresh in my mind. I remember stepping over the body of what must've been the ship's pilot, brownish skin stretched tight over its half-exposed face, rubbery suit untouched by time. I remember the strange cleanliness of the place, the sterile white floor that assured me I was the first mud-caked scavenger to raid this particular treasure trove. And I remember the smell most of all—it wasn't the smell of decay, but I couldn't place it at the time. It would take years, and a trip to the northern reaches of the habitable world, for me to finally recognize it as raw wheatrock. The walls were covered in it. Long tubes of glass and plastic pumped chunks of a green half-liquid through the ship like blood. They ran through rows of rounded aquariums swimming with flagellates, looping around tanks of a distinctive white substance that would one day enter my body through a pinprick under my navel.

I didn't know what to do with those sights, with the terrible smell, except to escape them. I grabbed what I could and climbed back out. Right before the rogue propeller hit my head, I watched the ship sink back into the river of mud and debris, lost forever.

Well, maybe not forever. Nothing is really lost forever, Medrah used to tell me. It's all a big ugly circle.

Someone will find those ships again eventually, just as I found them, just as plenty before me had found them. Maybe one had been a little scavenger girl in Satgarden five hundred years ago, who pricked her finger on a syringe containing the Institute. Maybe another had been a boy living in the caves of Verdira, who dug too deep when he followed a vein of nutrient-rich wheatrock to its source, releasing a monster into the caves.

"What a world our predecessors left us," Atiey would always

laugh, closing her book. "And all the Satgarden mackinae are just what they made out of metal and plastic. Pray you never meet the shit they tried to make out of living cells." Then she'd tuck her stacks of paper back under the floorboard and kneel on top of it, unmoving, in a moment of silent contemplation. I could never tell if she was thinking, or mourning.

XXIV

HERE'S A STORY EVEN Priest doesn't know. It's about you, and about Didier, and it starts with your tail.

Well, it doesn't really start with your tail. Didier had always been fond of you, for no reason you could fathom. He had always offered you sweets and mussed your hair and let you sit in his study while others were made to work. But when your tail grew in, his fondness turned into something else entirely.

It was during a storm of anatomical changes, when you sprouted upward, when your voice, if you'd had one, would've turned over itself to find a new register. With each cem you gained, so did your tail, and you had to adjust how you sat, how you walked. It wasn't particularly long, but no one had taught you how to have a tail, so you weren't quite sure what to do with it. At first you stuffed it down one pant leg, hoping the folds of cloth would hide it. Then you tried tucking it between your thighs, but that proved too awkward. Finally, you settled for looping it across one gluteus and letting it poke back up under your shirt, belt pinching it against your skin. At night you'd let it out, let it breathe a bit, wag it slowly in the safety of your room.

Your deformity, the château's doctor had told you, was not an uncommon one. He'd seen many such oddities passed down in families all across the habitable world: tails, polydactylies, supernumerary nipples, cartilaginous growths protruding from skulls like horns. Your extra limb was nothing more than a benign atavism, a fetal characteristic you had simply forgotten to discard.

So you had no explanation for the way Didier reacted to it. Early on, you'd occasionally catch him staring at it, when its tip twitched under your belt, or when you readjusted it to kneel and polish the stone floors. The first time he pulled you to your feet, coaxed it from under your shirt, and looked it over, an inexplicable distress descended on him. He paled, gritted his teeth, and disappeared. For weeks afterward he avoided you, retreating and rerouting when you turned the corner, locking his study door behind him so you could not enter.

What was stranger than his brief evasion was what came afterward. Gradually, he began to seek you out. He'd summon you for the most trivial tasks. He'd lay a hand on your shoulder, your back, when he spoke with you. Occasionally he would draw you aside and ask if he could feel your tail. If you loosened your trousers and let him brush its tip, he would reward you with some sweetened wheatrock. He'd take you with him on his summer walks, showing you the old Montish constellations in the sun-washed stars, crooning hymns no one left alive was supposed to know. During the autumn hunt, when you should've been merely a pack mule, he embarrassed the constable by naming you second marksman and letting you have the kill. When you'd returned from the woods, your face beamed so brightly the château's physician asked if you had a fever.

You should've smelled something amiss, you'd tell yourself years later, but at the time you did not mind the attention. Though you didn't understand Didier, you adapted to him, the same way you adapted to the other things in your life you could not control. You went about your duties, you cleaned up after him, you bowed

your head so he could kiss it. You were the closest you'd ever been
to content.

The first edge of Didier's wound tore open on an early winter
night. You had been cleaning ash from the fireplace in his study
while the tantrums of the château's weekly supper raged far below
you. The creak of a floorboard caught your ear, but at first you suspected it was only one of the château's many ghosts. You turned,
expecting to see an orb of ectoplasm. Instead you found Didier,
leaning against the doorway.

He swayed in the dim lamplight, reeking of gin, cheeks flushed
and tearstained. When he stepped into the room, his feet were
unsteady, his shoulders shook with sobs. You assumed the baron
must've sent him away, pelted him with a dismissal hideous
enough to bring him to tears.

But he did not complain of supper, as he usually did on these
nights. He only stumbled forward and opened his arms. "I'm
sorry," he said. "Good dead gods, I'm so sorry. It's not my fault. I
tried as best I could. I swear to you, I tried."

You had thought he was apologizing, perhaps, for his erratic
behavior of the past few months. That was your first mistake:
thinking he was talking to you.

"It's not my fault," he said again, earnestly.

Your second mistake, and this was the truly fatal one, was that
you pitied him. You stood, brushed the ash off your trousers, and
took his outstretched hand. You thought to comfort him, so you
squeezed it gently, a gesture just soothing enough for Didier to
misread it as an invitation. Something seemed to collapse inside
him, and he began to shake anew, his limp, drunk weight dragging the both of you onto the chesterfield in a puff of ash.

He wept into your neck. His hands wrung yours, his lips
brushed your collarbone. He told you that you looked and smelled
just like you should, just like he'd always known you would. He
showered your face with kisses, paralyzing you with every one,
and told you he'd missed you.

You didn't know what to think. You could never have guessed
you were in this situation because you were trapped in the body

your parents gave you, with their traumas and diseases and resistances and beauties. But the thought did cross your mind when, before he lost consciousness, Didier leaned in and whispered a name that wasn't yours.

The debate in the city is over. The Institute is going to reintegrate me, though of course it hasn't volunteered that information.

"That body will not stop speaking of dogs," I hear a host say. "It has clearly succumbed to madness."

"Is it malignant?" mutters another.

The Institute must think so. It must think I know too much, and I will talk too much. It can't let me continue as myself, regardless of whether my adult brain is neuroplastic enough to survive our reintegration.

The doctors know it's not safe to assimilate a new host outside the privacy of the Institute's walls, but I can see them in the laboratory next door, drawing the blood of one of their own. It'll take about thirty-six hours to prime the serum for compatibility, to cleanse it of its antibodies. I don't have much time.

It's gonna be hard, with my one eye against their forty. Three eyes, I suppose, if I can count Émile's. And I will, if I can get to him before the Institute drains him completely dry. Or before they catch me and pump me full of my old self again.

The door to my room creaks open. I can't see any physicians in the hallways or adjacent rooms, so for a moment I worry I've gone blind to their movements. I sit up and crane my aching neck to see if it's the piebald host again, but it's only Sylvie, shivering, holding up a rattling metal tray.

"They told me you could have real food," she says. As she approaches, the firelight illuminates the dark rings under her eyes. "It's cold, but it'll still fill you up."

She lays it at my bedside, and I can barely look at the burned bread and steaming wheatrock paste. I'd rather have Institute gruel, but I reach for it anyway. I know I have to eat. "Thanks, Sylvie."

She backs up, watching me closely—or allowing *Pseudomycota* to watch me through her eyes. I'm surprised the Institute would let her in here, in her state. But unless it bursts out of one of her orifices and makes it to a fire, I think I'm safe from reinfection.

"You're different," she says slowly.

"I lost an eye," I reply.

She stands there for a while, counting my reluctant bites. "They're saying you killed Didier. They're saying you hit him in the head."

I close my eye and see him lying in the firelight, breath flowing lifelessly through him. The Institute is changing his bandages, pausing to pull a thin length of *Pseudomycota* from his broken skull. His father watches indignantly, spouting insults, black liquid staining the curves of his gums.

"Didier isn't dead," I tell Sylvie.

She does not seem satisfied.

"It was Émile," I say. "Émile hit him."

"That's not true. He would never."

I don't bother explaining it to her. I know she never suspected a thing. It was not so much Didier but Émile who went out of his way to keep that secret.

"They're . . . I know they're not telling the truth about him, or about you," Sylvie continues. "Those doctors aren't telling me anything. And the children, they won't say where they took them."

I can no longer see the twins, but I can see the baby, a dozen strings of tubing crawling from his fat little limbs. He's peeled open like a ripe red fruit, organs laid out meticulously beside him.

"They won't let me see the girls," Sylvie whispers, clutching herself. "Or the baby. They're trying to tell me he died in the womb. But I saw him. I saw him just like you did. He was alive. He was alive, wasn't he?"

He certainly seemed so when he emerged from his mother, but I can't say if his screaming and kicking was that of a living child, or just the motions of the parasite that may have colonized him before birth. "I think so," I answer.

"They took him away, and they won't tell me what they've done with him. I need to see him, and the girls. I need to know, doctor."

"Sylvie . . . I'm sorry, I think the twins are already . . ." I swallow. *A distraction,* Atiey tells me. *That's what you need. Even if they can't see through you, part of their attention will still be on you.* I bite my lip, and before Medrah can stop me, I scrape away whatever is left of my good conscience. "I don't know where the twins are. But the baby . . . they cut him open."

Her hands rise to her mouth. She stares at me, tears welling in her eyes.

"He's in the north wing," I say. "But there's always a doctor in there with him during the day. If you want to see him, go at night. Late. Toward the morning." I hope she doesn't know there's always a doctor in there at night, too.

"Oh, dead gods." She shakes her head, releasing a sob. "What have they done?"

"I don't know, exactly," I say. "They don't tell me much. But believe me. He's there." She turns, and I reach for her. "Wait, Sylvie. Don't go now. Wait a day or two, learn when they come and go. If they catch you sneaking around, who knows what they'll do to you."

She is trembling, fingers at her cyanic lips.

"Promise you won't get caught," I tell her, and she nods.

There is a physician in the corridor now, masked, gloved, striding through the ripples of hot air. I wave her away, and make a show of eating my bread.

"Doctor . . ." She turns back to me before the door. "Why is this . . . why . . ." She seems to lose her question in a sea of others. Eventually she bites her lip, clears her throat, and settles on an answerable one. "Doctor, did Émile really kill Didier?"

"No," I say. "Not quite yet."

Didier remembered nothing of that night. He had awoken as he often did, fully dressed in the evening's clothes, disheveled and hungover on the chesterfield in his study. He thanked you when you brought him water, tousled your hair, and rewarded you with a little jade bijou that he found in his drawer.

Despite his absent memory, he was not quite the same after that. He seemed to sense something in you, some new tension, some nervous incertitude. His touches became a little more forceful, his kisses uneasy. Familiar hymns seemed to warp in his mouth. His gifts became stranger. He gave you a woven bracelet of cave grass, a relic of a clan you belonged to but never knew. He gave you the keys to his study. He gave you a ring of pressurized wheatrock that had once been the baroness's wedding band.

You had never been so unsettled in his presence before, nor had you ever seen him so volatile. His smile, once easy and warm, now fled as quickly as it arrived. His fancies tunneled into obsessions, his restoration projects grew in scope and extravagance. His fits of misery were as intense and frequent as his bouts of drunken elation, when he expounded on the glory of the château's past, before '97, before the thousand-year fires, before the sky fell. Whenever he restored another timeworn Montish tapestry, hoisted a new balustrade, or rescued another room from freezing decay, he would open a celebratory bottle of ancient red, then another. He would raise the rim of his glass to your lips, seating you beside him and guiding your hand across his skin, nuzzling you to the golden swells of a new Inultan phonograph or the pulse of revitalized lamplight. He was so earnest, so tender, that you truly believed him when he promised he would drag this cursed place out of the dust of its last disaster. He would rebuild its crumbling towers and fill its empty rooms with people, he would do it for you, for his daughters, for a past he never had. You looked forward to that day, you really did, when your home would be bright, warm, vibrant with the souls of the living. Until then, you would wait patiently for the château's rebirth, and you would wait for its master to finish his bottle, to vomit, to attempt to make it to bed and fail.

And on those strange nights when he broke down, when he could not stand to be alone in his silent, haunted suite, you stayed with him. You let him stroke back your hair, you let him slip that old ring onto your finger and weep, kissing your palm and telling you he could not live without you. You let him weave your tail between his fingers and bring its tip to his mouth, sending bolts of warmth up your spine. And even if he gripped you too tightly, if he burrowed too deep into a body that was not quite yours, when he asked if you liked it, you didn't say no. You couldn't say no to the heir to Verdira, and you couldn't lie to him for the same reason. So you said nothing, you did nothing, except remind yourself that Didier was handsome, he was kind, he fed you, clothed you. You belonged to him as much as any other appendage of the château. If anything, you were lucky to have him.

He said he loved you. No one had ever told you that before.

You'll die if you leave now, my mother says. *The winter's too deep.*

I tell her that I'd rather freeze in the wasteland than rot in captivity.

It's that little wildness Medrah gave you, Atiey replies softly. *Love her for it, but be careful.*

I focus on the blank space of my empty visual field, making sure of the Institute's positions. Most of its bodies are asleep right now, as we all should be. The one in charge of overseeing Émile left that room about an hour ago—it's now lying on its stomach in a distal chamber, feet next to the small fire. Another host is scraping saliva from a dog's tongue, and one is at Didier's bedside, rewrapping his shattered skull and drowning out the baron's voice with a hundred unreadable thoughts. Two more are standing over Hélène's last delivery, sifting through its abdomen for abnormalities.

Sylvie appears. The door to the baby's room flies open, and she tumbles inside, a billow of black velvet and pale, flinging fists. The Institute turns four eyes to her, shielding what remains of the infant. Its nearby bodies spin on their heels, redirecting themselves toward the baby's room. I sit up in bed, watching from their eyes as they rush down the hall, summoned like immune cells to a site of injury.

"How *could* you?" Sylvie screams, shoving the host nearest her. Another doctor comes in behind her, grasping her arms and pulling her as far off-balance as its small body can. They tumble to the floor, and she raises her fists again before two more bodies fly in to subdue her.

"I'm sorry, Sylvie," I say aloud, though I know she can't hear me.

My room is silent, the lab is empty, and my route is clear. My bandages have been changed, and I've eaten my fill of nauseating wheatrock paste. My legs are strong enough to carry me, and my wits are sharp enough to pierce through the haze of analgesics and anticonvulsants. I'm in the best shape I can possibly be at this point. There is no better time than now.

I swing my aching legs over the side of the bed, and the world spins. I let the feeling pass and pull myself upright, clutching the table for balance. When I'm sure I can make it, I slink across the room.

There are a thousand things I need, but only about a dozen are available to me. The Institute hasn't been kind enough to leave lock-picking tools lying around, but its collection of blades and hooks and pins and curettes might do me some good. I grab a few and wrap them in cloth to keep them from rattling, like the other Satgarden kids taught me. Quietness is a virtue in a scavenger. Some machines get woken up by noise, and those are usually the ones with the guns.

Can't believe you survived as long as you did, Atiey tells me. *It was only a matter of time before something bad happened.*

I fill a small bag with medicines, pledgets, decanters of antiseptics and ethers, and a few blades, just in case. After dressing myself as best I can, I shuffle desperately to the door. I pause one last time, feeling eyes on me. It is only my own, wide and dead and watching harmlessly from its tube on the shelf.

The halls are silent. They're hot, still febrile from the fires *Pseudomycota* has commanded us to build and throw ourselves into. I slip through the darkness far too slowly, injuries stinging with each movement. I keep my ears perked for any wandering servants, and every few steps I stop to close my eye and assess what the Institute sees. They're still occupied with Sylvie—two are holding her down and a third is fetching a sedative.

Somehow, I make it past the maids' quarters, into a hall of

perpetually unused guest rooms. I'm close now, close enough to know not to get too confident. Carefully, I step down the hall, past the empty sconces and frayed tapestries, reaching for my little bag of tools. I hope to all the dead gods my fingers remember how to pick a lock.

"Where are you going, doctor?"

My stomach drops. I spin and look to the end of the hall, where the starlight catches two pale, hairless spheres. The twins' heads shine like veiny pink grapes, pallid and bumpy and patched with discolored flesh.

"Girls!" My heart flutters and sinks. I'm unsure if it's driven by elation or terror. "I thought you were—what are you doing outta bed? You're paler than goddamn ghosts."

They shrug. They've still got all four of their eyes, but whether that's a good sign is up for debate. I know the Institute hasn't interacted with them for days. Either it's cured them, or given up on them altogether. "Do the doctors know you're up and about?"

They glance at one another and smile.

"Goddammit," I mutter. I narrow my eye, leaning toward the blank space across the bridge of my nose. Sylvie is still struggling against several pairs of hands, and I can't see anything beyond her. There appear to be no physicians in the twins' room, but I can't account for servants or gendarmes who might prowl the halls looking for missing girls.

In any case, five eyes are better than one. "Want to be the lookouts?" I ask them.

They perk up. "What are we doing?"

"Springing Émile. The other doctors locked him up."

"What for?" they ask.

For having a useful body, Atiey says, before I can. "If you want to find out, keep quiet and follow me." Their insatiable curiosity, on par with the Institute's, coaxes them into step behind me. "One of you at each end of the hall will do it. Run back to me if you see anyone coming."

They each nod a bald, flaking head and skip in opposite directions, bare feet floating silently above the carpet. I take one last look through the Institute's eyes, and situate myself before the door. I lean down to examine the lock, trying to remember everything this brain has not thought about for nearly ten years.

My hands haven't grown much since I last used them, but the muscles have been retrained for different purposes. When the tools fall into my palms, and then into the keyhole, two sets of memory fight over my fingers: the instinct to pull and twist in chaotic guesswork, and the well-trained habit of moving my fingers only with conscious, surgical precision.

It's no wonder I can't pick the damn lock. All I can do is rattle the metal inside the keyhole. I pause, wondering if I should give up and slam my fists against the door instead. It's not likely Émile is capable of answering, and with the constable out for both our blood, he'd probably show up sooner than anyone.

I twist the metal between my fingers, but it's no good. I'll need to send the girls away and think of something else. I glance to my left to see the shining bald head of one twin at the end of the hall, and at the other end—

Oh, great evil mackinae, she's gone. I'm not about to go chasing after her, but I twist to *psst* at her copy down the hall. I barely get half a hiss from my lips before something clicks in the door. Without any input from me or my tools, it slowly creaks open.

Fear springs through me, my heart clenches. I prepare for the constable's noseless face to appear from the dark, for his gun to thrust out at me. But it's just a pair of black-ringed eyes and a wry smile. A bald head leans out at me, reddish with dried flecks of blood.

I stare at the girl as she steps out into the hallway. "Shit," I breathe. "How did you get in?"

"I walked through the wall," she answers. She's hiding behind an unreadable simper, and I can't tell if she's playing with me or not.

"You've really gotta stop with the tricks," I say. "You nearly burst my heart."

The second twin drifts up to join us. "They're not tricks."

"And even if they *were*," says the other, "we can't help it."

"They just happen. Wherever we are, they happen."

"It's because we were stillborn. Like all the others."

"Don't start with me," I growl, pushing past them. "Go back to bed."

"Don't you remember, doctor? You were the one who delivered us." They glance at one another with mirrored, knowing smiles.

"Shush. Now is not the time."

I wave them away, but the cold draft of their presence lingers behind me as I step through the door. I creep across the scrubbed, tiled floor, glancing around for any sign of the Institute. The room is silent. Moonlight pours through the windows and lights the apparatuses of rubber and glass lining the walls. Before me is a narrow bed, white sheets rumpled, tubes and wires running across empty tables. One cannula dangles alone, dripping clear fluid onto the floor. Émile is nowhere in sight.

"Girls," I start, "you need to go. You need to get out—"

When I turn to address them, they too have disappeared.

XXV

THE FIRST TIME YOU entreated the dead gods to take Didier to join them was shortly after I had sewn the constable's nose back on. In the early gusts of winter, about two years before the collapse in the wheatrock mine released *Pseudomycota* into the world, you were caught with something you were not supposed to have.

You honestly expected the constable to be the first to discover you, to find your tail in Didier's hand or his gifts in your pocket. He'd been after you ever since that autumn hunt, looking for any misbehavior that would excuse a kick to a dog's side or a box to your ears. But that particular night he'd been in bed, acclimating to his reattached nose, and Hélène, heavy with pregnancy and insomnia, had suffered a midnight craving for raw bear meat.

You'd been the one awake, so you'd been the one to answer her call. It had been late, you had been careless, and you forgot to remove the gift that Didier gave you, the baroness's ring he insisted looked striking against the gray skin of your fingers.

You hadn't known it had been given to Hélène on her wedding day, despite Didier's feeble protests. Of course, she'd locked it

away in some gilded box a few months later, when her disillusion
set in. She hadn't seen it in years, but the moment you set down
the tray, she gripped your wrist, eyes wide. You expected her to
scream, to strike you. She only glanced up, recognizing something
in you, maybe the look on your face or the faint blotches on your
neck. Too knowingly, she grinned.

"Well, you're all kinds of a thief, aren't you?" she said, bright
with disdain. "How wonderful. Maybe you'll be the one to give
the baron all those heirs he wants."

She laughed, settled down to eat her meal, and sent you upstairs for your punishment.

In the tower, you stood before Didier and the baron, eyes lowered. The two of them lingered in silence for an agonizing few
minutes, Didier fidgeting as his father polished off a bottle of wine.
You prepared yourself for a blow, for a threat, for the baron to
hold you in place for an hour with a painful, carceral speech. You
were ready to take the beating, hide your wounds, and get on with
the day.

But when the baron's shout came, it wasn't directed at you.
Instead, the old man turned to his son, lifted the wine bottle, and
threw it at him. It missed, shattering against the wall, but you
flinched right along with Didier.

"You pathetic little cunt," the baron wheezed. "She's *dead,* do
you hear me? She's dead for good reason, and here you are trying
to bring her back."

You dared to lift your eyes. You were surprised but not relieved
to find that you were not the target of the baron's rage. Somehow,
it was almost worse to be a witness than it was to be the victim.

Didier stood perfectly still, hands folded behind his back. He
seemed to find the shattered glass on the floor worthy of his full
attention. "Pèren, look what a mess you've made—"

"*I've* made? *Me!* I clean up messes. You're the one who wants to
remake them." The baron rolled in his bed, nearly tearing himself
from it, blue-purple with rage. "I'll have him put down like the
rest of them. Shot in the head and buried in the garden. Maybe
you'll get over yourself then."

"Pèren . . ." Didier attempted.

"Or will you dig up his corpse and chew on his bones like a starving fucking dog?" The baron motioned to the fireplace, where a collection of pokers leaned against the andiron. "Well, go on, heat one up. Jab out his eyes, burn off his tail. Make him look a little less like her."

"He's done nothing wrong," Didier said weakly.

"Of course he has." The baron turned his gaze in your direction. "You should know better, you little shit. You're smarter than this. If this bastard gives you anything that's not yours, you put it back where it belongs. Come here."

You did. You regretted it every time, but you always obeyed the baron.

"Didier, get me something long. Hand me that poker."

He hesitated.

"Get it, or I'll use something heavier."

His gaze remained at his feet. With a slow, reluctant hand, he reached out and grasped the tool next to the fireplace. Wordlessly, he handed it to his father, and your stomach turned inside you.

"Good. Now forget about that insurgent bitch. Don't make mistakes, and for fuck's sake, don't repeat them." The baron leaned from his bed to grasp your hand, twisting the ring from your finger and jamming it over the end of the poker. A single eager swing downward crushed the fragile, ancient stone between floorboard and iron.

"Pèren!" Didier gasped, though he did not dare interrupt.

You were almost relieved, until the baron turned his weapon back to you. "If I hear of anything like this happening again, I'll break your knees and leave you for the ventigeaux, do you understand?"

Just to illustrate his point, he swung the poker into the outside of your leg, swifter than a man of his age and fettle had any right to be. Three more blows and you buckled, though not from the sting of the metal alone.

"You're a fucking embarrassment. Get out." The baron tossed the poker, and it clattered across the stained carpet to the pile of broken glass. "Not you, houseboy. You've still got to clean up in here."

You had no choice but to drag yourself up on your aching legs and comply. It wasn't so much the beating that did you in for the day, nor the baron's grumbling, nor the grueling work of cleaning up every shred of glass and drop of fetid wine. It was the swift and violent death of your rationalizations, the fragile shields you had raised against the world for so long.

You'd done your best to endure whatever Didier demanded, whatever the entire household demanded, because you thought, in some oblique way, that you were valued. But as you raked a tattered cloth over and over across the baron's floor, you realized that it wasn't even you Didier cared for. He loved a stranger, someone you would never meet. After all this time, after all his professions and gifts, after his rough hands and tugs at your tail, you were only the second-best thing, a warm body with something of a familiar face.

Things changed after that. Or, rather, you realized how dismally they stayed the same.

You went to great but inadequate lengths to hide from Didier. He always found you. The reluctant shakes of your head were met with caresses. When you looked away he would beg you to look back. Each time you would insist you had work to do, he would excuse you from it. Every line you tried to draw, Didier would overstep. He would apologize for it, profusely, but his contrition never stopped him from overstepping again.

You began to acknowledge what he had known his whole life: those lines were not yours to draw in the first place.

I know where Émile has gone.

He's not dead. The Institute has no reason to dispose of him, not with *Pseudomycota* crawling through just about every skull in town. And I refuse to believe the constable has managed to kill him.

I know him. I know how well he can manipulate the manor. He must've been thinking of escape as fervently as I have, enduring, dissociating, planning while the Institute prodded and sliced off tissues and withdrew fluids. He must've pilfered a key, or figured out how to open the lock without one, and slipped out of his room unnoticed.

I run. I don't care how much noise my feet make against the stone. I don't care who sees me rushing down the hall toward Didier's quarters, one-eyed and depth-impaired, slamming elbows and knees against corners and balustrades.

I grip the wall for guidance as I throw myself up a staircase, closing my eye and glancing through another. I can see the baron's face, mouth shaping his unceasing soliloquy. Didier's body lies in my peripheral vision, sunken gaze locked on the ceiling.

No sign of Émile. Good—if I can grab him and redirect him to the kennels before the Institute finds him out of bed, this whole thing doesn't need end in disaster. I need to hide him. I need to tell him that if one doctor sees him, they all have, no matter—

I skid to a halt. The hot air is thick with the smell of blood. A dark figure lingers at the end of the hall, slumped against the first steps of the spiral staircase. My heart hiccups and stutters, and I creep closer, fingers tightening around my tools. The shape does not move at my approach, but its hideous face comes into focus almost as savagely as an attack.

The constable is positioned dutifully at the base of his master's stairs. Blood drips behind him, easing down the steps to pool at the landing. His rifle is gone, and in its place is a bistoury, glinting red at his side. His head dangles on a limp neck, and his throat is nothing but a bubbling puncture, undulating with incoherent, desperate growls. The slits of his half-nose flare almost like nostrils, blowing flecks of blood and mucus with each shallow, dying breath. His eyes, deep-set and glinting, burn against me. I can almost see the reflection of Émile in them, blade clutched in one fist, flying over the length of his gun and sinking steel into him before he could even manage to miss. As I step over him, he reaches out to paw at my leg. He's not gone yet, but he will be soon.

I struggle up the stairs, and I can see a figure move in the corner of my blindness. The Institute's body turns, moving its eyes from Didier to the door. The crash of bursting wood echoes from the physician's ears to mine. I am too late.

Émile bursts rifle-first into Didier's bedchamber. From my angle at the bedside, I get a good view of his bloodshot black eyes, his calm frown, his sweat-plastered hair. I can see directly down the barrel as he points it in my direction—then that portion of my sight goes out like a snuffed candle.

My gasp emerges from twenty or so throats. I remember that feeling well—like having a fingernail suddenly and violently ripped off—and I can see other hosts rise from their beds, pull on their coats, abandon a now-sedated Sylvie to address the commotion in Didier's room.

I throw myself up the stairs, panting, hoping my feet will carry me faster than the Institute's. I can't see what's going on up there anymore, but I know I have to get there. I have to rescue that damn fool from himself before he ruins everything.

When I tumble through the door, Émile's back is to me. Down the length of his rifle sits the baron, reclining calmly at his son's bedside. The old man's eyes move from Didier to the corpse of the physician, burst head spilling blood onto the carpet.

"What a mess," he growls. "You killed my doctor, you little shit. If this sickness takes me, it'll be your fault."

The houseboy adjusts his aim.

"Émile," I say quietly, but he doesn't turn. He keeps the baron firmly in his sights. "Leave him. Come with me, we gotta go."

"Listen to her," the baron says. "You won't fix anything by prancing around and shooting up the place. Didn't work for your parents and it won't work for you." He shifts in his chair, slowly reaching for the bellpull against the wall. "Put the damn thing down, and wipe that hurt look off your face."

I step forward again. "We have to leave—"

His finger moves, still slick with the constable's blood, and the rifle discharges. The baron's thoracic tubing bursts, spewing serum and a cloud of bluish gas. The old man reels back in his chair, fist gripping the leather arm, knuckles whitening, breath pouring out in short, violent gasps. A stray duct spatters fluid with each harrowing wheeze of the baron's laughter.

"Good dead gods, you're a vicious little devil," he says. "I knew this would happen. Only a matter of time. I tried to tell Didier—"

Émile shoots the baron again. A quarter of his skull disappears in a spray of blood and brain, and the rest of his head lolls back and forth on his wrinkled neck. Strings of muscle dangle over his sunken cheek, hanging from the half-moon of what remains of his eye socket. That doesn't stop the baron from turning back to us, blue lips moving as they always are.

"I tried to help you, you know," he spits through blood and broken teeth. "I told him, I warned him. I told him not to start '97 all over again. But he never listens."

I can't move. Émile's shaking hands reload.

"Always trying to repeat everything," the baron says, his remaining eye rolling back into his head. "He thinks he can spit up his favorite morsels and savor them twice."

Émile aims once more, and I don't stop him. This time the baron's throat ruptures and his head bobs forward. It rolls past his clavicles, releasing another half-sentence before the ropes of cervical tubing and muscle pull taut, suspending it at his midline. He does not lift it again.

We stand in silence for a moment, heartbeat deafening in my ringing ears. I reach for Émile. "We have to go—"

He rips his arm away, swinging the rifle in my direction. Before I can move, before I can speak, something blunt hits my stomach and I collapse against the wall. When I regain my balance, the barrel's tip is hovering, too steadily, at my forehead. I tense, watching for the crook of Émile's finger, for the narrowing of his eye that always precedes his bullet. For an agonizing second he is perfectly still, picking me apart. His gaze is cold and sharp as a ventigeau's wind. It moves from my bruised, bandaged face, to my mismatched clothes, to the bag of supplies rattling in my hand. I do not know if through the crosshairs he sees the calculating monster that drugged and tried to infect him, or if he sees a human body, as desperate and vulnerable as his own.

"The Institute is coming for us," I start, carefully. "I can see them. They'll catch us if we don't leave now."

The gun does not move. Surely he knows that it would be better to shoot me now. For his own sake, or as retribution, he should crush me like all the other parasites in this cursed place.

Mackinita, Medrah gasps through racking sobs. *You deserve to live. Please live.*

"Émile," I continue softly. "I don't expect you to trust me. But . . . I'm still asking you to. They're coming up the east steps, past the drawing rooms. We can avoid them if we take the north passage, but we have to hurry."

He stares at me a moment longer. I can't tell if he believes me, if he thinks I'm insane, if he sees me as an ally, a distraction, a prisoner, or bait. Whatever he thinks, he lowers his gun. He does not let it fall to his side, nor does he follow me to the door. He gives me a knowing look, immovable. We both know why he is here, and he will not let me stop him.

He slips past the baron's still-wheezing corpse and approaches the wall. He slides the stone from his hiding place and removes a small container, filled with powder and ready to burst. He strides to Didier's bedside and struggles with the metal contraption for a moment, wrestling with Baker's delicate handiwork. The powder falls like snow as he pulls it open and shakes it onto his master's body, dotting his limp legs, his bare torso, circling it like a halo around his head. Didier's eyes are still on the ceiling, unmoving. But I think I can see his lips twitch as Émile hovers over him. He empties the metal egg over Didier's face last, and brushes off the final traces of flammable dust from his own skin. Then he steps back, lifts the candle from the bedside table, and throws it onto the body. A short series of pops rends the air, and within seconds the bed is engulfed in flames.

Émile lingers to watch Didier burn for a moment. Then he turns, rifle in hand, and marches me down the spiral staircase.

XXVI

"WHAT ARE YOU GOING to do when I'm gone?"

You glanced up from the ledgers at Didier, though that question was not your concern. You would be gone long before he sprouted another gray hair.

"Oh, don't look like that. I'm not going to prolong my misery like my father. But I can't imagine Hélène will want to take over the château when I'm dead. She'd run it into the ground out of spite."

He'd laughed, setting down his pen and brushing your shoulder.

It was an innocent gesture, but you numbed, readying yourself. The closer he came to your skin, the farther you fled from it. Though you did not intend to, you had mastered the art of stepping outside yourself, of removing Émile and letting someone else slip into his place. Sometimes it made things easier, even pleasurable. But often you would continue to be her, whoever she was, for days afterward—the world would remain pale, your thoughts dampened, and hours would pass you by without memory. You would find yourself in rooms you could not remember entering. You would spend hours shining the same piece of silverware. Each day somehow protracted into the same torpid, empty blur.

"And by that time I'll have rebuilt this place. The château will be a city unto itself, like the grand palaces in Inultus. Better than Inultus."

You'd tried so many things already. You hid in the shadow of the château's physician, in the safety of his sexless, constant busyness. You slept in the kennels when you could, using the dogs as shields. You even tried to strangle your tail with a piece of discarded piano wire, but you could not overcome the agony, the limb's anguished flailing, as if it were an independent creature struggling to survive. Eventually you sought Old Doc's help, undoing your belt and showing him where you wanted it cut. He'd only frowned and shaken his head, citing the danger of amputating a benign growth, especially one affixed to the spine. By the time he finished his monologue on the risks of infection and permanent paralysis, you knew there was nothing left for you but to let the damn thing be.

He never asked why you wanted to remove it, and I don't know what he could've done for you if he'd known. Offer you some sort of anodyne, perhaps. Some comfort, some useless advice, something that would not stir chaos in the château. The Institute is kind when it has to be, when it wants to be, but it wouldn't have compromised its only source of wheatrock for your sake. It had hundreds of mouths to feed, and you were only one servant. You were such a small, insignificant branch in its human taxonomy.

"And the girls . . ." Didier continued, though you didn't quite notice. "Well, I suppose they are mine, after all. I'll have to leave them something. But they wouldn't know what to do with the place. They certainly wouldn't manage it properly."

There was only one route left to you at that point, and it was into the winter night. You had no certain destination, but you sure as hell planned to get there. You tore a map out of an atlas in the study, and devised a route to the nearest town south. You stole a compass and an electric lamp, you slipped off with Hélène's bijoux and some of her strongest brandy, to use as barter or fuel. You refurbished an old dogsled and rescued every orphan ski you could, arranging them in mismatched pairs. You pilfered jackets and respirators, goggles and deerskin hats. You were more than ready.

"It should be yours. It's only right. You're the one who knows it best. But my father would never allow it, and he'll likely outlive us both."

The baron would be glad to see you go, you knew, but Didier would not. He loved you—or he loved whoever it was he sought inside you, and he would not let her go so easily. He would send out search parties and machines and uproot the whole town if he had to. He would send the constable, who would jump at the perverse opportunity to use the dogs as he saw fit, to shove their noses to the ground and their teeth into human skin. You had to cripple the manor somehow, to stymie and distract your pursuers. You had to make sure the household's eyes were elsewhere for long enough that you could ready a sled, or at least throw on some skis, and flee into the night. You needed some sort of disaster.

"Are you listening, Émile?"

You realized Didier was still talking. His hand grasped your elbow, gently shaking you back into yourself.

"Don't worry," he smiled. "It's not something to think about now. I'm not planning on dying anytime soon, and you're certainly not going first. You wouldn't do that to me. You wouldn't leave me alone in this madhouse, would you?"

He gently kissed your forehead. You decided to set the château on fire.

Émile's breath heaves, heavy and voiceless. His face is speckled with red droplets, his lean arms are bare and trembling, but he is fast and fierce and resolute. He drags me down the stairs at the pace of a near fall, rifle clattering against the walls. Every few steps he glances over his shoulder, ensuring that I still follow him and the flames do not.

We hurdle the constable's corpse, flee down the corridor, and emerge into the second-story grand hall. The tall windows cast winking starlight on the trail of bloodstains in our wake, but there is no time to hide our tracks.

A gaggle of maids scatters, shouting to one another as we fly past. At the base of the grand hall's curved stairs a few servants are clotting and signaling to one another like cells in a burst vessel. They've no doubt smelled the smoke—but I don't know if they're gathering to put out the fire, or throw themselves into it.

We take a sharp turn down a narrow corridor. A few steps across the faded carpet and I have to slow, shoulder throbbing, legs burning with effort. I lower my head to take a breath, and when I blink I see moonlit windows and torches streak past. They rotate in my vision, blurring as the eyes that see them rush down the hall.

"Wait," I hiss. "One's coming down the—"

I spring forward, reaching for Émile's elbow to drag him into the darkness of an adjacent room, but I'm too slow, too weak. The Institute appears at the end of the opposite hallway—alone, in its green-eyed, piebald body. Our gazes meet, and its lips twitch, eyes moving slightly upward. It's calling to the others that it has found the malignant host, the cancerous cell that has escaped confinement and is now spreading inflammation in its wake.

I almost turn around, I almost drag Émile down the opposite corridor, but he steps forward, lifting his rifle toward the Institute. For a moment, as the length of the barrel glints at the host, I can see us through its eyes. I see a hateful pair of sickly specimens, pale and thin and blood-covered—I almost chuckle at us, at the audacity of thinking we could escape the château in our state. Then Émile pulls the trigger, and the body flies against the opposite wall, clutching its stomach.

I cry out, pain searing my abdomen. Gravity pulls me forward, and I double over, staggering. Émile skids to a halt, returning to me with wide, dark eyes. He stares at me for a moment, clutching his rifle, but then bends to offer a reluctant elbow. He pulls me to my shaking feet, leading me across the hall as the last of the Institute's pain fades, as the last breath leaks from a nameless piebald child who will never recover his body, never overcome his chronic, agonizing infection. I don't want to look at him as we stumble past, but I can't help myself. I can't stop from glancing over my shoulder at a corpse that could easily have been my own.

Somehow, we reach the kennels. Panic, like smoke, has spread through the house, all the way from the tower to the basement. Howling snouts and scratching claws follow us down the ancient hallway, toward the farthest kennel, where Émile has stashed his supplies. He pushes through the door, releasing a pair of whining dogs, and throws aside a desk to dive for a gargantuan wardrobe scarred by centuries of gnawing teeth.

He nearly pulls the oak panels off their rusted hinges and dives inside, tearing through his cache. Deerskin trousers, furred parkas, masks, glass goggles, bits and pieces of ancient respirators, packs stuffed with cured meats, cheeses, wheatrock, ammunition, bracelets and alcohol and other sellable valuables. Leaning against the back of the wardrobe is a collection of skis in various states of repair—some with partners, some without—many too long, many too short.

He has more than he needs, a redundant collection of provisions of varying quality. Without pausing to think, he hands me supplies in my approximate size. I do not question him, I do not pause to thank him. I pull on the parka, the trousers, the gloves and the mask, face and shoulder aching, hands shaking with effort. Émile is faster than me, strapping his rifle over his shoulder and hauling the skis across the room while I'm still struggling into boots. When he makes it to the doorway, a deep rumble shakes the kennels. Somewhere above us, Didier's quarters are falling apart.

I pull on the last of my winter clothes and grab my poles. Weak, injured, I struggle to my feet and tell myself I'm ready. I've never skied before—at least in this body—but Stanislas had. I remember the jerks of his muscles, the movement of his feet as he lunged with one leg, then the other—*Shit, mackinita,* Medrah says. *Sure you're not bitin' off more'n you can chew?*

I stomp out into the hall, panting, sweat pouring down my forehead. Émile has piled his things by the door. He makes his way down the row of kennels, stopping to unlock every latch. Dust shakes from the ceiling as the flames upstairs set off another chain of incendiaries, but he doesn't flinch. He has planned a long time for this.

"Come on," I say. "It won't be long before the fire reaches—"

An outpouring of howls drowns out my voice. The dogs are flying through the dust, white bodies slamming against rebar and chicken wire as Émile pulls the last kennel open. He stands back to let the dogs rush past him, lifting his skis and chasing them only when he has made sure each is accounted for. Then he rushes back up the stairs, and I stumble after him.

All the doors are bolted or nailed shut, and the lower floors of the manor are buried in snow, so we have nothing to do but climb. I can barely breathe, barely see through the thick smoke, but I follow the streak of Émile's hair, I let the howls guide me. A sea of white fur buoys us back up the stairs, past the foyer, and up the stairs again, through the smoke and screaming servants, out into the upper hall.

Beyond the tall windows stretch blankets of untouched, blue-lit snow. The broken moon is full, the mountains glitter beyond the glass, streaked with ice and patches of frozen trees. The dogs rush forward, howling for the outside world, scratching, biting, wagging.

They whine encouragement as Émile drops his skis and swings the butt of his rifle against the glass. A spiderweb of cracks dances across the landscape, fragmenting the snow-light. Black eyes and noses and paws nudge his legs as he swings at the window again, adding a few more strands to the web, then a few more—and then, with a piercing ring, the glass shatters. A thousand flecks of light burst from the burning château, and a wave of dogs pours after it, churning whitely like milk boiling over the rim of a pot. They traverse the balcony, hurdle the balustrade, and flee across the frozen gardens, baying and leaping into the darkness.

Émile and I jump after them. We're not half as graceful, and we're certainly not as fast, but we drop from the broken window and tumble to the ground unharmed. I gasp as my boots hit the thick powder—the moment I sink into it, a shock of cold seeps through all my layers. Wind bites at my mask and goggles, and I can feel a crawling frost grip my bones, but I keep moving. I sling my skis over my screaming shoulder and stumble onward, pushing through the pain, the wheezing exhaustion. I do not dare to slow until I am well out of range of the catastrophe I know is coming.

An entourage of dogs panting at my side, I lurch through the orange snow, away from the burning manor. Flames creep across Didier's chambers, spitting smoke from the windows and lighting the looming, icy mountains a violent orange. Inevitably, the conflagration crawls toward the long, rigid-backed airship, frozen atop the highest tower.

I've been anticipating what happens next. Émile hasn't. I can't blame him. He hasn't been a doctor in the governor's aerostat lab; he hasn't treated the burns and eschars and lost limbs of the engineers. He doesn't know what foul gases go into that monstrous hot-air balloon.

I throw myself over him just as the explosion shakes the earth. The snow rolls under our feet like a wave, and I drag us both to the ground, an eruption of heat searing my back. When I glance over my aching shoulder, I see half the château launched skyward in a shower of stone and wood. Spheres of flaming gas and canvas engulf the other half, sending another burst of warmth through my shivering bones. A surge of sound and fire rushes toward the sky, lighting the night like a smeared sun, streaked with blue and orange and aglow with the writhing shapes of a thousand wailing ghosts.

For a glorious few seconds, all eyes are on the manor. Émile is paralyzed on the ground beside me, goggles lit by the dancing fires. The dogs pause, lifting their ears and tails, and silhouettes of townsfolk crawl onto their communal chalets' highest balconies to watch the spectacle. I can almost feel the gazes of children as they press their faces up against frosted, fogged windows, the indifferent blinks of goats and lynx in the mountains, turning their eyes to the distant column of smoke. And beside me, I sense the presence of my mothers, Medrah's hand over her mouth and Atiey's arms crossed in approval.

Great evil mackinae, Atiey says, before I can tell her I have no time for her commentary. *I spent years trying to prevent the resurgence of flight and you just blew that shit up in a second.*

I turn from her, handing Émile his skis as he sways to his feet. It takes him a few seconds to finally tear his eyes from the fire, but he shakes off his shock, steps onto his skis, and glides toward town. Before we go, I mutter to Atiey's shadow, "I'll tell you all about it when I get home."

Your plan was well thought out, meticulously prepared for, and a complete disaster. I'm not going to take all the blame—you're the one that had to go back and make sure Didier was dead.

It wouldn't have been too hard for you to slip from the château unnoticed, with all the fires you were going to set. Especially with the twins' help. Those girls could fit in tight spaces and access impassable rooms so well you suspected they could walk through walls. It was easy to get them to hide things where others would never think to look, and it was easy to keep them quiet, with their natural propensity for covert mischief. They would even interrupt the gendarmes' evening rounds while you slunk back from Baker's stores, cradling your pilfered incendiaries as reverently as any pyrotechnist. Poor girls, they truly thought you were helping them. You did not have the heart to tell them that even if you believed their stories, even if you saw those bloodied specters prowling the halls, a few flames could do nothing about them.

For months you mused on where to start your fire—perhaps the kitchens, where it would seem natural, perhaps in the foyer, where it would catch the most attention. No matter where it began, you had to make sure it spread outward in little bursts, just fast enough to keep the château occupied for a few hours, just slow enough that it would not be fatal.

In retrospect, you should've known you would burn Didier's chambers first, but you did not come to that decision until the day of the autumn's collapse. That day, when Baker lost his only love and the château lost more money than Didier thought possible, he sat you in the study for hours, handing you row after row of sums, hanging his head every time a foreman came by with news about what supplies and manpower had been lost, or how much wheatrock the earth had reclaimed. He wrung his hands and massaged his forehead, groaning well into the early morning. Each passing hour sank him deeper into misery and blame.

"Every blast, every goddamn blast," he moaned. He had given up trying to tally what he'd lost. Papers were strewn across his desk, scribbled with illegible fury. "Every blast, every collapse, every goddamn thing gone wrong." He lifted his eyes, glinting with grief. He was at the point where not even he could know what was inside his head, but what he said next surprised you. "It's because of what I did to you. It's because of what I let happen to you."

You stilled, but kept your head buried in your work. You hoped he would calm himself on his own, but you did not hope for long. He stood and swayed over you. "Shit, Émile," he said. "Say something."

You stared at him, because you could do nothing else.

"Tell me this wasn't my fault."

The distress in his voice was so keen, so accusatory, that for a moment you considered the possibility that, if the collapse was not his fault, it was yours.

"Please, Émile."

Afterward, you told yourself you should've known better. To offer Didier solace was to invite disaster, but you reached out anyway, allowing your compassion to mislead you. As soon as you touched him, something ripped open inside him.

"For fuck's sake," he growled. He threw out his arms and shoved documents and ledgers from the desk, scattering them onto the floor. "Just say something. Say *anything*."

You lifted your hands, but he would not accept that.

"No, *speak*, you little shit! Just for once, use words like a goddamn human being." He stepped toward you, arms open, face twisted by terror and grief. "Tell me I didn't do this. You can, I *know* you can."

You couldn't, so he tried to get it out of you. He grabbed your wrists, your collar, your hair. "Tell me," he kept saying, blurred, distant. "Please, *please*! Don't just sit there like a dog, *tell me*!"

You fled from yourself, but not fast enough, and not far enough. You stayed still, silent, not quite numb, so he resorted to the last thing he could do to get a reaction from you. He pushed you over the desk, grabbed your tail, and pulled as hard as he could.

Later, after you had stopped convulsing, when a feeling other than agony crawled back into your spine, he lay beside you and stroked your hair.

"Is it bad?" he asked. "Can you move your legs?"

You could, but the pain deterred you.

"Forgive me," Didier said. "Oh, hell, Émile. You know I meant none of it. That's not me. I would never . . . I would never do such a thing again." He lied so well even he didn't know it. He didn't know what you knew, that things would only get worse, that they would culminate in something irreversible, something you were not sure you could survive.

"I'm sorry. I'm so sorry." He buried his face in your neck, pulling you close, breath tickling your skin. You could barely hear his words over his soft sobbing. "I love you."

By now you knew he was not talking to you, but the person inside you that he dug for, relentlessly, like a ventigeau digging through a corpse. The one who had come before.

You recognized then, deeply but not consciously, that even if you fled, even if you burned down all of Verdira, it would not stop Didier. He would only replace you with another, like he would replace all the miners lost in the collapse, like he would replace Old Doc when, in a few weeks, *Pseudomycota* would free his hands for long enough to drive a scalpel through his own throat. Didier would crawl from the wreckage you made of him, wounded but ready to begin again, ready for another cycle of disaster and restoration. Mountains would wake and sleep and wake once more. There would be other collapses, other blasts, other miners, other houseboys.

You could not let it happen again. You had to take the dead gods' work into your own hands. If they weren't going to kill Didier, you had to.

The ground is turning black with *Pseudomycota*. I can feel them under my skis. I can see their little appendages writhe, rising like whiskers from the orange-lit snow. They're crawling from hosts,

slithering from the mouths and eyes and nostrils of those townsfolk who have braved the winter night to bathe in the heat of the
flames. They're slipping out of chimney stacks, through cracks
in cabin walls. They're pouring out of the exhaust chutes of
wheatrock refineries and the vents of warehouses, fattened with
weeks of rich nutriment. And they're all crawling toward the château, that massive conflagration, radiating heated gas and gargantuan blue flames—warmer than a human host, warmer than a
cabin's hearth, warmer than any fire for hundreds of miles.

It takes every ounce of my control to move past them. I slice
across their forms with the blades of my skis, my pole tips pierce
through the snow and into their wriggling arms. A few of the dogs
slow their sprint to pounce on the creatures, grasping them between
sharp teeth and shaking vigorously, tearing and tugging at the
squirming limbs. Émile and I ski onward, toward the night, surging
past the fight between Montish fauna and subterranean parasite,
the same fight that no doubt raged for centuries before my time.

Our course takes us past the remnants of Baker's hut, past the
warehouses, through the buried streets of Verdira pulsating gold
and black with fire and smoke. We ski over the mounds of rooftops, through forests of smokestacks, continuing westward. When
we pass the leaning old church spire, jutting out of the snow like a
tall, tiny house, I slow for a moment to catch my breath.

My shoulder is throbbing so violently it feels as if it might burst
open, and even with my respirator, the night air rips down my
throat in painful bursts. I think of the cocktails of analgesics and
anti-inflammatories I stole from the Institute, but before I can
throw my bag down and dig through it, a blur at the edge of my
vision turns my gaze toward the church.

Leaning against the slope of the warped belfry, thin robe blowing in the ashy gales, is the hunched figure of Priest. At least, I
think it's Priest. I can't tell if my panic has only conjured a mirage
in the rippling heat, but as the silhouette turns its hood to look
our way, I think I see a familiar glint in its eyes. The shape stands
immobile for a moment, then lifts a hand. Slowly, calmly, it bids
us farewell. Then it hugs itself, turns back to the spinning columns
of flame and smoke, and watches the château burn.

I turn to see if Émile has spotted the image of Priest as I have, but he is already lunging toward the trees. Poles raised against the terrors of the night, he plunges into the snowy woods easy as an itch-lizard into mud. I can only hope the Montish strengths and immunities passed down through generations of Verdiran winter will guide him, because they will have to guide me too.

I have no choice but to ski after him, muscles aching, lungs crackling with ice, away from the château, away from the safety of fire and heat, into the wilderness.

XXVII

TEN OR SO MILES southwest of the château a fissured arch of concrete sits tucked securely at the bend of what was once a river. It is
a broad, lichenous monolith, centuries dead but not quite gutted,
trabeculated with steel vanes and thick-walled chambers. Though
Émile is unsure of its intended purpose—I suspect it was once
some sort of hydraulic facility—he deemed it safe enough to mark
on his map, a small blue circle scratched with Didier's best foun-
tain pen. It is the first in a series of dots spanning southward, beginning at the château and ending at the nearest town. From there,
his course is unmarked. When he first tore out that map, he had
no idea where he would go—catch a train to the city, perhaps, or
a boat to the Wheslers, or run off to some undiscovered massif all
his own. Though I know better, a part of me wonders if he left his
route unfinished because he did not expect to survive the journey.

The night is bright, lit green with a retinue of stars and aurorae. As the first rush of adrenaline subsides, we slow to a steady,
agonizing rhythm. The weight of exhaustion too quickly returns

to my limbs, and with every lunge pain crawls from my shoulder downward. Still, I push through it.

The fires of Verdira have retreated to a vague, smoky glow beyond the trees, bleeding into the sky's dancing lights. I can almost see a sheen to it, a silvery shoal of *Pseudomycota*'s whorling progeny, and I shiver with something distinct from cold. A strange itch crawls through my parka and into my skin, like the legs of insects, a throng of watching eyes, a biting wind.

Émile seems to feel it too. He hesitates, lifting his nose to the air and his eyes to the trees, though I can see no movement in the tall shadows, no sign of animals or pursuers. He slides into a creek bed between two rows of forested knolls, out of sight, out of the glowing green of starlit snow. We move forward in silence, and the wind whistles through the pines, throwing glittering, freezing showers into our path. Émile stops to listen, head tilted. I know better than to ask what he's listening for. He redirects us, then loops back, feeling the breeze. When he thinks it's safe to continue, he takes off south. I pant after him, occasionally reaching up to clutch at my aching shoulder.

I know that he does not, and should not, have any intention of stopping for me. I can't rest, I can't veer from his wake, and I certainly can't retreat. Behind me stretches only the unkind wilds and whatever creatures prowl it—and even if I made it back to Verdira, into the heat and light, *Pseudomycota* would wriggle into my remaining eye the moment the smoke stings it.

Somehow, propelled by a cocktail of analgesics and dread, I'm able to slide one foot in front of the other. I keep my head down and my eye on Émile's tracks, counting my strokes. The wind picks up above the metal wheeze of my respirator and stiffens my sleeves, frosting the fur on my hood into silver needles. A thin ring of ice congeals at the rims of my goggles. Despite my strenuous movement, cold is seeping through me, clear and unstoppable as water.

It seems an age before the sloped corpse of the dam comes into view, and another before we reach its entrance, a nub of concrete concealed in bent and splintered pines. Émile, not yet panicking, ducks into the thicket and pulls off his skis, sliding to the base of a tree well. I follow suit, kneeling beside him and helping him unbury a tube of ancient steel and concrete. The wind takes a breath and blows again, twisting the creaking branches over our heads. Tufts of needles and spiked cones rain on our backs as we hunch into the metal crawl space.

The conduit is pitch-black and deathly quiet. I crouch behind Émile, flurries licking at my feet, and drag our skis into the stillness of the dark. Beyond the mouth of the tunnel I hear wood moan and a branch snap. We shuffle through the cramped darkness until the passageway opens up, depositing us into what I know is some sort of control room. Émile shuffles beside me, fumbling for his lamp. A bluish, weak light appears in his hands, illuminating the dusty consoles, the remnants of cables and circuitry he helped Baker dismantle and carry back to the château years ago, when the baron's liver decided to blow a fuse.

I drag our packs into a corner, gasping free of my respirator and hood. Émile positions himself at the mouth of the gloomy tunnel, gloves tightening over his rifle. He props himself up on his elbows and stares down the length of the barrel into the darkness. He doesn't like the sound of the wind outside, and neither do I.

He keeps his gun raised, tensing when a gust comes whirling through the conduit, but it dissipates into a harmless puff by the time it reaches him. Nothing follows: no braying, no snarling, no scraping of claws. The room falls mercifully still, and he allows himself to stand. His sigh echoes like a shout.

"We're . . . alive," I whisper, because I am suddenly struck with the absurdity of that fact.

Émile slips his finger from the trigger guard and turns from the passageway. When he removes his respirator, the device rattles in his fingers.

"I . . . thank you."

He leans against a sloped console, raising a hand to his forehead and melting into a slow, deep breath. The rifle still dangles at his side, but at least it isn't pointed at me.

"You could've left me behind," I say. "You could've shot me, and you didn't."

The tired look he gives me is perfectly clear in the dim lamplight. He has questions, and I'm the only one who can answer them.

"All right," I say.

He removes one glove, then the other. He slides a finger through the dust on the console, curling script starkly elegant against the primitive knobs and dials. *I do not understand you,* he writes. *You tried to poison me.*

My heart drops, and I rest a hand over it, the same that had offered him a drink, wrapped around his shoulder, and dragged him to the adjacent room. "I tried to do worse than that," I mutter.

Then you helped me. His fingertip hesitates. *In the study.*

Shame stabs at me. I cannot say if it was truly me that struck at Didier, or if it was the Institute, propelled only by self-preservation. "I'm . . . so sorry, Émile. I was late. Far too many years late." I rest my face in my hands for a moment. In the dark of my palms I see Didier's broken skull, *Pseudomycota* wriggling from clumps of coagulated blood. Fire engulfs him, crawling from his pale face to roof beams of the château, to the domes and pillars of Verdiran jade, the same jade that adorns the Institute's halls. "I know why you did it. I know—well, I might not know all of it. If I've learned anything in the past decade it's that every brain's got its own way of adapting. I can never truly understand. But I know what it's like to be paralyzed, at least. Trapped in a body that doesn't belong to you."

His finger hovers over the console, unmoving.

"What Didier did wasn't your fault. None of it was your fault." These are practiced words, words my mouth has repeated to thousands of patients who've suffered similar violations and injuries. "But I know you were struggling with it. And I know—"

Émile holds up his hand, and I fall silent. He writes a single word in the frosty grime: *How?*

"How do I know? Good question. It's never happened before." I pause, wondering how to convey to him his unprecedented immunity. Surely it would sound like nonsense to him. It sounds like nonsense to me. "When I . . . when the Institute made me—" I almost laugh at the strangeness of it. "I didn't mean for it to turn out the way it did. What I did to you is unforgivable. What the Institute has done to thousands of others is unforgivable."

There could be a way to right that wrong, Atiey says.

Don't make her, Medrah replies. *Not her job to fix others' mistakes.*

"But I tried to . . . I tried to inject you with something that I thought would help us—me—survive *Pseudomycota.* I did so without your knowledge or consent." I hesitate. I know how many meaningless apologies he's endured, how many times the burden of forgiveness was placed on him. "I am truly, deeply sorry."

He stares at me like I'm insane. He underlines his query with an insistent finger.

"While that happened . . . I . . . it failed. Something in you is resistant to infection—at least some infections. Maybe something passed down from your parents. And their parents, and theirs, considering where they came from. Considering the things they shared those caverns with." I pause, shivering. "In any case, you resisted the organism in that syringe, but while you were sick, there were . . . processes in your brain that I was made aware of. The thing I injected into you tried to rearrange your head, but you kept those pathways alive, and I got to travel them for a split second. I got to see—well, not *see,* but . . ." I sigh. "And you got to . . . well, I was you for a moment. And you were me. Us. I can't explain, but I can remember. I remember the autumn hunt, and the ring Didier gave you, and the night you released the lead dog. That was the first time he burned you both on the fire screen. You were frightened that he didn't seem to feel the heat."

I'd say Émile is speechless, if that meant anything. His fingers are tightly folded, his eyes wide—he's rendered gestureless, I suppose.

"I'm sorry. I did nothing. For years, I did nothing. No one ever told Stanislas what was happening. And I—he didn't notice at all. He should've. The Institute isn't nearly as astute as it likes to give itself credit for."

His hands are shaking now. His eyes are closed, and I couldn't read them if they were open.

"After half a millennium on this goddamn planet you'd think it'd know people better by now. But so long as it can use us to survive, there's no evolutionary prerogative for the Institute to change. Or so Atiey'd—"

He shakes his head, and I pause. He moves on to the next dusty surface and stares at it for a moment before lifting his finger.

What are you?

"I'm . . ." In truth, I'm not sure what to tell him. I am not quite myself anymore, and I'm certainly not the child who ascended the Institute's steps nearly a decade ago. I don't know if I'm even human, or if I'm only the synthesis of all my infections, if bits and pieces of *Pseudomycota* and the Institute and every other organism that has colonized me are still fighting in my blood, trying to conquer the territories of my muscles and consciousness. I don't know if I'm only an accumulation of organized cells that has deluded itself into thinking it's something more.

In the end, I decide to offer my hand. "I'm Simone."

XXVIII

IT FEELS RIGHT TO be in control again, to move my legs of my own volition, to think my own thoughts. But I miss having a body or two to spare. I wouldn't fear for my life so intensely if I had a few extras lying around, ready to take over when this one falls. My back is in agony, the rough wool is rubbing my shoulders raw, and I'd love to have a spare arm that knows exactly where I'm sore, to massage some life back into me, to nurse my wounds while the rest of me skis. I certainly can't ask Émile to do that. He's too busy keeping us alive.

He knew exactly when to slip out from the far end of the dam, sensing dawn without the aid of a timepiece. We have been skiing under a clear purple sky since. He knows his route by heart, the frozen lakes stringed like pearls, the scattered ruins and sanctuaries amid the wilderness. He knows the crevasses, the couloirs, where to tread carefully and where to scream across a valley before some creature sees prey in us.

So far we've outskied any pursuers. I can't see through any of

the Institute's eyes, and we haven't spotted a glint of the gendar-
merie. There are no pillars of coal smoke from stalking machines,
no roars of motors, no army of black tendrils slithering through
the snow. The only movement at our backs is a flurry whirling
up from a trough between the mountains' rocky knuckles. It is a
large but distant storm, a dome of icy wind blowing independent
of clouds or altitude.

As we snake across a frozen moraine, we turn to watch the billows of white-blue writhe and arch across the valley. It is miles away,
hovering steadily above the dam. The feeble rays of the sun streak
through it, beating it back, but I have a terrible suspicion that at
night it will quicken, howling across the tracks we leave in our wake.

I can hear thoughts churn in Émile's head, stories and warnings
echoing in Priest's gravelly voice. He holds his gloves up, measuring in fingerbreadths the distance and size of the eddies. We
both know it is not just a gust of paranoia. The more I stare at the
strange blizzard, the surer I become that it is living.

We don't rest until a ridge rises between us and the storm. Even
then, we linger only for a few minutes at high noon, in a copse
sheltered enough that we can remove our respirators and breathe.
Lunch is a palmful of powdered wheatrock, washed down with
stolen eau-de-vie. I retch, but it'll fuel me for another few miles.

Émile rolls a clump of wheatrock around with his tongue, eyes
on the wilderness behind us. Beyond the fitful blizzard, the sky
billows sickly gray, an oncoming cloud front or the last coughs of
smoke from the château. I stare with him, and it takes me a moment to realize he is waving to ask me something.

What will happen to Verdira?

"I don't know," I admit, warming my throat with Hélène's
brandy. "The smoke is going to spread *Pseudomycota,* though
who knows how long it'll stay airborne. Anyone not infected already will be soon." I swallow a few congealed capsules of a potent analgesic. "I dunno if any of the Institute's hosts lived through
the fire. Either way, a whole lot of them are gonna ride up here in
spring. They'll have the governor's men with them, and they'll be
looking for us. Me for knowing too much about them, and you for
having the only viable remedy for *Pseudomycota.*"

Only two people in this goddamn world who won't be out to kill you, mackinita, Atiey says.

Émile stuffs the cork back into the bottle and glances my way. *Is that what they took from my eyes?*

"I think so. I'm sure they tried. I don't know if they managed to concoct some sort of medicine out of it. If they did, it's burned up with the rest of the château." I shove my aching feet back into my skis. "But the Institute won't forget what it learned here."

He considers my words for a moment, staring out into the trees. Slowly, he blinks, thin mounds of his corneas twitching under his lids. I recognize the movement, as if he is glancing askance at a memory in the dark, a kaleidoscopic scene projected from hundreds of eyes, hundreds of miles away. He is parsing through information, tiny fragments of both myself and the Institute he glimpsed when we tried to take hold of him. For a fraction of a second, or so he told me last night before we collapsed on the floor of the control room, he could see an echo, a conglomerate palimpsest of the Institute's many neural networks as it tried to override his own.

He had thought it was a nightmare, induced by whatever strange drug the château's unhinged doctor had injected into him. The flashes of Satgarden's bubbling mud-river, Inultus and its shining palaces, the feeling of being spread thin, ubiquitous, like air, the sting of an itch-lizard's bite. Two women's faces, unfamiliar, inexplicably beloved. Fleeting shards that he did not understand, febrile and delirious with his brief infection.

I'd tried my best to explain to him what he'd witnessed. He had seen very little, and nothing with the remotest degree of clarity, but it was enough to warrant an account stretching back half a millennium. He was receptive, at least. He's used to these kinds of stories, full of Priest's fables of falling dogs' noses, of dark creatures in the caverns who are tempted by fire. He's already been introduced to half the characters in the Institute's tale. Either things are falling into place in his head, or falling apart entirely.

A flurry lifts from the valley, stinging our skin. The blizzard has rounded the hill. It moves with purpose, and so must we. Before he dons his respirator, Émile turns to me and mouths one last question I can't answer. *Will it spread to the city?*

It's possible the billions of *Pseudomycota*'s progeny floating above Verdira will ease back into the snow. It's also possible those unseen, weightless coils will catch an updraft, buoyed along the tracks on an infective, invincible cloud, slithering through every station and town on its journey southward. I can hope *Pseudomycota* doesn't chase me to Inultus, or worse, meet me there—but there is no telling. The winter winds have been peculiarly strong this year.

The second circle on Émile's map is Didier's hunting lodge, straddling the southern tip of his father's demesne. Our shared memories of the route are blurred with heartache and the changing seasons, but I recognize the thickening woods, the chipped prominence in whose shadow it hides. Émile had only toyed with the idea of stopping there, unsure if it would be a strategic waypoint or simply a convenient place to get caught. Now, we have little choice. The day is not long, and the snowstorm is gaining on us.

We ski along a winding river, passing under bridges, crumbling metal towers, and abandoned lifts. The trees creak with snow, and the pebbles of the moon tumble across a purple sky, lighting the slopes and glaciers. It's almost tempting to stop and contemplate the landscape, to take in the vastness of Verdira and its strange beauty, but dusk is plummeting toward us in evil streaks of indigo.

The first stars appear. The knife-tip of a distant summit stabs the sun, then splits it into two weakened slivers. My body's heat flees with the light, and a sharp breeze tickles our backs. It follows us up the slopes, whistling through the couloirs and shaking snow from the trees around us.

Émile quickens his pace. I feel him straighten, alert. I hear him tell himself not to slow, not to look behind him—some residual part of me may still be privy to his thoughts, or I am loudly thinking the same thing. Our panic rises with the wind, but we keep our gazes and our ski tips forward, between the frosted trunks groaning in the coming blizzard.

It shouldn't be moving this fast. No storm should move this

fast, appear this suddenly, this violently. But the one that follows us is carried on four legs, as fleet-footed as a deer. Once it sees its quarry, Priest assured me long ago, it slows for nothing. And its sight is sharp.

The gales have begun to howl, falling from a high whistle to a deep trill, as a dog's might. Trees shake and bend, shedding needles and frozen cones in our path. The ground disappears, concealed in eddies of ice and debris. Somewhere behind me wood creaks and snaps. The sound shudders through my legs, painful as a fracture. Émile ignores the branches falling around him, and rushes forward in a desperate, straight line. He does not veer; he abandons any plan to double back, to hide ourselves, to attempt to outwit the Verdiran night. He knows better.

Too far ahead, there is a clearing. A long, geometric mound rises there, the buried slope of a pitched roof. I know there's a row of dormer windows on the south side, a series of attic lead lights under which Émile once daydreamed, files and polish and disassembled firearms neglected in his lap. He used to stare for hours in the bright afternoon, unable to imagine the colored panels buried and lightless even in the depths of winter. I hope the weather doesn't prove him wrong.

Émile lunges and the wind follows, stabbing through our layers and into our freezing backs. I slide after him, wheezing and off-balance, blinded by the shadows of trees as they bend and retract across the snow. I try to focus on the two unswerving, dark lines of his tracks, even though the wind is screaming now, blowing them away the moment they appear.

Something glows in my vision. I know better, but I look up to the sky, to the stars and broken moon beyond the swaying trees, hoping to see a pink arc of Verdiran dawn. But the glow is behind my sight, inside my sight: the dancing shapes are only the warnings of a brain on the cusp of a spasm.

"No—" I breathe, muffled by the wheeze of my respirator. I try to shout through it, to Émile's rolling back, but a wild gust sweeps a sheet of snow between us. He disappears into the haze, and I throw myself after him, stumbling between the black trunks that spring up in his place. They warp and stretch, entangling me in a maze of infinite, featureless snow. Émile's tracks are gone, and so is he.

Trembling with cold, blind, winded, I take my last deep breath. Then I pull down my respirator and shout his name into the blizzard. My mouth freezes instantly, my lips split, my tongue curls in agony. A wave of tiny needles pierces the mounds of my gums, the fragile mucosa of my nose. I taste a surge of blood, but I shout again, words raspy and incoherent like a death rattle.

The wind snatches my voice and rips it apart. It pierces my ribs, my spine, the tendons in my throbbing legs, blinding me, numbing me. For a moment gravity vanishes, and I can't tell if my feet are still in my skis or my skis on the ground. A scream deafens me—my own, or the gale's, or the rusted hinges of a machine as it turns, undead, in the mud-river. The world brightens and spins, and I tumble forward, wherever forward may be.

For a fraction of a second, the wind dies. Through the glittering vapor of the blizzard's stilled breath, the trees briefly come into view, haloed by starlight and the glowing tips of the high mountains.

I see it.

Four long, silver-white legs emerge from the snow, converging into a narrow, skeletal body. A thin neck bends past the treetops, past the needle-sharp crags, bisects the broken moon and keeps climbing, until it terminates in a bony, antlered head. A pair of eyes arches over me, wide-set and vivid red.

I scurry toward the cover of trees, but the ventigeau has seen me. I can barely cry out before it charges, throwing its tiny head downward, antlers glittering. Flurries swirl around its multi-jointed legs, and every shining edge of the animal is sharpened in the light, keen enough to cut through skin and bone as easily as they cut through the heavy snow. When it releases a bellow, stinging wind slices across my face, freezing my blood as soon as it leaks from my skin.

I can't move. The circling flurry holds me in place, pushing in forceful gusts against my legs, arresting my consciousness even as it tries to slip from me. Gleefully, the ventigeau begins to tear me apart.

The wind bites through my clothes, the glint of an antler tilts toward me, but what pierces me first is a sudden longing, deep and cold and impossible to soothe. My nose fills with Satgarden mud, my skin with the warmth of Medrah and Atiey, kissing the place on my head where the propeller hit. I hunger for home and I dread it, knowing that I will never see it again. I will never feel the touch of my mothers' hands, smell their soaps or hear them laughing in the adjacent room, and they will never know me, or what became of me, what I have learned and fought and survived. They will never know how close I came to escape, that I died on my way home to them, ripped to pieces in a sleet-shrouded wilderness. My heart spasms in agony, every cell in it seems to rip open, and I beg the ventigeau to finish its work.

Then, Émile is beside me. I can't see him, but I feel him raise his rifle in the glinting aurorae. I feel his movements, his breath, the echo of his mind, of memories we once shared—Didier's hands around mine, his voice breathing calm in my ear. The trick is not to stay steady, he whispers. The trick is to move with your unsteadiness. There is no such thing as a perfect shot. Only an adaptive one.

The constable's outrage burns me, his glare hot on my back, but I keep my eyes on the buck. It moves steadily through the trees, ready for my shot. Everything else evaporates—the men behind me, the woods, the gun, myself. There is only the animal, Didier's breath, and a long, invisible shaft of energy in my palms, waiting for my command. *Now,* he says.

Émile's trigger finger tenses, his tail bends, an ache of loneliness twists inside him, twisted more by Didier's gentle cruelty, unassuaged no matter what refuge the château offered him, no matter what lives once lived inside him.

A gunshot rings out. The ventigeau staggers. It does not fall—it lowers its head, two shafts of icy air curling from its nostrils, and sweeps toward him.

The howl that sails through the night is vicious, familiar. Something white emerges from the shadows of the woods and darts between the tall, thin legs, swift as the fell wind. The giant turns, skeletal head following the movement of its assailant, twisting its neck once, then again, red gaze scanning the trees.

Deep in my brain, a light shudders.

Again, Didier says. Another shot pierces the air.

Circles of white shrink inward from the edges of my vision, swallowing the night. My last image is four silver legs shifting in the moonlight, and then I hold tight, like Medrah always told me.

XXIX

I WAKE IN THE CHÂTEAU.

I jolt upright, nose itching with the smell of dusty linen. My head throbs, my face and lips sting with every movement, but I am warm and, strangely, alive. Through the bits and pieces of light still floating at the corners of my eyesight I can make out a small, sparse stone room. I am on the floor, under a mountain of fur blankets. A gas flame burns on a timeworn end table, and an empty bed frame is propped sideways against the wall, draped in cobwebs. It is not a room I have seen before.

I rub the hazy glow of exhaustion from my eye and see a thin tapestry hanging over the doorway. Lying beneath it, licking her paws, is a familiar dog. She lifts her head when I move, torn ear twitching, and follows me to a stand. Slowly, I stumble to the door and into the hall. With each unsteady step I regain a little more of my mind, though it feels as if some invisible hammer has tried to make a fine dust of my skull.

I round the corner, under the dead stares of mounted bear skulls and portraits of barons past. I creak down a staircase and emerge into the great room of what I now know to be Didier's hunting lodge. The place has been put to bed for winter. All but the highest windows are boarded, the girandole is stripped of candles, the furniture covered and pushed to the peripheries. Before the empty hearth, leaving prints and smears in the dust, Émile sorts through our packs. He counts and rearranges rations, medicines, ammunition, and some provisions that appear to be pilfered from the lodge's pantry. He hasn't gathered much: only a bag of sugar, two bottles of wine, and a few bars of pressed wheatrock.

The dog's paws click against the floor, and Émile lifts his eyes to us. He gives me the telltale twitch of his mouth that marks an attempt at a smile. He almost seems relieved to see me.

"Did you . . ." I pause, tongue stinging. "Did you carry me here?"

He nods. He looks at the dog, then mouths me an explanation. I can't parse out the details, but it seems the dog bought him enough time to pull me through my postictal haze and into a high window of the lodge. Judging from the animal bones and piles of white fur, it looks like the lead dog has been living here for a while. She must've sniffed out the familiar, following the same faded memories we did.

"And is . . ." I creak, lifting a finger to dab at my oozing lip. "The ventigeau . . . did you kill it?"

He gives me a disappointed frown. Of course he didn't.

"Then . . . is it gone?"

He tilts his head toward the ceiling, and I strain my ears. Only the faintest wind buzzes outside—no rattling boards or shingles, no thumps of falling trees. I can't tell if the breeze is only a trace of the ventigeau's presence, like a wake rippling behind a boat, or if it's still nearby, shaking off the bullets and circling the lodge, waiting for cold or hunger to drive us to the surface.

I seat myself beside Émile, reaching into my bag for a tonic that can soothe the burns and abrasions of the Verdiran night. I pop open a bottle, gargle, and spit, numbing my mouth as much as I can. "Thank you, Émile. And thank you, chennie."

The dog curls in the dust, watching us from behind her bushy tail. Émile's hands ask if I'm all right.

"As much as can be expected," I answer. "Hell of a time for a fit. It's just . . . my old injury. From the accident. Just a spark. A tough, long spark." I intend to force a smile, but it comes easier than expected. "My mamans used to call me mackinita because my little machine kept short-circuiting."

Émile looks at me for a moment. He offers me a jar of musty unguent.

"Is it still night?" I ask, bathing my face.

He nods, placing the food carefully in his bag. I know he was hoping for a much better haul. His memories of this place are colored by the abundance of feasts.

"Shit. We'll have to hurry." I lean back, glancing at the stuffed head of an elk mounted above me. "The last point on your map—do you think that's far enough south that the ventigeau can't follow us?"

He frowns.

"Perhaps the train, then," I sigh.

He stills, thoughtful. Then he rises and disappears into an adjacent room. When he returns, he's carrying a small sheaf of paper and a worn pencil.

You're going back to Inultus, aren't you? he writes.

"I want to."

The Institute is there.

"Most of it, I know. But I have to get to Satgarden. I have to get back to my mothers. They'll be able to help me—or, at the very least, they won't hand me over to the Institute."

What he writes next sends a sharp pain from my heart to my shoulder. *They did once already.*

"What do you know about it?" I snap. "They had no idea. They had no idea what it was, what it would do. No one did. Did *you*?"

He shakes his head, holding my gaze, but that does not lessen the sting. Suddenly I am certain he sees me for what I am: a motherless child, too old, too knowledgeable, and still so terrified, captive in a body that has grown without her.

I'm sorry, he writes.

"It's . . . all right. You're right. But it's not their fault. I was hurt. They didn't know what else to do." My empty socket begins to ache. "I have to see them again. I have to tell them what happened to me. What's been happening."

Don't fool yourself into thinking those parasites will leave you be, Atiey warns me. *Even if you make it back to us, even if you share everything you know, you're still in the Institute's backyard.*

She's right. It's not like the Institute hasn't faced human threats before, ideological enemies, those who have come too close to discovering its secrets. All those bodies have disappeared, some into the ground, some into the furnace, some into the Institute itself.

"I don't care," I whisper to her. "The whole world is its fucking backyard. I'm still going home."

Émile glances up at me.

"I . . . once we reach the station—" *If we reach the station,* Atiey corrects, and I wave her away. "Once we reach the station . . . where will you go?"

He stares at his paper for a few moments, anguished. It was cruel to ask. We're both well aware he has never planned that far. *I don't know. I have nowhere. I don't know what to do.*

I give him a moment to breathe, watching him bite his lip. "I . . . I know there's nothing I can do to erase what happened to you. But if you'll accept help, I'll give it. We can hide you. Atiey has friends who may be able to take you wherever you want to go. You can stay with us as long as you need, until you move on, or come back north."

A lump travels down his throat. He stares at his fingers, slowly twirling his pencil. *Old Doc invited me to the city, once.*

"I know. The Institute planned to do to you what it did to me."

I wanted to go. Didier refused, told me my place was in the château. He pauses. *I think He was afraid of losing me.*

"He was terrified."

Émile closes his eyes, raising his hand to his forehead and leaning into it. For a long while he doesn't move, brow furrowed in thought. Eventually, he turns back to me. He flips the paper and begins to write on the back.

I have another question.

I know what he's about to ask. I also know he has avoided doing so because he's deeply afraid of the answer. It's either the threat of the ventigeau or the hope of escape that spurs him to slide that paper over to me.

Who was Útolie?

Émile spends the remainder of the night destroying everything on the ground floor. I lie on our piled blankets, watching the tapestry in the doorway ripple with the breath of his fervent activity. Echoes bound up the stairs, of glass shattering, thumps of overturned furniture, the ripping of oily portraits. The dog barks and howls down there with him, growling gleefully with every new sound, with every thrown object.

He had been anticipating it. Of course he had. He'd always had some inkling, some vague, sinister recognition of her. He sensed the woman whose skin he was softly forced into, as intimately and inescapably as Didier. He felt the fragmented shape of her coalesce around him, despite the prohibitive silence, the sealed lips of those who had always known far more about him than he had.

Clenched jaw over clenched fist, he listened attentively, each confirmation sending a new crack through him, until silently, utterly, he broke apart. He stood, dry-eyed, and disappeared with the dog, leaving me with nothing to do but climb upstairs alone.

For an hour at least he traverses the lodge, unmaking every memory, every finely crafted treasure. He knows the barony is invincible in oblivion, and will never lament the losses. That does not stop him.

I'm still awake when he returns. He pulls aside the tapestry and throws himself onto the blankets, silent. The dog settles between us, dragging the preserved head of a buck behind her. She chews on one antler, tail wagging at my face, as Émile runs his fingers through her fur. Briefly, they touch mine. He recoils on instinct, drawing his arm back across the panting flank of the animal.

He lies perfectly still for a few minutes. I whisper his name into the flickering darkness, and he doesn't answer. His face is buried in the dog's back, his breath slow and steady. His hand hangs, limp and untroubled, a few cems above my own. I speak again, to silence. He is deeply, resolutely asleep.

XXX

IT TAKES US FOUR days in the frozen wilderness to run out of food. We've been unable to scavenge anything but a few hares and a single bottle of whiskey left in the warped remains of a télécabine pod. All I have left in my bag are tinctures of vitamins, so I drop a few on our tongues and call it lunch.

The storm claws at our wake, injured, furious. Every day it creeps a bit closer, blowing down from the jagged northern horizon and licking at our backs. I hear it in distant stone-sharpened whistles, in the bone-aching cracks of glacial ice. Twice now I've collapsed in its shadow, rigid, trapped somewhere beyond the world. Émile has helped me sway upright each time, dragging me through my daze as my exhausted brain rattles its parts back into place.

He says it's because he's taken me up on my offer. He can't leave me for the ventigeau. Someone has to be his guide, his interpreter. Someone has to show him how to hop a freight.

Until then, the lead dog watches over us. She slaloms between trees, leading us away from thin ice and around the freezing hollows of sleeping creatures. She occasionally disappears and reappears, looping back to howl at our rear, covering our tracks, dispersing invisible scents this way and that. She leaps through the snow as easily as air, eyes and nose a lively threesome of black dots against the endless white. Émile is just as swift, skiing close to the ground, hunched almost on all fours like a lycanthrope.

I can't stop thinking about home. Medrah'd be delighted to see us glide through the glens and forests, guided by the piercing howls of an ancient animal. She'd read a book about dogs once, when Atiey was teaching her to read. Soon as I get back, I'll add a few stories to that collection.

The light is short-lived, and the feeble sun barely slips over the ridges before dropping down again, drawing a small but slowly widening circle in the pink sky. Somehow, we cover a few precarious, arduous miles before sunset forces us underground. We dive into abandoned cabins, village ruins, caves, every shelter that has lived through the mountains turning over in their fitful sleep.

During the long nights, we listen for the sound of the wind, and I change my bandages and rub salve on my sore legs. Starving, we share our warmth, dog curled safely between us.

Every so often I feel a tail against my leg—sometimes the dog's, sometimes Émile's. His seems to move on its own, twitching and wiggling as if excited to have some room. He apologizes for its ceaseless activity, and I tell him not to. I know he has no control over it.

It's not like my own body is normal. With the damn thing catching up on nearly a decade's worth of lost time, I'm not so sure what's happening with it. My menstrual cycle is at a dry point, and one breast is inexplicably sore—*Always end up with one bigger than the other,* Medrah assures me. *No two're the same, not even on the same person.*

Late bloomer, Atiey laughs. *Past twenty and finally going through puberty.*

A little knot of dread turns my stomach. I tell myself not to think on it, but I don't know if my mothers are still alive. Worse yet, I don't know if they'd recognize me. Maybe they won't know the hard-faced little thing I've become, one-eyed, too literate.

Maybe they won't understand the accent this tongue has acclimated to, or they'll wonder why I haven't grown a cem. They'll ask where I've been, who I've been, why I've got a Montish refugee with me. They'll ask if he belongs to me the same way Atiey and Medrah belong to each other, and I'll say no, but that I love him, that I've been him, that he's something much more peculiar than a friend. Or maybe I'll say none of that. I'll just tell them he's here because of a family issue. Something to do with his medrah. Atiey will raise an eyebrow, and Medrah will laugh. *No runnin' from your mama's trauma,* she'll say, like she often does.

When I close my eye, I try to imagine their smiling faces. Instead, I see jade pillars crumbling. I see bodies in the streets of Inultus, thousands of them, civilians and Institute, crawled through with trembling coils of black. I see dog-nose ships rising from the mud-rivers, scattered miles of wheatrock seeping nutrients into the Inultan soil, sleeping mountains waiting to wake beneath the city streets. I see the world ending all over again.

The dog refuses to go any farther.

In the distance we can see the chimneys of a settlement. It's a town I recognize from the windows of a rattling train car, though I have passed it only a few times the last twenty years or so. The clouds hang low and heavy, but I can see a column of engine-steam billowing in the fog.

Distantly, the ventigeau follows, sluggish in its rage. The townsfolk will see it coming, they will retreat to their houses and shut the doors and blinds. They may offer us sanctuary if we pound at their doors. But surely, they will try to send the train off south well before the blizzard hits.

Émile tries to coax the dog down the hill, toward the village, but no matter how he claps and whistles and slaps his knee, she is obstinate. She paces and pants, watching him with worried black eyes. When he makes to grab her she jumps out of reach, barking and growling.

So we leave her. Émile looks behind us every few strokes of his skis, clearly hoping she'll follow. She only lingers at the crest of the hill, pacing and releasing long, despondent wails. I tell Émile that it's for the best, that dogs don't belong on trains or in cities, that she will be happier up here in the wild north. It's all bullshit. I'm sure she'd be happier with Émile, no matter where he is.

Reluctantly, he gives up on the dog and follows me to the edge of the settlement. Hidden behind a series of latrines, we remove our skis and throw them into the snow, congratulating whatever lucky soul finds them in the spring. Then, carefully, we make our way into town.

The houses are only half-buried, and the wind is still mild enough that we can walk without masks. A few townsfolk are even wandering outside, thickly bundled and red-cheeked, watching the storm in the distance. When I close my eye, I don't see through any others nearby, but I can't be too careful. With what happened in Verdira, the Institute might already be crawling all over this place.

I buy a few loaves with one of Hélène's bracelets before we tiptoe toward the station, ducking under windows glowing with firelight. Beyond the sloping cabins shudders the shape of the massive engine, rounded belly shining with sheets of ice. A few people are clumped on the platform, puffing billows of frozen breath like the train itself.

Émile and I make our way past the station, to the train's lagging end. We duck behind stacked boxes of cargo, keeping low, keeping silent. I still have my pilfered tools in case we need to pry anything open, but when we reach the tracks, the door to the boxcar easily gives way.

I keep watch as Émile scrambles up one gargantuan wheel. He pauses, perched toward the northern horizon, but after a moment's hesitation he tumbles into the darkness. I haul myself up after him, heart in my throat. As I step over the wheel, I can't stop myself from imagining all its moving parts, all the crankpins and drivers ready to crush and break and slice a scavenger's limbs as eagerly as any Satgarden mackina. Émile stares back at me from the shadows, giving me the same nervous look he gave the dog before we left her. Slowly, earnestly, he mouths *Simone*.

Just as I finally pluck up the courage to throw myself in beside him, I feel eyes on me. I glance over to the snowy platform and see a boy standing there, round red face haloed in the frosted fur of his parka. I freeze in place as his eyes widen, suspended in the wind. He's got his finger in his mouth, and he's wearing the Institute's gloves.

We lock gazes. For a moment I'm sure he's going to scream, I'm sure he's going to point us out to the prowling conductors. But he doesn't. He only stares at me, silent, transfixed. I give him a smile, then I raise my finger to my lips in a gesture of silence. He blinks, agonizingly slowly, then mirrors me. He bites down on his bare forefinger, kicks a little snow at his feet, and turns away.

The freight car rattles and jerks, and the shriek of a whistle rends the icy air. The cargo shifts as the train struggles to pull out of the station, agonizing in its heaviness. A few pigs shiver in cages opposite us, stumbling with inertia.

I'm cold, exhausted, and every muscle is sore, but I'm comfortable enough. I'm not so sure about Émile—he's pacing back and forth, climbing over boxes and crates. I think he's anxious. He's never been on a train.

"It's all right," I tell him, ripping the heel off a rye loaf. "We can take turns watching for conductors or gendarmes. We'll be in Inultus in a few days, at most. If it doesn't snow too much, and if the tracks don't need any repairs. If the train gets stopped we'll find another way south. We can buy a ride with a trading caravan. I was a physician with one, once, I know them—they'd love to get their hands on some of the baron's jade." I shift, stretching my aching back and sore shoulder. "Just a little while longer and we'll be in Inultus. My mamans'll be overjoyed. You'll see. Just a few more days."

Émile is not listening. He's made his way to the boxcar door, and now he shoves his weight against it. Before I can jump up to stop him it wrenches open, screeching along its tracks. A gust of freezing air fills the car, setting the pigs to screaming.

"What are you doing?" I yell. "They'll catch us!"

He leans out, one gray hand gripping the steel, the other dangling freely in the open. It traces the shapes of buildings as they roll past, accelerating in streaks of firelight.

I scramble toward him, hurdling a collection of portmanteaux. "Close the door—"

Flakes of ash and snow whip through his hair as he arches his neck, craning to watch the mountains fly by. He lifts his arm in the wind, untroubled by the icy gales, and when he glances back to me, a grin crawls across his face, wide, genuine, unpracticed.

He mouths something to me, earnestly, slowly, but I cannot read it. A skewed column of afternoon sun falls across the valley, setting the snow alight.

He begins to shake. Independent of the rattling train, his shoulders tremble, his mouth opens, he almost doubles over. I grab his furred shoulder, holding him steady as he leans into the empty air, convulsing in breathless laughter. He heaves a silent shout, narrowed black eyes wet with something more vehement than relief. In the shifting haze of gold-lit snow, I can see two streaks of tears fall across his cheeks, smeared by the brilliant wind.

Acknowledgments

A HUGE THANK-YOU TO:

My agent, Alexander Cochran, for seeing something in this little book.

My editor, Carl Engle-Laird, for fixing many things in this little book.

My sensitivity readers, M. Evan MacGriogair, Ollie Hennis, and Ronkwahrhakónha Dube.

Matt Rusin, Oliver Dougherty, Irene Gallo, Troix Jackson, Lee Harris, Michael Dudding, Samantha Friedlander, Amanda Melfi, Desirae Friesen, Christine Foltzer, Dakota Griffin, Steven Bucsok, and the rest of the folks at TDA.

Sam Weber, for the killer cover.

Jack Hadley and Suzannah Dunn and all my fellow writers at Curtis Brown Creative.

Helen and Stan, who asked to be characters. I'm sorry. You asked.

My family, biological and chosen, for everything.

And Mick. You know what you did.

About the Author

HIRON ENNES is a writer, musician, and student of medicine based in the Pacific Northwest. Their areas of interest include infectious disease, pathology, and anticapitalist healthcare reform. When they're not hunched over a microscope or Word document, they can be found playing in the snow or playing the harp (though usually not at the same time). They're queer in every sense of the word, and they really want to pet your dog. *Leech* is their first novel.